MAKING UP

Elizabeth Harrington was born on the Isle of Wight in 1957. At the age of sixteen she moved to London where she worked for a magazine editor before moving into public relations work.

She now lives with her family in Herefordshire, where she is concentrating on her writing career. *Making Up* is her second novel, following *The Corporate Wife*.

Acclaim for *The Corporate Wife*:

'A fast-paced, warm-hearted romantic thriller: the sex and skulduggery will keep you racing from start to finish.'
SALLY BEAUMAN

D0774828

ELIZABETH HARRINGTON

Making Up

HarperCollins*Publishers*

HarperCollins*Publishers*
77–85 Fulham Palace Road
Hammersmith, London W6 8JB

A Paperback Original 1995

1 3 5 7 9 8 6 4 2

A catalogue record for this book is available from
the British Library

ISBN 0 00 647327 X

Typeset in Palatino at The Spartan Press Ltd, Lymington, Hants

Printed in Great Britain by HarperCollinsManufacturing Glasgow

For Peter

To wake at dawn with a winged heart and give
    thanks for another day of loving;
To rest at the noon hour and meditate love's ecstasy;
To return home with gratitude;
And then to sleep with a prayer for the beloved in
    your heart and a song of praise upon your lips.

The Prophet
Kahlil Gibran

Chapter One

Taking a seat in the glossy reception area, Fern leaned well back into the slippery red leather sofa, its surface squeaking beneath her bottom, stretching her long legs out in front of her.

She noticed, with vague satisfaction, that her shoes still carried mud splatters from her crazy morning dash through the park, and she met the eyes of the receptionist challengingly. Fern knew the woman had been watching her – weighing her up – wondering what business Fern had untidying the place with her less-than-perfect footwear and tatty jeans.

The air was laced with sweet but cloying scents that caught in Fern's nose. She wrinkled it, fighting the urge to sneeze, and at the same time dipped into her pocket to pull out the remains of a crumpled tissue. Looking around the walls, observing the perfect faces that stared haughtily down at her from the various product posters, Fern felt, for the first time in a long while, just a touch self-conscious. She studied the receptionist surreptitiously over her tattered tissue. The woman was immaculately painted, powdered and primped. Large gold orbs sat on her ear lobes, and a mass of gold chains jangled and swung around her neck and wrists as she shuffled elegantly through paperwork on the desk in front of her. Her neat little button-through dress exactly matched the rich scarlet of the velvet-soft carpet, emblazoned in silvery grey with the intertwined O and R of the Oscar Rees insignia. The windows were starkly dressed with

Venetian blinds of glittering chrome, echoing the livery of the large display of Oscar Rees products, proudly boxed in their glossy red packaging and effectively adorned with the silver initials of the man responsible for it all.

As the minutes ticked by, various employees passed through reception, some meeting visitors from other leather sofas or pushing packages at scruffy messengers. Fern couldn't believe how like clones of each other these women were. Save for the difference in hairstyles it was almost impossible to tell them apart, with their perfectly made-up faces and slickly coloured lips. But then to work for an organization like Oscar Rees one almost needed a degree in the art of facial deception.

In spite of her sprawled legs, scrubbed face and take-me-or-leave-me persona, Fern felt just the teensiest bit gauche, though she hardly dare admit it to herself. She spread her fingers out in front of her. Her nails were uneven, squared at the corners. Manicures simply weren't a priority in her life. Then she stared again at the receptionist's dainty fingertips playing along the paperwork, and scrunched her hands up into fists, tucking them safely out of sight under her armpits.

Fern tapped her foot with mild impatience. She'd been waiting here fifteen minutes already. She still had to finish off the piece on Singles' Dining Clubs and the production department were screaming for it. Plus she had another two interviews to carry out after Mr Johnny Sharpe deigned to put in an appearance. If only she could collect up all the wasted time she'd spent hanging around waiting for interviews! One day soon she'd make sure she was the one back at the office deciding what features were going to be run, and who was going to write them, and how.

2

And 'soon' might be in the next couple of weeks when Edwina announced just who was going to sit in the newly vacated Assistant Features Editor's chair. Until then she had to smile through adversity and work her little butt off to prove it was made from exactly the right material to fit the seat!

She delved into the large ex-army canvas rucksack and pulled out a dog-eared notebook so that she could gen up once more on the Oscar Rees Corporation.

Of course, old Oscar himself was no longer around. He'd shaken off his last puff of powder a couple of years back, leaving his son, Hugo, to run the show. Fern hadn't actually met Hugo, but she'd heard he was quite a tough cookie, as perhaps befitted the head of a major cosmetics house, with a ruthless determination to push Oscar Rees onwards and upwards into the twenty-first century. Photographs she'd seen showed him to be rather handsome in a cool, almost austere, way. He didn't seem to smile much in his pictures, but looked a bit mean and moody. Clearly he was nobody's fool. Several other members of the Rees family, and for that matter, the Eastons (with whom Oscar had merged back in the thirties) were part of the team, keeping their fingers in the dream creams and potions that made Oscar Rees the successful house it was today. And now here she was, sitting self-consciously in her own brand of street chic in this den of face couture, feeling increasingly like something the cat had dragged in and shamefully abandoned. Fern crossed her legs, noting her exposed pink kneecap poking through the strips of worn denim and wondered, not for the first time, whether this story was the good idea it had been cracked up to be. The lift doors hissed, and a tall, slim, in fact painfully slim, young man rushed out. His shock of straggly black hair added to his resemblance to an anorexic floormop.

'Johnny!' The girl behind the desk half-shouted then, gesturing to Fern as if she were hoping the cat had indeed come back to retrieve its debris. 'This, er, person is here to see you.'

Johnny frowned, confused for a second. 'What? Yes . . . sorry . . . you must be from *Faces*. Um, Fern, isn't it? Fern Donleavy?'

Fern knew from his reaction that up until approximately sixty seconds ago Johnny Sharpe must have totally forgotten her existence, and the fact that she had a 9.30 a.m. appointment with him.

'Fern, yes, Fern. Come on, so sorry to keep you waiting.'

Fern grinned at him. His own smile spread infectiously across his boyish face, his blue eyes glittering at her from somewhat dark-looking sockets. She stood, and Fern could see Johnny was surprised to find she was nearly as tall as he. There weren't too many five foot eleven women around town.

'I'll lead the way, shall I?' He picked up a pile of papers that Miss Daintytips was holding out to him and Fern followed him through the hallowed corridors, Johnny chatting over his shoulder to her.

'Great idea . . . really pleased . . . '

'What?'

'I'm really pleased you felt able to help out.'

'I haven't yet,' she shrugged.

'But you will.' He grinned at her again, acknowledging the cheek of his statement.

She couldn't help but grin back. 'We'll see.'

They arrived at an open-plan area where more glitzy girls sat at desks and hunched over telephones. As Fern passed they glanced up, giving her the receptionist's look of curious acknowledgement, followed by haughty dismissal. Clearly she posed no threat to these lipsticked ladies.

'In here, Fern.' Johnny disappeared through a doorway and Fern stepped smartly in behind him. 'I take it you drink coffee?'

'Thanks, black.'

'Two black coffees, please, Janie.' One of the willowy creatures unfolded herself and tripped off in a swirl of clinks, jangles and scents. Fern sneaked a look through the large floor-to-ceiling window that held a grandstand view of New Bond Street below them. Just next door were the hallowed windows of Hermès, while opposite one could watch the comings and goings through the discreet front entrance of Sotheby's. The sun bounced off the car rooftops, cheering up the otherwise drab sight of a typical jam. As she turned back to Johnny, she pulled off her battered leather jacket, and her hair, which had previously been neatly tucked inside it, swung free around her shoulders. Johnny looked up and his breath caught in his throat. The sun poured through her hair, turning it into liquid amber that swung heavily to cover her breasts, almost down to her waist. She flicked it back behind her shoulders, kind of shrugging it away, revealing the simple white T-shirt underneath, and then with boyish movements plonked herself down on the chair opposite his desk. Her legs, even while seated, seemed to go on forever, and he could tell, through the tightness of her jeans, they were slender and shapely. This was indeed a pleasant surprise.

Fern gestured to the pile of photographs on his desk. 'How many have you seen already?'

'Don't ask. All I can say is it's been hell. They're all pretty, desperately pretty. But there's just a certain

5

something that I know when I find it, I'll know, if you see what I mean.'

'But you can't tell what it is.'

'Nope.' He tapped his forehead with his finger. 'It's something up here, a feeling I've got. The right girl's got to be pretty special. After all, there's a big contract waiting for her.'

Fern nodded and began scribbling in her notebook. 'It's not something *Faces* would normally involve itself in, given that it's so commercial. I mean, you're getting guaranteed plugs for Oscar Rees and the new line, but we felt it was quite a novel idea and the magazine, too, would get a lot of mileage out of it – *Faces* searches for The Face. But I'd like more details before we finalize anything.'

Johnny sat down on the desk, resting his foot on Fern's chair. He had a very direct way of looking at her, and at the moment she wasn't sure whether she liked it or not.

'Okay. What does Vitale mean to you? What does it suggest? What identity do you feel a product of that name would have?'

'I'm afraid I'm not well up on product identities, but I guess it's got to have something to do with health and vitality.'

'Correct!' Johnny said delightedly, as if she'd just cracked the meaning of life. 'Health and vitality, and what else?'

'Young, vibrant, maybe sporty . . . '

'You've got it!'

'But it's all a bit simplistic, isn't it? I mean it's not that difficult to assume with that kind of name. Of course, on the other hand it could have doggy associations.'

'Doggy?'

Clearly she had blasphemed. 'Yes, health and vitality. Sounds like a bouncing puppy.'

Johnny winced. 'I think we'll forget about that. We're searching for girls, not dogs.'

'Let's hope that's what you get, then,' Fern teased.

'So, the idea is that you run a competition for the search for The Face. Of course, there'll be age limits, height and weight guidance and so on, otherwise we'll have every girl in the country applying.'

'I should think whatever restrictions you put on it, you'll probably have every girl in the country applying in any event. A million-pound contract is quite a carrot to dangle.'

'Yeah. That's the problem, sifting the wheat from the chaff. Let's say between fifteen and twenty-one.' Fern scribbled as he rattled on. 'Height between five eight and six foot. Applicants should have good complexions, no scars et cetera – oh, and a fit and well-proportioned body. Two colour pictures to be sent – one of head and shoulders and one full-length body shot, okay?'

'Fine.'

'As we discussed on the phone, we'll divide it into regional heats to be held in big hotels where they can have an Oscar Rees makeover and the winners of the regional heats will get a cheque for £500 and £100 worth of Oscar Rees products – and of course their picture will appear in *Faces*.'

'Got it. What about the time limit?'

'Let's hold the first heat a month after publication, then we'll stage the heats at fortnightly intervals around the country. So the entry for the first ones have got to be in two weeks after publication. Okay?'

Fern nodded.

'Good.'

'What about judging?'

'You?'

'Wouldn't have a clue.'

7

'Sure you would. I'll be judging too, and so will Hugo Rees himself. I might dredge up a couple of others, but I'll let you know before your copy deadline.'

'There's just one thing that bothers me about all this.'

'What's that?'

'You haven't actually told me anything about the product itself.'

Johnny touched the side of his nose conspiratorially. 'Secret, Fern. It's all cloak-and-dagger stuff in this business. I'm afraid I'm not at liberty to divulge – '

'Look, I'm not after the formula or anything, but so far all you've told me about it is what it's going to be called. I think I need a bit more to go on. Like is it cosmetics in terms of paint – you know, lipstick, eye colour, et cetera, or are we talking skincare? I feel I need to give some kind of a hint in this competition to the poor girl who's going to end up promoting the stuff for a living.'

Johnny stared at her thoughtfully for a few moments, then he picked up his telephone. 'Lucienne!' he barked into the mouthpiece. 'Listen, I need a copy of the draft press release about Vitale . . . Yes, that's it, the one that says what the range is going to be all about. I'm in a meeting with a journalist from *Faces*, so I'd like it now, if possible. Thanks.'

He turned back to Fern. 'You can take the press release away with you. Lucienne's going to pop it down to me – that's if she agrees that you can use the information at this stage. You'll have to check it out with her.'

'Lucienne?'

'Yeah. Lucienne Easton. She's Hugo's niece and she looks after all the PR and marketing stuff. I'm products and faces . . . ah, here she is. That was quick.' Johnny stood up to make the introductions. 'Lucienne, this is Fern Donleavy from *Faces*.'

Fern held out her hand and stared into a pair of deep brown, almond-shaped eyes. The sleekly arched brows lifted slightly as she took in Fern's torn jeans and her scrubbed face, and she offered her hand limply to Fern.

'Hello,' she drawled through blood-red lips. 'I'm afraid I must ask what you intend using this for.' She held the press release back from Fern, clutching it to her abdomen protectively.

'I think it will be okay,' Johnny interrupted. 'Fern is running the competition for us, and naturally she feels she wants to give a clue as to what Vitale will be all about. It's all good publicity, Lucienne.'

Lucienne had one of those unfortunate tilts to her nose that seemed as if someone had dropped a dog turd not far below it. Fern eyed her suit and focused on the intertwined Cs on her jacket buttons. Being part of the Rees/Easton dynasty was clearly lucrative.

She smiled directly at Lucienne. 'I can be pretty vague about it, if it's a problem, but I'd like to say, "The new skincare range from Oscar Rees, based on extract of exotic seaweed . . . " or whatever it is. You know the sort of thing. I do feel people will want to know what Vitale is all about. Are there lipsticks, that sort of stuff, what's new about them. You tell me as much as I can put, and I'll do my best with it, okay?'

'Well . . . ' Lucienne continued to regard Fern suspiciously. After all, this rather messy-looking creature was nothing like the normal fashion PRs Lucienne had to deal with. 'I'm not at all sure it's appropriate to release any details at this stage. You see, our competitors are dying to know what we're up to, and we'd really like to save it all for a big splash at the time of the launch. All I suggest you say is simply that it's a new product line in skincare and cosmetics from Oscar Rees, and leave it at that.' She flicked her sleek black bob behind her ears. 'I'm sorry if it causes you a problem, but these things are rather sensitive, you see.'

'Fine.' Fern's smile drooped and she acknowledged the challenge in Lucienne's eyes. She caught sight of Johnny's frown through the corner of her eye, and sensed this had more to do with a power play between Johnny and the arrogant Lucienne than with the secrecy of some daft product. Still, she had enough for her story.

'I'll work round it.'

'Thanks, Lucienne,' Johnny said with barely disguised sarcasm.

Lucienne spun round on her neat little calf-leather pumps. 'So sorry . . . ' she murmured vaguely. 'And thank you so much, er . . . Miss Donleavy.'

'Fern. And not at all.' Lucienne caught the hint of mockery that darted across Fern's eyes.

After Lucienne had gone, Fern collected up her jacket.

'Sorry about that,' Johnny said. 'Lucienne can be a bit over-protective at times, but don't worry about her.'

'I won't.' She stood up. 'I'll be in touch if I need anything else.'

'Fine. You're coming along to the ball tomorrow night, aren't you? Hugo will be there. I'll introduce you if we get a chance.'

'I'm looking forward to it. It's not often we struggling journalists get the chance to go to such glamorous events.'

Johnny tried to imagine what she would look like all dolled up. He looked at her face more closely. There was an almost perfect translucence to her pale

10

skin. Her clear green eyes were framed by long dark lashes, unusual for a redhead, he thought. She had a wide brow and a neat straight nose, and when she smiled her even mouth showed a row of perfectly straight, pearly white teeth.

A thought crossed his mind and for a fraction of a second he stared more intently at her, then he told himself not to be so foolish. It was too early in the morning after such a heavy night before. His mind was playing tricks on him. Coincidences like this simply didn't happen.

He led the way back to reception. 'Thanks for coming in, Fern, and I'll see you tomorrow.'

'Yeah. 'Bye, Johnny.'

But as Johnny made his way back along the corridor to his office, he found himself unable to get Fern Donleavy's face out of his mind.

Fern was weeping over the onions when she heard Paul's key in the lock. She wiped her eyes on her sleeve, chopped the last offending piece and chucked it into the frying pan. The hot oil hissed and spat angrily while she went to greet him.

'Darling . . . ' he crooned. God, he had such a sexy voice. It never failed to make her feel shivery all over. She couldn't understand why in his job he didn't get snapped up for voice-overs all the time. He kissed her firmly on the lips, slapping her rump as he broke away. 'You look as though you've been crying.'

She laughed. 'Onions – really strong onions for supper.'

'They smell delicious.'

'And so do you,' she said happily burrowing her nose into his neck. 'What have you been up to? You look pretty cool.' She stepped back to get a better view of him. He was wearing his 'country' suit, all

Harris tweed and brogues, and she had to admit, squire-like or not, he was rather gorgeous. Clean, blond and edible.

'Casting session – again,' he sighed, bored.

'And?'

'Oh, I dare say nothing. They wanted someone to demonstrate a carpet shampoo and the machine was long and thin, I was long and thin, so they decided to get a short stubby actor to balance it. The whole thing was rather a waste of time, except for the statutory expenses for turning up.'

'At least you've still got the play.' Fern threw the mince into the frying pan and chased it round with a well-worn wooden spoon.

'Yes, that's true. What would I do without a run of *Love's Labours Lost* along the south coast?'

'It's work.'

'Too damn right it's work – bloody hard work.'

'Good experience for you.'

Paul put his hand to his head dramatically. 'Great actors need to feel as well as experience, so how about letting me have a feel of you.'

'Paul!' Fern shrieked as he pulled her into his arms, sliding his leg adeptly between hers. 'For goodness' sake, I'm trying to cook supper.'

'The only thing I want to eat right now is you!' His hand slipped down to her crotch, and squeezed suggestively. She slapped at it playfully. 'Do stop it, otherwise we'll end up not eating and I don't know about you, but I'm absolutely starving.'

He shrugged and spoke lightly. 'Okay, have it your own way. Just remember, there's thousands of groupies out there desperate for a grope, and you've turned me down in preference to a plate of mince.'

Fern couldn't help but giggle. 'Hard to believe, I

12

know. But I guess it's something I'll eventually come to terms with. And there's always later.'

'I may not be on offer later.'

'Watch it, I just might remind you of that.'

'You cruel women journalists are all the same . . . Hey, what's this all about?' He picked the stiff white card out of the small front pocket of her rucksack which she had abandoned in the corner earlier.

She swore inwardly at her oversight. 'H'm?'

He waved the card under her nose. 'You didn't tell me you'd been invited to this.'

'Oh, didn't I?' Fern tried to sound casual. She had a feeling her attending the Cosmetics Association's annual ball might not go down too well with Paul.

'It's tomorrow night, Fern.' His previously warm tone had changed to one of icy accusation.

'I know that.'

'And it says Ms Fern Donleavy and guest on the card. Just who were you thinking of taking?'

'A photographer, of course. I need pix of the evening to back up my story.'

'What story?' He was playing games now, putting her through her paces.

'You know very well, Paul. Oscar Rees, remember? The search for The Face to launch a thousand products. I told you all about it.'

Paul looked vague. 'Did you? Oh well, if you say you did, then I suppose you must have done.'

'Paul, you're a shit! You know damn well I did.'

Part conscience and part hurt was making her angry. Paul had a rather irritating habit of forgetting entire conversations when it suited him. Sometimes she wondered if he ever really listened to her. It was almost as if he treated her career as a bit of a joke. And as for telling him about the invitation! She knew him too well to risk another of his jealous tantrums.

Had it not been for her stupidity in leaving the invitation around for him to find she knew she would have got away with telling him she had to go to the damned ball by herself.

Paul was grinning at her benignly. 'Anyway, I'm sure you were about to break it to me.'

'Over supper. And it's work, Paul. It's no big deal. It'll be boring as hell, full of stuffed shirts and bimbettes. I just need to get a feel for the industry – the types of people involved in it.'

'I understand, sweetheart.' His voice was velvety soft once more. 'Don't worry. And to prove I don't mind I'll take you out for a little drink after supper.'

'I don't want to be too late, though. I need to be razor sharp for tomorrow.'

'Little Cinderella will be delivered back by her Prince Charming well before the witching hour.'

'Oh shut up, you mad idiot,' she laughed.

They got back to the flat at 11.30 p.m., much later than Fern would have liked. Paul flicked the small knob on the Yale lock, and started shutting off the lights.

'So you're staying?' she said, trying to sound light. Truth was she would much rather he had gone back to his own flat, but to argue now would make her even later to bed, and she couldn't afford to be tired tomorrow.

'You do want me to, don't you?' His voice sounded hurt.

'Of course,' she said quickly. 'It's just that I thought that . . . well, it doesn't matter. Let's go up, shall we?'

Fern must have been in bed for at least half an hour before Paul joined her. God knows what he had been up to, but she had just drifted off into a light sleep so her body started when the door clicked closed firmly behind him. He slid into bed beside her and stroked her nipples lightly, so that the sensation was a mixture of mild arousal and bearable tickling. She moved away, hoping he might take the hint and notice that she was, to all intents and purposes, asleep. But Paul was noted for his persistence and soon Fern found herself very awake and very aroused.

Paul's tongue licked down over her body, tickling and teasing with its wet slippery warmth. He spread her legs out and dropped his head, burying his nose into the soft curls that formed a pretty triangle, and sucked hard on her clitoris, lapping at it like a mewling kitten, his tongue one minute hard and rasping, the next hot and deliciously wet.

Fern's hips bucked involuntarily, willing Paul to swallow her, consume her totally with his exquisite tongue. But just then he broke off, and paused for what seemed like an age before planting a kiss smack on her lips, forcing her to taste her own subtle saltiness that lingered on his tongue.

'Do you love me?' he asked suddenly. His eyes pierced with a fierce intensity.

'You know I do,' she gasped. 'I love you, Paul.' She pulled his mouth back towards hers.

He pressed his penis between her legs and then in the same marvellous way it always had, it slipped easily inside her. Fern clutched at him, pulling him harder into her, spreading herself against him.

'Take me,' he cried.

'Oh yes.' Her voice was a sob, caught in her throat.

'Tomorrow . . . ' he finished – his thrusts getting shorter, faster, furious.

She was powerless, out of control, thrown against him again and again. 'Yes . . . oh yes . . . ' she cried. And then it was over.

Paul pulled out of her almost immediately. He cuddled up beside her. 'I knew you wouldn't really do it.'

'Do what?'

'Go to the ball without me!'

'What?'

'You just said – '

'When?'

'Just now – when we were making love. I asked if I could, and you said yes.'

'Paul!' She hammered the pillow in frustration. 'Sometimes you're a bastard, you know, a spoilt little boy bastard. What the hell am I supposed to tell the editor? How am I going to get my photographs?'

'I'm an actor, I'll pretend to be your photographer. What could be easier?'

'I need pictures, not lines! Oh, I give up, I really do!'

Chapter Two

Fern was tearing her hair out. Three frantic calls to Johnny hadn't managed to produce an extra ticket to the blasted ball. She'd coerced and cajoled the lady at the Cosmetics Association but there were simply no tickets left. She had been told there was absolutely no admittance whatsoever without an invite, so that was that. And it had been no fun learning that a photographer cancelled at three hours' notice is not a happy photographer. Paul could really piss her off sometimes. The real reason he wanted to be at the ball, she guessed, was sheer ambition, coupled with the fact that he couldn't bear to think that she might be able to have a good time without him. No doubt he thought there would be some influential people there who would 'notice' him, or maybe a chance meeting that would turn into a useful contact at some time in the future. It wasn't what you know, but who, and Paul wasn't going to pass up such a potential opportunity as this, even if it meant screwing up Fern's story.

She used to think she was ambitious, but boy, Paul really took the biscuit. Although she tried not to analyse their meeting too much, she wondered if the real reason he had plied her with so many post-theatre drinks, late suppers, chocolates and flowers was because he wanted superior reviews and a special mention in the magazine, not, as he said, because he had fallen immediately, hopelessly and passionately in love with her.

It was ironic that it had taken Paul a good few weeks to discover that Fern had nothing to do with the Arts pages – she was news and features. But she hadn't been too hard on him. After all, some of the best relationships started like that.

Finally resigned to taking her own 35mm pocket camera to the ball, Fern did a last-minute dash round the shops to pick up something suitable to wear, assuming that on this occasion she would not be able to get away with her tatty 501s.

Paul was in the bath when she got back to the flat. That meant there'd be little hot water left for her planned scented soak. No doubt Paul would have indulged himself fully. Quickly pressing her 'new' outfit, she settled down with a small pack of freshly purchased emery boards, and set about trying to get her nails to a uniform length. In effect this meant filing them down as short as possible. At least that made any thought of nail varnish out of the question.

In spite of her gentle contempt for the cosmetics business, Fern still wanted to hold her head high – to be just as attractive as those painted ladies. And, strangely, the Oscar Rees magic seemed to be casting its spell over her. Her mother would have been most surprised to see Fern furtively drawing lipstick stripes on to the back of her hand at Fenwick's this lunchtime. But there it was, in its shiny red and silver box that probably cost three times as much as the lipstick to produce, emblazoned with the OR of Oscar Rees. She felt as though she had concluded some rite of passage through purchasing her first lipstick – albeit at the age of twenty-three – a bit like the feeling when she had raided the condom dispenser at the age of seventeen. Funny that she should need condoms before lipsticks.

She could hear her mother's voice whispering at

her accusingly. 'Traitoress!' it said. She laughed at it. 'Where's your sense of fun, Mum?'

'Who are you talking to?'

She nearly jumped out of her skin. Why did Paul enjoy doing that so much?

'You scared me half to death. I was talking to myself.'

'Well, you know what they say.'

'Yes, I know,' she muttered, turning away from him. 'Any hot water left?'

'Masses. I didn't take much.'

Fern knew sure as hell that meant there would be none left. She ran up to the bathroom and put her hand on the cylinder. Just as she thought: barely warm. Oh well, cold was supposed to be good for the skin, wasn't it, and the soul? Luckily she'd washed her hair this morning.

As Fern shivered in the tepid water, she realized with a jolt just how far she had come, taking such things for granted. Up until the age of sixteen electricity had been a luxury available only to other people. Lights, central heating, immersion heaters, hair dryers and stereos, all things she now completely took for granted, had not featured in her life until she had left the cottage in County Cork.

'Jaysus, gurrl,' she told herself, 'you'll be goin' soft, so yer will.' She shivered and lathered, bringing back memories of icy cold mornings going off to school, with Rowena threatening to turn a bucket upside down over her. Those were the days all right. She wondered how Paul with his coddled English Home Counties background would survive the rigours of an Irish winter in a time-warped cottage.

Fern towelled herself down roughly, letting the friction liven up her circulation and bring some warmth back into her chilled skin. Soon she began to

19

feel invigorated, wonderfully refreshed, a very different feeling to that languid warm mood a hot soak put you in. She felt more alive and tingly all over. Perhaps she'd recommend it to the beauty tips columnist.

Paul, naturally enough, was still drying his hair by the time she joined him, fully dressed except for one small finishing touch. He still had the power to make her stomach lurch over with lust – six-foot-two solid hunk, soft blond curls, beautifully even features, piercing pale-blue eyes – maybe she could excuse him his self-indulgences. His cuffs flapped loosely around his tanned wrists, the wing collar was invitingly open at the top, the yellow silk bow tie dangling round his neck. She imagined themselves at the end of the evening, just about to strip off their glad rags. Well, at least that was something to look forward to – and maybe the ball would be a lot more fun with Paul in tow rather than some photographer from work.

'You look pretty good,' she conceded, admiringly. For a moment she'd totally forgotten her own outfit until she noticed Paul's slow gaze travel from her high heels, up to her cheeky little black net skirt and her *pièce de résistance* – the bum-freezer naval jacket she'd picked up in Oxfam this afternoon. It had wonderful gold braid epaulettes and braided buttons.

'And you look . . . interesting,' he grinned.

She pulled open her jacket.

'Fern, don't you think that's a bit rude?'

'Don't be daft. You can't actually see anything.'

'Well, it doesn't leave all that much to the imagination.' He was referring to the sexy little black-and-red bustier that hid underneath the jacket. Dainty lace and bones pushed her boobs under and over, forming a decent-sized cleavage.

'So! Since when has that been a problem?'

'If you get yourself molested, don't blame me.'

'Unless of course you're the one who molests me,' she said, coquettishly.

Fern was happy to take the bus, but Paul insisted that they must take a cab and, to give him his due, it would be his treat. So they were deposited safely outside the stately entrance to the Grosvenor House Hotel.

There was a sort of ill-formed queue of similarly attired folks waving their invitation cards at the strategically positioned flunkies. Paul placed his hand lightly and proprietorially in the small of Fern's back to guide her through the foyer. The bright lights made them blink as they were directed towards the ballroom. Literally hundreds of jewel-coloured gowns in every style and length decorated the women around the place. No Laura Ashley numbers among this lot, Fern decided. These were the genuine article. Five-figure couture, no doubt. Fern could kick herself, and Paul. She desperately needed a serious photographer. Her pocket camera would no way do this justice. The event would make a terrific diary piece to earn her revered editor's approval, and Fern needed all the approval she could get. She wanted that promotion to Assistant Features Editor. Here was a golden opportunity to catch the really big names at play and here she was, with no sensible camera.

'I'm just going to find the loo,' she told Paul. 'I'll see you in a minute, okay?' Before he had chance to reply she disappeared between several yards of taffeta and tule. She simply had to get hold of someone. She found a telephone and, taking a deep breath, called directory inquiries and got hold of Anthony, the photographer's, number. The guy was going to think she was a complete schizoid having cancelled him earlier today.

'Please, please, be in,' she pleaded as the phone rang and rang. After what seemed like an age, it was picked up.

'Anthony,' she fought to keep her voice smooth, 'it's me, Fern. Yes . . . again . . . um, thing is, Anthony, it looks like I might need you here after all.'

She could hear the exasperation in his voice. Thank God she'd always had a decent working relationship with him up to now, otherwise she'd have no cred left whatsoever.

She tried to appease him. 'Look, I know I've messed you around and it's all my fault, but the thing is there's some great opportunities here and so I wonder if you could get over here.' She crossed her fingers and prayed, at the same time looking forward to the moment when she might cheerfully strangle Paul.

At last she sighed with relief. 'Anthony, you're a doll. Thanks. I'll see you in what, half an hour? I'll meet you outside.'

How on earth was she going to smuggle him in? Fern wandered nonchalantly through the foyer. The flunkies stood behind two desks on which they were piling the handed-in invitation cards. An enticing pile of white stiffies beckoned her. She needed two, one to smuggle out for Anthony and another to get herself back in. Question was, how to steal them?

Fern hovered for a few moments, hoping for inspiration, when she noticed something going on outside. A large black Daimler had pulled up with a royal crest at the front. It must be Princess Michael, Fern realized. Her name had been on the invitation as special guest of honour. The flunkies left the table and sped out to the waiting car, stopping any other guests from coming through for a few moments, and moving people aside to allow Her Royal Highness access. Now was her chance. Fern sidled over to the table and whipped a couple of cards from the top of the pile. She stuffed them both inside her jacket, then hugged it tightly around herself. She stepped briskly away from the table and out of suspicion's reach. When the hand fell firmly on her shoulder she nearly fainted with shock. She could feel 'GUILT' written in six-inch-high letters across her forehead as she turned around.

She looked up into the darkest pair of eyes she believed she had ever seen. Above them thick black brows knitted together, and a face glowered at her fiercely. The top of his head was covered with jet-black curls, giving him an almost Italian appearance. His huge frame made even Paul seem slight. She guessed he was maybe just a few years older than herself.

'What, if I may ask, were you doing?'

Fern's face flushed the colour of the carpet. 'I . . . er . . . um . . . ' she stammered guiltily. 'I was just . . . '

'Yes?' One brow raised in stern curiosity.

Fern took in his clothes. Like everyone else he was wearing a white dinner jacket. He looked more like a guest than a security man.

'I'm not sure it's any of your business,' she answered curtly, and tried to move away from him.

'Wait a moment. Not so fast, young lady.'

Fern's green eyes turned even greener, and the man noticed that her delicate little nostrils flared ever so slightly.

'What were you doing stealing a card off the table?'

'As I said, I really don't see why I should tell you. Do you actually work here?' she said in the haughtiest voice she could summon.

He burst out laughing. 'What an idea,' he said, as if he found it intriguing. 'But, no. I don't work here. He does.' He pointed to a flunky. 'I suppose I could just tell him.'

Fern thought she detected a hint of amusement in the man's eyes. Dear God, he's playing with me, she thought angrily. And laughing at me, too. 'You could if you wanted. Why don't you then? Go ahead. I suppose he can only throw me out.'

'And that,' he said, 'would be a pity.'

Again Fern flushed. What an impudent person. She was just about to come up with some clever retort when a gorgeous brunette appeared at his side. 'Ah, Leo, there you are. I was wondering where you'd wandered off to.' She regarded Fern dubiously. 'I'm sorry . . . have we met?'

'I don't believe so,' Fern said quickly and seeing her chance of escape, she almost sprinted out through the front door, leaving the woman gazing open-mouthed behind her.

By the time she had smuggled Anthony in, and briefed him on exactly what and whom she wanted, the couple had long disappeared. Now she had to cope with Paul.

True to form, Paul hadn't been idle. Fern eventually found him sitting at a table between two rather young and very pretty ladies. He was engaging them with his theatre stories, playing the role of famous actor and name-dropping. Although he smiled at her cheerfully, she could tell he was not happy about her absence.

'Sorry,' she breathed, 'I got caught up. There was something I had to do. I hope you've been all right.'

'Oh, I've been more than happy,' he gushed. 'Fern, let me introduce you to my new friends.' He turned to his right. 'This is Annabelinda, whose daddy has

something to do with Harvey Nichols, and this,'
turning to the girl on his left, 'is Catriona, whose
daddy runs a little pharmaceutical company. And
this, ladies, is Fern, our bright young journalist,
whose father . . . What was it Daddy did, darling?'

Fern glared at him. The bastard! He knew damn
well about Fern's father. That was certainly a direct
hit below the belt, and he knew it. But she was not
going to show her anger in front of these two lemon
tartlets. However, fortunately Paul had noticed someone over Fern's shoulder and had been distracted,
wondering just who the gangly young bloke was who
seemed to be taking such an interest in Fern.

Johnny Sharpe had thought about Fern Donleavy
on and off for the last twenty-four hours, not least
because she had kept on pestering him for an extra
ticket for the do. Everyone knew they were like
bloody gold dust so he had had to disappoint her. But
there had been something else bothering him about
her which he hadn't quite been able to put his finger
on. Ever since he had first noticed her come into the
ballroom he hadn't been able to take his eyes off the
woman. She looked stunning, so stunning that she
sent shivers down his spine, and the tell-tale tingle in
his testicles. The more he looked at her, the more he
wanted to see of her. He had one of those hunches
growing in him that could develop into a dead cert.
The little touch of what looked like 'Burning Red' on
her lip was the finishing touch. Her whole face came
alive. As he approached the table, he noticed the big
guy giving him the evil eye. As usual when he got
these hunches, he'd have some explaining to do.

Fern looked around and Paul noted her face light
up at the sight of the man. She had a respite, for the
moment at least.

'Johnny, come and meet Paul,' she said brightly,

'and the girls. This is Johnny Sharpe, Product Manager at Oscar Rees. Johnny, this is my boyfriend, Paul, and . . . er, Annabelinda and . . . Catriona.'

'We know each other,' the girls said in unison.

'Oh, one forgets, it's a small world, isn't it?'

Paul and Johnny shook hands and Paul poured both Fern and Johnny a glass of wine from a bottle that had appeared from somewhere. Attempting not to be either rude or obvious, Johnny continued to try and examine Fern's face. In the end Fern felt she had to say something.

'Look, Johnny, do I have a spot on my nose, or something? It's just that you keep looking at me rather strangely.'

'What? Oh no . . . ' Johnny laughed, a little nervously. 'No, no. I'm thinking, that's all.'

'And you have to stare at me for that,' Fern said with amusement.

'I have to talk to you,' he said.

'I knew it. It's my lipstick, isn't it? It doesn't suit me. The first time I wear it, and I get it wrong. I should have known. Look, I'll find a tissue and get rid of it – that's if it hasn't set indelibly. Just my luck, eh?'

'Are you serious? This is the first time you've worn it?'

'Sure. I couldn't come to a do like this without some concession to the business, now could I?'

'Go on. Make my day. Tell me it's by Oscar Rees.'

Fern opened up her tiny, purse-sized handbag and pulled out her proud new purchase.

'Now I do believe in miracles,' Johnny cried.

'What are you both going on about?' Paul interrupted.

'I really don't know,' Fern giggled, 'but I do think Johnny must be a teensy bit mad – aren't you, Johnny?'

26

'Not mad, merely inspired. I'll explain everything later, but right now there's someone I really want you to meet, Fern. Would you excuse us for a few moments, Paul?'

'But – ' Fern started to protest, but Johnny was already pulling her up out of the seat.

'Why not?' Paul shrugged. 'I seem to have excused her for most of the evening.'

Johnny pulled Fern across the empty dance floor, past the queue that had formed for the buffet supper, and towards the front of the ballroom. 'Where on earth are you taking me?'

'Trust me.'

'Why should I?'

'Okay, don't trust me. Just come out of curiosity. I'm going to introduce you to Hugo.'

'Hugo Rees?' Fern squeaked. 'Then why all the secrecy?'

'Just for fun.'

'Let me get a notebook, and I want my photographer to come . . .'

'You won't need either for this, I promise.'

In spite of her long legs, Fern was almost trotting to keep up with Johnny. There was a gap between the tables, and then a much larger table than the standard ten-seaters. Fern assumed this must be the top table.

She recognized Hugo straight away. He was much like his photographs, only perhaps a little softer looking. He was seated next to a beautifully groomed sophisticated brunette, whom Fern assumed to be his wife, Olivia, clad in what could only be Valentino.

Hugo smiled up at Johnny, at first not noticing Fern. 'Johnny, my dear chap,' he drawled. 'How nice to see you – you're enjoying yourself, I trust?'

'Enormously, thanks, Hugo. Listen, there's someone I'd like you to meet.' Johnny pulled Fern forward.

27

Fern started to speak, to acknowledge Johnny's introduction, saying hello while Hugo's mouth opened and shut wordlessly, like a goldfish. Eventually he thrust out his hand, mechanically, and muttered something incomprehensible.

Fern looked at Johnny, confused. She wasn't sure what to do next. Johnny, too, seemed to be taken aback by Hugo's obvious frostiness.

'I'm going to talk to Fern about Vitale, Hugo.' While Johnny spoke he grinned at Fern. 'I think she's the one, in fact I'm sure of it.' He squeezed Fern's hand with excitement.

'Indeed,' Hugo said flatly.

'What?' Fern could hardly hear what they were talking about over the noise of the band, which had just started up.

'Come on. See you later, Hugo.' Johnny pulled her away. ' . . . I'll explain everything.'

'Well, if it isn't the artful dodger again?'

As Fern turned to follow Johnny she had almost smashed head on to the arrogant so-and-so who had baited her over the invitation card. 'Still here, I see. Haven't been thrown out then?'

'No thanks to you.'

'On the contrary, it was completely thanks to me. I can only assume you must have had some very good reason for gate-crashing this evening.'

'I'm not a gate-crasher.'

'No, no, of course not.' The man looked at Johnny as though he and Fern were a couple of conspirators. 'I hope you have a pleasant evening.'

Fern swung away from him, only to witness the suspicious gaze of his girlfriend upon her. 'For God's sake . . . ' Fern muttered under her breath.

'What was all that about?' Johnny demanded. As he spoke Fern watched the couple saunter over to where Hugo Rees was seated. So that was why Hugo had been so unpleasant to her. The horrid man had obviously gossiped about her. How very mean!

'Don't ask. It's a long and rather boring story.'

'Do you know Leo Eden, then?'

'That's a familiar name. Isn't he something to do with Cooper Jefferson, the soap conglomerate?'

'Oh, Fern, where have you been? He's the UK Managing Director. Everyone knows who Leo Eden is. I'm surprised you didn't recognize him straight away.'

'Huh! Arrogant pig, anyway, wouldn't you say?'

'I wouldn't know. I don't mix in such exalted circles as you clearly do.'

Fern tossed her hair back and laughed. 'Well, I'm doing really well judging by tonight. I appear to have achieved notoriety with Leo Eden, and the cold shoulder from Hugo Rees.'

'Yes, I've never known Hugo behave like that. He usually oozes charm and diplomacy – out of the office, anyway. You obviously have quite an effect on people, Fern.'

'But not necessarily a good one, it would seem. I think I'd better find Paul. I guess I'm probably in trouble with him, too.'

'But I have to talk to you. It's desperately important.'

'Okay, but let's find Paul first. Then we can all sit down.'

Johnny didn't think it was the kind of conversation they should have in front of the boyfriend. Paul didn't look the helpful type. 'He seemed very happy with Annabelinda and Catriona.'

'Maybe, but I ought to check.'

They reached the table, but Paul was nowhere to be seen. Fern eventually sighted him in the food queue.

He was gesturing to her, telling her that he was getting a plateful for her. She beamed at him, realizing he must be having a good time to be so benevolent towards her.

She turned to Johnny. 'Okay, so what did you want to talk about?'

Johnny took a deep breath. 'I'll come straight to the point. It's the Vitale girl. I've found her. I told you yesterday I'd know when I did – that certain something – something very special – '

'And indefinable,' Fern interrupted. 'Well, don't keep me in suspense – and you do realize you might well have ruined my story.'

'It's you!'

Fern shrieked with laughter, causing several heads to turn in their direction. 'You can't be serious. My God, I thought I'd misheard you back there!' she howled.

Johnny had hoped for a more positive response. 'You didn't mishear me and I'm quite serious.'

'Don't be ridiculous,' she managed to splutter once her laughter had died down a little. 'You can't possibly think that – '

'Fern, I've never been more serious in my life. I know it. You're just perfect.'

Fern looked at him as if he'd gone stark staring bonkers. 'I believe you really are serious, aren't you?'

'Yes, deadly'.

'Johnny, I'm a journalist. I have a job other young journalists would kill for. I have a degree in English and I like to use my brain to make a living. I hardly ever wear make-up. The answer is no. Not in a million years, Johnny. Now let's forget about it and concentrate on this wonderful competition I'm going to put together for you. But first I think I should find

Paul and try and enjoy the rest of the evening. After all, I've still got a lot of ferreting to do. Now where's that photographer . . .'

Chapter Three

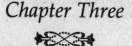

'I thought she was going to stay all night.' Olivia tapped her foot in irritation. Hugo had phoned for the car, and rather than wait inside in the warmth, Olivia had insisted on their coming out onto the front terrace of the hotel. Hugo rocked backwards and forwards on his heels, trying to keep warm. Although it was late April there was still a chill in the air.

'Who?'

'The Princess. I was simply dying to leave and one simply can't leave until she does.'

'Perhaps it shows she was enjoying herself, my dear – which is obviously more than can be said for you.'

'Hugo, you can be unbelievably tiresome at times. It's not often we attend these sorts of occasions together, and as you know, I always do my utmost to put on a good show, yet you ogled that young woman shamefully obviously all night long.'

'What woman?' Hugo snapped, stopping his swaying abruptly.

Olivia's thin lips twitched, and her eyebrows lifted with impatience. 'You know perfectly well which woman I'm talking about. The one, as you seem to have forgotten, with the ginger hair down to her waist. You couldn't take your eyes off her.'

At that moment the car arrived, giving Hugo a few much-needed moments of reprieve. He had never seen the young woman before, but there was something about her which he found extremely disarming. Maybe it was her striking red hair. He had been mesmerized by her – but not for the reasons Olivia was implying.

At last, as they settled back inside the car, Hugo said, 'I should think a lot of men were watching her, Olivia. She's a very attractive girl. However, the real reason I was looking at her so closely was because she has been proposed as The Face to launch Vitale.'

'I see!' Once more Olivia's lips tightened. 'Then that will make life convenient for you, won't it?'

'I really can't imagine what you're talking about.' Hugo stared out of the window. He hated Olivia's moods. She could be a vicious bitch at times, and for no real reason.

'You've got the hots for her.'

'Olivia, I'm seriously wondering whether it's you, not I, who has the hots for her. You do seem to be making an awful lot of fuss about this.'

'Trust you to say something as predictable as that, Hugo. You're not even funny. My only point is that on the few occasions we do go out together it would be nice to think you could try just as hard as I do to put on a good show.'

The car drew up outside the gracious five-storeyed, St James's house. Thomas, the chauffeur, jumped out to open Olivia's door.

'I shall be spending the night at my club, Olivia. I'm sure you'll understand.'

'You always have to run away, don't you, Hugo? Can't stand any emotion. Yes, of course I understand. Goodnight.' Olivia turned to the driver. 'Mr Hugo will be going to his usual haunt, Thomas. If you could just see me in first . . . '

She glared at Hugo and spun away through the vast double doors and safely out of sight.

Hugo let out a large sigh of relief, and untied the bow around his neck. How he hated these scenes with the woman. She had about as much warmth as a freshly filled ice-bucket. Poor old Olivia. She was one to talk about showing emotion.

'Drayton Gardens, Mr Hugo?'

Hugo smiled and nodded, hoping to get a warm welcome at the other end. He glanced at his watch – nearly 1.15 a.m.

When they pulled up outside Ricci Pembroke's flat, Hugo could see immediately the place was in darkness.

'Damn!' he swore under his breath. Perhaps, after all, he should go to his club rather than risk disturbing her. He thought for a moment, checking his pockets. Ricci had given him his own key although he was loath to use it, always preferring to act as a guest and not presume too much in her home. Perhaps tonight he should use the key and not drag her out of bed. He could give her a nice surprise instead.

'Thanks, Thomas. I'll make my own way into the office. Don't bother to pick me up.'

'Very good, sir.' Thomas watched his employer disappear through the dark doorway, and thought how lucky he was to have dear old Nancy to go back to. It was nice to know which bed you were going to wake up in every morning. But with a wife like Olivia he could hardly blame the poor bugger.

Hugo let himself in and tiptoed through the flat. The door to Ricci's bedroom stood slightly ajar. He thought he could just about hear her soft breathing if he listened hard.

He slipped out of his clothes and crept into her room. Her soft form lay curled up under the cotton sheet. Her pale blonde hair, though fading, spread prettily across the pillowcase. She looked much younger than she was, and rather vulnerable. Hugo stood and watched her for several moments, then abruptly she turned over and her eyes flew open in fear. Two huge blue saucers gazed at him, wide with shock and amazement, but when she came to enough to realize, she started to laugh.

'Dear God, Hugo, you nearly gave me a heart attack. I thought I must be having a visit from the local rapist!'

'I'm sorry, darling. I wanted to spend the night with you. Then I realized how late it was, and the flat was in darkness, and I didn't want to disturb you. I suppose I was just hoping I might have been able to slip into bed beside you and give you a nice surprise tomorrow morning.'

'A wonderful idea, Hugo, but I think I might have noticed you.'

'Did I do the wrong thing?'

'No,' she said, matter-of-factly. ''Course not. But you're not expecting me to get up and entertain you, are you?'

Hugo eyed the bed covetously. 'Actually, I was wondering if you might like to entertain me from there. It does look jolly inviting.'

Ricci threw back the sheet to reveal her skimpy crêpe de Chine nightgown. 'Why don't you come and make yourself comfortable?' she giggled, softly.

Hugo obediently lay down beside her and did what all good guests should do: he took great care to amuse his hostess.

Hugo was awoken by the smell of fresh coffee and newly baked bread. Ricci appeared with a tray on which sat a large coffee pot, two breakfast cups and saucers, and a basketful of warm rolls, butter and honey.

'Mmm,' Hugo sighed appreciatively. 'You spoil me, Ricci. And how did you manage to bake bread at this time of day?'

She laughed. 'I took them out of the freezer, plonked them in the oven, pressed the right buttons and, hey presto, freshly baked bread.'

'Listen,' Hugo said, through satisfied munches, 'I'm sorry about last night. I really shouldn't have turned up so late.'

'I'm glad you did. You were most attentive, Hugo. I had a very interesting night.'

Hugo looked at her mischievously. 'Would you like an interesting morning, too?'

'Love one, but you've got to get to the office, and I've got to show a client a mountain of swatch books so that she can change her curtains for the *third* time this year, and she's expecting me in precisely one hour's time.'

'Ricci, I – '

'Don't say it, Hugo. I don't want to hear it. No commitment, remember, no excuses. That's our deal. You've got Olivia, I've got . . . well, I've got my interior design business and I'm very happy with the way things are. I like my independence. So, let's have our coffee, shall we?'

Hugo often wondered how he'd been fortunate enough to find a woman like Ricci Pembroke. She was the most perfect mistress material imaginable. Her late husband, much older than she, had actually been a close friend of Hugo's father. Hugo had accompanied his own father to Lord Pembroke's funeral, and there noticed the soft-faced, gentle widow who had seemed so dignified. Several months later, after what Hugo deemed to be a respectable amount of time, he had invited the lovely widow to lunch, and steadily over many months their friendship had developed into the easy affair it now was. In truth, Hugo wasn't sure if he was in love with Ricci. He wasn't sure he even knew what love was. In his view it was no more than a vapid romantic notion that caused a lot more misery than happiness.

Convenience was more the crux of happiness of the sort Hugo and Ricci shared. No demands were made and therefore there arose few dissatisfactions. Even his marriage to Olivia had its benefits. Most of the time she lived very much her own life, and between them they found the arrangement worked.

Ricci disappeared into the bathroom and Hugo finished his coffee and the last of the bread.

'Your bath is drawn, Hugo. And I'll put your things out for you while you're in the bathroom,' she said, emerging.

'Thank you, my love,' Hugo sighed, contentedly. Perhaps, though, if things were different he might well want to make some kind of serious commitment to this gentle and giving creature.

Chapter Four

No sooner had Fern settled down, bleary-eyed and wrapped around a large mug of bitter black coffee, than her phone rang.

'Fern!' It was Johnny's anxious voice. 'I have to talk to you . . . about last night. This is really important.'

'I'm just about to start working on the article about the search for The Face and I've had a few ideas since last night. Maybe a profile on the Oscar Rees empire? Might be rather complementary, don't you think?'

'That's the point, Fern. I need to speak to you urgently about what I said last night.'

'You were serious, then?'

'Of course I was. I told you I'd know when I found the right girl, and I know it's you.'

Fern swallowed hard, barely able to believe what she was hearing. The characters on her VDU screen danced out of focus.

'Let me come and talk to you.'

'I really don't think there's much point, Johnny. I'm a journalist, not a model.'

'I'll be around in half an hour.' He hung up.

Fern pushed her chair back from the desk and ran her slim fingers through her thick mass of gleaming copper hair, sighing in frustration. Life was always so damned complicated. It had taken months of hard slog and a lucky break to get into the business, and twenty-three years of age was hardly the time for a career change. All the same, her dog-eared notebook sat enticingly on the corner of the desk. She snatched it up and flicked back through her scribbles, hastily finding the notes she had made about the Oscar Rees competition.

The figure of one million pounds zoomed in front of her eyes, underlined three times. One million pounds for a two-year modelling contract! What would she earn from scribbling during the next two years? Twenty thousand a year if she was lucky. If she got promoted to Assistant Features Editor maybe she'd get twenty-five thousand. That meant she'd have to work for forty years to earn the same money.

And what would Rowena say? Fern's mother had studiously raised her to question what she classed as man's deliberate attempt to subordinate women by making them feel so inferior as to need to paint themselves up before being fit to be seen out. Fern shook her head and smiled. All those feminist books her mother had lent her . . . And what about her education, her determination to make her own mark in the world to the extent that she had won a scholarship to study for her A-levels in Dublin and had then gone on to read English at Trinity? Fern had rejected a lot of Rowena's more extreme ideas, but she couldn't reject the fact that, through witnessing Rowena's bitterness and through never knowing a father of her own, she felt she could never place herself in a position where she would have to be reliant on a man's whim. Fern would be stronger than Rowena, more worldly, and more temperate in her attitudes, but the strange thing was that just wearing the lipstick last night had been almost a betrayal of her roots.

Fern didn't want any more complications in her life right now. She had enough problems trying to sort out Paul's jealous tantrums, her fight for promotion, and producing some really hot articles, without the necessity of being seduced by outrageous offers for jobs with impossibly short shelf-lives, and which would be undoubtedly dominated by men. By the time Johnny Sharpe arrived, she had sorted things out in her own mind.

She smiled at Johnny sympathetically. 'I'm afraid you've had a wasted journey. I really can't consider the offer, Johnny. I'm well and truly flattered – if that's the right word – but it isn't me.'

'But you don't know what's involved – '

'I can guess. And we have talked about it.'

'What about the money?'

She laughed. 'I wouldn't know what to do with it.'

'Let me at least buy you lunch, and we can talk about it.'

'I don't think I'll be eating lunch today, somehow.'

'A drink, then.'

'No. Thank you. Sorry, Johnny.' She saw the look of disappointment cover his face and softened slightly. 'Tell you what, how about a compromise? I'll sit here and fiddle about on my screen, while you talk.'

Johnny raised his hands upwards. 'Progress! Thank you, someone up there! So you know the bare bones of it. A million-pound minimum, two-year contract – to be renegotiated at the end of the period. During that time you will be available at all reasonable times to promote the product. You will be photographed, dressed and treated like royalty. All your expenses connected with promotion will be taken care of. Of course, you'll have a car, travel round the world and fame thrown in.'

Fern looked up from her screen and realized that Alix, one of the other staff writers, had been listening to every word. When she saw Fern look at her she grinned. 'Is this for real?'

Neither of them answered.

'Are you seriously being offered the Vitale contract?'

Johnny butted in. 'Yes, she is, and the silly girl doesn't want to take it.'

'Look, Johnny,' Fern said softly, ignoring Alix's interruption, 'I'm grateful to you for asking me and I know you think I haven't given the offer a proper consideration, but you should understand that all my life I've wanted to be a journalist and I've worked incredibly hard to get here. I'm very ambitious and I guess I have a fairly clear idea of where my career map will lead me.'

'But this offer could make you world famous!'

'I realize that, Johnny, but it's not the kind of fame I want. You know as well as I do that people would take me less seriously if they thought it was my face that had opened doors for me rather than my brain. I don't mean to say that models don't have brains, I'm just stating that that is the way things are. I've seen what happens on fashion shoots. The last person to have a say in what's going on is the model. She's just paid to look nice. Aren't I making sense to you?'

'I think you're being unfair on yourself and your potential. You could carry on writing if you wished. You could think of becoming the Vitale girl as taking a sabbatical. Just put your career on hold. You might even enjoy it.'

'I enjoy being stimulated, Johnny. I enjoy researching and writing good stories. I enjoy the variety this job gives me. One day I might be interviewing a bunch of kids on the street about their favourite movies, and the next day I might be interviewing the star of the movie. If I stopped what I'm doing now, I'd lose my footing. People would forget me all too quickly.'

'No one would forget you if you had millions of pounds behind you pushing your face on giant posters in every city.'

'I'd never be taken seriously again. I'm sorry, Johnny.' She smiled at him warmly. 'I'm really looking forward to running the story. I'm sure we'll find someone far more suitable.'

'To hell with the story, Fern. This is a chance in a lifetime and I think you should think very carefully before you turn it down.' Johnny's tone had changed.

Fern's mouth was set firm. Bullying was certainly not going to get him any closer to his objective.

'You have my answer. But I promise to deliver you a great article. Now I really must get on with it.'

Johnny rose from his chair. 'Then kill the article!'

'But what about the search?' Fern regarded him in astonishment.

'Sod the search, I'll go elsewhere.'

'You know it's just right for *Faces*. There's no need to be silly about this, Johnny.'

'You know where I am if you change your mind.' He swept out of the office.

Alix decided to keep her head down for the moment. Fern was obviously not in a mood to chat it over. She had slammed her notebook into her drawer and snapped that she was going out for a walk. Hopefully to cool down, Alix thought.

Alix had seen Fern's temper once before and it was not a pretty sight, but by six o'clock Alix's natural curiosity got the better of natural tact and diplomacy.

'Let's go and have a drink – you look like you could do with it.'

'What? Oh no, Alix. I really ought to get back. I'm bushed after last night and I've got some work to do on the Oscar Rees story.'

'But it's been killed.'

'Yeah, I know, but that doesn't stop me finding another angle. There's enough material in that family for a book, let alone an article.'

'Go on, just a quickie. I thought we might go to Casper's.'

'I shouldn't really . . . and besides, we always go there. It might be nice to try somewhere different.'

'Fern, don't be dull. It's much more fun than some boring old pub.'

Fern finished packing her desk up and threw her dog-eared notebook into the canvas rucksack by her chair. She stood up, shaking her hair out. Alix viewed it enviously. What she wouldn't give to have her face plastered all over Oscar Rees's new range. Still, she was hardly the type herself with her own 'individual' looks. But Fern . . . well . . . Although Alix would never admit it to anybody, she wasn't at all surprised by the suggestion.

When Fern caught sight of Alix's dejected face, she immediately felt guilty. Poor old Alix didn't have anyone to rush home to, which was precisely why she wanted to go to Casper's.

'To be honest I wasn't exactly looking forward to the empty flat. Paul's got rehearsals tonight so okay, just a quick one.'

'Great!' Alix rubbed her hands together gleefully and Fern wondered privately whether she'd ever have the courage to suggest that if Alix stopped shaving her head Sinéad O'Connor style, then she might be a lot more successful with the opposite sex.

Alix was extremely clever, but sometimes not particularly bright. She'd been on the magazine just a short time less than Fern, by way of local papers and journalism courses at college. While Fern tended to gravitate more towards diary and style-type pieces, Alix was into exposés and celebrity gossip. She could be like a ferocious terrier when she was on the scent of a scandal.

They weren't exactly what Fern would call real friends. They'd been thrown together through work, but they had enough in common to drink together on occasion.

Casper's was packed, as usual. There was no space at the bar, so Fern and Alix attached themselves to the end of the table queue. 'We might as well eat, then,' Alix said.

Fern opened her mouth to protest, and then quickly shut it. By the time they got themselves a table she could be weak with hunger, and as she'd already agreed to go this far, she just might as well go the whole way and be done with it.

'Why not?' Fern relaxed and started to take in her surroundings.

Most tables seemed to be single sex – that is, they either were full of women, or full of men. On some the phone placed in the centre of the table was being put to good use, while on others the occupants waited rather pathetically for someone to ring their bell, as it were, presumably finding the object of their own desires otherwise engaged. The whole Casper's pick-up gimmick was based on the ability of diners at each table to telephone to other tables, and thereby chat up anyone they fancied from a distance, through the relative safety of black Bakelite – a new dimension in safe sex.

It took at least half an hour to be seated, but the phone rang almost as soon as they sat down. Alix grabbed at it eagerly, and then drooled hello in her sexiest voice. Fern could hear the voice coming out clearly. It made her cringe with embarrassment. 'Can I speak to your friend,' it said. Alix thrust the phone towards Fern.

'Hello,' she said.

'I'd like you to tie me up in your hair and crush me between your legs, then I'd like – '

Fern slammed the phone back down. 'Disgusting person!' she hissed.

'But I thought it was a woman,' Alix said.

'It was.'

Fern looked around the restaurant and there, over in the far corner, was a lady who looked remarkably similar to Alix, complete with leather cap, and thigh high boots. She waved at Fern.

'Dear God,' Fern sighed. 'Funny old place, isn't it?'

'Casper's?'

'The world!'

Alix looked longingly at the phone for a few moments, then they scanned the menus and gave their order. Two glasses of wine appeared from nowhere. Fern looked at the waiter, confused.

'Two gentlemen over there,' he explained.

The phone rang again. Alix picked it up. 'Table 10,' explained the voice. 'Cheers!'

'Oh, you bought us the drinks,' Alix said in her best breathy voice. Then she turned around to try and see Table 10. Two wrinklies, who looked as if they'd been let off bingo with the wife for a night, sat in their suede car coats, waving.

'We'd like you to join us,' the voice said, eagerly.

'Sorry, too old. But thanks for the drink,' Alix said, bluntly, ringing off. 'We're doing really well, aren't we? A dyke and two geriatrics.'

'I suppose the night is young,' Fern said encouragingly.

Alix drew pictures with her fork in the top of her spaghetti carbonara, clearly deflated by the other guests at Casper's that night. Then she brightened up suddenly.

'Tell me all about that guy – the one in the office. It sounds very intriguing, Fern.'

'It's not at all really, Alix. Hey, d'you know who this tape's by. It's good, isn't it?'

'Bonnie Raitt.' And you're not getting off that lightly, thought Alix. 'Lots of girls would give their eyeteeth.'

'Then they wouldn't make very good models, would they?'

'Ha-ha, very funny. This guy is seriously offering you the Vitale contract?'

Fern shrugged. 'I guess.'

'Have you any idea what that means?'

'Sure. I do wish everyone would stop treating me like a total bimbo-head and thinking that just because I haven't jumped a mile high in delight at the offer there must be something wrong with my intellect. I do understand, Alix, but it's something I just can't see I'd get any enjoyment out of.'

'But just think of the money.'

'What's the point of earning lots of money and being miserable?'

'With that amount of money you couldn't possibly be miserable.'

'Then you're the one that's being daft. I can't think of anyone rich who's truly happy.'

'The supermodels look pretty chirpy to me. I grant you it may not necessarily make you happy to be mega . . . I mean really Onassis-style rich, but, Fern, you'd just be, well, well off, wouldn't you?' And besides, thought Alix, if Fern walked from the mag, then she'd be next in line for Assistant Features Editor. This offer could be extremely good news.

'I don't wear cosmetics.' Fern tried to stifle a yawn, unsuccessfully.

'So?'

'What's the point of hiring someone like me to promote cosmetics?'

'They want someone natural, I suppose. Anyway, why should I want to talk you into it? I'm jealous as hell. I just wish they'd asked me.'

'So do I,' Fern laughed, and at the same time she rubbed her forefinger lightly over her bottom lip, remembering the silky, sensuous feeling of last night's lipstick.

There was certainly no lack of material on Oscar Rees for Fern to get her teeth into, though some of the things she had uncovered in the last few days were going to be too hot to handle, with such diverse things as the sexual preferences of Hugo Rees's wife and the fact that the company was potentially on the receiving end of a hostile takeover bid at this very moment. She stood, full mug of black coffee in hand, and surveyed the mass of press cuttings that now covered the dining table. She was just itching to get her nose into them. Paul was out at rehearsal and the whole evening stretched ahead of her – pure undisturbed bliss.

Fern had already sorted the cuttings into semiorganized piles, starting with city performance and shareholder information, then moving through the whole gamut of cosmetics preparations and spectacular perfume launches to the enormous amount of scandal which seemed to hover like a sour scent around the family.

When Johnny had first vetoed The Face story Fern had been so angry that she wanted nothing to do with the company, but she had allowed her instinct to lead her into what she knew was going to be a very impressive piece about the company's slick marketing strategies and the image-making processes employed by major cosmetics houses such as Oscar Rees. If this didn't land her the post of Assistant Features Editor then she might as well seriously consider looking round for another job. She loved the interviews and the writing, and she never intended to stop doing either, but she wanted to be stretched and that meant she had to be given more of an editorial role on the magazine than simply being a staff writer. Edwina, Fern's boss, would see from this what a great story she could put together.

Hugo and Olivia Rees's marriage struck Fern as an altogether sad affair. There was no heir apparent from Hugo's loins. Whenever they had been pictured together, the couple gave the appearance of being extremely awkward in close proximity to each other. They looked brittle and unhappy. Nothing had ever been confirmed, but there were hints (and Fern was reading very closely between the lines) that Olivia enjoyed the company of women more than men, but then that wasn't so extraordinary. On Hugo's side, there were several society diary-type pictures which showed him in the company of a certain Lady Pembroke rather often. It amused Fern to compare Hugo beside his wife, and Hugo beside whom she presumed to be his mistress. He looked a far happier person with the latter. Fern guessed these pictures had some very interesting stories to tell.

It seemed that the company was very tightly held in the family's hand, albeit a slightly extended one. Alfred Easton had arrived in England from depression-hit America in the thirties, bringing his cosmetic formulas learned at the apron of a certain famous Hungarian lady in his pocket, so to speak. In New York, having deserted the salon of his mentor, he had tried to make a go of his own business by

48

setting up a chain of salons, but the great lady had proved too much for him and had vowed to ruin his every attempt, still being very sore at his audacity in stealing her formulas.

Every time Alfred opened a salon, very soon one of hers would appear in close proximity, and this was at a time when American women were not yet used to having their cosmetic needs provided by a humble man. Alfred went bust, and headed for England with what little he had left.

Soon he realized that the small but well-established and highly respected house of Oscar Rees could perhaps do worse than to team up with someone of his experience and expertize, and after several months of protracted negotiations over name, royalties and so on, a deal between Alfred Easton and Oscar Rees was struck.

Sixty per cent of the company rested with Oscar Rees, and the rest went to the brash American. They soon needed to borrow money from the bank to expand their production facilities, so the bank took a ten per cent stake from Oscar, and a two per cent stake from Alfred. The partnership had thrived spectacularly over the years, not least because of its insistence on continuing to manufacture lipstick during the war years and classing it as an essential item. Keeping high the morale of the women at home was a vital part of the war effort. They might have to go without their nylons, but they certainly shouldn't pass up their lipstick!

When Oscar's heir, Hugo, married Alfred's daughter, Olivia, it seemed like a marriage made in heaven. The two patriarchs couldn't have wished for a neater join between the sides.

Then, of course, there was the Foundation, the splendidly prestigious Rees Foundation for Remedial

Cosmetic Surgery, founded by the dogs of war upon their return from the action. So many horrendous injuries resulted from the war. Pilots had their faces burned off, soldiers were shattered by shrapnel. Oscar and more especially Alfred, not satisfied with merely manufacturing the powders and paints to camouflage the scars, decided, with charity and individual sponsorship, to bring together leading specialists in the new field of cosmetic surgery, and so the Foundation was born. Now, over forty years later, it was an institution world famous for its pioneering work in the field, and for the fact that many patients were never charged a penny for their treatment. An illustrious board of governors oversaw the running of the place, with the token family presence filled by Olivia. So far as Fern could gather, the Foundation now owned approximately fifteen per cent of the shares in Oscar Rees, bequeathed to it from both Alfred and Oscar, upon their demise.

Fern wondered whether she might fit in a visit to the place and see what else she could learn about it.

She scribbled some notes and then flicked through the cuttings on the Easton family. Olivia's brother, Julian, figured heavily amongst them. He was a notorious playboy and he didn't seem to do very much in the business at all, other than promote the name through his infamy. It appeared that he had been married at least three times, had brief sporting careers in motor racing, yachting and polo, and a continuing interest in the art of bonking as many beautiful women as possible.

The twins, from his first marriage, were now grown up and well ensconsed in the family firm. Lucienne and Alexander were as alike as the proverbial two peas in the pod and, according to the cuttings, they too had had fairly chequered careers both at school and then university. And from what she was reading, and the way some of the stuff had been written, Fern had the feeling there could well be a lot more that had stayed out of the press. Again she resolved to try and dig further.

When Fern heard Paul's key in the lock she looked at her watch and was astonished to realize that the last three hours had whizzed by. Her cold mug of coffee still sat on the table, untouched and forgotten.

'Hi!' she called out to him, and stretched, easing out the tense knots in her shoulders. God, she could do with a good work-out. Hunching over desks wasn't the best way of exercising the muscles.

Paul came in and bent over her, plonking a light kiss on the top of her head.

'What a night! If half the cast bothered to learn their lines it would do us all a favour. We were trying to struggle through Act Four and Dull fell asleep backstage, while Nathaniel was trying to get his leg over the princess. What a bloody shower. Any drink in the house, Fern?' Almost as an after-thought, he glanced back at the table where her own labours sprawled in front of her. 'Oh, and what have you been up to?'

Fern laughed quietly. 'This.' She pointed to the mess by way of explanation.

Paul glanced at one of the press cuttings. 'Not bloody Oscar Rees again. I had enough of them the other night. Still working on that daft story of yours?'

Fern bit her lip, struggling to keep her temper. 'As a matter of fact, no. This is a slightly different story. The Face story has been killed by them so I thought

51

I'd ferret around and see if I could come up with something else.'

'But I thought they were pestering you to run it.'

'They were. Now they've changed their minds.'

Paul helped himself to the last of the whisky, filling the tumbler half full and replacing the empty whisky bottle back in the cupboard.

'Are you disappointed?'

She shrugged. 'I guess. I thought it would make a good story.'

'So why did they change?'

Fern took a deep breath. She had deliberately not mentioned the subject to Paul, knowing he'd probably be upset about Johnny coming to see her, and more than likely would fly into one of his jealous tantrums. He hated anyone paying her attention.

'Because Johnny wanted me to consider becoming The Face.'

Paul nearly spluttered a mouthful of whisky over her. 'What?' he screeched. 'Are you serious?'

'He said he was serious.'

'You?' He said it with such derision that Fern began to feel seriously offended.

'Yeah.'

'I've never heard such a daft idea. You? A model?' He squealed with laughter.

'It's not so daft,' she muttered defensively. 'They thought I was fresh-faced, and that's what they wanted.'

'You're too old!'

'I'm only twenty-three.'

'In that business, that's old, believe me.'

'Then if I'm "too old", why would Johnny ask me?'

'You're so naïve at times, aren't you? Because,

dear Fern, he's got the hots for you. Any fool could work that out.'

Fern's cheeks burned with anger, but she bit her lip. Instead she glowered at him, her green eyes narrowing venomously. When she spoke, her voice was low. 'So you're suggesting it's a kind of casting couch scenario, then – all this trouble purely to seduce me? Give the guy more credit than that. He does have some professionalism, I'm sure.'

'There's no such thing as professionalism in cosmetics. It's a contradiction in terms.'

Fern started to collect up her papers, shuffling them angrily. 'I just wonder what you'd have said if they'd asked you!'

'At least if he'd asked me I'd have guessed straight away what his motives were.'

'So now you're suggesting he's gay, are you?'

'No. I'm merely pointing out that if he'd wanted to lay me, he might well have used the same ploy. That's not the same as saying he is.'

'I think you're jealous,' she snapped.

'Oh do grow up,' Paul said. He drained his Scotch and picked up his coat which he'd only just cast off onto the sofa. He yawned obviously. 'I think I'll head on back to my place. I can see I'm not going to get a peaceful night here.'

God! How could he be so selfish! Fern was fuming too much to speak. Surely he must see she had steam coming out of her ears. If he made a move to kiss her she would probably thump him. Luckily for him he headed straight for the door.

Then he turned back to her, throwing his scarf dramatically over his shoulder. 'Farewell, mad wench, you have simple wit!'

Fern picked up her notebook and threw it at Paul as hard as she could, but he ducked through the door quickly, leaving the book to hit the wood with a resounding thud.

'Oh!' she screeched. 'That man is the end!'

Chapter Five

Edwina Butler leaned back in her conspicuously large leather chair and rested her fingers, prayer-like, beneath her chin. Not for the first time, Fern found herself wondering how long it would be before she could occupy the same, or a very similar, chair. Edwina's coolly intelligent eyes fixed steadily on Fern.

'It's not bad, but I wonder whether it's quite right.'

Fern raised her eyebrows, and cursed the lurch in her stomach. She waited, swine-like, for Edwina's pearls of wisdom to fall before her.

'I wonder,' she repeated in her smooth voice that cloaked a razor-sharp tongue, 'whether this is snappy enough for us. It's perhaps a little supplementish, not tight enough, Fern.'

'I felt there was so much good information there that to have made it too tight would have been an injustice – '

'Yes, darling. But I just feel . . . I don't know . . . ' Her voice tailed off, and she examined her fingernails intently. 'Such a shame about the story. I rather liked The Face idea. Nice and glamorous.'

'I think this is better,' Fern said boldly.

'It's very good. There's plenty of sharp writing, but then that's what I would expect from you, Fern. Why don't you shorten the piece by, say, a thousand words or so, and then I'll take another look at it? I'm sure you'll agree with me.'

Fern started to rise. 'Edwina, I wondered if you'd had any more ideas about the next Assistant Features Editor. David leaves at the end of the month and, as you know, I was hoping – '

'Of course you were,' Edwina said lightly. 'I quite understand, Fern. But I must be straight with you and tell you that I am obviously considering others as well as yourself. It's an important step, and I want to be sure that whoever takes it is going to benefit *Faces* as fully as possible. But rest assured, Fern, I'm taking into account all you've achieved so far.'

'Thanks.' Fern let her hair swing around her face, shrouding the flush of humiliation on her cheeks. Edwina had hinted that the job would be hers. There was no other person with as much experience as she had. She managed to control her temper until she reached her desk, then she threw herself down onto her chair, swearing under her breath.

'What's up with you? Edwina in one of her moods?' asked Alix.

Fern bit her lip. 'Not really. She was just being a bit vague. That always irritates me,' Fern lied awkwardly. She sensed it was not a good idea to broadcast around the office what had just passed between herself and Edwina. And she had no doubt that telling Alix was tantamount to putting it over the paging system.

Fern fetched a coffee and then grabbed the newspaper from her desk. She flicked through the pages until she found what she was looking for. Perhaps it was fate that it happened to be 'Media' day.

Alix would often dally in the office at the end of the day. She liked to draft her stuff when all was quiet and everyone had gone home. Besides, the deserted desks brought other advantages: she could practise her powers of espionage. With the skill and efficiency of one venturing through well-charted territory, Alix flicked through Fern's drawers, checking out the pad on which she scribbled her ideas. Then she leafed through the small V & A diary, scanning Fern's appointments. She squinted with concentration at the new entries, then something caught her customary curiosity.

'Broadgate Street,' she muttered aloud. 'What on earth would she be going there for?'

She closed the diary and replaced it in the drawer. Then moving from the desk, she stumbled over the wastepaper basket. The *Guardian* spilled onto the floor. With a well-honed spirit of detection Alix quickly found the appointments page. 'Tut-tut, Fern, you really should be more careful,' she laughed to herself.

There in the centre of the display ads was a neat circle of red ringing an ad placed by *A La Mode*, International Magazines' flagship glossy. Alix tucked the newspaper under her arm, humming lightly to herself.

The vast International Magazines building made even Oscar Rees's prestigious headquarters seem diminutive. The main receptionist had directed Fern to the fifth floor, where she had stepped out from the lift into the heart of a bustling magazine empire. A wall display listed the major titles impressively and succeeded in filling visitors with awe. The large coffee table in front of her was neatly stacked with the latest editions of the top ten women's titles. Phones buzzed, printers clicked and ludicrously pretty young girls darted about the place, parading the hottest and latest off the fashion pages. Fern thought back to the time of her interview on *Faces*, when she had considered the glamour and sophistication of Edwina and the couple of floors occupied by the mag impressive. *Faces* would probably just about fill up the ladies' loo in this place, it was all so huge! Fern smiled up as a young girl approached. She had the classic bone structure of the English aristocracy, small oval face, wedge-like cheekbones and a nose designed only to detect the most refined of smells.

'I'm Fenella, India Duncan-Forrester's assistant,' she said haughtily, in a voice that could chisel lead crystal. 'Miss Duncan-Forrester can see you now.'

'Thank you,' Fern said politely and followed the gorgeous creature through a maze of desks and partitions until they reached a smoked-glass tabernacle at the far side of the room. Fenella held the door open for Fern, who obediently stepped through – then halted in her tracks.

'Oh!' she blurted, before she could stop herself. She hesitated, cursing her luck. Here was Leo Eden's girlfriend, the one who had been so jealous at the ball the other week.

'You'd better come and sit down. Fern, isn't it?' Miss Duncan-Forrester's nose wrinkled visibly as she stared at Fern's jeans. Fern tossed her hair back, and waited for the woman's eyes to level with her own, unable to disguise the look of challenge. 'Did you bring a CV with you?'

Fern nodded and, almost reluctantly, handed over her life. While Miss Duncan-Forrester scanned the pages, Fern sat ramrod straight, watching the woman's expression. Every few moments her eyebrows would lift, and then a kind of sneer of disdain crept across her over-made-up visage. Eventually she let go of the pages and let them fall, unaided on to her desk.

Twisting her lips as if wondering where to start,

she regarded Fern with that same hint of suspicion. Fern bet herself £100 she wouldn't get the job.

'So,' the woman said at last, 'you've worked on *Faces*.'

'Yes.' Fern coughed to remove the treacherous note of nervousness from her voice. 'For eighteen months. Before that I was – '

'Yes, yes,' the woman cut her off. 'I can read, you know.'

Fern snapped her lips shut and waited.

'*Faces* is far removed from *Mode*. I wouldn't necessarily call what you've done an apprenticeship. I'd have thought you might be better off going a bit more downmarket, really.'

Fern felt the angry flush flood across her cheeks. 'We have a circulation of 400,000 and a readership of just over a million. *Faces* reaches an audience with the largest disposable income per capita, i.e., the under twenty-fives. I've been producing lead articles on a regular basis for the last twelve months. I think that's quite an apprenticeship.'

'But not for us,' the creature hissed. 'You see, what we're looking for in Assistant Features Editor is someone who will instinctively know what's right for *Mode*. Someone who will simply blend in.' She laid heavy emphasis on the words, then smiled at Fern. 'We're a very tightknit staff. We all have to get on, well, intimately. We need a certain element of sophistication and quite simply, to put it bluntly, I just don't think you're the type, dear.'

'What do you mean?' Fern could feel her hackles getting dangerously high.

'Your background and experience, charming as they sound, won't have given you the necessary polish needed to succeed on this magazine. I'm sorry, but I have to think of the other staff. And your style is, well,' her eyes roved over Fern's jeans once more, 'a little streetish for our tastes.'

'But what about all my achievements, all my stories? Don't you want to ask me about them? Don't you want me to tell you about the great ideas I have for *Mode* articles?' Fern fluttered a folder at the ghastly female. 'I spent a long time putting this little lot together.'

The woman laughed. 'I can't see that there'd be any point in taking any more of your time. I'm sure you'll agree when you've given it some thought. Why don't you try one of the women's weeklies?'

Fern stood up and snatched her CV back from the desk. 'This wasn't an interview at all. From the moment I walked through that door you had no intention of considering me for the job. This is all because your creep of a boyfriend spoke to me at that ball the other week. Well, rest assured I wouldn't touch a man like him with a barge pole. You have nothing to worry about. And, for the record, I wouldn't want to join a magazine that employs people as unprofessional as yourself.'

'My dear girl, the very fact of your outburst makes you wholly unsuitable for such a prestigious job. And quite frankly, until you'd mentioned it I'd quite forgotten that I'd met you before. Now, if you'll excuse me!'

Fern swept out of the office and didn't stop until she was safely back on the street where even the polluted, fume-filled air tasted sweet in comparison to that viper's den.

It took Alix several attempts to gain Fern's attention. She was staring out of the window, lost in some secret world. 'Fern!' Alix tried again, more insistently.

'Oh, Alix, I'm sorry. I was miles away.'

'So I can tell. I've been standing here for two minutes.'

Fern sighed and her shoulders drooped despondently.

'Want to talk about it?' Alix asked solicitously.

'There's nothing to talk about really. It just seems that suddenly everything's going wrong in my life, ever since that bloody Vitale story.'

'But I thought you'd come up with something better.'

'So did I,' Fern said morosely. 'And Paul's being a pain in the butt. I think maybe I'm losing my sense of direction a bit. Do you ever feel like that, Alix?'

'Never.' Alix shook her head decidedly. 'Mostly I know exactly where I'm headed.'

'Then you're very lucky,' Fern forced a smile.

'Well, whenever I'm feeling down, I take a break. Just a couple of days or so. Maybe that's what you should do. Why don't you pop over to Ireland, get some fresh country air into you? You haven't had a holiday in months.'

'Sounds more like running away to me.'

'Nonsense. I can cover for you here. Anyway, there's a bank holiday coming up next week. All you'd need to ask for would be a couple of days. Even stingy old Edwina can't object to that.'

'Yeah, maybe I will,' Fern said thoughtfully. 'Right at this moment the idea of getting out of London sounds like good news.'

'That's settled then,' Alix said triumphantly.

That should give her the time to get her plans into action.

Chapter Six

Olivia Rees lay face down on the hard massage couch, her chin propped on her hands, luxuriating in the feel of the professional hands on her body, easing and pummelling her oiled flesh. The small hands worked expertly over her back, down onto her buttocks, pressing and kneading all the tension away. Her skin felt electric: ultrasensitive and delicious. She stretched, like a satisfied cat, letting out a purr of contentment. 'Mmm, Linda . . . that feels so good . . . ' she sighed.

'Turn over, then,' the younger woman ordered. Olivia eased herself onto her back and let the small towel that had lain across her lower pelvis slip onto the floor. She stretched her arms above her head, pulling her breasts taut, thrilling at the pleasure flooding through them. She closed her eyes and concentrated on the path the woman's fingers were taking. The masseuse gripped one foot firmly, and kneaded the sole of it, causing a discomfort which was strangely pleasurable. Next her hands slipped up the length of Olivia's leg, almost to her crotch, and Olivia shuddered with an excitement that was purely sexual. She lifted her lower torso, teasingly, willing the girl to continue her exploration, daring her to search a little further. But the hands retreated once more, down to her other foot, and from there started their tortuous journey back to the point where almost, but not quite, they would enter a dangerously forbidden place.

Shamelessly, Olivia moaned with the sensuous agony of frustration. Her cunt throbbed and turned liquid and still the blasted girl teased her. The hands came to a rest against Olivia's lower belly and lay motionless for a moment, the warmth turning into a burning heat. Then, oh so agonizingly slowly, they slid up her stomach, over the tight-stretched skin of her ribs, and then firmly grasped each of her breasts, the adept fingers flickering over the stiff buds of her nipples. A strange, strangled sound came from Olivia's throat, and she writhed on the narrow bed, pushing her buttocks high, demanding release. She bit her lip until she tasted blood.

Olivia opened her eyes and saw Linda's knowing smile. The girl's eyes travelled over Olivia's body, and she very slowly started to unbutton her sterile white coat. Her breasts fell out of the garment, and Olivia stared, marvelling at their milky whiteness. Linda laughed a low sound full of promise and anticipation.

At last she stood naked before Olivia, and Olivia reached out for her, pulling her towards her. 'Damn you, you're such a bloody tease,' she hissed at the younger woman.

'That's why I'm so good for you,' the other countered. She came closer to the bed and bent over Olivia's head so that her breasts swung over her face. Olivia's tongue darted and flicked over each breast, enjoying the sweet taste and smell of them. Then she grabbed the girl's hand and pushed it down to the space between her legs that ached so unbearably and longingly. Suddenly Linda thrust her fingers deep inside Olivia, slipping into her cunt easily, spreading the wet, silky flesh apart. Olivia's hips bucked and writhed, demanding more and more from that small, searching hand. She wanted to engulf it totally, to swallow it up inside her; she pushed higher and higher, until the girl's four fingers were thrusting into her. Then, as Linda climbed on top of her, placing her naked skin against Olivia's body, Olivia reached her shattering climax, exploding wildly, almost toppling off the narrow bed. Linda's mouth closed over Olivia's nipple, but Olivia flinched, and pushed her head away. 'I'm too sensitive. Wait a minute . . . ' Then: 'Did you hear that?'

'What?'

'The bloody door.'

'Won't Thomas let them in?'

'That's the trouble. Thomas will undoubtedly let them in, and that means, my dear young thing, that they might just trek up the stairs to see me. Sorry, my love, but I think you'd better put your white coat back on pdq.'

'Just when it was getting to the best bit,' the young masseuse sighed.

Olivia stroked her cheek, gently. 'I'll make it up to you next time, promise.'

Linda bent down and kissed Olivia firmly on the mouth, and then picked up the crumpled uniform off the floor and quickly buttoned it back on. Olivia had never known Linda to wear anything underneath it, winter or summer. The girl was such a hussy . . .

Olivia retrieved the small towel from the floor and draped it over her so that her body was covered. Loud footsteps rang out across the marble tiles on the landing, then there was a heavy knock at the door.

'Come in,' Olivia cried out.

A tall, slim young man entered the room. He had the same jet-black hair and fine, aristocratic features as the woman who lay semi-naked on the couch. His eyebrows echoed the distinguished arch of Olivia's, and beneath them, dark, almost black eyes reflected back at Olivia's own. She could have been looking at her own son.

'Aunt,' Alexander gushed, 'I'm so sorry if I interrupted something.' His voice was heavy with insinuation, but Olivia ignored it.

'Alexander,' she sighed languidly. 'Whatever brings you here at this time of day? I thought you'd be busy wrestling Oscar Rees away from my darling husband, not giving aged aunts house calls. Something frightfully important must have happened for us to be so honoured.' She gestured to Linda, who was collecting up her bottles of oil and packing them away in a small, quilted bag.

'Linda, darling, have you met my nephew, Alexander? He can be quite charming, so I'm told.'

'Hello,' Linda said shortly. She was still sulking from her missed orgasm.

'So you're the one who keeps Aunt Olivia in shape. I hear you're awfully good!' Alexander eyed Linda from top to toe, then brought his eyes to rest on Linda's ample bosom, which was fighting against the tight buttons of her coat.

'Well, unfortunately for you, Alexander, you'll never know. I'm afraid Linda only does women.'

'Such a pity,' Alexander sighed, and flicked an imaginary piece of fluff from his immaculate dark pinstriped sleeve. 'Linda, my dear, I'm sure you won't mind if I have a quick word with my aunt, will you?'

'It's all right, Alexander. Linda was just going, weren't you, darling?' Olivia ignored Linda's petulant pout. 'Don't worry, we'll make sure we finish off properly next time.'

'I'll make sure we do,' Linda said, collecting her bag and glowering at Alexander as she reached the door. Alexander closed it firmly behind her.

'Pretty little thing, isn't she?'

'Delightful.' Olivia sat up, so that the towel dropped from her breasts, refusing to be drawn by Alexander's mockery.

Alexander walked back to the couch and stood over Olivia, his eyes roving freely over her naked breasts.

'You have a marvellous body, you know, Aunt.'

'Really?' Olivia's voice sounded bored.

'It's a shame to waste it.' Alexander reached out and placed his finger on Olivia's shoulder. He drew it across the top of her neck and then down towards her nipple. She shrugged it off, matter of factly.

'Look, Alexander,' she said, rising so that she stood before him totally naked. 'I'm sure you didn't come here to discuss my physique.' She picked up a robe off the bed and pulled it around herself. 'So, what brings you here? You'll forgive me, of course. I've got a Foundation lunch I simply must get to, and I'm running a bit short on time.'

'Of course, of course. Same old Aunt Olivia, always rushing off doing good deeds. Well, I won't hold you up. I just wondered if you'd heard about the offer.'

'What offer?'

'Ah . . . ' he said rather smugly, 'so you mean Hugo didn't mention it?'

'Damn you, Alexander. Stop being so obtuse. What on earth are you talking about?'

'I'm talking, my dear, about the offer Cooper Jefferson has made for Oscar Rees.'

'Oh, come on, Alexander. Don't be a silly boy. We all know Coopers have been sniffing around for years. They'll never make a serious offer, and if they *had*, Hugo would have told me about it.'

'Well, be that as it may, the fact is they have.'

'They couldn't afford us. Hugo would never agree – '

'£100 million pounds sounds to me as if they can afford us.'

'You're not serious!'

'Believe me, Olivia, I don't joke about that sort of money. You realize, of course, what this means?'

Olivia was still reeling. She sank down onto the bed. Why on earth hadn't Hugo told her? She had a right to know, if what Alexander was saying was, indeed, true.

'Ten per cent of that could be yours, Olivia. At a rough calculation, that means you'd be worth, let's see, a cool ten million. Not bad, eh?'

'He'd never agree to it, though. Hugo won't sell. He'll never give up the "Rees legacy", as he calls it. You know that as well as I do, Alexander.'

Alexander came to sit beside her on the low bed. He spoke very quietly, conspiratorially. 'Olivia, just think what freedom you'd have with all your assets released. You wouldn't even have to stay with Hugo – if you didn't want to, of course,' he added quickly when he saw Olivia's lips tighten. 'And then there's the Foundation – your precious Foundation. What could they do with the money right now? Interesting proposition, isn't it?' His grin was almost a leer.

'Thing is . . . ' he studied his fingernails, casually, 'the decision could perhaps be taken from Hugo.'

'What on earth do you mean?'

'Put it this way: my lovely sister and I between us have thirteen per cent, you've got ten per cent, our old man's got ten per cent, and we mustn't forget the bank and their little stake of twelve per cent. Between us all that makes forty-five per cent.'

'I'm not a complete imbecile, thanks, Alexander.

And Hugo's left with a measly forty per cent, with fifteen per cent having gone to the Foundation.'

'Exactly. So you see what I'm getting at?'

'We sell regardless of Hugo's wishes.' Olivia sounded horrified. It was unthinkable. Hugo *was* the company.

'It's a thought, isn't it, depending on what we all want at the end of the day.'

'This offer from Coopers, it might be a straight share swap, rather than cash.' Olivia struggled to get more information.

Alexander shrugged. 'I'm not exactly sure,' he lied smoothly. 'I have a feeling it's hard cash.'

'Nobody's got that sort of cash available just like that.'

'Coopers have, and besides, even if they didn't they'd borrow it. You've only got to look at Oscars' profits to realize that any bank would put up for it.'

'Even if I agreed to it, who's to say the others will? The bank have been deliriously happy with Hugo's management. They won't agree if Hugo doesn't want to. They'd never vote against him.'

Alexander smiled, pleased with himself. 'You can never be sure of anything, these days, Auntie. It's not what you know, it's who you know.'

'You're a devious little shit, Alexander, always were. Your parents should have had you put down at birth. Actually, I've always considered Hugo eminently sensible for not selling out, you know.'

'Don't be silly. No one in their right mind would resist an offer like this one.'

'You'd better go and read your history books, young man. If it were a share deal, you've only got to look at what happened when Helman-Palmer bought Caterina Grey. Things went dramatically wrong. They lost a fortune. And if those were our

68

shares we could end up losing a fortune, not gaining one.'

'Caterina Grey was already flagging.'

'Not so. It flagged when they started getting the products wrong – and even you've got to admit that's something Hugo's never done. We've all got that to be grateful for. Why do you think my father and Hugo's father were happy to let Hugo jump into the driving seat? Julian couldn't have done it. Your father was always bored with the business. He likes to enjoy himself too much.'

'And what about Lucienne and me? We're in the company. We know which direction it's got to go in.'

Olivia stood up and walked through to her dressing room. She was beginning to tire of Alexander's presence, for all his news. He could be desperately naïve at times.

'Darling nephew,' she called from the next room, 'don't think that just because you and your twin sister attended Harvard Business School it qualifies you to run a company like Oscar Rees. You've got to learn to walk first. And you could learn from Hugo.'

'If he'd let us.' Alexander's voice carried through to her. He sounded like a sulky child.

'Maybe he's a lot shrewder than you think. After all, the reason for your visit is to do some dirty dealing behind his back, is it not? Therefore you can hardly blame the man for being a little wary in letting either of you have a free hand. Hugo is not stupid, Alexander, and quite frankly, if he feels this offer isn't right for the company then I shall probably abide by his decision.'

Alexander stood in the doorway and watched his aunt slip a long, slender leg into a sheer film of nylon. She attached two lace suspender clips to the top of the stocking.

'I'm sure I've surprised you, haven't I?' she went on. 'Just remember, Alexander, Hugo's built up Oscars. That's how we all manage to have such privileged lifestyles. I warn you, don't bite the hand, it just might stick in your throat and choke you!'

Olivia had no doubt of whose hand fed her, and she had no intention of cutting it off. For all their marital problems, life with Hugo was extremely comfortable.

She was going to ask Alexander to zip her up, but he had already left.

'I suppose it's "after" Mondrian.'

The man looked around, and the girl who had spoken sighed, still staring at the painting.

'Is it? I wouldn't have known. It just looks like a lot of squares to me. Is that what they call cubism?'

'No. Picasso and Braque were cubists. Piet Mondrian was abstract,' she said knowledgeably.

'Really. Do you know a lot about it . . . art, I mean?'

She turned around, and Charles Allen found himself looking into a pair of the deepest brown eyes he had ever seen. They were shaped like two large, perfect almonds, and the brows above them rose in a steep arch, giving her a look of almost haughty disdain. Then she smiled at him, and he found himself mesmerized by her face. It was beautiful – desperately beautiful. Her perfectly painted crimson lips drew his eyes, until finally he realized he must be gawping.

Her eyes twinkled at him mischievously, and he was glad not to have missed this ravishing woman in the crowded rooms.

'Not that much, but perhaps a bit more than you do,' she laughed.

70

'I don't suppose you'd consider showing me around, would you? I'm sure I'd find it a lot more fun having the stuff explained, as it were.'

The girl looked at her watch. 'I'm sorry, I'm supposed to be somewhere else in a few minutes. I've already stayed longer than I should,' and suddenly she was gone, swallowed up by the hordes of people attending the Royal Academy Summer Exhibition's Gala Reception, all eager to be seen starting off the season in the right place.

As soon as Lucienne got into her car in St James's Square, she made a telephone call.

'Xan,' she said quickly, 'so far so good. I think he's interested. I suppose you want me at Grosvenor House, too.'

'Why not? A bit of culture shouldn't do you any harm at all. You can show off your knowledge of antiques to our banking friend as well.'

'He's not very attractive, Xan. I hope I don't have to go all the way.'

'Just think of Coopers, darling Sin, and ten million smackeroonies. For that kind of money you can fake it, I'm sure.'

'Bastard!' Lucienne hissed at him as she switched off the phone.

Chapter Seven

Leo Eden never particularly looked forward to the New York sessions with his egomaniacal Texan boss, and this occasion proved no exception. Leo declined the proffered glass of mineral water and fixed his gaze on Lowenstein's fleshy lips. At least the man had managed to shed some weight since Leo's last visit, and his skin appeared to have an unprecedented hint of colour. Must have found himself a new mistress, Leo mused.

Lowenstein was reaching the end of his speech. 'I want that company, Leo. I want a controlling interest. Do you think you can get it?'

'As you and I both know, Bob, a lot can happen between negotiations and signature. I can only tell you what the situation looks like and that is that we could have over fifty per cent of Oscar Rees's shares in our control.'

Bob listened carefully to Leo. He liked and respected the man very much and had quickly learned that he was nobody's fool. The son of a Swiss pharmaceuticals magnate, he had chosen to carve his own niche in the industry, without resorting to what the Texan considered to be unhealthy nepotism.

'Damn me, but that would be a shit-hot acquisition, Eden. I reckon I could get us some serious real estate inside Macy's with a name like that to entice those slimy buyers. Why, they'd be begging us for the rights to sell Oscar Rees. I could never understand why old Oscar didn't launch the product over here before now.'

Leo coughed in embarrassment. Still, with two hundred companies under the Cooper Jefferson flag perhaps Lowenstein could be forgiven for not knowing this small piece of information.

'He has, Bob. All the lines are available at Bloomingdale's. They have been for ten years or so.'

Lowenstein burst out laughing. 'Hell, Eden, just goes to show how often I buy perfume. But I don't need to, that's the sort of thing I employ people like you to tell me. Anyway, I want you to get this thing sewn up tight, understand? No cock-ups, Eden, no screwing. Get me Oscar Rees,' Leo stood up, 'however much it takes. Got it?'

'Sure, Bob, $150 million. I suppose we'll get it gift-wrapped for that sort of money.'

Bob looked at his London MD sideways. Sometimes he had the strangest feeling that the odd sense of British humour was way over his head.

Leo acknowledged the stewardess's broad grin and thanked her for the pre-publication copy of *Vanity Fair* which she handed to him. He placed it on the empty seat beside him and tucked in to the quenelle of sole and julienne of carrots, washing it down with a highly palatable bottle of Chablis. After his tray had been cleared and he was served a delicious cup of fresh coffee, he idly picked up the glossy and flicked through it.

As the fan of pages flashed in front of his eyes, something made him stop and turn back. He could barely believe what he was seeing. There on the page in front of him was a piece cheekily entitled 'A Butch Batch' – the so-called pick of industry's most eligible bachelors. Leo groaned. He was staring at a glossy

73

blow-up of his own face, joined by a small group of other unfortunates, who for some strange reason featured a lot less prominently than he himself. He peered into the background of the photograph to try to track down where he had been when the picture was taken, but it could have been at any number of black-tie affairs. He stroked his chin ruefully, resting his thumb in the faint groove at the base of it. It wasn't a bad picture at all. One could just see a small white hand nestling in the crook of his left arm, but whatever female it was would remain a mystery, as the magazine had decided to block her right out.

The copy ran like a job CV:

Place of birth: Somewhere in middle Europe
Education: Eton, the Sorbonne, Cambridge
Hobbies: Skiing, sailing, tennis, hot-air ballooning, acquiring as many companies and women as possible.

Leo grunted. Damned cheek of it. He read on.

Achievements
School: Ten O-levels, four As, in Economics, Chemistry, Maths and Business Studies
Sorbonne: Certificate of Distinction
Cambridge: First Class Honours Degree in Economics and Business Studies
Sporting: Rowing blue

Well, well, someone had been very busy on his behalf, and so far they'd got it right, give or take a few bits here and there. He closed the magazine and slid it into his briefcase. He caught the eye of the stewardess.

'Thanks,' he said. 'I didn't know.'

Again she gave him the benefit of her broad smile. 'It sounds fairly impressive. Should I believe it?'

'Every single word of it,' Leo laughed.

'I don't think we've got anything more to discuss, gentlemen.' Hugo was trying very hard to maintain his cool. Coopers had been hounding him for weeks and he had finally agreed to what he hoped would be the last meeting on the subject. To this end, Leo Eden, Coopers' MD, and Larry Kerson, the company accountant, now sat at either side of Hugo in Oscar Rees's grand conference room in the basement of the Bond Street headquarters. For almost an hour both Eden and Kerson had been vainly putting their case to him.

'I will not sell, gentlemen. That has always been my position, and it will continue to be my position. At the risk of repeating myself, as I'm sure you all know, Oscar Rees was my father. Oscar merged wth Easton back in the thirties. Since its inception, Oscar Rees has been a privately owned and run corporation, and it is my intention to keep it that way.' Hugo stood up, by way of dismissal.

'The other shareholders might disagree with you, Hugo,' Larry Kerson, the ferret-faced accountant, pointed out smugly. 'Let's face it, it may not be your decision to make.'

Hugo didn't bother to hide his distaste for the man. 'I already know what their answers will be.'

Leo Eden grinned amiably at Hugo. Hugo admired Eden. He was extraordinarily young to have scaled the heights of such a huge operation as Cooper Jefferson. Hugo guessed he couldn't be any more than thirty or so. His skill at acquiring complementary companies was partly the reason for his success, though sometimes he had almost lost his position through his acquisitiveness. Three times deals of his had been referred to the Monopolies Commission.

In some ways Eden reminded Hugo very much of himself. There was a cool assurance about him that one could respect. He didn't get overexcited when things got a bit heated around the table. Unlike his sidekick, Kerson, he managed to maintain his charm, even when Hugo himself was swearing at him. Perhaps if things had been different Hugo might well have enjoyed working with this younger man. He would have enjoyed guiding the likes of Leo Eden . . .

Eden's shrewd gaze brought Hugo back to reality. This young man didn't seem to be in need of much in the way of guidance at the present time.

'I wouldn't be too sure, Hugo. Things have a way of turning out unexpectedly when it comes to cash offers.'

He snapped his briefcase shut and put his hand out. 'Hugo, I've always had the utmost respect for you. I know what you've achieved for Oscar Rees and that's why I want you on the Board at Coopers. It's not as if we're giving you a cheap offer. I firmly believe that you could be in for a very tough time ahead. You're going to need us soon, but by the time you do, you won't receive anything like the offer we're making at the moment. You'd better think hard about it.'

Hugo knew the man was sincere, but what Eden didn't realize was that without Oscar Rees, Hugo's life would be pointless. He had chosen the company above everything else, and if he gave it up now then his whole life would be a mockery. He would fight it all the way.

One last spray of perfume, a quick lipstick check and Lucienne was ready. She smoothed down the fine jersey of her diminutive black Jasper Conran cocktail dress and headed through the reception area of the Grosvenor House Hotel, following the stairs down to the Great Room, from where she could already hear the excited buzz of people attending the private preview of the famous antiques fair. As far as she could see, visitors were milling round, admiring the vast assortment of treasures assembled on the hundred or so stalls. Lucienne took a glass of champagne from a proffered tray and slowly walked across the room, pausing every now and then to glance at an interesting piece of furniture or *objet d'art*.

All the while she was watching out for Charles Allen, hoping to catch sight of his tall, blondish head among the crowd. Perhaps Grosvenor House hadn't been such a good idea after all. She should have chosen another known haunt of Charles Allen's, such as a nightclub, where it would have been much more intimate and easy to spot him. Several people had noticed her. She smiled back or mouthed a quick hello, trying to look as if she had a purpose before her, and couldn't stop and chat at this moment. She sipped her champagne, her eyes scanning the faces over the rim of her glass. Damn! This was hopeless. Perhaps she'd try the gallery. She found the stairs and made her way up to the mezzanine level where there were even more people and stalls.

Lucienne walked around for a bit, and then leaned up against the balcony, looking back over her shoulder at the crowd below. She flicked her long red fingernails against the glass in irritation. All she could see was a swarm of dinner suits.

'Hello!'

Lucienne nearly jumped out of her décolletage. She turned and came eyeball to eyeball with Charles Allen. She looked at him blankly, although a very small smile played around her lips.

77

'We've met, haven't we?' he said, a little uncertainly.

'Have we?' Her eyes glittered at him. He was grinning broadly.

'The Royal Academy, the other night. You ran away from me.'

'I did?' she feigned ignorance.

'Yep. Quite ruined my evening,' he laughed. His blondy-reddish hair was plastered flatly to his head and parted neatly to one side, and his grey eyes puckered at the corners in delight. He looked more pleasant than she remembered.

'You're on your own again.'

Lucienne shrugged. 'Perhaps.'

'Let me find you a refill.' He took the empty glass from her.

'Thanks,' she said and smiled at him, giving him the full benefit of her sloe-coloured eyes.

'Don't go away,' he ordered.

So far so good, Lucienne thought. He was back in a moment, and handed her a full glass.

'Cheers,' he said.

She raised the champagne to her lips and sipped it, glancing up at him from underneath her thick lashes.

'Perhaps you'd show me around the fair? I'm afraid my knowledge of antiques is about as full as my knowledge of art.'

'It's so awfully crowded, I don't think there'd be much pleasure in it,' Lucienne sighed, glancing back over her shoulder to the mass of people milling around below them. 'Where do all these people come from? Everywhere seems to be such a crush these days.'

Charles Allen murmured his agreement. He was clearly disappointed.

'I wasn't going to stay on much longer,' Lucienne said, as suggestively as she could.

'Perhaps . . . ' he spoke very tentatively, shyly, ' . . . perhaps you'd like to join me for a drink somewhere else?'

'Um . . . well, I'm not sure if I should. After all, I don't even know your name.'

'Charles,' he said quickly. 'Charles Allen.' He held his hand out to her.

'Lucienne,' she said. 'Lucienne Easton,' and before he had time to think: 'Okay, Mr Charles Allen, tonight I feel like taking risks. Let's go.'

He chose Trader Vics. It was convenient, dark and intimate. Lucienne had chosen the Grosvenor House Antiques Fair because it was next door to Trader Vics.

Both for the moment well satisfied, they searched the long list of cocktails. 'Well? What would you like?' Charles asked solicitously after a few moments.

Lucienne looked him full in the eye. 'I'd like a long slow screw up against the wall,' then her tongue flicked over her upper lip.

Charles Allen's cock stood to attention like a guardsman. He hadn't noticed how sensuously generous her mouth was. A small, teasing smile lifted it.

'Then I shall organize one for you,' he said smoothly.

Interesting, thought Lucienne. Perhaps he might be more fun than she'd initially suspected. Bankers weren't renowned for their entertainment value normally.

Preferring not to stand up because of the bulge in his trousers, Charles summoned the waitress over.

'A screwdriver and a long slow screw, thanks.' He returned the waitress's cheeky grin.

Lucienne's short black dress rode high over her

thighs, affording Charles a feast of Lycra-ed limbs. His erection throbbed, making it hard to concentrate on small talk.

'You're obviously very interested in the arts,' he tried.

'I have a small collection, nothing very grand. Usually I just go for what I like.'

'Like what's his name the other night?'

'Mondrian? Lord, no,' she laughed, making him feel cloddish and dim. 'He's a bit too modernist for me. I like representational stuff that tells me what I'm looking at. There's nothing like a good nude painted well, is there? It can be deeply erotic or innocent, but always sensuous. The curves, the colours, the slopes. The bits of shadow, the way the light catches the form . . .'

Charles listened, mesmerized.

'I'm sorry, I'm going on a bit, aren't I?' she sighed. 'Artists have so much passion inside them.'

She uncrossed her legs and the Lycra hissed sexily. Her skirt seemed to have slid even further up her thighs.

Charles's hand shook slightly. Lucienne leaned well back, stretching her arms along the top of the banquette seat, knowing only too well that her cleavage would be set to best advantage by so doing.

'Are you married?' she asked bluntly.

'No. Divorced. And you?'

Again the deep-throated laugh. 'God, no. I can't imagine getting hitched for years. I'm quite an independent sort of girl. I like things my own way.'

'I can see that.'

'How long have you been divorced?'

'Six months, that's all. We were separated for much longer. It took an age to get the whole thing sorted out.'

'So you haven't been snapped up? I *am* surprised.'

Charles was beginning to feel very good indeed. He ordered a second round of drinks. 'I've been too busy. Pressure of work and all that.'

'But you do manage to get out, Charles. Otherwise we wouldn't be sitting here now, would we?'

'All corporate stuff. I work for a bank,' he explained. Lucienne raised her eyebrows in polite interest.

'I've abandoned my colleagues tonight. I'll let you into a secret,' he said conspiratorially. 'I didn't tell them, either. I've done a runner!'

'You naughty boy!' Lucienne mocked, and crossed her legs once more. If her skirt went any higher he'd be staring at her crotch.

Charles couldn't remember the last time he'd felt so wound up and horny. He hadn't had any sex for months. Up until now it hadn't bothered him, either. Tonight, though, all he wanted to do was to get this girl bucking underneath him. She was such a strange mixture. She was coming on as strongly as a common little tart, but she dripped class and style. Her voice was educated, smooth as satin, and she had some very impressive-looking rocks round her neck.

'Have you eaten?'

Lucienne bit her lip and let her neat little teeth drag slowly back across the surface.

'I'm not sure I'm very hungry, Charles. I seem to have lost my appetite for food.' She put her empty glass back on the table and slipped a finger over the creamy flesh that swelled out of her plunging neckline. The finger circled around slowly, while the almost-black eyes watched Charles's expression.

Jesus! The woman was going to have him coming

all over the inside of his trousers. He was going to explode any second.

'Let's get out of here,' he said gruffly.

Once outside Charles couldn't control himself any longer. He grabbed her arm and pulled her towards him.

'What . . . ' came Lucienne's muffled protest, but Charles's mouth was covering up any words. Soon her tongue was sucking on his, pulling it harder into her mouth. She moaned, between her harsh breathing, breaking away from his mouth.

With a mammoth effort, Charles stood up straight. He looked around. There was a dark alleyway down the side of the club. Without a word, he pulled Lucienne into the opening. He shoved her back against one wall, and pushed his body between her legs. They were both panting, almost grunting. Lucienne's legs climbed the wall behind him so that she straddled him. He grasped her underneath her taut little buttocks. Lucienne's hand reached down and ripped at the gusset of her tights until there was a hole large enough to accommodate Charles's searching penis. Then she slipped her thumb between the crotch of her knickers and the soft, wet flesh, holding the tiny piece of silk aside. Charles's penis thrust inside her furiously, pounding her against the wall. 'This is what you ordered, isn't it?' his voice rasped in her ear.

'Long and slow,' she moaned, 'but this will do . . . ' She clawed at his head, frantically pulling his face into hers, licking and sucking at him, all the time trying to open herself to him so that he could drive deeper and deeper inside her.

Charles came in a shattering explosion. Lucienne felt him contract and she, too, convulsed into a shuddering paroxysm of orgasmic pleasure. Her legs

82

shook uncontrollably and she clung on to Charles's shoulders while she lowered her legs back to the ground. Charles buried his head in her neck. 'Jesus Christ!' He was almost sobbing. 'My God! Lucienne . . . I was out of control . . . I couldn't help myself. You're marvellous. Fabulous.'

She cradled his head with her hands. What felt like gallons of warm liquid ran down her legs. The guy mustn't have done it for years! He must have been full to the brim. She smiled like a self-satisfied cat. And she hadn't even had to fake it!

'Are you all right?' she whispered to him. She felt him nod his head.

'I think I'd better get home,' she said softly, 'sort myself out.'

'I'll come with you.'

'Better not. I've got a big day tomorrow.'

'But will you be all right? I mean, I can't just let you go alone, after . . . after this.'

'Of course you can. I'll be perfectly all right. Listen, I'm in a bit of a mess. It's best if I go quickly. God knows what I must look like,' she giggled. 'And it's all your fault.'

He smiled back, rather sheepishly. 'Sorry.'

'Don't be. It was worth it.' For once, she actually meant it. It had been extremely exciting. Unusual for a banker, too.

'Give me your phone number.'

Lucienne fumbled in her bag which she'd just retrieved from the ground. Her grin widened as she handed him a small white card. A very satisfactory conclusion to the deal. Xan would be impressed. Charles looked at the card but he couldn't read it properly in the darkness. He popped it into his top pocket.

'I'll call you.'

'Fine. Do.'

What a woman! He watched her stride off and hail a cab, cool as you please. He zipped himself up, but his cock was already fighting to come out again. Celibacy, clearly, had come to an end.

Chapter Eight

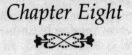

The spanking new minibus pulled over and Fern
thanked Seamus O'Leary very much for the ride
from Cork. She threw her large rucksack over her
shoulder, jumped down from the steps and waved
goodbye. The vehicle pulled away with a hoot,
leaving a smell of diesel fumes and hot engine
behind it. The noise remained for some moments
as the bus negotiated the steep bends further
along the road, until eventually it faded away into
the silence.

Fern stood still, breathing in the smells, revelling
in the feel of the pure air around her. She ran both
her hands through her hair, and then shook her
head, joyfully. She felt free! Alive! Rejuvenated,
already. The journey had taken most of the day, and
her legs had been so cramped up that they now felt
stiff, and disjointed, but nothing could take away
from the sense of release she was now feeling at
being back on Irish soil – home, again.

On either side of her treeless purple-covered
slopes rose skywards, littered with rocky outcrops
that forbade gentle strolling. The sun bleached the
stones white in places while laying dark shadows
across the patchy heather and yellow-tipped gorse.
Where the ground flattened out between the hills,
miniature lakes had formed from the almost-daily
feeding of rainwater.

It was fresh, pure and irresistible. Fern took a
deep, deep breath, pushed her hands down into the

front pockets of her Levi's and set off, up the lane towards her mother's cottage.

Situated, as it was, just beyond a sharp bend in the road and settled on the top of an incline, the house came upon Fern as it always did, all of a sudden. It had a neatness to its worn and weathered façade, with its symmetrically positioned windows: one either side of the forever-open front door, and the three square mullioned windows on the first floor.

It had been several years since the elevations had been limewashed, and the original stone of the cottage bled through the white like grazes. The garden, as ever, was riotously overgrown. The climate and position of the place had hardened Rowena's heart against any desires she may have had for tender roses and herbaceous borders. Instead, a lone clematis struggled against the wall to the left of the door, its green flower buds showing a tiny tip of purple through the pinnacle.

Fern stepped through the front door and stood for a few moments, letting her eyes get accustomed to the dim light. The air felt still and cool. A well-worn and very old oak table stood to the side of the door, its top covered with piles of dog-eared sketch pads and an assortment of jam jars stuffed full of brushes and pencils. Behind the table, propped against the wall, were two vast canvas stretchers, new and unused, presumably waiting for her mother's attention.

Fern dumped her rucksack. Out of habit she glanced at the table where her mother put the post. There was a stack of brown envelopes ominously abandoned unopened, but nothing for Fern.

She walked through into the kitchen. The range sat comfortingly against the far wall, a wooden chair positioned next to it covered with a faded patchwork cushion. Fern shook her head affectionately at the large oil lamp which hung low over the long pine table. The electricity supply was far from the cottage and her mother had for so long not been able to afford the luxury of it, that now she could, she no longer felt the need. Instead she relied on lamps and candles and, besides, here the day started with the sunrise, and bedtime came not long after the sun had gone down. Sometimes Fern had surprised herself at how easily she had adapted to London life and the everyday things that people took for granted, like taps that poured out piping hot water, and milk that wasn't forever 'on the turn'. Here batteries were an essential part of living, if you wanted anything to do with the outside world. Radios went quiet for weeks, and in the London flat music was one of the things Fern appreciated most of all when she could press a couple of buttons and listen to tapes to her heart's content.

She filled the kettle and placed it on the range. A small tabby cat jumped down from his hiding place on top of the dresser and marched over to her, his tail held aloft. He miaowed loudly and rubbed hard up against her legs. She bent down and stroked his silky fur.

'Feeding time, is it, Bono, or are you just pleased to see me, hey?' Fern had named the cat after U2's lead singer, back in her serious teenage crush days. She picked up the feather-light creature and cuddled him to her chest. He purred loudly and pressed his nose against her hand, demanding to be stroked once more.

Fern made a pot of tea and poured out two mugs, then, one in each hand, set off in search of her mother.

Rowena's studio was tucked away at the rear of the

cottage, down at the far end of the garden. Originally it had been a pig-shed, but one of the few luxuries Rowena *had* allowed herself was the redesign of the place in order to provide her with a decent studio. Almost an entire wall, and most of the roof was made of glass. The remainder of the building was made up of weather-boarded timber, stained with black pitch. Fern could see her mother through the glass, but so intent was Rowena on her work, that she didn't notice Fern's approach.

'Hi, Mum,' Fern shouted matter-of-factly, as if she had just come home off the school bus.

Her mother looked round, and blinked. 'Good God!' she screeched. 'I thought for a moment I must have gone right off my head and you were a ghost.'

'Could be, but I'm not. Anyway, you went off your head years ago.'

'No, you're not a ghost. A ghost wouldn't be so damned cheeky!'

Fern popped the two mugs down carefully on the table. Then she almost swept Rowena off her feet in a great big bear hug. Her mother always smelled wonderful: the scents of lilies, and fresh bread smothered with melted butter and honey but mingled with an evocative whiff of turps and oil paint. Eventually Fern released Rowena, and the two women stood and examined each other closely. Often when Rowena looked at Fern, she had the uncanny sensation of looking in a mirror, only the mirror had been suspended in time some seventeen years ago when she, too, was only twenty-three. They both had the same blaze of flame-coloured hair, and piercingly green, Irish eyes. Rowena's freckles had faded with age, and her pale skin had a slightly weathered look about it, but Fern's skin had a delicate translucence like that of a winter bloom. To her mother's artistic eye, albeit a slightly biased one, Fern's skin had an extraordinary perfection to it. Rowena reached out with her hand, and stroked her daughter's cheek lightly, thrilling to the soft, velvety feel. She grinned at Fern delightedly. 'Am I glad to see you,' she laughed. 'Tell me what you think of this painting I'm up to my neck in. Tell me you think it's hideous – I wouldn't be at all surprised.'

There was one thing Fern knew only too well, and that was her mother's work was *never* hideous.

Rowena stood away from the canvas so that Fern could get a good look at it. Fern was silent for a few moments, taking in the work. She could all but feel the warmth of the August sun radiating out from the canvas. Rowena had somehow managed to capture perfectly the essence of a ripe cornfield, half-harvested and edged with a mass of scarlet poppies. In the foreground the blood-red heads almost burst out from the painting, fighting for dominance over a mass of tumbleweed, cow parsley and white-flowered valerian.

'It's a very happy painting, don't you think?' Fern said, eventually.

'It's a bit of a bloody cliché. But it sells. Anthony's coming down in a few days to collect this one, and a couple of others I've knocked up. I expect he'll be pleased with it,' she said, matter-of-factly.

Anthony was Rowena's agent. He was based in Cork, and from there he marketed her paintings both in London and New York. Years and years of struggling were at last beginning to pay off for Rowena and her canvases were now selling at between £5,000 and £10,000, depending on the size. In artistic circles she was beginning to make quite a name for herself.

'Have you eaten?'

Fern shook her head.

'Come on, then. Let's go see what we can find.'

Later, when they had stuffed down enormous quantities of Rowena's home-made bread, and the lemony goat's cheese that she had pressed herself, Fern realized that not once had her mother asked what Fern was doing here.

That was typical of Rowena. She never had interfered in Fern's life, almost to the extent that she could appear uninterested, though Fern knew it was her innate sense of personal privacy that kept her from prying. Rowena knew that they would have a much better relationship if she let Fern come to her when she was needed, rather than pushing, and pressurizing and alienating her. Rowena had always reasoned that children were like animals: you had to earn their trust, it wasn't granted as some God-given right purely by accident of birth, and as with any small creature, you had to show through kindness and understanding that you could be trusted.

Instead Rowena filled Fern in on the village news and made her scream with laughter over the fact that the tourist office's latest idea was to turn Rowena into a local attraction, complete with a signpost at the end of the lane stating the whereabouts of the famous local artist, and other such anecdotes.

Eventually, relaxed and yawning, Rowena set about clearing the table. 'You can lie in in the morning if you want. I expect you're a bit tired. I'll be up bright and early to catch the best light, but I won't wake you.'

As she watched her mother move about the kitchen, setting up the candles and rinsing the dishes, Fern dearly wished that Rowena could meet somebody. It had been so many years since she remembered anyone important in her mother's life. In the early years, when Fern was small, and Anthony would visit them bringing lots of wonderful sweets for Fern, and clothes and wine for her mother, it did cross Fern's mind that Anthony could be her father. But then she spent a lot of her childhood looking at and wondering if this one or that one could be the one. She wouldn't have minded if Anthony had been her father. Anyone who could bring such excitement into Rowena and Fern's lives when he visited was an okay sort of bloke. He would stay for a couple of days or so, and then depart with a parcel of Rowena's paintings, and her mother would be very quiet and withdrawn for a few hours, and Fern knew she had to play by herself until her mother's mood lifted. As Fern grew older she came to realize that every painting her mother parted with was like removing a tiny piece of herself, and she always hated it. But Anthony had done his job on Rowena's behalf faithfully, so at least she didn't have to worry about money any more. Fern had hoped that something might develop with Anthony, but eventually she learned that although Anthony had previously been married, he now preferred spending his time with young men.

Being so remote from anywhere, it was difficult for Rowena to meet anybody else. She hated going up to Cork at the best of times, and she didn't seem to miss a social life. The locals considered her to be a bit of an oddity. In their books, if you hadn't caught yourself a husband by the age of twenty-two, things were looking pretty bad. There were plenty of middle-aged bachelor farmers around who were only too ready to take themselves a wife. You could meet them in the village bars when they'd take a few hours off from their toils to scour the place for any opportunities amongst the tourists. Many a marriage proposal got

91

turned down around eleven o'clock on a Friday night in a noisy bar.

For these poor old so-and-sos marriage was essential. Without an heir the fields would be lost, and they'd be condemned to darning their own socks and boiling their own potatoes until the day they died.

What the locals couldn't understand was how Rowena had managed to stay manless. She was a real beauty to look at. Her copper-coloured hair had lost none of its lustre, and her body was as slim and willowy as her daughter's. But, Fern reasoned to herself, she seemed quietly content, so not having a man around wasn't necessarily such a bad thing.

Fern had managed to get through the best part of the novel she'd been promising herself she'd read for the past six months. The shadows had deepened and she was just beginning to find it difficult to focus on the print when Rowena appeared from the studio. Fern set the book aside and squeezed her mother's hand.

'Come on, I'll get you a drink, and you can tell me how my soda bread tastes.'

After Fern had poured the tea Rowena pulled out a crumpled brown paper bag from behind the bread bin. 'I went to the bank the other morning.'

'And you didn't just cash some money, I'll bet. You're incorrigible.'

'Does that mean you won't be joining me, then?'

Fern was already unscrewing the lid of the small, unlabelled bottle. She splashed a few drops of the clear, white liquid into both their mugs. Then she picked up her own and sipped it with satisfaction, feeling the burn of the poteen in her throat.

'I'm surprised nobody's caught on to Donal yet. After all this time, there can't be anybody left who doesn't know what he's up to.'

'You're right, but that's good for his business and for the bank. Everyone uses that branch now. They must know he's handing out the liquor along with the cash. There isn't a soul in town who doesn't go to him for supplies. There's nobody'd wish to turn him in now, and what would be the point of all that fuss?'

'I'm really glad I came home, Mum.' Fern sighed contentedly, taking small sips of the fiery toddy.

'Me too. It's kind of quiet around here these days. Oh, not that I'm saying I miss you or anything. Well, of course I miss you, Fern, but I don't want you to feel guilty or anything . . .'

Fern spluttered with laughter. Poor Rowena, she tried so hard to be an independent kind of mother.

Rowena laughed too. 'I shouldn't try to be subtle, should I? It's never worked yet. Okay, I do miss you, but I'm very content in my own little world.'

'I can tell. I'd have to come home more often if I thought you were miserable, anyhow.' Fern teased.

'Is everything all right?'

'Fine. Everything's absolutely fine. I just needed to think some things through, and it was really difficult in London. It all seemed so confusing.'

Rowena's voice dropped with concern. 'Do you want to talk about it?'

Fern saw her look of worry. 'Oh no, don't get the wrong idea. There's nothing the matter. It's just work. There was a promotion I really wanted and I'm not sure I'm going to get it.'

'Why ever not?' Rowena snapped, full of indignation.

'I don't know. That's the problem. I know I've done good work. The editor's been really pleased with most of my stuff. It's odd.' She sighed heavily. 'Anyway, there's still a chance I might get it. No decision's been made yet.'

'There you go, probably worrying your daft head over nothing. Is that all you're fretting over?'

Fern considered whether to tell Rowena about her ill-fated interview. It was all too complicated, and Rowena probably wouldn't understand about women like India Duncan-Forrester.

'Yeah, I guess. Maybe it's time for me to move on from *Faces*. You don't get really successful by staying in one job. I've been there for eighteen months and I guess it's time to do something new, so if they don't promote me to Assistant Features Editor I'll just have to do something else.'

'Well, It's no good asking me what I think, it's all foreign to me. You'll have to make your own mind up. Anyway, you usually do.'

Rowena helped herself to the bottle. She pushed it over to Fern. Fern shook her head. 'I'm not used to it. You'll have me on the floor. I'll tell you something that'll make you laugh, though, I've been offered a modelling contract!'

'On the magazine?'

'No, with a cosmetics company. It's a bit of a long story, but I was doing this article with them on the search for a face to launch a new product line, and the guy who's the product manager there asked me if I'd do it. Of course I said no. I'm not about to chuck away my career in journalism to smile into a camera all day.'

'Bloody right too. Exploitation, that's what it is, pure and simple.'

'The money's quite good, though.'

'But money's not everything, Fern. It won't buy happiness.'

'That's what I said. I told them I didn't want a million pounds. I knew you'd be proud of me.'

Rowena choked on her toddy. 'What did you say?'

'I said I told them I didn't want a million pounds.'

'Is that what they offered? Holy Mary, Fern, what did they want you to do? It wasn't some porno job, was it?'

Fern laughed. 'No, it wasn't. And I don't think the blue movie industry would offer that sort of money in any event. It was to promote a new product.'

'You're pulling my leg!'

'Nope. Crazy, isn't it?'

'Crazy . . . it's downright immoral, Fern. Who in God's name would be that stupid now?'

'Oscar Rees – '

'Who?'

'Oscar Rees . . . that's what the company's called.'

'Is that the name of the man who runs it, Oscar?'

'No. It's Hugo actually. Hugo Rees.'

Rowena slowly picked up the bottle of poteen. She unscrewed the top and then placed the neck of the bottle into her mouth, taking a great gulp of the burning liquid.

Fern watched her mother in astonishment. Her reflex action was to pull the bottle away from her. 'What are you doing?'

Rowena's face turned a deep beetroot colour and she started to splutter, at the same time trying to wrestle the bottle out of Fern's grasp. Between chokes she gasped, 'Give . . . me . . . that . . . bloody thing!'

'No. Not until you tell me what's wrong.'

'There's nothing, I just want a drink.'

'You're not having one. Tell me what's wrong.'

Fern's face swam in and out of focus. Rowena's breathing came quickly and she tried to steady it. She studied her daughter intently, taking in every strand of hair on her head, every curve of her features, the way she smiled, the slight tilt of her head . . .

95

'Rowena?' Fern's voice was low and gentle. 'Are you okay?' She had never seen her mother hit the bottle like that in her life. She was certainly a heavy drinker, but she never took her poteen neat, even if a goat had passed on or the like.

Rowena struggled to compose herself. 'It's shock,' she tried to keep her voice even. 'Shock at the thought of you being offered a million-pound contract.'

'You think I should take it?'

'Jesus, no. It's tantamount to prostitution. Don't even consider it, Fern,' she hissed urgently. 'It'll corrupt you. You'll change. Forget it. It's wicked money.'

'I wouldn't go so far as to call it wicked, Ma, but it's certainly a bit immoral.'

'That's right. I don't want you ending up as some painted face. I gave you a decent upbringing, my girl, decent values. I knew you'd be corrupted if you went to live in that hell hole!'

'Ma!' Fern started to protest. 'I told you, I turned it down. I didn't want the job.'

Rowena seemed to be barely listening. 'No daughter of mine would do a thing like that. No daughter of mine would bring shame on this house. You'll stay away from them, Fern Donleavy, or else stay away from me!' Rowena stood up, taking the bottle with her. 'Goodnight!' she hissed. She lit a candle and waited for the flame to settle, then headed out of the door, leaving Fern speechless with amazement, alone in the kitchen.

In the small timber hut, just beyond the end of the cottage, Rowena sat rocking slowly and rhythmically on an old oak rocking chair. At least twenty candles burned around the room, making it churchlike, almost like a shrine. Her eyes were fixed on a point in the distance where she gazed unblinkingly, tears spilling silently down her cheeks. On the far wall a large wooden chest stood open and a painting had been propped up against the open lid. A young man stared back at her across the years, his lips lifting slightly at the edge, knowingly, as if he were about to surprise her, as lovers do, with a kiss, or a gift, or a secret, or even just soft words of love.

'Oh, Hugo,' Rowena murmured, 'you've got so much to answer for.'

As she sat, rocking in her trance, Rowena's memory was allowed, for this night at least, to tear her to pieces.

Fern was up well before the sun. The kitchen was engulfed by deep shadows as she padded in her thick socks across the chilly stone floor. The cat crawled out from his nesting place, and rubbed himself lasciviously against her shins, so that as she walked she was forced to kick him out of her way lest he trip her up.

'Bono, it's not time for breakfast yet,' she whispered as she put the kettle on to the range. She rubbed her cold hands together above the hot plate, feeling with pleasure the warmth rising. The sky to the east was slowly changing colour from a deep, blackish navy to a paler shade, heralding the forthcoming dawn.

Everything was so still and silent. Unlike London there were no sounds of traffic, or of commuters trudging past the house. The sky had no orange city glow. All was peace and tranquillity. Fern made the tea and carried a mug through to her mother's room. The curtains had not been drawn, so in the brightening gloom Fern could see immediately that the bed had not been slept in. She carried the tea back out and placed it on the table, lighting the oil lamp which hung overhead, and watched as the glowing aureola bathed the kitchen with its gentle light. A few minutes later, as she sat by the range sipping her hot tea, the latch on the back door lifted, and Rowena appeared, looking absolutely ghastly.

'Oh!' she said in surprise. 'I thought you'd be in bed.'

'I couldn't sleep,' Fern said. 'Here, I've just made you a tea. I took it into your room, but of course you weren't there.'

'No, I . . . er . . . was working.'

By the state of her mother's face, and the swelling around her eyes, it was fairly obvious to Fern what Rowena had been doing all night, and that certainly wasn't working.

Fern stood up and crossed the room. She wrapped her arms around her mother's slim frame, shivering as the cold transferred itself from Rowena's body to hers. 'You're absolutely frozen. Come here and get warm.' Fern led her over to the stove. Then she fetched a blanket off the bed, and carefully placed it around Rowena's shoulders.

Rowena smiled gratefully. 'Thanks. You're being very understanding, considering.'

'No, I'm not. I don't understand at all, but I would like to, Rowena. I'm worried about you. I want to know what all that was about last night.'

Rowena continued to sip her tea silently. Fern waited for her to speak.

'Rowena,' she said finally, 'whatever was the matter?'

'Nothing.'

'Look, I told you last night, I'm not going to even consider the offer.'

Rowena seemed hardly to be listening. She continued to stare at a point somewhere beyond Fern's feet.

At last she looked up at Fern. Her mouth was a thin line of contempt. 'Good. I'm glad, because it stinks!'

'I think you're going over the top, Rowena. It's not that bad.' Fern felt sick and tired. She wished she'd never set foot inside Oscar Rees's bloody office in the first place. Life had really been ticking along quite nicely. Now she seemed to have lost all sense of direction. She sighed and put her mug down on the kitchen table. Clearly, given the mood Rowena was in, she wouldn't get anywhere by arguing. The woman was irrational. 'Well, if I should change my mind, I'll remember not to let you know.'

Rowena seemed to slump further into her chair. She shrugged carelessly. 'It's up to you, Fern. It's your conscience,' she added cuttingly.

At last Fern's eyes filled with tears. Rowena had gone too far. There was nothing wrong with Fern's conscience; it was more like Rowena's own troubling her this time. There was something deeper, Fern was sure of it. Maybe her mother was jealous. All those years of struggle for Rowena to give Fern a proper home and upbringing, and here was Fern being offered a million-pound deal at the age of twenty-three. If only Rowena could, just for once, behave like a normal mother.

'Why must you make me feel so damned guilty, Rowena? It's the money, isn't it? That's what you can't stand. The thought that I could be successful without slogging my guts out like you did all your life. Well, I'm tired of feeling guilty on your behalf. Look, I know it's been hard for you bringing me up on your own, but I didn't ask to be born. For Christ's sake, I hardly know who I am, even. Half of me is missing. A mystery. You won't tell me, will you?' Fern's voice rose and the tears gushed down her cheeks.

'Do you ever wonder what it's been like for me looking at every man who walked through our door wondering if this was going to be the one. If one day you'd say to me, "Oh, by the way, Fern, that was your Da that just walked out"? You've given me a conscience all right, Rowena. Why the hell do you think I put up with your secrets?' She glowered at her mother's anguished face. 'Because I have a conscience and because I feel so damned guilty.'

'Secrets? We don't have secrets, Fern.'

'No, not small ones, Rowena. Only the major, important ones in life. Oh, for God's sake, have it your own way. You obviously just don't trust me.'

Fern stormed out of the kitchen and into her bedroom, and then, fighting the tears, she threw her clothes into her bag. She reappeared a few minutes later.

'Look, I need time to sort myself out, too. I'm sorry if I've upset you,' she sniffed loudly.

Rowena looked hunched and distant.

'I'm going back to London. I'll be in touch . . . '

Rowena turned then, and Fern glimpsed the sparkle of tears in her eyes. She quickly went over and kissed her mother, and then without looking back, she left the house.

Her anger kept her going. Why, why, why did her mother have to be so damned difficult at times? Couldn't she see how much it hurt to be shut out like this? Maybe she was behaving like a child, but then so was Rowena. God, it was like stepping back in time. On the few occasions that Fern had tried to broach the subject of Rowena's past – Fern's past, too – she had got the same kind of brick wall treatment.

She didn't know where she came from, she didn't know where her grandparents were, and if she had them at all, whether they were alive. The whole history of herself had gone missing, except Rowena knew exactly where it was, but she was just too bloody-minded and selfish to tell.

One day Rowena would have to face up to whatever it was she was so desperate to hide. As Fern stomped off down the lane, knowing she had a good long walk ahead of her, she dug deep into herself and realized that maybe she, too, was just as frightened of learning the truth as Rowena was of telling it.

Chapter Nine

The silver Bentley purred quietly into the kerbside along Holland Park Avenue. Thomas jumped quickly out of the driver's seat, and trotted around to open Olivia's door. She uncrossed her long, slim legs and unfolded herself from the car. She stood up and brushed down her sleek beige Chanel skirt, nodded to Thomas, and then paused for a moment outside the tall black doors that marked the entrance to the Rees Foundation.

The small brass plaque to the left of the doors gleamed brightly in the sunlight and Olivia's mood lifted. She always looked forward to these Foundation luncheons with a pleasant sense of anticipation. This was her domain. She had taken over her father's role as the figurehead of the now internationally-renowned clinic.

The trustees had a bi-monthly committee lunch at which the general running of the place and the funding of it would be discussed. Olivia was the Fund's director.

She pushed the heavy door open, hitting the hallowed calm of the place. It was almost like stepping into a discreet gentleman's club with its gloomy mahogany panelling, vast overhead chandelier and black and white tiled floor. There was a smell of wax polish and lavender, but lingering just below was the faintest whiff of antiseptic.

Olivia caught sight of herself in the huge ormolu mirror that covered the wall to the right of the entrance. Not a single hair rose out of place from the sleek French bob that stopped just short of the point of her jawline. It was as sleek and shiny as melted wax. Her skin looked pale, luminous in the shadows of the dark hallway, and her eyes glittered back at her like polished coals. She permitted her reflection a small, self-satisfied grin before following the corridor through a series of tight little twists and turns to the directors' dining room.

The others stood up as she entered. 'Olivia . . . ' Their voices blended together in gushing greeting.

'Gentlemen,' she smiled back at the four of them. Professor Alan Cox came forward and kissed her on both cheeks. 'Olivia, my dear,' he said, 'come and have a drink – there's still time before lunch.' Olivia was handed her gin and tonic.

'What do you think of the new wing, Olivia?' Lewis Bloomfield spoke quickly, excitedly. 'Those ten new beds are going to be full this time next week. Isn't it marvellous?' he enthused.

'It is marvellous, Lewis, but it's gone way over budget,' Michael Ginn interrupted. Olivia always felt mildly repulsed by the man. He looked overstuffed, as if he might burst out of his reddened skin at any time. He had a large nose plonked like a badly shaped potato in the centre of his face and when he spoke his lips shone with spittle.

'Spoken like a true accountant,' Lewis Bloomfield, the Clinic's director, reprimanded him gently. 'Building works are always over budget. None of us seriously thought it would be within, did we?'

'It's not a problem, is it?' Olivia looked at the accountant over the top of her glass, trying to hide her distaste in the lemon slice.

Michael Ginn spoke rather pompously, now considering he had been granted a serious hearing. He

103

spoke more than a little condescendingly to Olivia, the only woman present. 'Should we luncheon first? Perhaps we might discuss all matters over coffee?'

Olivia shrugged. 'I dare say the situation won't have changed by then, and I confess I am rather hungry.'

They settled themselves around the large circular table that obviated the need for any jostling for position. Edward Hunter, the suave young administrator, sat at Olivia's right, and Alan Cox to her left. Edward had only been with the Foundation for a few months, but he had managed to keep everything running beautifully smoothly while the building works had been in progress, a project which had taken some eighteen months. Coming in halfway through all that had been a trying time for a new administrator – in fact the whole project had proved so trying that the old administrator had found it all too much and walked out. At twenty-eight years old, Edward was young and energetic and deeply committed to the work the Clinic carried out. It was important to have some young blood amongst them. Olivia was the next youngest at forty; the others far older.

Olivia had got used to their patronizing ways in the past. She knew she had enough clout when it really mattered. Had it not been for her father and father-in-law, the place would never have come into being.

'We need an immediate injection of at least a million,' Ginn said bluntly. 'The new wing has come in at a hundred per cent over budget, and we simply can't afford to keep going unless we get some cash in very quickly. Frankly, I'm loathe to open the wing at all.'

Olivia felt the colour drain from her face. 'That's ridiculous. For God's sake, we've got huge dividends coming in from the shares, plus all the funds I've raised via the charity. How on earth can we be so desperate?'

'Because we have more beds than we've ever had before; because the consultants' fees are rising, because the rates are so high. It costs a fortune to keep a building like this running – remember the roof repairs that came as a total surprise to all of us? And then there's all the research chairs that we've so generously sponsored.' Ginn threw his hands up in despair. 'We're broke!'

Olivia tried to keep the cool that she was so famous for. She sipped her coffee delicately while inside her gut was doing treble somersaults. Why had she not known about this before? She'd been a bloody idiot not to make it her business to find out. Her job was always to raise the money; make all the right noises to the right people; be seen a lot. She wasn't supposed to do the bloody book-keeping. Trouble was, if the Foundation collapsed, so did her kudos.

'And do you have a proposed solution to this?' she asked, frostily.

'Sure. We raise some more money, fast. That's your department, isn't it?'

'Then I'd better get to work, hadn't I?' Olivia was already rising from her seat.

As Thomas sped Olivia away from the Foundation, her mind was working overtime. There had been so much damned publicity about the funding of the new wing, and how successful Mrs Hugo Rees had been at raising such funds, that if word got out that the new wards weren't even going to open she would end up being the scapegoat because *she* was the figurehead of the blasted fund-raising. She had to come up with something fast. She bit her lip sharply as the conversation with Alexander resurrected itself inside her head. He had said her shares would be worth £10 million. Then that could mean a cash injection of something in the region of £15 million just from the sale of the Foundation's shareholding alone.

Hugo would somehow have to be dealt with. Somehow he'd have to be made to think that Olivia was against the sale but had been swept along by the other shareholders who were intent on selling, and that it was for Hugo's own good that she was doing it . . . No, it would never work. Hugo wasn't that stupid.

She stared hopelessly out of the window, feeling the knot in her stomach tighten. Perhaps if she just had a quiet chat with Alexander they might, between them, think of something. Not that she'd give anything away, of course.

Alexander Easton was, from Hugo's rather cynical viewpoint, just another of life's cruel little jests, placed on this earth, like so many of the Easton family, purely to torment him. Hugo often wondered just what he had done in his life to deserve such poisonous relatives. Take today, for instance. Not content merely to spend the morning fighting off Cooper Jefferson, Hugo had escaped for a quiet hour to his regular table at the Connaught, only to be hounded by bloody Alexander.

Having studied the menu, he had looked up to find his nephew standing there.

'Mind if I join you, old chap?' Before Hugo had chance to reply, he sat himself down on the chair opposite.

'Yes, as a matter of fact I do,' Hugo said bluntly.

'That's what I love about you, Hugo. Always so honest.'

'Wish I could say the same for you.'

106

Alexander picked up the menu and scanned it quickly.

'Don't tell me you're staying.'

'We all have to eat, Hugo.'

'Yes, but not necessarily at the same trough, Alexander.'

'I'm glad I found you,' Alexander went on, unruffled by Hugo's hostility. 'I thought I'd see how you got on this morning.'

Hugo raised one dark eyebrow sternly.

'With Coopers,' Alexander added.

'I'm surprised you didn't ask them yourself.'

'As a matter of fact I tried to contact Leo, but he had gone straight on to another meeting. I thought I'd try the next best thing. After all, Hugo, as one of the shareholders I do have a right to know.'

The waiter arrived and Hugo snapped out his order.

'I'll have the same,' Alexander said quickly. 'Oh, and a bottle of the '89 Puligny-Montrachet.'

'So, tell me, did they manage to talk some sense into you?'

Hugo found himself twisting the starched linen napkin, which had been spread across his knee, into a tight ball. He dearly wished it was Alexander's scrawny little neck.

'No.'

'You refused. Again.'

'Correct.'

'It's a fantastic offer.'

Hugo sighed. 'Alexander, we have an extremely profitable company. We do not need to sell ourselves to some soulless conglomerate in order to make a fast buck, as I'm sure you would put it. It simply isn't necessary to sell out. The products bear our own personality; they are highly prestigious. Do you seriously think it makes economic sense to reduce the "exclusive" factor on the products? We don't want to be mass-market grot.'

'Then I think you're being blinkered. It's true that many of Coopers' products are low-priced mass-market, but that's precisely why they're after Oscar Rees. They'd want to capitalize on that exclusivity, wouldn't they? For God's sake, the average woman on the street would never know the products had been taken over – '

'There's no such thing as an average woman.'

'Try telling that to the market researchers, Hugo. You're living in a dreamworld. You've got to move with the times.'

'And I suppose,' Hugo said quietly as he started tearing at his filleted sole, 'under Coopers you might be given an opportunity to develop your own products, bearing in mind that so far I've vetoed your ideas.'

'Leo Eden appreciates that I am an extremely talented chemist.'

'Does he also appreciate the direction which your talent chooses to follow?'

'He knows that the road to success in cosmetics is through sound product development and a nose to spot trends, to be one jump ahead. Cell replenishment and rejuvenation is the future – the fountain of youth, Hugo, and all that,' he added facetiously.

'So you haven't told him, have you? Well, he might just find the whole thing as distasteful as I do.'

Alexander shrugged carelessly. 'If you were to change your mind, give us more of a free hand – a say in what's going on – then Lucienne and I might be persuaded to back you on this bid. Otherwise . . . ' Alexander drained his glass, and savoured the fine wine before continuing ' . . . we owe it to ourselves to follow our destinies.'

Hugo laughed, but it was an empty, bitter sound. 'Do as you please, Alexander. Your and Lucienne's combined shareholding is not going to force me into a corner, now is it?'

'You assume the others wouldn't be attracted to the offer?'

'I can't answer for Julian, but the bank will stay with me, the Foundation won't want to take a risk, and I imagine Olivia will stay loyal to her husband.'

'I'm not sure that you're right there, Hugo. I think the other shareholders might well be persuaded, in different ways, of course. You may have your head too deeply in the sand to dig out this time.'

At that moment Alexander's pocket let out an alarming buzz. Hugo sniffed distastefully as the younger man reached into his jacket and pulled out a small telephone. 'Excuse me, Hugo,' he muttered.

The voice that rang out from the instrument across the table, muffled as it was, startled Hugo. He heard quite clearly his wife announce herself.

Alexander grinned slowly, the kind of grin a snake might wear to reassure the mouse it's about to swallow, and pushed his chair back, regarding Hugo impudently.

'So,' he said, making his delight abundantly clear, 'you want to hear more about the offer, Aunt Olivia?'

Hugo slammed down his coffee cup and stood up. He threw his napkin so that it landed slap-bang in the sugar bowl, then without a backward glance, he stormed out of the restaurant.

Hugo was not having a good day. Actually, he wasn't having a good year . . . or a particularly good life, come to that. It wasn't enough that his father had, in

109

his will, passed voting shares to the Foundation which could now be used against him; it wasn't enough that the bank's twelve per cent of stock could swing the other way when the bidding became serious and he could end up losing the company as a result; it wasn't enough that he was married to a raving lesbian who was also intent on selling out on him. Oh no, none of that was enough. Now, his damned brother-in-law had got himself into trouble again.

Hugo raced up the wide stone steps to the front door of number 23 Queen Anne's Walk. He turned his key in the lock and pushed open one half of the vast double doors, then he shrugged off his jacket and placed his briefcase on the hall table.

'Hugo!' Olivia's shrill voice exclaimed from somewhere out of sight. He heard the sharp clicking of her heels on the wooden stairs as she raced down to him. 'Hugo,' she continued, sounding breathless with anxiety, 'thank God you're back. David's in the library waiting for you. I've delayed dinner until eight o'clock. The family are coming to discuss everything. What a mess . . . ' she muttered, turning away and then, suddenly remembering, 'Oh, and how was Julian?'

For the first time she looked at Hugo. His face was pale and baggy, appearing older than his forty-two years.

'Well, he seemed very fit indeed, actually. I don't think he has any idea of the trouble he's causing us.'

'Oh.' At least she had the grace to sound embarrassed.

'I had to fight my way through the tabloid press camping out on the doorstep of the hospital. I knew something like this would happen one day, Olivia. I dearly wish you could have kept your darling brother under control.'

Olivia's eyes narrowed. She spun away from him and click-clacked across the hall in retreat.

It wasn't often that Olivia was rendered speechless – she usually had the last word – but she was going to find this latest event extremely hard to live down if Hugo had anything to do with it. He pushed open the library doors, and managed a weak smile in the direction of his friend who also happened to be his lawyer.

'David!'

The man rose from the winged armchair, putting down his half-full whisky glass. 'Ah, Hugo. Good.' They shook hands firmly.

'Thanks for coming over,' Hugo's voice was almost a grunt.

'I came as soon as I heard. What's the news? Is Julian all right?'

'Yes, so they say. He's got to take it easy for a while, and they want to keep him under observation for a couple of days, but apart from that he seems to treat the whole messy business as some jolly jape!'

'Well, that's Julian for you. But that doesn't exactly help Oscar Rees, does it?'

'God, David, I wouldn't be at all surprised if he didn't end up turning the whole thing to his advantage, make himself out as some kind of Casanova.'

'Hardly. Not when he has a heart attack on the job! I would have thought the opposite sex might find the idea a little off-putting. Imagine it, a discreet little afternoon assignation, and suddenly your partner starts dying all over you.'

'Happens all the time, apparently,' Hugo said bluntly. 'Except it wasn't a heart attack. It seems he's suffering from executive stress.'

'Executive stress?' David nearly choked on his Scotch. 'Signed his name too often, you mean? Got too excited at the polo?'

'Quite.'

'Things could have been worse,' David said, brightly. 'He could have dropped dead.'

'That would be worse?' Hugo murmured, almost to himself.

Julian had plagued him for too many years to evoke in him charitable feelings. The only good thing about him was that, mainly through his *amour fou*, he generated a racy kind of publicity for Oscar Rees. He was a gossip columnist's dream, and a publicist's nightmare. One never quite knew what he would do next. Or, on occasions, whom.

'What about the woman?'

'Well, we could do without that, of course. You know who she is?'

'Caro Littleton? Yes. Wife of Stephen, the honourable member for Chalfont Rising, Minister for the Environment. Oh it's tasty, all right, Hugo. I'd guess this story is going to run for several days.'

'Years, probably,' Hugo said morosely. 'Daft girl went in the ambulance with him. She could have let the hotel manager deal with the whole business. They're awfully used to that sort of thing. Instead she acted like a guardian angel and remained at his bedside, gave a statement at the hospital, that sort of thing.'

'You never know. It might all be good for business at the end of the day. Women like a rogue like Julian. He's sexy and romantic. Dangerous – isn't that the buzz word these days?'

'You sound like a copywriter, David. Perhaps we should have Oscar Rees tattooed across his dick. That way we'd get more exposure than a year's worth of advertisements in *Vogue*. Anyway, thanks, again, for coming over.'

'It's the least I could do.' They raised their glasses to each other.

David and Hugo had met at Cambridge back in the early seventies where they had both been reading law. Now David had one of the most successful commercial practices in London and a major client was Oscar Rees. Over the years, their friendship had mellowed and deepened, and David knew Hugo relied on him heavily to provide clear, unbiased advice. Because of Hugo's rather exalted position, and the power of money, there were few people around Hugo who liked to be as honest with him.

'I wanted to talk to you about Cooper Jefferson,' David said.

'It seems everyone wants to talk to me about Cooper Jefferson,' Hugo replied morosely.

'I checked out your father's will. It seems completely watertight.'

'I know. I've already looked at it myself. It seems to me, David, that it all hangs on the bloody Foundation. If the silly old fool hadn't passed voting shares over to the damned place, then I'd probably be all right – either that or I should have had a brood of children. Then the shares would never have gone there.' Hugo didn't add that in many ways he was quite relieved at not having risked the cloning of his treacherous wife.

As if on cue, the library doors swung open and Olivia appeared, looking glossy and brittle. Her sleek black hair, short and straight, never moved. To Hugo's mind it hardened her face and made her seem unapproachable and sterile. She wore a beautifully tailored red woollen dress that finished just above her

113

kneecaps, revealing her slender legs, but the sight did nothing for Hugo.

'The others have arrived, Hugo. I've put them in the dining room already, so if you and David would like to join us when you're ready . . . '

Hugo noticed the change in her tone. Her voice was softer than usual. Normally she would have snapped the words out, but she sounded almost meek – like a child that's about to be chastised. Maybe it was her conscience. One could almost feel sorry for her, Hugo thought. Almost.

Hugo and David knocked back the last of their whiskies and followed in Olivia's footsteps. Hugo hardly thought it necessary to summon the twins, but for some reason Olivia had gone straight ahead and done it. When he saw them he thought he detected a kind of amused smugness about them, despite their father being in hospital.

'Lucienne . . . Alexander . . . ' Hugo grunted the perfunctory greeting.

'Uncle Hugo,' their voices blended together silkily. 'How are you?' The words slithered out of their mouths.

'Marvellous!' he snapped. 'Couldn't be better!' Then, feeling a little sensitive to any feelings they might have for Julian and his copious affairs, he mellowed a little. 'I'm sure you'll both be relieved to know that your father is fine. He didn't suffer a heart attack. He is merely suffering from, er, stress. Or at least that's what the doctor says.'

Lucienne sighed. 'Thank goodness,' she gushed. 'God, I've been so worried. We both have, haven't we, Alexander?'

Alexander nodded. 'Very worried. We didn't know what to think. What happened, Uncle Hugo?'

For some reason, whenever Hugo heard Alexander

114

speak to him like that, especially when he said Uncle Hugo, all the hairs on his back prickled, and he could feel himself tense up. Maybe it was just Alexander's voice, which had a slightly effeminate touch to it. He didn't trust either of them further than he could throw them. It was bad enough having to tolerate them at the office without having to put up with them at home as well.

Hugo knew he was being decidedly uncharitable and grumpy this evening, but taking into account all the problems his wife's family had brought him, he felt he had damned good reason to be. They all sat down at their appointed places: Olivia nearest the doorway, David to her right, and the twins to her left, while Hugo took the head of the table at the opposite end. A vast gilt-framed mirror covered the wall behind the twins, reflecting the dozens of tiny lights spilling from the chandelier, and three candelabra containing twelve candles burned in the centre of the table, casting flickering points over the glass and silverware.

Each place had been carefully laid with the Rees Minton, designed especially for Hugo's grandfather. Thomas deftly unfolded Hugo's napkin with a flick of his wrist and laid it across his employer's lap, before ladling the consommé into Hugo's soup plate. Thomas and Nancy were the only staff they kept on these days, apart from the daily. Nancy did the cooking and general running of the house, while her husband, Thomas, combined the roles of butler, driver, handyman and gardener.

'I'm so pleased you could come, David. Dragging you out at such short notice like this . . . '

'Think nothing of it, Olivia. It's always a pleasure to have an excuse to see you. I'm only sorry it's under such circumstances.'

115

'God, David, you sound as though there's been a death in the family,' Alexander said, somewhat arrogantly, Hugo thought. 'It's not as if there's been a huge disaster or anything. Just Dad having some stupid old fit or whatever while he was bonking some bird. I mean it's no big deal, is it?'

Hugo replaced his spoon in the soup plate noisily. Olivia seemed not to have noticed her nephew's insolent rambling.

'If you ask me,' Alexander continued, 'I think it's all rather a hoot. I expect Dad will, too.' He started to laugh. 'He's going to have to live it all down, isn't he – '

'Alexander! That's quite enough of that, thank you. Your father was not "bonking some bird", he was bonking a cabinet minister's wife. And what's more she's the Minister for the Environment's wife. The DoE could make life pretty difficult for Oscar Rees if they chose to. I'm sure I don't have to tell you what I'm talking about. The man's hardly going to be sympathetic to us after the publicity about his wife, is he?'

'Depends how he feels about her, I suppose. Some men might be relieved by it. Gives them a free rein, doesn't it, Hugo?'

Hugo looked down at the table for a moment, having no doubt as to what Alexander was referring, the irritating little shit. Fortunately for him, and for Olivia, they both knew about the other's activities.

'Let's hope you're right, Alexander. Maybe no mention will be made of it. I expect Caro will just go home, and he'll ask her what she did today, and she'll say, "Darling you can read about it in all the tabloids tomorrow," and he'll turn back to the newspaper and say, "Oh good, darling, I'll look forward to it."'

'It's a thought.'

116

'Not a very clever one!'

'Poor Daddy's always getting into such scrapes,' Lucienne chirruped. 'In a way, Uncle Hugo, Oscar Rees are lucky to have someone like Daddy around. He's awfully glamorous, and terribly wicked. If only our PR department could generate as much publicity in a month as he does in five minutes. I hope you're the same as him one day, Alexander.'

Hugo shook his head, bewildered. Had the whole world gone quite mad? Or was it just Julian and his family? Probably the latter, he thought.

'There's good publicity and there's bad publicity, Lucienne. Your father seems to be more expert at the bad sort.'

'Oh but, Uncle Hugo, that's not quite correct. No publicity is worse than bad publicity! I'll bet you our sales will go up after this.'

Hugo had a feeling she could be right.

Chapter Ten

Charles Allen had never had it so good! He lay, dreamily staring at the ceiling, watching the small cracks in the plaster fade in and out of focus. He wriggled his pelvis slightly so that his cock slid further down Lucienne's throat. She gagged slightly, pulled away, and then started to lick furiously over the tip, sending shock waves of pleasure through his groin, up into all his nerve endings. He would come any second if she carried on like that. She snapped her lips shut around his shaft, and slid them down, engulfing him in her soft, warm mouth. He could feel the razor-sharp edge of teeth, both threatening and exciting. He was entirely at her mercy. She sucked hard on him, making little choked noises. Her hands crept up over his abdomen, on to his chest and sought out his nipples, teasing her fingers lightly over them. He groaned and thrust harder into her mouth, wave upon wave of ecstasy pouring through him and flooding into Lucienne's throat. She continued to suck, swallowing him, savouring every last little drop of him. Then, when his thrashings subsided, she lifted her head and smiled at him, triumphantly.

'Amazing . . . ' he sighed. 'You're just totally amazing. Come here.' He pulled her up to him and wrapped his arms around her, then he kissed her long and hard. Her tongue tasted salty and slightly bitter.

'I'm glad you liked it,' she said, her lips curling up

at the corners in feline satisfaction. She snuggled into the curve of his arm, and stroked the hairs on his chest, tracing her fingers across, circling and playing.

'It's a very small world, isn't it?' Charles said, sighing. 'Imagine you being with Oscar Rees. I had no idea.'

Lucienne lay back on the pillow, still smiling. Charles Allen had called her the very next day, after their session in Trader Vics. She'd stalled him for a while and then finally agreed to meet him. First they'd had a preliminary, sexy lunch and then Charles had brought her back for coffee at his flat.

The kettle didn't even get switched on. Charles had ripped her clothes off the minute they got through the door. There was a trail of garments leading from the kitchen, through the sitting room and into the bedroom. Her La Perla camisole lay torn at the side of the bed. She wondered idly if she should reclaim it under expenses.

Charles kissed her lightly on the shoulder and slipped out of bed. 'Be back in a minute, darling.'

She watched him move away. He had a very nice body. Wide shoulders tapering into a neat little waist, and very squeezable, firm buttocks. His long legs were muscular and, as she well knew, very strong. All in all, seducing Charles Allen had been a very pleasant experience, and contrary to all her expectations. In his pictures he looked the archetypal neat young man: ambitious, arrogant and desperately dull. She never would have guessed he'd turn out to be as eager for sex, and as adventurous, as she herself was. She was beginning rather to like him.

Charles reappeared with a bottle of champagne and two glasses.

'Thirsty?'

'Should I be mixing my drinks?' she giggled, narrowing her eyes and running her tongue across her lips suggestively.

'Champagne's probably not quite as good for you, but just as refreshing, perhaps.'

'Then I'd love some.' She watched while he quickly popped the cork, and filled the glasses. Then she drank the ice-cold liquid, ready for a refill straight away.

'You were thirsty.'

'I just like getting high,' she said, pulling her knees up under her chin, giving him the full benefit of the enticing flesh between her legs. Already he could feel his cock growing hard again. He just couldn't get enough of her. Never had he met anyone like her before. She just oozed sex.

'When I was married,' he began, hesitantly, 'I never . . . we never . . . did anything like this.'

'I can't believe that,' Lucienne giggled.

'Truly. My wife only liked doing it in the missionary position. She would lie under me, never moving. You know, I could feel her almost willing me to get it over with. I don't think she ever enjoyed a moment of it. And as for what you did just now . . . well, she'd probably have been ill just thinking about it.'

'What a waste!' Lucienne sighed. 'She never knew how delicious you are. I guess you must be fairly out of practice then?'

'I wouldn't say that.' Charles sounded hurt. 'Did I seem to be out of practice?'

God, how fragile men's egos could be! She extended a long graceful leg and rubbed her toes along his shin. 'No. Out of practice is not the same as saying no good. I just meant you might need a little refresher course . . . in a number of options . . .

120

alternatives, should I say. We could experiment a bit, if you like.' She looked at him from under the crescent of thick black lashes.

Charles couldn't stand it any longer. He grabbed the glass from her hand, placed it on the table at the side of the bed, and threw himself on top of her.

Lucienne protested. 'That's just what I mean. Not like that, Charles.' She flipped over onto her stomach and then pulled her knees up under her so that she was on all fours. 'Like this!'

'You're like a bitch on heat, all sex and cunt!'

'Then you'd better hurry up and service me, hadn't you?'

Charles didn't need any encouraging. He was already in there.

It was dark when Lucienne woke up. Charles was kissing her face, saying something. She turned over and remembered where she was. She felt sticky and very well used. Her limbs were heavy and relaxed. She looked at her watch.

'I have to go.'

'Why?'

'I can't stay here all the time, Charles. I've got things to do at home.'

'Let them wait. I need you here.'

'You've had more than enough of me for one day. Any more and you'll start to tire of me.'

Charles snorted. 'Don't be ridiculous. I could never tire of you. You're far too exciting.' He was already running his tongue across her shoulders. She brushed him away, gently.

'Charles! Stop it.' She slid out of the bed. 'I'd like a shower.'

'Sure. Go ahead.'

When she had finished, Charles came into the

121

bathroom and sat down on the loo seat, watching Lucienne towel herself dry. She bent down and rubbed her long, slender legs. He marvelled at the creaminess of her skin, remembering the soft, velvety feel of it. Then she dabbed at the small dark triangle at the point where her legs met. Her full, neat breasts bounced enticingly, forming a deep cleavage when she leaned forward.

'I wish you didn't have to go.'

She stopped towelling herself and stood up, giving him the full benefit of her perfectly formed body. Lucienne knew no shyness. She had nothing to be ashamed of.

'The office is going a bit crazy at the moment. All sorts of things are going on.'

'Like?' Charles couldn't think what things could possibly be going on that he wouldn't already know about.

'It's Uncle Hugo,' she said, wrapping the towel around her and tucking a corner of it between her breasts to secure it. 'He seems very vague at the moment. We're all a bit worried about him.'

'Worried about Hugo? What on earth for?'

'He just seems a bit removed, as if he's not really with us half the time.'

'Oh come on, Lucienne. Hugo's always been very with us. That's why he makes such a brilliant job of running the company.'

'I know, you're right. It's probably nothing.'

Lucienne left the bathroom and Charles followed her. She picked up the remnants of the camisole from the floor and frowned at it.

'I don't think this is going to be much good. Ah well.' She threw it into the bin tucked under the small desk in the corner of the room. Then she stepped into her dress and asked Charles to zip her up.

Charles's curiosity was stirred. 'What do you mean?' If he could find out some inside information about Hugo, it might well be to the bank's advantage. Collingwoods held twelve per cent of Oscar Rees's shares, and had done since the time that Alfred Easton and Oscar Rees had merged back in the thirties. It had always been an extremely lucrative holding, and up until recently it had been overseen by old Patrick Collingwood himself. He'd been a lifelong friend of Oscar's. In fact the two old men had died within the space of a year of each other. Now the Rees holding came within Charles's own department. Not that he was in charge of it or anything – that was all down to the committee. Still, it might be of value to find out what Lucienne was getting at.

'H'm? About what?'

'About Hugo?'

'Oh, as I said, it's probably nothing. It's just that a few of us have noticed lately that he just seems to be in another world. I think Dad's latest escapade didn't help matters much. And then, of course, there's Aunt Olivia and her lesbian entourage getting him down. Frankly, both Alexander and I feel he's heading for a breakdown. He's losing touch with reality. We can't get any decisions out of him about the business, so it's all rather difficult. Still . . . ' she said, stepping into her high heels and peering into the small mirror on the table, ' . . . I expect things will sort themselves out. I hope they do. It would be a shame to see a company like Oscar Rees going down the pan, wouldn't it?'

She picked up her bag and came over to give him a very deep kiss. 'Call me,' she said.

He watched her slim body sway beautifully out of the room and heard the click of the door closing behind her. She'd certainly given him something to think about.

The Cooper Jefferson building occupied a big slice of Berkeley Square. Although the company hid behind the thirties façade, there was nothing about its philosophy that belonged to the past. It was a hugely successful conglomerate, with fingers in all sorts of pies. Way back it had made its name out of toothpaste and soap. Now it boasted many of the leading cosmetics houses under its vastly diverse umbrella.

Alexander's feet sank into the plush carpet as he moved noiselessly along the corridor to Leo Eden's office. The walls were covered with maple-framed blow-ups of the various product lines. Soon Oscar Rees would be joining them, Alexander thought with smug satisfaction.

Alexander congratulated himself on his smooth bit of manoeuvring. Leo Eden had not been quite as keen to jump on Oscar Rees as Alexander had at first thought. Although Leo had a reputation for acquisition on a grand scale, he had many reservations about the wisdom of his corporation adding Oscars to its portfolio, annoyingly echoing Hugo's opinion. While he had no qualms about buying up mass-market lines which could be sold through high-street chains and supermarkets, he doubted whether Coopers would find it as profitable to concentrate on the select marketplace which Oscar Rees occupied. But Alexander had managed to persuade Leo that with the combined expertize of himself and Lucienne on board, the fate of the company would be safe. It was only to be expected that Leo should also want Hugo as part of the deal, but Alexander knew his uncle well enough to predict that if the bid by Coopers was successful, Hugo would be too proud to share the control of his great love in life, and he would, in all probability, retreat into retirement. That would leave the way clear for both he and Lucienne to get on with the job of masterminding Oscar Rees on behalf of Cooper Jefferson.

Hugo was such a bloody old fool. If he'd allowed Lucienne and himself just a touch of control in the company Alexander wouldn't have been so desperate to play the Judas. Hugo deserved everything he was getting. Just look at Leo: nepotism had certainly played a part in his rise to corporate stardom. Not that anyone ever admitted it openly, but if your family couldn't give you a helping shove along the way, there wasn't much point in having one, was there? As many doors had been opened to Leo Eden because of his background as they had through his ability, and Alexander was after his job in the not-too-distant future. That was all part of his grand plan. First of all a seat on the board of Oscar Rees, and Hugo's gentle removal via resignation or distress, then he would work on Leo and, more importantly, Leo's boss in the States, Bob Lowenstein.

Leo's door opened just as Alexander reached it. This was the second time Alexander had paid Leo a visit, and Alexander knew that Leo would be well pleased with his news.

And it had been so bloody easy! Poor old Hugo. He was already a dinosaur, little did he know it. The King is dead . . .

'Leo!' Alexander said, smoothly. 'Good to see you.'

'Alexander.'

Leo's reception wasn't as warm as Alexander would have liked, but he'd soon change once he heard what Alexander had got to tell him.

'Come in. Sit down. How's it all going?'

'Terrific,' Alexander beamed at him. 'Really good, thanks, Leo. I think you'll agree with me.'

Leo sat back in the vast leather executive swivel chair, and regarded the other man. There was something about Alexander Easton that rather unnerved him. He was totally ruthless. That in itself shouldn't have bothered Leo – he himself hadn't got where he was without a touch of hardness now and again – but there was something else. He couldn't quite put his finger on what it was, but he would have been a lot happier if the deal hadn't been so closely tied up with Alexander. When Alexander had first approached him about a potential buy-out, he had felt distinctly uneasy about the deal. Initially he had turned it down flat, but Alexander had been annoyingly persistent, eventually managing to convince Leo that a massive fifty per cent of the company could be up for grabs. However, Leo wanted Hugo Rees to remain on the board.

'So, what have you got for me? This good news of yours – let's have it.'

'I believe I've got the deal in the bag.'

'Oh yes?'

Alexander patted his jacket pocket. 'Fifty per cent of the shares are sitting in here, metaphorically speaking.'

Leo managed a small smile. 'That's very interesting, Alexander. How did you manage that so quickly? A bit of gentle coercion, no doubt?'

Alexander shrugged. 'Perhaps,' he chuckled quietly. 'You know how it is – you see, people like cash these days. It's comforting, I suppose, to know it's there rather than having it tied up in some mouldering old company.'

'Quite.'

'My aunt called me yesterday. It seems both she

and the Oscar Rees Foundation could be prepared to sell.'

'Funny. I always thought Olivia would stick with Hugo.'

'It seems the Foundation could do with a cash injection right now. Then, of course, there's my sister and myself – though technically we won't actually be selling, will we? And the bank. I believe Lucienne's dealing with that and hopes to have confirmation that they'll run with the bid very soon.'

Leo couldn't help smiling. 'You have been busy, haven't you? So that just leaves Hugo and your father. Which way do you think he'll jump?'

Alexander glanced at his beautifully manicured nails for a moment. 'Hard to say. The thing about my old man is that he doesn't actually need the money. He's got enough even without the shares in the company.' Alexander caught himself thinking aloud. 'But I'm sure he won't be a problem. As I said, we're okay even without Dad's agreement. We'd still have a majority vote. At the end of the day, that's all we need. Then I expect Hugo will go.' Alexander brushed his hands together as if the deed were as good as done. 'And we can look forward to Oscar Rees with Lucienne and me at the helm. Then we can really get to work on some most interesting products. The labs are doing the preliminary testings at the moment, behind closed doors, of course. But it's all looking very promising indeed.'

'Aren't you being a bit premature, Alexander? Hugo will still have fifty per cent of the company. I really don't think we should assume he'll resign. That would hardly be good news for Oscars.'

Alexander's eyes narrowed, but he answered Leo evenly. 'No, you're probably right. In fact, it would be best for all of us if he stayed on. I must say, I'm all for it, really. But I simply feel that he won't take kindly to sharing the running of the company. I'm only trying to warn you, Leo, that he might choose to resign.'

'I shall endeavour to make sure he stays on, Alexander. Of course, we haven't exactly defined the particular roles you and Lucienne will fill in the new company, have we?'

'I must have your agreement that we have a seat on the Board, and I want my own research department so that I can concentrate on some stunning new developments. I couldn't think of pushing this deal through if I imagined for one moment that wouldn't be the case.'

Leo eyed Alexander sternly. 'It seems to me that you have no other option than to trust me at the moment. You don't have another buyer lined up, and you know that our offer is on the table. I've indicated to you that I'll give you both a place on the Board and the rest will have to be negotiated once we have signed a deal. I want to know if there's any surprises looming, Alexander. Any trusts attached to those shares that you say are in your pocket? This whole exercise could cost me one hell of a lot of money if it falls through. I don't want any last-minute hiccups.'

Alexander stood up, and Leo knew he'd got him on the defensive.

'Look, you can take my word. I know there's nothing hidden away. As I said, it's simple. Watertight. Just a matter of time.' He looked at his watch. 'I must dash. Lots of things to do.'

Leo grinned to himself as Alexander disappeared through the door. The man was a bloody fool – a dangerous bloody fool. He'd string Alexander along for the time being just to get the deal signed, but after that he'd make sure that there'd be a watertight let-out clause to jettison the Easton twins if they proved to be a liability. Anyway, it was time the bid was made public. The official approaches could now be made, according to Alexander's latest news.

Chapter Eleven

Alix definitely looked shifty. She was not her usual nosy self when Fern bumped into her by the lift, each of them on their way into the office.

'Er, hi,' Alix said, swallowing hard and avoiding Fern's eyes.

'Hi, Alix,' Fern returned cheerfully. 'How's things?'

'Oh, fine . . . fine.' Alix nodded as if to reassure herself of the very fine-ness of everything.

'Great.'

Fern was expecting the normal barrage of questions from Alix about where she had been, but instead Alix stared uneasily at her feet. The lift doors pinged open on the second floor. Fern stepped out and waited for Alix to follow her, but Alix grinned sheepishly, pointed her index finger skywards, and sort of half waved to Fern as the doors slid closed.

Funny, Fern thought. It wasn't usual for Alix to pop up to see the higher echelons this early in the morning. Few of them tended to be in yet, for one thing, and for another, if they were, it wasn't politically safe to visit until they'd stoked themselves up on sufficient quantities of caffeine.

Fern shrugged off her jacket and threw it around the back of her chair. For all the noise and bustle, and the often difficult job of concentrating on one's scribbling amid the fracas, Fern enjoyed being a part of the office. At least she had done until she'd grown out of the job. Now she had to wait at Edwina's pleasure to see what would happen about the promotion. Fern's few days away had hardly helped. If anything she felt even worse than she had before. Now on top of all the office problems, she had to deal with the guilty feelings she had over screaming at her mother like that.

She turned on her WP, and waited for the relevant files to come up on the screen. Then she turned to her in-tray and to the pile of post that awaited her. Out of the corner of her eye something, or rather the lack of something, caught her attention. She turned around and took in a full view of Alix's desk. It was empty – clear, bare – positively uninhabited. Fern stood up slowly from her chair frowning uncertainly.

She walked across to the deserted desk and started to check tentatively through the drawers. All were empty. What on earth had happened? Was that why Alix had appeared so sheepish this morning? Had she been ordered off the magazine for some misdemeanour and right now was collecting her P45 from upstairs? Poor Alix! How dreadful!

A burning sense of injustice fired Fern's temper. How dare they? After all she had done for the magazine. Well, Fern wasn't going to let it go just like that. She intended to tell whoever was responsible that you didn't dismiss good staff as easily as that, not without causing a rebellion in the ranks. She intended to demonstrate her solidarity right now.

Fern raced upstairs two at a time, her wild hair flying. She pushed it back absently and stormed through the swing doors, hesitating only to decide which direction Alix might have gone in. She decided to start with the Managing Editor's office. She strode down the corridor and knocked on the closed door. After a few moments' silence Fern realized there was no one in. She shrugged, and spun around, heading for the Editor's exalted environs. Again, after knocking, she realized this too was deserted. A couple more abortive attempts at giving the senior executives a piece of her mind and she headed down to the Features Editor's patch. She pushed the swing doors open in front of her and stopped short as the doors crashed together behind her.

Alix looked up from a rather large desk, and shifted her swivel chair around with her feet, while her bottom nestled nicely in the expensive-looking padded seat.

'What are you doing up here?'

Alix seemed to gulp. 'I . . . er . . . got a promotion, Fern.'

'A promotion! Jesus, I thought they must have fired you! Your desk was empty so I assumed . . . ' Fern glimpsed a hint of smugness on Alix's face.

'Fired! Oh no . . . ' she laughed at the ridiculousness of the idea. 'I've been made Assistant Features Editor.'

'What?'

'Assistant Features Editor.' Alix rolled her tongue deliciously around the title, savouring it fully.

'Congratulations,' Fern managed to splutter. 'I'm thrilled for you. You . . . er . . . deserve it, Alix.' Fern thought she was going to throw up. She felt physically sick.

'Thanks, Fern. I'm glad you're not upset.'

Fern's answering smile felt remarkably like a snarl.

'I thought you might be upset. I guess we all thought you'd be next in line – '

'No, no,' Fern's voice squeaked. 'You deserve it, Alix,' and for want of anything better to say: 'Let's have a celebratory drink at lunchtime, shall we?' She backed out of the room, managing to keep her plastic smile stuck in place.

That should have been *her* job. Everyone knew that Fern was next in line. What had gone wrong? She stared at her blank screen for most of the morning, trying to tell herself that she shouldn't feel bitter, especially bearing in mind she was more than half thinking about chucking in the job anyway, while another voice kept telling her that simply wasn't the point.

At 11.30 a.m., she got summoned to the Editor's office. Edwina Butler invited Fern to sit down. As she did so, Fern couldn't resist a sneaky glance around the room, the same room that had often illustrated her fantasy in 'one day when I'm editor . . .'

Once over the formalities, Edwina came straight to the point, her dark, weasel-sharp eyes glittering intelligently at Fern.

'I expect you've heard about Alix?'

Fern cleared her throat, doubting her voice. 'Yes.'

'I really would have liked to offer the job to you, Fern, but Alix told me of your plans.'

Fern's eyebrows shot skywards. 'Sorry?'

'Your plans,' Edwina repeated politely.

'I'm not exactly sure what you mean. What did Alix tell you?'

'About *A La Mode*, of course. If you're going to leave us it would be rather short-sighted of me to offer you the job.'

'But if you had offered me the job, I wouldn't leave,' Fern protested.

Edwina pouted her famous scarlet lips at Fern. 'Darling, you know how I need all my troops to be utterly loyal. I had no idea you were so dissatisfied with us. I really thought we were a close team. I'm sure you'll understand how difficult it was, but at the end of the day I have to do what's best for *Faces*. I have to know that the team is pulling together.'

Although Edwina spoke matter-of-factly, Fern knew damn well there was a hint of venom there. Edwina was angry that Fern had supposedly betrayed her – angry that she'd learned of it through Alix.

'But . . . ' Fern started to protest. She wanted to explain that she had been set up, that Alix had no right – that it wasn't true. What a bitch Alix was! Fern fought hard to control her anger. Her fingernails dug into her palms as she struggled to speak.

She stared at the pile of articles sitting neatly stacked in the centre of Edwina's desk. Plastic wallets of transparencies spilled out of another pile. She looked at the little pot of chinagraph pencils, kept permanently sharpened so that Edwina could scribble over the layouts. These were the Editor's tools and trappings. How often had she imagined herself at the other side of this desk?

Now there seemed little point in protesting. The decision was made for her and her position on *Faces* was untenable. She bit the proverbial bullet.

'I would have talked to you, but I needed time to think, to be sure. That's why I went away. I needed to see what your decision would be. You know I'm ambitious, Edwina. I'm sure you of all people understand that. I knew I was right for that job, and you led me to believe that I might not get it. I had to cover my options.'

'Quite, yes. I suppose you did. So no doubt you'll let me know in the next day or so what your plans are. It's clear to me that you won't be satisfied with your position as Editorial Assistant for any longer. Do let me know.' Edwina picked up her diary by way of dismissal.

Fern strode down the corridor to Alix's new office. She picked up the glass of mineral water sitting on

Alix's desk, and holding it over Alix's shaved head, tipped her hand and watched with satisfaction the drenching of the cow. As Alix screeched in protest, Fern spoke: 'There's that celebratory drink I mentioned.'

Laura, Hugo's PA, poked her head round the door to tell him that Olivia and Julian had arrived. He quickly scanned his desk to see if there was any sensitive paperwork lying on it and then went to fetch his wife and brother-in-law into his office.

'Thank you so much, both of you, for agreeing to come and see me in the office. I do think it's sometimes more convenient to talk in an environment other than one's home, don't you agree?' he said, leading the way without waiting for an answer.

Hugo could not detect any signs of Julian's illness. He looked the absolute picture of the healthy playboy, tanned, blond and extremely relaxed. How on earth the man could have been suffering from executive stress was quite beyond Hugo. Julian had never done a day's work in his life – unless, of course, you classed running a polo team and swanning around South America for half your life as work.

Olivia, on the other hand, was looking distinctly unhealthy. She had the ivory pallor of a vampire. Hugo had considered asking her whether she actually felt all right, but then, on second thoughts, decided that he really wasn't particularly bothered enough to inquire.

'Please do sit down,' he invited, as he plonked himself in his giant leather seat. 'I want to talk to you both about the offer from Cooper Jefferson. Naturally I need to know formally which way you intend to vote so that I may know what my future position will be. Julian, you first, if you wouldn't mind.'

'I am very tempted. Ten million's a lot of dough, Hugo!' How Hugo hated Julian's pseudo-hippie expressions. One would think that at the age of forty-eight he'd grow up a bit. And really, those tight white jeans . . .

'But then I think, hell, what do I want that kind of money for. I get everything I need as it is. We're all rich enough, aren't we? And I like promoting the company. Makes me feel as if I'm doing something worthwhile.'

Hugo's mouth twitched as he remembered the conversation he and David had had a short time ago about Julian's ability to gain the company exposure. 'That's very noble of you,' he murmured.

'Hell, it's not noble, Hugo. You know me, I just like to have a good time and I can't think I'd have a better one if I cashed everything in. I need more space to consider. I guess I'm still weighing up my options.'

'What about you, Olivia?'

Hugo was astonished to see his wife dab at her glistening black eyes with a small lace handkerchief. She sniffed daintily. 'I don't know what to say, Hugo,' she said pathetically.

Hugo felt nothing – no sympathy or affection for this snivelling creature he had called wife for so many years.

'Then why don't you just tell me what you intend to do?' he said curtly.

'I intend to sell,' she said quickly. 'And so does the Foundation – and the twins!' she garbled.

'I see. I would have thought that as my wife you might show a little more loyalty to me.'

'I've thought about that, too. I really can't see how Cooper Jefferson will affect you that much. You'll be all right, Hugo, but I've got to think about the money.'

136

'Olivia, you've never had to think about money in your life!'

'Not *my* money – the Foundation. This sale is vitally important for the Foundation's survival.'

'I would have thought some decent management would do more to help the Foundation's survival.'

'I take that as a personal insult, Hugo.'

'It was meant as one, Olivia.'

She glanced quickly at Julian, who seemed to be regarding his brown leather Docksides intently.

'And what's more Olivia, I want a divorce!'

Julian looked at the pair of them, aghast. 'A divorce!' he and Olivia said in unison.

'Yes,' Hugo said, almost relishing Olivia's anguish. 'I've decided, Olivia. Our marriage is a total sham and I wish to have some life of my own.'

'But you entirely have a life of your own. And what about me?'

'Come, come now, Olivia, you know as well as I do that our interests lie in opposite directions.'

julian stood up. 'I think it would be better if I left.'

'No!' Olivia almost shouted. 'Stay, Julian. I want you to hear this.'

Hugo seemed to have forgotten Julian's presence. He continued, clearly enjoying himself, 'I suggest you collect your things and move out of the house. No doubt you will be consulting your lawyers. I shall expect to hear from them.'

'Now wait a moment!' Anger seemed to be assisting Olivia's recovery from the shock. '*I* move out! I have no intention of doing any such thing. *You* can move out, Hugo. After all, you spend most nights with your *lady* friend, so it really wouldn't make much difference to you, would it? It would be too inconvenient for me. It's out of the question.'

'Well, we can't live there together,' Hugo cried.

'Suit yourself. It's you who's asking for this, not me. I'm quite happy that we maintain the status quo. I do not want a divorce.'

'I'm sure you don't. Life's far too comfortable for you. But, Olivia, you seem to forget one thing – your little act of betrayal. Wives aren't supposed to do that.'

'You treat the bloody company as if it's yours by divine right. You forget that half of it was *my* father's,' Olivia hissed. 'Therefore the Easton family can do as they see fit.'

Julian stood up again. 'Look, I really must go.'

Olivia pushed him back into his seat. 'Julian, stay!' she commanded, and Julian sullenly returned to contemplating his shoes for strength.

'I will not move out of the house,' Olivia continued. 'It's large enough to accommodate the pair of us if you choose, otherwise you will have to make your own arrangements, Hugo. That is all I will say on the matter. I think you should think very carefully about the ramifications of this course of action.'

Hugo had had enough. 'Julian, Olivia.' He stood and turned his back on his odious wife and ineffectual brother-in-law. He stared gloomily out of the window, only turning round when he heard the final click of the door.

Mid-morning Johnny Sharpe arrived back in the office tired and irritated. He dumped his calfskin briefcase down by his desk and saw the hand-scrawled note on top of the pile of paperwork. 'Hugo wants to see you,' it said simply. 'That's all I bloody need,' he said, under his breath, running a flustered hand through his long, dark hair.

Johnny was getting very tired of vainly trying to find the woman to launch Vitale. His life was becoming a bit of a joke. Each morning had found him prowling the railway platforms from Paddington to Waterloo, scrutinizing the sea of commuters for a likely looker. He had seen fit to approach only three girls, and that had been a no-fun job. Who wouldn't be suspicious of some jerk coming up to you at eight o'clock in the morning asking if you'd like to have some pictures taken? It had demanded all his diplomatic skill to convince the ladies in question (well, almost convince them) that he was who he said he was, and the best he could then hope for was that they would follow his request, and call him up at the company, having first checked him out with reception – if they were interested, of course. There had been no way he could possibly have asked *them* if he could contact them.

Then he had worn down some more shoe leather traipsing round the drama schools, hanging around the classrooms, peeping like some demented letch. The things he did for the bloody company – and no one, but no one, appreciated it. All he needed now was a meeting with Hugo. Oh yes, just like a hole in the head.

Janie, his secretary, appeared. 'Johnny . . . ' Her voice sounded breathy and nervous. Her hands fluttered about in front of her. 'Thank God you're in. Hugo wants to see you, *urgently*!'

'When is it ever not urgent with him?'

Johnny flicked the message aside and scanned the pile of post. He slipped off the leather jacket hung round his shoulders and gave it to Janie. 'Hang this, will you, darling?'

'Shall I tell him you're here, then?' She stood in the doorway, waiting for his answer. It was quite clear that she was not enjoying her role as go-between. Hugo could be quite monstrous when he was in one of his moods.

'Let me get a coffee first, lovey. I need an infusion of something to pep me up, and short of a stiff brandy, I'd better make do with the disgusting stuff that masquerades as coffee.'

'I'll get it for you,' Janie said, knowing the sooner she did that, the sooner he'd see Hugo, and the sooner Hugo would be off her back.

Johnny ripped open the post, and quickly glanced at the latest show cards sent from the model agencies – just in case. He flipped them aside quickly, then stopped. Something caught his eye. The last card, which now looked up at him from the desk . . . there was something about the girl's look, a sort of cheekiness, almost a defiance, that caught his attention. Feeling a very slight flutter in his abdomen, he picked up the card and viewed the model more carefully. Her hair was short – perhaps that was why he had cast it aside so quickly. After Fern, the idea of long flowing locks was hard to dismiss. But the girl had a lovely, pert look. Her hair bounced and shone, even in the still photograph.

Johnny grinned. And then it started. The tingle between his legs. He shifted in his chair and blew a kiss at the young face on the photograph.

'Where the hell have you been?' Hugo was in a filthy temper. 'I've been trying to get hold of you all week. Not even Janie knew where you were. You're supposed to be running a product launch, not doing a damned irresponsible disappearing act. It's at a crucial stage, we're already behind schedule, and you've gone AWOL. I think you've got some explaining to do.'

Johnny felt he'd been transported back in time.

Hugo was like the headmaster about to beat the shit out of him for escaping to the local pub for a quick one. Johnny cleared his throat, and told himself not to be a wimp.

'What's happening about the casting session? When am I going to see some photographs? The advertising agency are champing at the bit. They really need to get going.' Hugo's thick brows knitted together in a worried frown.

'Don't worry, Hugo,' Johnny said calmly. 'I've been on to that. I haven't been idle. I've been hunting,' he said cheerfully, 'and this,' he placed the model card triumphantly down on the desk in front of Hugo, ' . . . er, there's nothing definite as yet. Obviously I want your approval before I go off and do anything, but I have to tell you, Hugo, I can feel it in my – '

Hugo struck his own head lightly with his palm. 'I don't believe it, not the balls feeling again.'

Johnny glanced into his lap for a fraction of a second. 'I can always rely on them.'

'Really. Well, I'm very happy for you, Johnny. Now what about this girl?' Hugo cleared his throat, faintly embarrassed by Johnny's scrotal signals. He picked up the card, then said curtly. 'This isn't the girl you had in mind!'

Johnny shifted uncomfortably in his seat. 'Well, no, but – '

'What about the girl you introduced me to at the ball? Redhead, wasn't she? I thought you told me she was the one.'

'Well, yes . . . but – '

'What's the matter, man?' Hugo barked.

'She didn't want to do it.' Johnny managed to get out eventually.

Hugo's face reddened, very slightly. 'Didn't want to do it?'

'That's right.'

'But no girl in her right mind would turn down an opportunity like this!'

'I know. I did tell her that, several times, actually.'

'But she didn't want to know?'

'That's right.' Johnny shrugged. He went on quickly, 'So I thought perhaps we might try – '

'H'm.' Hugo studied the card. He remembered the striking redhead quite clearly. This one had a fresh-faced beauty, certainly, but she didn't have the same kind of head-turning qualities.

'Is it worth trying again – the other one?'

'I could, but I don't think I'd get anywhere. She's a fairly strong-willed lady, and she was very insistent.'

Hugo's foul mood seemed to settle into an even deeper level of despondency. He felt profoundly and inexplicably disappointed. He hadn't realized until this moment quite how much he wanted to see the girl again.

'What's her telephone number?' he barked.

Johnny's jaw dropped open. 'Why?' he blurted before he could catch his tongue.

'Why?' Hugo's voice was a headache-inducing boom. 'Because I intend to persuade her otherwise.'

Johnny tried not to let the fact that Hugo had quite obviously flipped his lid reflect on his face. Finally Johnny shrugged and riffled through his organizer. Hugo scribbled the number down.

'Fine. And by the way, Johnny, I want the mock-ups for the Ozzie posters on my desk by this afternoon. Sometimes I wonder just what kind of an operation I'm running, for God's sake, man. We have a product launch without a face, and a perfume boost without the bloody posters.'

Johnny backed off, leaving Hugo bad-temperedly punching numbers into his telephone.

Fern sat in the tiny bar, sipping a glass of iced mineral water, trying very hard to fade inconspicuously between the respective backs of a pinstriped suit and a piercingly loud woman intent on telling her companion every detail of her arduous morning's shopping in Harrods.

When the exalted Mr Hugo Rees had called her yesterday and invited her to meet him at the Capital Hotel for lunch she had wondered whether someone was playing some kind of prank on her. 'Hugo,' she had repeated uncertainly, '*the* Hugo Rees?'

'That's the one,' the beautifully modulated voice had assured her. 'I wonder if we might chat over one or two things . . . over lunch. Tomorrow at one, say?'

Fern had smiled to herself. She had nothing left to lose.

Already Hugo was seven minutes late, and seven minutes sitting in this place felt a good deal longer. Fern was now wishing she had spent more time wandering around Joseph instead of endeavouring to make the appointment on time. She sneaked a glance at her watch, for the third time in as many minutes, and tried to look as though she spent every lunch-time comfortably perched in her jeans among a sea of Saint Laurent and Armani.

'Waiting for someone?'

The voice startled her, making her almost spill her drink. She looked up into deep, dark eyes below thick black brows. Annoyingly, she felt her cheeks turn pink in embarrassment. She shook her hair around her face, attempting to hide her blushes. What on earth was the matter with her? Leo

143

Eden's dark eyes crinkled at the corners in amusement.

'Or are you gate-crashing someone's party again?'

'No, I'm meeting someone,' she said quickly, and then realized she was almost confirming his accusation. 'And I'm not a gate-crasher.'

Leo Eden laughed, and Fern was surprised at how attractive the sound was. His voice had a smooth, velvety depth to it, like rich dark chocolate. But there was something about him which made her uneasy, nervous, like a gawky teenager. Then she realized he was not alone. India Duncan-Forrester slid to his side. 'Leo, sorry, I bumped into a friend in the – ' She halted, mid-flow as she noticed Fern. 'Oh!' She didn't try to hide her distaste. 'You again!'

'You know each other?' Leo inquired curiously. India wore an immaculate emerald-green linen suit, which finished a flattering inch above her slender knees, with a royal blue and emerald green blouse underneath. Gold chains dangled round her neck. Long slim fingers curved possessively around Leo's arm, revealing to Fern the scarlet-painted talons which no doubt would do a slick job of scratching Fern's eyes out.

'Not socially,' India stressed, letting her eyes sweep conspicuously and disapprovingly over Fern's faded jeans. 'She came to me for a job.'

Leo Eden's brow raised as he turned his attention back to Fern. 'Did you get it?' he asked, failing to hide the mockery in his voice.

Fern shook her head. 'The odds were against me.' She looked directly at India. 'There was too much competition, wasn't there?'

'I do hope you have better luck elsewhere,' India simpered insincerely. 'I hear via the grapevine that your job at *Faces* is on the market. Did you decide to go to one of the weeklies?' Her syrupy voice couldn't quite disguise the malice behind her words.

Fern felt the colour drain from her cheeks. How the hell did India know that? She'd only spoken to Edwina a couple of days ago. Grapevine my arse, she thought. Bloody Alix, no doubt spreading the word.

Fern was struggling to find a suitable retort, given that she was now technically out of work, when Hugo's arrival diverted their attention. The conversation in the bar seemed to lull as Hugo politely pushed his way through the over-crowded room. Hugo appeared not to notice the many heads turning in his direction. Even disallowing the fact that he was the internationally recognized head of Oscar Rees, with a substantial personal fortune, his tall stature and dark good looks afforded him many admiring glances, particularly from the female quarter. Unlike his brother-in-law though, Hugo was not a playboy. That much Fern had gleaned from her previous research on the family.

He smiled warmly at her, taking her hand in his. 'Ah, Fern . . . so sorry. I got held up.' He glanced into her jade-green eyes and for a moment it was as if time had stopped. There was something so remarkably familiar about the girl. And her hair, so rich and vivid, swinging loosely over her simple white linen shirt. Her hand shifted in his, and remembering himself, he released it. He coughed to disguise his fleeting lack of composure.

Leo unwittingly rescued him. 'Hugo. Well, well. Now we can at least solve the mystery.'

'And what mystery is that, Leo?'

'The mystery of urchins having lunch dates at the Capital.'

Hugo frowned, not having the faintest idea what Leo was going on about. 'India . . . ' He nodded politely to Leo's companion, having only just noticed her.

Leo persisted. 'Aren't you going to introduce us formally, Hugo?'

'Er, yes. Right. Fern, I'd like you to meet India Duncan-Forrester . . .'

India stepped backwards, away from Fern and smiled coolly. 'We've already met.'

'And Leo Eden. This is Fern Donleavy.'

'Delighted,' Leo drawled in his husky voice. Then he lifted Fern's small and rather chilled hand, and raised it gallantly to his lips.

Fern caught his eyes as he placed his lips to her hand, and she saw the hint in those depths of something which looked extraordinarily like mischief. Contrary to her feelings for him, she found her mouth betraying her. It lifted into an answering grin.

'Come along, Leo, our table is ready.' India bustled him away, glaring accusingly at Fern.

Hugo apologized once more. 'I do hope you haven't been waiting long, my dear.'

Fern lied. 'No, not at all.'

'Good. Well, let's see the menu, shall we? I've ordered you a glass of champagne. I do hope you like champagne.'

As he spoke the waiter arrived carrying a tray which bore a couple of glasses of bubbly and a large bowl of black olives. The two people in front of Fern had, thankfully, vacated their seats, creating more space for herself and Hugo.

'So good of you to come,' Hugo murmured as he clinked glasses with Fern. She sipped at the pale honey-coloured fizz and savoured the delicious, buttery taste of it. After two or three more large sips she was feeling much warmer, and much more relaxed. After Hugo's abruptness at the Cosmetics Association ball, she had expected him to be colder than he appeared today. She studied his head as he bent over the menu, noting the silver threads in his dark hair, and the hollow, aristocratic line of his cheeks. He was certainly attractive, though much too old for her taste. For the millionth time she wondered what on earth he had invited her here for.

'I can thoroughly recommend the duck – if you like duck, of course. And the lobster salad as an hors d'oeuvre is excellent – again, if you like lobster.'

'Sounds delicious,' Fern said, grateful to be relieved of the task of struggling through the menu. In any event, she wasn't at all sure of how much she'd be able to eat. Hard as she tried to act calm, the anxious butterflies in her stomach refused to settle down.

The waiter seemed to have some mysterious sixth sense and he appeared the minute Hugo put the menus aside. Once they were alone again Hugo smiled benevolently at Fern.

'I expect you've guessed why I wanted to see you.'

She took a flyer. 'I can only imagine it must have something to do with Vitale.'

'I gather you told Johnny you weren't interested.'

'I did. And I wasn't . . .' Fern's voice tailed off.

'Wasn't?' Hugo jumped in, hopefully. 'Could there be a change of heart, perhaps?'

'Put it this way,' Fern said bluntly. 'I'm looking for a job now. If you'd asked me the same question a few days ago I would have told you that I had no intention of ever leaving journalism. However, I've had my eyes opened to a few things which led me to believe I could maybe consider a change of direction.'

Hugo's smile broadened. 'How very interesting. Come, my dear, let's talk some more over lunch.'

The waiter led them through into the dining room. Fern was relieved to find that Leo Eden and India Duncan-Forrester were seated at the far side of the room, well out of earshot, and almost out of sight. A bottle of very dry, but deliciously light white wine accompanied the beautifully prepared lobster. Fern picked her way delicately through the shellfish as Hugo recounted the details of the contract.

'I doubt you'd find many jobs offering you a million pounds for two years' work.'

Fern set aside the miniature pair of pliers she had been using to crack open the lobster's claws and wiped her mouth on the napkin. She regarded Hugo levelly.

'I'm not much of a materialist,' she said. 'To be quite honest, the money frightens me. I was never brought up to believe it bought you happiness. It's such a huge amount, too much for me to imagine. It's almost an immoral amount of money,' her eyes sparkled mischievously, 'though I've always thought it would be nice not to have to worry about the phone bill. But what concerns me most is that I wouldn't be exercising my brain enough. I'm afraid I might get bored.'

Hugo roared with laughter. 'You simply wouldn't have the time, my dear. If you *were* to decide to take up the offer, you'd be whisked off for photographic shoots, publicity campaigns, the launch itself . . . You see, you would be the ambassador for Vitale, at the very front line of the product, as it were. People would identify Vitale with you, with your face. You'd be dealing with the press, answering their questions, learning all about the product.'

'You make it all sound very exciting. But I'm a

148

journalist. That's what I've spent years training to be and I feel very unrelaxed about throwing it all away. Like I said to Johnny, I might never be taken seriously again.'

'Then you are underestimating the job. Don't you realize, Fern, that once the contract is finished, all sorts of doors would be open to you? You'd become an international celebrity. It wouldn't be the finish of your career, but the beginning of many new ones, if you wished. There's nothing to stop you writing, is there? It's my opinion that people would be far more interested in what Fern Donleavy has to say when they really know who you are. You'd become a household name – the Vitale girl.'

'You mean I'd be known as the Vitale girl, not Fern Donleavy.'

'No, I mean everyone will know exactly who the Vitale girl *is*. It would be *your* product.'

'But would I have any say in it? My job would be all about the promotion of Vitale, not about the actual strategy of it, the way it's developed, the way it progresses . . .'

Hugo refilled her glass and studied her benevolently. 'Your expertize is in journalism, not in cosmetics. These things are highly specialized. Oscar Rees has many different departments, employs many specialists, to devise and plan what you've just mentioned. I have to be frank, Fern, and tell you that this wouldn't be some sort of graduate training course to qualify you to run the company at the end of the day.'

'Don't you see, that's the worst thing about it? I'd be treated as some clotheshorse, or blank canvas, or whatever, that people can use as they like. I just don't think my personality is suited to that. I need to be involved, really involved, with whatever it is I do. I want to use my brain, Hugo, and I don't believe that the job you are very kindly offering me would do that.' Fern pushed the wine aside and picked up the glass of mineral water. 'I'm not suggesting I run the company, Hugo, but I'm suggesting I would like to be more involved with the job than simply having my picture taken and handing out press packs to ligging journalists.'

'But you have no training in cosmetics!'

'Nor in modelling, yet you're prepared to offer me a million to do it. If I were to consider the offer then I'm suggesting that you get more than your money's worth and I have a more fulfilling role. Let me learn the business as well! I've a quick mind, I'm reasonably ambitious and I learn fast. If I were to accept this contract then I would want a career that's going to develop along with my commitment to you.' She smiled her most dazzling smile. 'All I'm suggesting is that you make best use of your assets.'

Hugo shook his head. 'I can see you're a very determined young lady and I am going to be the one who now has to think about things.'

Hugo was not going to admit to Fern at this stage that he was seriously impressed with her and that his decision was already made. From the way she'd put up her arguments today, he had no doubt that she could develop into a formidable member of his team. A lady this headstrong might well require a short rein and a fair bit of schooling. Hugo smiled to himself. Johnny Sharpe might find his work far more interesting when he learned who his new assistant product manager was going to be.

'Then with your agreement,' Hugo mocked her lightly, 'I suggest we get you into the studio pdq for some test shots.'

'I'll look forward to it. And then we can talk about

my possible role within the company.' She grinned cheekily back at him.

Hugo laughed. Johnny had made a wise choice.

Chapter Twelve

❦❦❦❦

Fern recognized Johnny's voice immediately. 'Hello,' she said hesitantly, wondering how on earth he would treat her now that she had done a complete about-turn, and not thanks to his persuasion either.

'I heard the news from Hugo,' he said matter-of tactly, his voice betraying no emotion. 'I gather you're interested.'

'Listen, I'm sorry, Johnny, about the other week. You must think I've been leading you a merry dance.'

He laughed quietly. 'I'm used to it. Nothing's ever straightforward in this business. I'm glad Hugo managed to talk you into it.'

Did she detect a note of sarcasm? 'It wasn't just Hugo. It was a combination of lots of other things – the most important being the fact that I decided to move on from *Faces*. Everything happened rather quickly – not as I had planned. I thought my next career move would be to Assistant Features Editor and it didn't happen, but that's another story.' She might as well be honest with him from the start. She owed him that after all his running around.

'Yeah. Well, that's life for you. Now about this shoot . . . ' God, he really did sound cold.

'Johnny,' she said softly, 'do you think we could try and start again? I really did have good reason to turn your offer down, and I had good reason to reconsider. Please don't think I was just being bloody-minded.'

'Oh, to hell with it,' he laughed. 'I never could hold out this kind of act. The fact is, I'm thrilled that you've agreed to the shoot, and I'm mad that Hugo pulled a flanker over me. It's just my wounded male pride. That and the fact that when you're world famous I won't be able to say that you were all my own work.'

'That's just the kind of thing I want to hear,' she laughed. 'Guaranteed to make me change my mind.'

'Hey, hold on, let's get you booked into the studio. First thing tomorrow morning suit you? I can't wait to see these test shots and I dare say neither can you! I'll pick you up around ten.' Johnny was surprised at how much he was actually looking forward to it. 'Get a good night's sleep.'

''Night, Johnny,' she said quietly, 'and thanks.'

The floor of Fern's bedroom seemed to have disappeared under a sea of T-shirts, jeans and a strange assortment of dresses. She was beginning to wish she'd never agreed to this. The whole idea was crazy. She held up a long black tube of Lycra, placing it against her, and then chucked it back onto the bed. It was no good. She just didn't know what to put on. The doorbell rang and she swore aloud. She picked up a T-shirt and threw it over her head. When Johnny entered the flat he was confronted with the sight of Fern's endless legs disappearing tantalizingly under the long white T-shirt. She turned away from him and stomped up the stairs. 'It's no good. I haven't got a damned thing to wear!'

'You've got a pair of jeans, haven't you? Just put those on. We'll be dressing you in something else when the shoot starts, so what you wear really doesn't matter.'

'So now I'm a clotheshorse as well as a plastic

bimbo. Whatever happened to my ideals in life? Fern thought.

'Hurry up,' Johnny called after her. 'We don't want to keep them all waiting.'

Fern stopped in her tracks. 'All?' she asked suspiciously. 'Who's all?'

'Oh, just the whole of Oscar Rees. I invited them along to have a look at you.'

Fern shrieked in horror. 'Johnny! You didn't! How could you? I'm not coming.'

'Come on, I'm joking. But we have got a hairdresser, a stylist and the photographer's assistant all waiting for you.'

'Terrific,' Fern sighed in resignation and bounded up the remaining stairs.

She pulled a clean pair of jeans from the bottom of the untidy mountain of clothes which covered the bed and then threaded a thick tan leather belt through the beltloops and pulled it tight. Then she stepped into her thick-soled Doc Martens, threw her hair back over her shoulders, picked up her bag and joined Johnny.

'Okay then, what are we waiting for?'

Johnny shrugged, and followed Fern out of the flat. His step was lighter than it had been for days. All his instincts told him that this girl was going to be fantastic, even if she might also turn out to be something of a handful!

Truth to tell, Johnny was surprised at how meekly Fern succumbed to all the attentions necessary before the shoot commenced. Firstly the hairdresser took one look at her hair and threw his hands up in despair. 'Do you never have this cut?'

'Well, I trim it occasionally, when it gets particularly raggy at the ends. But I like it kind of messy. It's me!'

'Would you mind,' he said as diplomatically as he could, 'if I perhaps trimmed a little bit off it now? Just the teensiest, weensiest littlest of bits?' he wheedled.

Fern wriggled uncertainly in her seat, in front of the vast mirror surrounded by lightbulbs. 'Johnny,' she called, 'he wants to cut my hair.'

Johnny appeared next to her reflection. 'What do you think, Frank?'

'Just a little tidying up. Not much.'

Johnny picked up a piece of the unruly red mass. 'Not too much, off. It's rather glorious, isn't it.'

Frank sighed, not at all sure about that. A haircut was a haircut, after all, and he had a reputation to think about. 'Whatever you want,' he said and got out his scissors and began his attack.

In the meantime a girl appeared with an enormous case which she proceeded to empty onto the table in front of Fern. 'Hi,' she said brightly. 'I'm Louise!'

'I'm Fern, I think,' Fern added uncertainly. 'And I hope I still will be by the end of this.'

Louise laughed. 'Don't worry. I've been told to make you look natural. So you shouldn't notice too much difference.'

Fern screwed her nose up. 'If I've got to look natural, then maybe I don't need to wear any make-up.'

'You can't promote a product range without wearing it,' Johnny said, a little impatiently to Fern's mind.

'Seems daft to me. You want women to go out and spend money buying something they're going to wear on their faces which is going to look like they're not wearing anything on their faces.' She grinned at Louise. 'The whole world's gone potty!'

While Frank pulled and teased her hair, brushing and snipping and pausing every few moments to take a look, Louise matched her palette up to Fern's colouring, holding shades up to her, examining her eyes, tutting and umming as she went through them. Fern eyed the row of bottles which Louise had lined up on the dressing table in front of her. 'So this is it?'

'This is it, the first samples of Vitale. Smart bottles, aren't they?'

Fern reached over and picked up one marked Vitalize. The clear plastic bottle was filled with a milk-white lotion. The product looked clean, almost clinical in its simplicity with its silver ball-shaped cap, and the tall, thin jade-green capital letters which marched neatly around the base of the bottle, contrasting very well with the white contents. Next Fern examined the squat jar of something marked Vitality. Again, the screw top was the same glittering silver, with tall green capital letters adorning the circumference of the jar. She unscrewed the top and smelled the contents. She was surprised at how fruity the fragrance was.

'Mmm,' she sighed to Louise, 'it smells almost edible.'

'I wouldn't advise it. Let's see how your face likes it, shall we?'

Frank, finally satisfied with Fern's hair, gave Louise permission to begin. First of all she lathered Fern's face and neck with the cream cleanser and massaged it into all the curves of her face. Then, just as Fern was beginning to enjoy the feel of Louise's hands playing around her face, she started to tissue it all off again. Having finished that, she repeated the whole thing, from start to finish. 'I'm just cleansing your face,' she explained.

'I washed it this morning!'

Louise showed Fern a piece of the tissue and Fern was ashamed to see how black it looked. 'That can't be from me!'

''Fraid so. You just can't get into the pores without a proper cleansing routine. You're lucky you don't get spots.'

'My face feels really tingly,' Fern cried a few moments later. 'Is it supposed to do that?'

'Yep, that's the fruit acids getting to work on all your dead cells. You wait and see how good your skin looks when I've finished with you.'

Then Louise put a deliciously refreshing cold tonic over Fern's face, wiping away any trace of the grease left from the cleansing routine. Next she put some lotion onto her fingers and again started to massage it into Fern's face and neck, starting off with quick little strokes that started near the base of her neck, on up to her chin, and high over her cheekbones, finishing in light circular movements over her forehead and nose. Still Fern didn't look any different, but her skin felt smooth and soft. Then came the foundation. Louise squirted a tiny bit of the light, beige-coloured mousse on to her palm and began applying it to Fern's skin, evening out the tones of colour on her face and disguising the freckles.

'Don't get rid of too many freckles,' Johnny ordered.

Then came a powder to set it all, by which time Fern felt as though she'd got a mask three inches thick plastered over her face. She grimaced at her reflection, expecting the whole lot to crack up. Surprisingly, it didn't.

Louise added some colour to Fern's cheekbones, just a touch of faintest pinky brown, followed by some outlining to her eyes and some mascara that made her eyes water while Louise told her to look up, and then to look down as she brushed it on and, finally, some pale, reddy-pink lipgloss.

When at last Fern took a good long look at the

whole picture she could hardly see much difference from her 'normal' face.

'Well?' Louise asked, a little nervously.

Fern shrugged. 'Yeah. It's okay!' Her eyes seemed larger and greener, and maybe her mouth a little fuller, but she didn't look half as painted as she felt.

Frank put down his copy of *Faces*, which he'd been intently studying all the while, and started to brush Fern's hair out. He turned to Johnny. 'Do you want it up, or anything?'

'Not for the moment. Just long and natural, and maybe a bit wild-looking, okay?'

'Stand up, bend over and let your head drop forward,' said Frank.

Fern bent double and Frank knelt down and began brushing the underside of her hair. He gave a few squirts of something which smelled totally revolting and then asked her to stand up. Fern's hair looked twice as thick as it normally did.

'Wow!' Johnny said, in admiration. 'Terrific!'

A few more squirts from Frank and Fern was led through to the studio. She looked so natural, dressed as she had arrived, that Johnny had decided to keep her in her own clothes for the initial session.

Dressed all in black, the guy who appeared from behind the backdrops looked about as thin as a wire coathanger. It seemed a remarkable feat of human engineering that his legs could actually hold him up at all.

'Zak, this is Fern,' said Johnny.

'Hi, Fern. How're ya doin'?' He sounded slightly American, or something.

'Okay so far, thanks.'

Zak was doing a Johnny on her, pressing his nose almost up to hers, squinting into her eyes, following the lines of her cheekbones as if he were trying to follow an A to Z using a torch with dead batteries.

'Yeah. See what you mean, John. She's pretty special. Okay,' he almost sang, 'let's get to work.'

An equally stringy though younger-looking assistant appeared from the secret place behind the backdrop and brought a small black box up in front of Fern's face. He showed it to Zak, who was busy looking through his lens, ducking up and down, swivelling the tripod around, fiddling with the spotlights and generally setting up. He had a huge lens fixed onto the camera, with a big hood attached to the end of it.

'Sit over there, would you?'

Fern looked to see where Zak was pointing. There was a stool next to the backdrop. She sat on it and pouted at him, feeling dreadfully self-conscious.

'Can you sit up?' He talked down into his camera but Fern guessed he must be speaking to her. She straightened her back and flicked her hair over her shoulder. The bulb flashed. She turned her face around to see where the others were, and again the bulb flashed. She turned back to the camera, flash. The shoot seemed to have started.

'Lovely . . . lovely . . . ' she heard Zak croon. Again, she wasn't sure if he was talking to himself or to her. 'Now look at me. Great. Stick your chin out . . . no, too much. That's it! Perfect.' Flash. 'Okay, look around, towards the doorway, slowly, very slowly. Hold it!' Flash. 'Great!'

On and on it went until, through boredom, she began to relax. She tried pulling faces. She smiled. She tilted her head. She frowned. She smouldered. She turned around and looked back at the camera over her shoulders, and all the while Zak was encouraging her. 'That's marvellous. You're doing great.'

After a while he swapped cameras. 'Now we're going to do some body shots. Stand by the stool, Fern, lean forwards as if you're talking to me . . . That's it. Yeah, hold it there!' On and on, she was posing and turning, almost dancing to the camera's tune. Soon she was lost in the strange relationship that was building up between her and that small black piece of glass that kept winking at her over and over.

Johnny couldn't believe it. She was a natural, a real pro. She looked as if she'd been doing it for years. He laughed, his heart feeling very light indeed.

Johnny didn't want to break in on what was going on between them, but eventually he knew he had to. 'Look, Zak, we're going to have a hair change, and a different look. Give us five minutes, would you, when you're ready?'

Fern was pleased to have the break. She was feeling quite hot and very thirsty.

Frank pulled her hair tightly back and wound it up into a knot which sat on top of her head. Louise put some more shadow on to her eyes, and darkened the gloss.

Fern was stunned by the change in her appearance. She looked very sophisticated – much older, a different kind of woman altogether. She realized with a start she had never thought of herself as a woman before, but the person staring back at her from the mirror was no girl. She was some sexy-looking woman!

'Okay,' she said, suddenly feeling in control and very confident, 'I'm ready. Come on, Zak. Let's get to work!'

*　　*　　*

Johnny followed Fern into the airy sitting room. Their shoes clumped noisily over the stripped boards. There was a pretty Victorian cast-iron fireplace filled with an assortment of feathers, flowers and grasses, and over the mantelpiece hung a portrait of the young woman who had just plonked herself down cross-legged on the floor. Johnny walked over to the canvas. The girl who looked back at him pouted with an almost self-mocking attitude of rebelliousness. Her wild red hair billowed out from her head in tangled ringlets. Her hands rested in the front pockets of her faded jeans, and the small, graceful curve of her young bosom could be faintly seen under the soft white shirt. Now Johnny knew, stronger than ever, that this was the right girl to launch Vitale. The painting was magnificent. It conveyed all that he wanted to say about the product, about the woman behind the product, its character, its personality, its essence . . . everything. The face captured on canvas was young, and yet there was a hint of worldliness, a sexiness about her, but naïve, sprung from a core of naturalness, rather than artifice and calculation. Yet through the innocence there was a wildness, too, the sense that she embodied a spirit unwilling to be captured. A feeling that this girl would be a bit of a handful, but a whole lot of fun. Johnny wondered whether Fern would let the advertising agency have a look at the painting.

'Who's the artist?' he said.

'Rowena . . . My mother. She's an artist.' Fern shrugged as if it were of no consequence.

'Ah,' Johnny said, as if everything were now clear. 'She obviously knows you petty well.'

'Who's to judge?' Fern said coldly. 'Only those who know me pretty well themselves. And there aren't many of those around.'

161

'Shame,' Johnny shrugged, ignoring her defensiveness. 'Perhaps I'll soon be in a position to judge.'

'Hm, maybe. Oh, I'm sorry, Johnny. It's nothing against you, it's just that my mother and I aren't exactly on good terms at the moment. We had a row.'

Johnny grinned. 'Forget it. I don't take offence easily. I thought you'd know that by now.'

'I guess I should. Nobody could be as pushy as you and stay sensitive.'

'Hey . . . ' he started to protest mildly. Fern was laughing. For the first time she looked at Johnny Sharpe properly, as more than just Oscar Rees's Product Manager, an irritating but sometimes amusing little pest who had coerced her into considering some pretty daft notions. She looked at him as a man, and hard as she tried to stop him, he was forcing her to like him. There was such an air of warmth and openness about him. But her life hardly needed any more complications right now. She forced her attention back to the business in hand.

'Well? What do you think?' Johnny asked, trying to keep the excitement out of his voice.

Fern flicked through the proof shots, then laid them out on the floor in front of her like playing cards. 'More to the point, what do you think?'

'They're okay,' he said nonchalantly. 'I guess they're okay.'

'H'm,' she agreed, noncommittally, 'I do look very different, don't I?'

Johnny couldn't contain himself any longer. He produced the bottle of champagne which had remained hidden inside his leather jacket. The cold glass had probably given his ribs frostbite. Zak had dropped the proofs round as soon as he'd finished printing them, and Johnny had wanted to give Fern the good news. Judging by the bemused look on her face, his nonchalance had taken her in.

'Fern!' he cried. 'They're fucking fantastic. Even Zak said so, and praise from Zak, believe me, is unheard of. Hugo is going to *die* when he sees these.'

Still sounding uncertain, she continued to pore over the photos. 'You really think so?'

'Take my word for it. Now go and find some glasses and let's drink to your first million.'

Fern shuddered with excitement. 'I can't believe I'm even thinking about this. I'm sure I'll wake up and find it's all been some daft dream.'

'Once you've seen the contract it'll seem real enough. You'll have to find yourself a good lawyer to get everything checked out. It might be a good idea if you got yourself an agent . . . ' Johnny mused quietly.

'Dear God, I'm not some supermodel, you know.'

'Fern,' Johnny said softly, 'I don't think you quite realize what this contract will mean. I wouldn't be at all surprised if you soon found yourself in the same league. Vitale has a launch budget of £12 million. You are going to be the face behind one of Europe's most prestigious cosmetics houses' new lines. Believe me, there'll be supermodels out there who'd love to be in your shoes.'

Fern shook her head sceptically. 'Sure, sure,' she said. 'Well, it's a good job I've got big feet because I intend to keep them firmly on the ground.' She stopped and listened. 'Oh God,' she groaned as she heard the slam of the front door. 'Not tonight of all nights. That guy's got perfect bloody timing!'

She hadn't seen Paul since he'd stormed out after being so rude to her about the Oscar Rees offer, and surprisingly, she hadn't actually missed him. There'd been far too many things other than his childish tantrum to occupy her mind.

'It's Paul,' she explained to Johnny, who was beginning to shift about uncomfortably. He drained his glass.

Paul entered the room. 'Hi . . . ' his voice broke off as he noticed Johnny. 'Oh! I didn't know you'd have company.'

Fern smiled at him graciously. 'Paul, you've met Johnny haven't you – at the ball, remember?'

Paul grimaced at Johnny. 'Sure. I remember. I hope I wasn't interrupting something . . . '

'No, no, not at all.' Johnny struggled to his feet, watching Paul's eyes take in the empty champagne bottle. 'I was just leaving.'

'Don't rush off, Johnny. Wouldn't you like a coffee or something before you go?' Fern asked solicitously.

Johnny looked at his watch conspicuously. 'No, thanks. I've got an early start tomorrow, loads of things to do, contracts to draw up and all that sort of thing. Umm, nice to see you, Paul.'

Fern helped Johnny gather up the photographs. Paul snatched one out of her hand.

'What's this?' he demanded.

Fern raised her eyebrows at Johnny. Johnny winked back. 'I'll tell you all about it in a second,' she said. 'I'll just see Johnny out.' She picked the photograph out of his hand and gave it to Johnny.

'Thanks,' he said as he stuffed them into his jacket pocket. 'I'll call you tomorrow. 'Night, Paul.'

'Would you like to tell me what the hell's going on?' Paul hissed when she came back into the room.

'Well, that's a nice way to say hello, isn't it? I

haven't seen you for ages, and then you march back in here like some possessive keeper.'

'I've been busy. And you were hardly hospitable the last time I saw you. I thought you'd like some time to cool off.'

'I've been busy too, as it happens, and Johnny and I were having a meeting to discuss my new job.'

'Your new job! At this hour?'

'Yeah. I've decided to accept the Oscar Rees offer, the one I told you about, remember? I'm going to be the face behind a thousand bottles. Exciting, isn't it?' she grinned at him.

Paul let out a long sigh and sat down heavily. 'You're crazy! I told you what that guy was after. Looks like he's getting it, as well.'

'Oh, don't be so stupid.' She yawned and started to pick up the empty bottle and glasses.

'It all looked very cosy, just the two of you and a bottle of champagne. I wonder what I'd have found if I'd come round a bit later.'

'Shut up!' Fern murmured as she left the room. She was certainly not going to let his jibes get to her. His jealousy was becoming ridiculous. Soon he'd be getting mad if she even spoke to another man. And the fact that she was going to be famous – and rich – would probably send him over the edge. It was hardly as if their relationship was going places at the moment. All they seemed to do when they saw each other was row. Whereas in the beginning she had found him wildly sexy and couldn't wait to jump into bed with him at any time of the day, the thought of sleeping with him these days was like a chore. Her lips tightened angrily. She called upstairs, 'I'm going to bed in a minute. I think you ought to go.' Her shoulders tensed as she heard his footsteps clump down the steps towards her.

'Fern,' he said softly, 'let's not fight!'

'I'm not. I'm perfectly happy. I would like a good night's sleep and I'm sure you'll understand if I don't leap into bed with you just because you've deigned to turn up at midnight.'

He put his arms around her and she pushed them away. 'Don't!' she snapped. He grabbed her arm and his fingers tightened painfully around it. She winced. 'Paul, you're hurting.' He pulled her towards him and pushed his mouth down onto hers. She struggled away.

Just as suddenly, he let go. 'Suit yourself, but I'm not going to put up with this for much longer, Fern.'

Her eyes opened wide in disbelief at what she was hearing, but there was no point in answering back. She just wanted to get rid of him.

'Goodnight, Paul,' she said. 'Call me tomorrow. We'll talk then.'

'I'll call you when I'm ready,' he muttered and slammed the door behind him.

Fern let out a long sigh and slid the security chain into place. Why couldn't life just be simple, for once?

'I really must congratulate you, Fern. Your face, I gather, will be worth a fortune. Perhaps we'll do an interview with you shortly. It's an interesting snippet for the magazine.'

Fern took a deep breath and managed to smile back at Edwina. This was one meeting she'd be very glad to put behind her.

'Why not?' Fern smiled. 'It's going to be quite a change of direction for me. A bit of a challenge, perhaps.'

Edwina raised her eyebrows. 'Modelling?' she said

as if Fern must be off her rocker to consider modelling a challenge.

'I intend to get very involved with the product. You know me, Edwina, I won't be content to take a back seat.'

'No. Well, we know that, don't we, Fern? So,' she said fixing her dark eyes on Fern, 'I'm afraid I shall have to ask you to clear your desk. Magazines aren't the places to work out notices. Anyway, I expect you've got masses to do.'

'I've already cleared my desk. I've just got a couple of things to sort out and then I shall be off.'

Edwina stood up and offered her hand. 'So, Fern. I'd like to thank you for all your help over the past eighteen months. You've been a great asset to the magazine and the world of journalism will miss you. I felt sure you had great things ahead of you. Perhaps – who knows? – your new career will herald even greater things. Now you'll be truly famous, Fern.'

'Thank you, Edwina. I'm sure I'm making the right decision.'

'We'll send on all the necessary bits and pieces. For now, good luck and goodbye.' Edwina retreated back into her office, closing the door behind her.

Fern had just one more thing to do. She walked back to her desk feeling a new lightness in her step. She opened up her computer, typed in the security code and located the piece on Oscar Rees. Alix's by-line had replaced her own. She had guessed it: the little cow had wanted to pass the piece off as her own. Fern pressed delete and then confirmed her command. In seconds the whole article ceased to exist.

Fern's fingers flew over the keyboard. Then she pressed in Alix's code and waited for the screen to confirm its linkup with Alix's computer. Fern smiled at the screen. 'I'll see you around, Alix.' The green cursor flashed satisfyingly at her. Then it moved.

'Bitch!' it said simply.

Chapter Thirteen

Laura, Hugo's personal assistant, stared at the envelope which had just landed via a messenger on her desk. The Cooper Jefferson logo decorated the edge of it. From the look on her face, she seemed to be expecting it to jump up and bite her. This was turning into one hell of a day. Hugo had arrived at the office late, looking as if he had spent the night on a clothesline. He was crumpled and unshaven. When she had called out her usual cheery 'Good morning' he had totally ignored her and slammed the door of his office shut. Twice she had tried to put calls through to him, and twice he had snapped her head off, saying he wouldn't speak to anyone. Perhaps he had had another of his rows with Olivia, though in the past two years or so there had been far fewer, given that both Hugo and Olivia seemed to be very much leading their own lives. The letter bore the word 'Urgent' in large red letters. There was really only one thing Laura could do. She tiptoed into Hugo's office and found him staring out of the window in what appeared to be a trance. She uttered a polite little cough. 'Um, this just arrived for you, Hugo, by hand. As it said says "Urgent" I thought I'd better bring it straight in. So sorry to disturb you.' She beat a hasty retreat, closing the door quietly behind her.

Hugo ripped open the envelope. Not only was it marked 'Urgent', it was also 'Strictly Confidential'. On any normal day Hugo would probably have felt a lot more apprehensive about opening the thing. Today, though, he felt so low already he didn't think anything else could happen to make him feel any worse.

He scanned the ominous-looking letter, then reread it slowly. It was an official approach from Cooper Jefferson to all the shareholders of Oscar Rees: the family, the Foundation, the bank, the lot. So, battle was about to commence. Hugo shoved the letter into his inside pocket, then on impulse, he picked up his telephone and punched out Ricci's number. Perhaps if he was lucky he might catch her working at home, or between clients. She answered almost immediately.

'Ricci, oh, I'm glad you're there. Not too busy? Look would it be okay if I popped round? . . . When? Oh, right now . . . Jolly good, see you shortly.'

He collected his briefcase, told Laura he was unavailable for the rest of the day, and then set off to find a comforting bosom.

Hugo nestled up to Ricci, pulling her wonderfully warm naked body close to him. She stirred, stretched and then opened her eyes.

'I must have dropped off,' she said.

'You looked terribly peaceful.' Hugo stroked her hair gently.

'I am, you're the troubled one.'

Hugo closed his eyes again, considering whether he should tell Ricci his news. Bloody Olivia! It was enough that he had the Cooper Jefferson deal looming.

Ricci uncurled herself. 'I'll get us some tea, keep my space.'

He grinned his acknowledgement. When she returned a few minutes later, Hugo pulled himself up on to the pillow and gratefully took the dainty teacup she offered. He sipped carefully at the steaming liquid, admiring the curves of Ricci's breasts which showed subtly through the sheer satin of her gown. She regarded him over the rim of her cup.

'So,' she said briskly, 'feeling better now?'

'A bit. I had a letter from Olivia's lawyers yesterday. It seems she wants the bloody house. Coopers want the bloody company and my wife wants the bloody house. It really does make one wonder, Ricci, what the hell one has been doing with one's life.'

'Ah, I see. Hence the visit.'

'Can't stop the old brain whirring round. We had the most fearful row last night. Do you know, she had the cheek to accuse me of impotence.'

Ricci stroked his hair soothingly. 'Would you like me to give you a reference, darling?' she cooed lightly. He had the grace to chuckle.

'I told her that she's not having the house. It was my father's house and that's that. She also had the bloody nerve to tell me she wants half the company, too.'

'But that's impossible.'

'Well, not quite as impossible as I'd like it to be. I may have to buy her off. I tell you, Ricci, it's going to cost me a bloody fortune. Right now I need this like a damned hole in the head. It's bad enough having to fight off Coopers. Sometimes I feel tempted to jack the whole bloody thing in and run off.'

Ricci squirmed against him. 'You mean we could run away together to an idyllic little island in the sun where you'd shake the tree and I'd catch the coconuts? Or maybe we'd fish in a crystal lagoon . . .'

'I don't think you're taking me seriously, are you?'

'Not in the least. You'd never survive without the company, so do stop being so defeatist, darling, and let's work out what can be done. Now then, who's prepared to sell, and who isn't?'

'Those bloody twins would auction their mother, if she hadn't committed hari-kiri already. I guess anyone who'd borne a pair like that would want to top themselves.'

'Hugo!' Ricci admonished him gently. 'But that's only a little slice.'

'Yes. Then there's Olivia.'

'I know, whose name shall be poison on your lips . . .'

'The Foundation, and as for the bank and Julian, well, I really can't say for sure. I don't think Julian will sell. He did tell me he was happy to stick as he was. But you just never know how much these people can be persuaded by the scent of ready cash.'

'I wouldn't worry about Julian. I can sort him out.'

'How on earth would you propose to do that?'

'It's a long story, but ever since that messy business with Caro Littleton, the pair of them have been having a hell of a time meeting up. The tabloid press have been camping out at Caro's house night and day. It seems her hubby has had the telephone tapped, too. Anyway, Caro came to see me. She was hysterical, absolutely beside herself. It seems she believes herself to be head over heels in love with Julian and she begged me to help her out.'

'But why on earth would you do that?'

'Caro and I go back a long way. We were at school together.' Ricci giggled. 'She hasn't changed much either. She was always getting into scrapes even then. I did think that once she'd made this rather successful marriage she might settle down a bit, but, of course, Julian does seem to make a habit of wreaking havoc in people's lives. I do hope he's serious this time, Hugo.'

'But you might get into awful trouble if anyone finds out.'

'I might, but quite frankly I don't have any loyalty to her husband, and Julian can be frightfully endearing.'

'H'mph. I wouldn't know about that.'

'No, I don't suppose you would. Be that as it may, they've been meeting up here.'

'Why you devious baggage! You don't mean they've been having it off in our bed?'

'No, in the spare room. So you see, my dear Hugo, I rather doubt that Julian would want to upset me, and therefore you, at the moment, do you? I'll have a little chat with Caro and sort it out.'

'You think it'll be as simple as that?'

'Don't underestimate the power of lust, especially not where Julian's concerned.'

'How would you know about Julian's lust?' Hugo quipped lightly.

'I just do.'

Hugo suddenly felt awash with affection for this delightful lady. He took her teacup from her and placed it carefully on the table. Then he pulled her down onto the bed, and wrapped her tightly in the circle of his arms.

'Soon I shall take you to dinner,' he promised softly, 'but first I have some unfinished business to attend to.'

His lips stifled Ricci's giggle.

Charles Allen was looking forward to this morning's meeting. He held the file tightly to his chest as he took the lift up to the number 3 conference suite. His report had come together very well, thanks to Lucienne's assistance. In fact he had circulated it to the Board a couple of days before the official offer from Cooper Jefferson had arrived on Humphrey Morrison's desk. Now the word was out that Hugo's days were numbered. It was Charles's opinion that the deal could be very lucrative indeed for Collingwoods.

Charles pushed the door open. The room was already quite full. He saw Hugo in the distance. His aristocratically gaunt face looked leaner and meaner than it normally did. He barely glanced at Charles as he found his seat. So, Charles thought to himself, I suppose he thinks I'm some underling judging by the amount of notice he's taking of me. You're going to have a rude awakening, Hugo old chap.

Hugo might well look worried. The old boy network was a thing of the past. In the real world of the 1990s, decisions are made on commercial realities, not on how long you've dined together at White's. There wasn't room for gentlemanly agreements any more. Collingwoods were waking up to the fact through necessity. Hugo was about to do the same.

Eventually, when all were assembled around the grand rosewood and walnut conference table, Hugo shuffled some papers and then rose to his feet, clearing his throat, a little nervously, to Charles's mind.

'Gentlemen, I know you are all aware of why I am here today. Cooper Jefferson has made an official approach to all Oscar Rees shareholders with the intention of persuading such shareholders to sell their stakes in the Oscar Rees Corporation, thereby giving control of the company to Cooper Jefferson.' Hugo paused and looked around the table, waiting for the answering nods of understanding.

174

'I'm sure it will come as no surprise to any of you to know that I am a hundred per cent against this takeover. It is my lifelong intention, as it was that of both my father and Alfred Easton, to keep the Oscar Rees Corporation within the family. We have traded on our cachet of exclusivity, and perhaps it's fair to say, a fondness for a family name that can be traced back more than sixty years, to stimulate brand loyalty for our products. So many of our competitors have been bought out in this way over the years, only eventually to lose all the mystique and glamour that has kept such companies on top through the years. It is my gut feeling that if Oscar Rees is taken over by some huge conglomerate like Cooper Jefferson, it won't be too long before we are sold in every high-street supermarket in the country. We will be downmarket, over-accessible and therefore supreme-ly unattractive to all those women we have catered for throughout many decades.

'I believe that my wife, and my nephew and niece are going to accept this offer from Cooper Jefferson. I know that my brother-in-law, Julian Easton, and you yourselves will be loyal to me. Therefore I propose that with your help, instead of allowing this deal to go ahead, we must find alternative buyers for those willing to sell, and make sure that my position at the company is not threatened. Naturally we shall have to find a buyer willing to spend more than Coopers are offering, and I should therefore think it possible we shall have to approach more than one potential buyer. I can't think, bearing in mind our excellent record, that would provide us with too much of a problem.'

Hugo took his seat, and smiled confidently around the table.

Charles Allen stroked the report in his hand

possessively. Humphrey Morrison coughed and looked embarrassed. Then he stood up.

'Hugo . . .' He hesitated and then looked around the table, his eyes narrowing as they rested on Charles's face.

Charles smiled up at him impudently. Let the old fool frown. His days were nearly up, anyway. It was time for relics such as Morrison to take early retirement. That was to be Charles's next recommendation.

'. . . We've had sight of a rather disturbing report. It would appear, Hugo, that your personal life may be encroaching on your business life.'

'What?' Hugo's snap rang across the room like a cracked whip. 'I don't have any personal life, for God's sake!'

Humphrey Morrison couldn't bring himself to look at Hugo directly. He respected the man – and liked him. He knew there must be a mistake here. Collingwoods never used to conduct business like this. He felt sure Charles Allen had embarked upon some dirty tricks campaign. The bank had always been above all that – up until recently, of course. Now where had the trust gone that used to be so tacitly taken for granted between the bank and its clients? These young sharks such as the Charles Allens in the business were overturning all that. Money and commercialism were the only gods for these boys. Forget loyalty, for this is banking. And when the going gets rough, a good banker cuts. Simple!

Very simple for someone such as Humphrey Morrison, who had watched over the company for so many years he had developed an almost proprietorial pride in its achievements. And now he was positioned as chief hatchet man. Perhaps his retirement was a little overdue.

'There are suggestions contained in this report which the bank must consider very seriously.'

'What suggestions?'

'About your present state of health, Hugo.'

'I've never been fitter. I had a medical six months ago. You can look at a copy of it, if you like. Knowing you lot you've probably already got a copy.'

'It wasn't the physical side we were worrying about.' How Humphrey hated himself as he voiced the words.

'Oh?' Hugo laughed drily. 'Of course, how silly of me. Then it must be my mental state. Ha! I should have guessed, shouldn't I? But then I suppose I should expect *my* bankers to be one step ahead of me. Then am I cracking up?' He looked around the table, searching the faces intently. Not one man had the courage to raise their eyes to meet Hugo's. 'I suppose my nephew and niece might have something to do with this?'

Charles Allen shifted in his seat a little uncomfortably.

Hugo hissed, 'It's a ridiculous suggestion.'

'But unfortunately one we have to take very seriously. According to this report there are several product development areas which are crucial to Oscar Rees's continued success and which you have seen fit not to pursue.'

'I knew it. It *is* Alexander, isn't it? Alexander and his revolting formula. I stand by my decision not to embark on any such course of action for Oscar Rees. It would be a disaster, morally and financially – '

Charles Allen butted in, unable to contain himself any longer. 'But your competition are actively following it!'

'Are they? I suppose Alexander told you that, too. I would dispute it. And I would like you all to understand precisely what it is my nephew and niece are so hellbent on exploiting. I hope your stomachs are strong, gentlemen . . .' Hugo stood up and leaned forward, resting his hands on the table in front of him. He looked very tall, and suddenly quite menacing. Charles Allen moved back in his seat.

'It is my nephew's intention to collect foetal tissue and use it to formulate an anti-ageing cream which he believes women will pay a fortune for. Our more enlightened French neighbours have, of course, outlawed this practice. Unfortunately we have no laws against such exploitation at the moment. Alexander believes that if women can happily plaster placental extract over their faces, then they'll certainly be happy to do the same with cells taken from aborted babies.' There were gasps from around the table. 'So, I suggest you consider again my state of mind, and that of my nephew.'

Hugo picked up his briefcase and popped his paperwork into it. 'There is just one more thing before I go, gentlemen . . .'

Humphrey Morrison had turned a rather nasty shade of green. 'Yes?' he said quietly.

'Am I to assume then, taking my deranged mind into account, Collingwoods would be choosing to sell out?'

Again Hugo searched the faces. No one spoke for what seemed like a full minute. Humphrey Morrison cleared his throat. The sound of the ancient grandfather clock ticked across the room, like a hushed final knell.

'Am I to assume, then, that the bank would not be looking for a buyer on my behalf, because it has already decided I should be replaced?'

Humphrey's voice cracked nervously. 'Well, we mustn't be too hasty.'

'I'm sorry, Humphrey, I didn't quite catch that.' Hugo's hate burned into Humphrey.

'I said perhaps we should have more time to consider . . .'

'Then I am afraid that there is most certainly a conflict of interests, here, gentlemen. And therefore I shall be conducting my business elsewhere.' He pushed his chair out noisily. 'Good day to you!' he snapped, as he swept out of the hushed room.

Charles guessed even before he picked up his direct line just who would be on the other end of it.

'Lucienne,' he laughed, 'I knew it would be you.'

'Darling,' Lucienne murmured huskily, 'I couldn't wait. I had to call you. How did it go?'

'Fine,' he said reassuringly. 'Nothing to worry about. Hugo's definitely running scared. I thought old Humphrey Morrison was going to shit himself with fear. Poor old bugger. He just can't get used to the idea that the old boy network's dead and buried. He looked as if he was going to have a heart attack when Hugo stood up and told the Board what Alexander was up to.'

Lucienne's voice sharpened. 'What did he tell them?'

'Oh, some nonsense about abortions – foetuses – pretty unsavoury stuff.' Charles laughed. 'Just shows how desperate the guy is, trying to frighten the bank with ridiculous horror stories. Of course, I didn't believe a word of it, and in any event it really won't make much difference to the bank what happens to the company. If we sell, we sell. Oscar Rees can do what it likes, can't it?'

'Yes, you're right darling, well done. So what does Hugo intend to do?' She tapped her fingers in irritation, willing Charles to get to the point. It was lucky for them that Charles Allen was such an idiot. Manipulating him had been a complete doddle.

'Well, he stormed out of the meeting, threatening to take his business elsewhere.'

'And?'

'No one would pick up the account just like that, not when there's a deal like this in the offing. And the account is of little importance given that we hold the shares.'

'So you think the bank will agree to sell?'

'I have no doubt of it, Lucienne. With you and me working together we can't fail to show Hugo Rees his time's up. I'm going to make damn sure the bank sells. Just leave it to me.'

'Well done, darling. I'll see you at eight.'

'I can't wait. Eight o'clock at my place.'

Humphrey Morrison was very pleased he had followed his hunch, and equally pleased that Allen had forgotten to close his office door. He listened for a few more moments and then tiptoed away, back down the corridor. So, Hugo had been right. It seemed that Mr Allen's report might well involve a degree of bias towards certain members of the Easton family. Stupid young fool. Humphrey knew what he had to do.

As soon as he reached his own office he arranged for a meeting with the head of the security department. He needed a bug put on Allen's phones, and he had to alert the rest of the Board. He could feel the adrenalin pumping through his veins, and it felt good. He had work to do.

Chapter Fourteen

'So I take it you two are happy about working together?'

Fern and Johnny grinned at each other. 'Yes, Hugo,' they said in unison.

'Well, that makes life easier. So from now on, Fern, you will be styled Assistant Product Manager for Vitale. You will act as Johnny's back-up, and you will be expected to come up with ideas and plans regarding the marketing of Vitale. I trust that is satisfactory to you?'

Fern's grin stretched from ear to ear. 'More than satisfactory, thanks, Hugo. I'm really looking forward to getting my teeth into the work. I'm sure that with Johnny's guidance I shall be able to make a positive contribution to the marketing side.'

'Quite. I hope so,' he smiled back. 'Now run along you two. I understand you have a shoot to attend at some tennis club.' Both rose from their seats. 'Oh, and Johnny, hang on a minute. I want to have a chat about the retailers' presentation on the Ozzie boost.'

Fern closed Hugo's door behind her, hoping that Johnny would be kept for a good long time. The more the tennis shoot was delayed the better. She had been dreading the whole thing ever since Johnny had come up with the bright idea of putting her in a pair of shorts with a racquet in her hand in the vain hope that she might look sporty.

'Still after your story, then?'

'I'm sorry?'

'Aren't you the one running the competition . . . to find The Face?' Lucienne regarded Fern distastefully. 'I hope you're not sniffing around for our company secrets. You know, if you need information you really ought to make an appointment to see me. I look after the PR for Oscars. Johnny Sharpe is products, not publicity, and Hugo is far too busy to be bothered by such things.'

Fern's mouth tightened, but she chose not to reply. Instead she sat down on the conveniently positioned sofa outside Hugo's office door and picked up a copy of *Vogue*.

'What was your name again?'

Fern looked up and sighed heavily. She remembered Lucienne's unhelpful attitude from the day when she had first met Johnny. She also remembered what she had read about her in the cuttings. And if this was the lady Oscar Rees chose to deal with the press, the company had a serious problem with its presentation.

'Fern Donleavy. You're Lucienne, aren't you?'

'Miss Easton,' the girl said arrogantly.

Fern flicked over another couple of pages while Lucienne remained standing over her, tapping her toes.

'Well?'

'Oh, I'm sorry,' Fern smiled disarmingly. 'Um, was there something you wanted?'

'Yes. I want to know what you're doing here.'

Fern's smile didn't falter, but her green eyes glittered with as much ice as a crème de menthe frappé. 'I'm waiting for Johnny . . .'

Thankfully, Johnny appeared just then. 'Ah, Lucienne. Have you two met?'

'Yes,' they said, in unison.

'Yes, of course you have.' He scratched his head

and hopped from one foot to the other, as if he wasn't quite sure what to say next. Clearly Johnny felt very awkward in Lucienne's company. 'Um, Fern, come on. We've got to go.'

'Just a moment,' Lucienne drawled. 'I was explaining to, er . . . Miss Donleavy that if she needs any information on Oscar Rees she should be talking to me, not to you.'

'Oh, no. Don't worry about that, Lucienne. Fern's not after publicity. She's my new Assistant Product Manager. Hadn't you heard?'

'What?' Lucienne sounded horrified. 'But that can't be. She's a journalist. I thought – '

Johnny beamed broadly. 'It's all agreed. Oh, and I nearly forgot to mention it, but Fern is also going to be The Face for Vitale.'

Lucienne flushed. 'Nobody told me about this.'

Fern couldn't resist it. 'Perhaps that's because you're publicity, Lucienne.' She linked her arm through Johnny's and grinned sheepishly at Lucienne as Johnny pulled her towards the corridor. 'Sorry, Lucienne – must dash. Lovely to see you again.'

Lucienne shot Fern a look of what could only be described as pure poison.

'Phew . . . what's up with her?' Fern and Johnny were sitting in an interminable traffic jam, attempting to get from Bond Street to Chiswick. So far, after half an hour, they had reached Hyde Park corner.

'Lucienne? Yes, she's always been a bit of a cow.'

'I suppose it's good to know it's not just me.'

'I don't think Lucienne likes anyone really – apart from her darling brother, that is.'

As Fern stared into Harrods' windows she remembered reading something which had bothered her. Now that Johnny mentioned it, the story came back to her, along with her natural journalist's curiosity.

'There was some article I read about them. Didn't they go off to Harvard together?'

'Yes. It was most unusual for a brother and a sister to be accepted at the same time. It seems that as well as being rather unpleasant people, they're also extremely gifted. Unfortunately for everyone around them they haven't put their brains to the best use.'

'What do they do in the company? Will I have much to do with them?'

'Well, they both studied chemistry, and then business. Alexander's based down at Southampton where he helps the R & D boffins. But Lucienne decided the formula side wasn't glamorous enough for her. She's now on PR, though thankfully Hugo has mostly kept her off Vitale. She does a lot of the perfume stuff. You'll probably remember things like her father on the polo field in his infamous sweat shirts emblazoned with La Petite Mort, leaving night-clubs, photographs in the paper, that sort of rubbish. The "photo opportunity" I guess would be Lucienne's way of putting it.'

'So she might get transferred to Vitale?'

'Unlikely. Vitale is one of Hugo's pets. He won't want the tortuous twosome involved if he can escape it. So don't worry about it. Besides, you'd handle her.'

'Yeah. But I'd rather stay cool. I could do without that sort of agro.'

They were silent for a couple of miles, each left to their own thoughts.

'I've remembered the story!' Fern said. 'It was when the twins were at Harvard. *People* magazine published something. I read it when I was doing some research. It seems they went to some society ball with the Long Island set or something like that. Anyway, apparently the twins were dancing together and a photographer took a snap of them. They were snogging!'

'I think anyone you spoke to would say their relationship was a little strange.'

'But incestuous?' Fern was repulsed by the thought.

'I don't know about that. I'd guess not. Probably they lark about together to shock everyone. They like to think they're a frightfully risqué pair.'

Fern shuddered. 'I think I'll stay well clear in that case.'

At last they reached the Riverside Club, Johnny's local tennis joint. He parked the little Peugeot 205 between a Mercedes and a Volvo.

'I'd no idea the place would be so busy. Don't these people have jobs to go to?'

'Wives, Fern. This is where the ladies come to get out of the way of the nanny.'

'Oh my God! I feel quite sick. I thought we would be doing this thing in private!'

While Johnny signed them in, Fern had a chance to look around. A posse of Lycra-limbed ladies who exercise emerged from the glass-walled studio to the left of reception. Fern shuddered inwardly at the thought of herself turning into what she could only imagine to be a sort of Jane Fonda clone by the time Johnny finished with her.

Then she felt Johnny's hand in her back, guiding her through to the small but well-stocked shop where she was to be kitted out in the very latest line of tennis wear. She had exactly two hours to learn how to play the game before the cameras were due to arrive to picture the Vitale girl giving her best shots on court.

'Rosie, this is Fern,' Johnny announced, handing Fern over to a bubbly-looking girl who grinned at her warmly. Her thick black ringlets were captured in a high ponytail on the top of her head, but they fell forward over her face, making her look like a woolly sheepdog.

'Remember, Rosie, just a classic pair of white shorts – boyish, if anything, and white socks and shoes. Here's the polo shirt, Fern. Hope you approve of it. I'll pop back in ten minutes to see how you're getting on.'

As Fern took the specially designed shirt out of its wrapping Rosie stood back to get a better look at her hips. 'What size are you? Ten, I'd guess, or even an eight. Now, let's see . . .' Rosie flipped through the rails while Fern drifted over to the stack of racquets. She pulled out a rather fancy-looking shocking pink number that was speckled with glossy blue spots. She swung it round for effect.

'How do I look?' she asked her new friend.

'Fine, but you need a tennis racquet. That one's for squash. Don't worry, we'll sort you out with one later. I expect one of the coaches will decide what you need.'

'I don't suppose you get many people here who are quite so green as me.'

'Lovey,' Rosie confided, 'at least you'll use the racquet, even if it's only for a couple of hours. Some of our customers only buy one so that it can be seen sticking out of their sports bag or displayed on the back seat of the Merc. You'd be surprised.'

Fern giggled. 'Are you serious?'

'Sure. Come on, let's see how these look.'

By the time Johnny reappeared Fern was trying on tennis shoes. She stood up to show off her pristine polo shirt and immaculately cut shorts. Johnny grinned from ear to ear. She looked gorgeous – like a fresh young colt, all leggy and lovable. 'Right, turn around.'

She obediently did as she was told and Johnny nodded admiringly at the way the shorts did justice to Fern's neat little bottom. She did a little hop in her new shoes, to see how they felt. Her body was full of such natural grace that Johnny secretly couldn't wait to see her on the tennis court. The white polo shirt had the tall thin logo of Vitale spread across the chest in soft jade green. The colour was echoed in little stripes around the short cuffed sleeves and around the white collar. It was simple but stunningly effective.

'Okay, so what about my hair?'

Johnny reached into his sports bag and pulled a small package out. 'Wait till you see this, the *pièce de résistance*.' Having unwrapped it, he flourished its contents under Fern's nose.

'Oh no!' Fern cried. 'You have to be joking.'

Johnny put a green-and-white baseball cap onto his head. Again, it had the Vitale logo scrawled across the front of it. He turned around to show Fern the hole at the back. 'You can push your hair through here.'

'It's really naff.'

'It's perfect.'

'A real cliché.'

'Try it.'

'Oh, all right.' She pulled the hat over her head and struggled to pull her hair through the gap at the back. Johnny was thrilled to see how good she looked. He had had the hat specially designed so that the peak wasn't too large. He wanted to be able to see her eyes. Her neat nose looked cheeky below the pea, and he knew exactly what shade of lipstick he would suggest to the make-up girl. But the main thing was that with her endlessly long legs, and her slim, lithe frame, Fern would look exactly as he had envisaged: young, healthy, cheeky, sexy and vital – with a sparkle of her 'what the hell' personality shining seductively through.

Johnny had no doubt at all in his mind that they would come up with some great advertising shots this afternoon, and was equally certain that there would be an awful lot of women keen to use a product associated with this fresh-faced beauty.

'Oh, and I nearly forgot . . .' His hand dived into the bag once more and pulled out a pair of green wristbands. 'The finishing touch, and at the rate you'll be made to run around, you'll probably need to mop up your sweat!'

'Terrific! I feel as if I'm about to be fed to the lions,' she said, after they had thanked Rosie and said their goodbyes. 'And I'm a real fraud all dressed up like this.' Then she shrieked. 'Johnny, the courts have got glass sides! You never told me. That means people will see us.'

They had walked through to the bar, and just beyond were four indoor tennis courts, stretching visibly one behind the other towards the back of the vast, hangar-like hall.

'Don't be daft. Everyone's far too busy worrying about what they look like themselves to notice you.'

'Ha-ha! With Vitale plastered all over my head and breast, and an entire photographic crew, that's really funny.'

'The shoot is in a different court, next door. They're already setting up. Now calm down, you're getting paranoid.'

They waited on Court 1 while the coach finished off on Court 2 next door to them. Fern watched as the ball whistled over the net, almost scraping the top of it, as coach and pupil rallied together. That was one hell of a good pupil, Fern decided. Either that, or tennis was a lot easier than she'd always been led to believe.

Robin was tall, blond and gorgeous. He shook Fern's hand and she had to stop herself from wincing, concentrating instead on the soft blond hairs that covered his rather tasty and, unlike her own, tanned legs.

'Hi, Fern,' he said cheerfully. 'Johnny's told me all about you, and in two hours you'll be a real pro. But first let's find you a racquet.' He looked at her hand, sized her up and then disappeared, returning a couple of moments later with what Fern considered to be an offensive weapon.

'Now, tell me how this feels,' he said, holding it out to her.

'Like a racquet,' she said unhelpfully, turning it over in her hand.

'Does it feel too big or too heavy?'

'For what?' she asked innocently.

'Fern,' Johnny cautioned.

'No, truly. I'm not being difficult. It's just that I don't think I can judge either of those things bearing in mind I don't know what it's supposed to feel like.'

'Okay, okay,' Robin said. 'I think it'll be fine. Let's get started.'

Several hours later, after Fern had been released, she collapsed exhausted into the jacuzzi. Her whole body hurt. She felt as if a giant hand had scrunched her bones together, wringing her out like a piece of wet washing. She closed her eyes and concentrated on the feel of the powerful bubbles pounding against her flesh, and helping to massage the tension away. All she had to do was clutch on to the sides every now and then to stop her bottom from floating off the submerged seat. The water roared and gurgled in her ears, soothing her and helping her to unwind, at last feeling the profound relief that the dreaded 'tennis shoot' was behind her. So relaxed had she become that she had drifted off on a daydream which took her to some secluded beach, away from photographers' lenses and make-up artists, where she could swim naked in the water, accompanied by some sexy, but so far faceless, male.

'This seems to be becoming something of a habit, doesn't it?' The voice startled her.

Fern's eyes flicked open and a distinctly uncool gasp flew out of her mouth.

'I'm not sure I believe in as many coincidences as this. What do you think?'

Before she had time to reply, Leo Eden stepped down and plonked himself beside her, casually placing his hands behind his head, and settling himself back comfortably.

'I . . . er . . .'

'Yes, that's what I think, too,' he muttered, before giving her a chance to speak.

She had to take control of the situation, before the arrogant man thought she was a total wimp.

'Are you following me?' she asked curtly.

'Following you? What on earth would I be doing that for?'

'As you said, it seems these chance meetings can't be put down to coincidence. So I assume you must be.'

'I merely stopped off at my sports club for a quick swim on my way home from the office, as is my wont. And here you are, settled in my favourite spot of the jacuzzi. I assure you I have better things to do

190

with my time than follow you.' He stared at her, and seemed to be giving something a good deal of thought. 'I'll retract that. I wouldn't be surprised if there were quite a few men who wanted to follow you. However, I am not amongst them.'

She could get up and walk out, but she was enjoying the jacuzzi so much, and her body felt so tired. Damn Leo Eden. Why did he have to turn up?

Fern closed her eyes again and tried to pretend that he wasn't sitting, nearly naked, nine inches or so away from her. It had not escaped her notice in the few seconds that she had stared at him that he had a pretty powerful body. It had muscles and hair in all the right places. And now, hard as she tried to ignore it, she felt painfully aware of his physical presence.

Why did he always have to be so damned clever? Each time she had met him he had been so sarcastic, and really she'd done nothing to offend him. Perhaps he was just one of those men who liked to pick on women.

She peeked at him, finding her curiosity getting the better of her, and opened her eyes fully when she realized he had both of his closed. His nose was long and straight, an aristocratic kind of nose, and his thick dark brows formed two neat crescents above his closed eyes. A shadow of whiskers showed through the skin around his chin and jaw, and Fern was shocked to find herself wondering what it would feel like if she ran her finger over it.

She stood up quickly, suddenly in a hurry to get away from him. He opened his eyes and they travelled lazily and somewhat impertinently upwards from her slim ankles, up over her endless legs, and her temptingly curved hips up to her breasts which now showed clearly through the thin cotton jersey swimsuit.

When his eyes finally met hers, he grinned. 'Johnny should be congratulated.'

'I'll tell him,' she hissed, and swept off towards the women's changing rooms and away from Leo Eden's taunting words.

The thought first occurred to Fern as she helped Johnny clear off the table, after they had waded their way through the delicious pizza he had insisted on preparing for them. Not once had he tried to make a pass at her. She wasn't at all sure whether she was pleased or not.

She watched him surreptitiously from the rear as he worked over the washing up. She liked the way his dark hair fell into little curls just below his collar. He had a nice, comfortable face, but he was so dreadfully thin she suspected that if they ever did get into a clinch she'd be terrified she might break him in two. He made her laugh, though. At times he exasperated and irritated her. He could be bossy and dogmatic, but he could also be considerate and patient. As they settled down with coffee, Fern sat on the floor, leaning against the sofa upon which Johnny sat, his knees a couple of inches from her nose. She grinned up at him. 'That was a delicious meal. Where did you learn to cook pizza like that? Every time I try and do one, the dough turns out like a biscuit.'

'I spent a summer in Rome when I was a student. I fancied myself as being a bit of an art scholar, saw a few antiquities, ran out of money and got a job in a café. It was hard work but I learned about pizza-making.'

'And what else?' she said softly, wondering what adventures he must have had while he was there.

'I fell in love, at least twice,' he laughed. 'Nothing serious, though.'

'And now?' She stared down at her shoes, unable to look him directly in the face, fearing her eyes might betray a little too much curiosity.

'Given it all up. It's much healthier to be celibate. Fewer complications, less hassle. Far easier.'

'I know what you mean,' she said with feeling. 'Paul's driving me mad at the moment. He's getting so stupid about what I do, so jealous. I don't think I can stand it for much longer.' She drained her coffee cup. 'I'll have to sort it out. I guess I've put it off for too long already.' She glanced at Johnny's concerned face. The conversation was in danger of getting very morose.

'So,' she said brightly, 'what other ordeals have you got lined up for me?'

'Paris!'

'Oh!' she squealed with excitement. 'When, and what for, and for how long?'

'In a month's time and you're going to do a catwalk show for Chanel.'

'You can't be serious!' Fern's voice was filled with horror.

'You'll breeze it. All you have to do is put one foot in front of the other, sway your hips a little, and parade the pretty clothes.'

'It's all fixed up then?'

'Yep. I got it confirmed yesterday. I was just waiting for the right moment to tell you. I knew you'd be pleased.'

Fern slapped his knee playfully. 'You mean you knew I'd be horrified.'

Johnny ruffled the top of her head, and she caught his hand. Then, very gently, he pulled her up beside him onto the sofa. Fern held her breath, unsure but at the same time knowing what would happen next. Johnny's face was closing in on hers. She felt her eyelids drooping, the warmth of his lips brush against hers. She surrendered herself, for a moment enjoying the sweetness of the kiss. Here was a man who really liked her, and delighted in her success. Johnny was kind, gentle and trusting, all things that Paul could never be. Then slowly she pushed Johnny away. She giggled to hide her uncertainty of the situation.

Johnny reached out and stroked her hair. 'I wasn't expecting that to happen,' he said simply.

'Me neither.' She stood up, feeling awkward. 'Maybe I'd better go. I don't know if I'm ready for anything, Johnny, what with Paul and work – '

'Hey, stop looking so worried.' Johnny stood up and clasped her hands in his. 'I really like you, Fern, you know that. Let's not get too carried away with what just happened. It was lovely, but I guess we've both got unfinished business to deal with.'

'Sure,' she said, smiling nervously. 'I . . . er . . . had better go. We've got an early start tomorrow. Thanks for supper. I hope I didn't make too big a fool of myself today.' She spoke quickly, anxious to be away from him so that she could think about what had happened, about how to deal with it. All she needed was another bloody complication in life.

Chapter Fifteen

It had taken well over an hour to reach the factory, which was situated just outside Southampton on the south coast and, during that time, neither Johnny nor Fern had spoken a word about what had happened the previous night. Though at first they had each been a little shy of the other, as the miles slipped behind them and they sped into the countryside, they had eventually fallen into their former easy companionableness. In truth, Fern would have dearly loved to have asked Johnny what he meant last night when he said that they *both* had unfinished business to deal with. Clearly he was talking about Paul for her, but what problems did *he* have? She was far too embarrassed to ask him outright in case he might think she was chasing after him. She'd just have to control her curiosity. Whatever Johnny's situation was, she had to sort her own out before she could begin to think of entering a relationship with anyone else, and especially someone she worked with. It was hardly ideal to leap straight from one man's arms into the next. She needed some time to herself, to reappraise her situation, otherwise she'd be in danger of losing all control over her life. The most sensible option was to push any thoughts of Johnny, other than work thoughts, right out of her mind.

Setting her resolve, Fern clambered out of the passenger seat and stretched her long legs, smelling the salt in the air. The Oscar Rees factory stood six storeys high – a vast block of mirrored windows, red paintwork and grey brick, echoing the red and silver insignia of Oscar Rees's packaging. She was eager to get inside and see with her own eyes the birth of her product. They made their way through the twelve-foot-tall heavy glass doors. The cool, air-conditioned interior sent a chill through Fern. They introduced themselves to the receptionist who then led the way through the building past the tempting exhibit of all the Oscar Rees products. The walls were covered with advertisement shots showing unbelievably beautiful creatures pouting with lipstick, or smoothing immaculately manicured nails over peaches-and-cream skin.

Johnny caught Fern's gaze. 'You'll be up there soon,' he said.

Fern shook her head. 'They all look so perfect. Not a blemish, or a spot, or even a freckle . . . I just can't imagine how this can be happening.'

'You shouldn't be so modest. Anyway, it's remarkable what can be achieved with a bit of retouching here and there. Ah, here we are.'

They entered a world of white coats, making the place appear more like a laboratory than a factory. The receptionist took them into a small room where a row of freshly laundered and starched white coats hung on a rack.

'I'm afraid you'll have to put these on,' she explained. 'It's all to do with hygiene. And I'm sorry, Miss Donleavy, but if you wouldn't mind putting this cap over your head . . .'

'I feel as if I've come to an operating theatre.'

'It's a bit like that,' the girl laughed. 'We have to be very careful about product contamination. There's a basin over there, if you'd like to wash your hands, and while you're doing that I'll tell Dr Chapmån you're here.'

'I had no idea it would be like this,' Fern cried as she set to work scrubbing her perfectly clean fingernails which were now beautifully manicured crescents.

'Just imagine if someone opened a pot and found a very long, red hair wrapped up inside it! I don't think they'd be too impressed, would they?'

'I guess not.'

Johnny helped Fern scoop her hair up into a bun which she then hooked up into the elasticated mob cap. 'I look as if I should just be starting my shift on the deli. Ah well, let's go.'

Dr Chapman, the Factory Administrator, was waiting for them. In spite of the risk of contamination, he shook Fern's hand. 'I'm delighted to meet you, Miss Donleavy. I expect you want to hear all about Vitale. We're extremely pleased with the way the products have been formulated. The production is on stream right now, so of course we're all holding our breaths, ready for the launch date. Do you have any idea as yet when that's going to be?'

'September,' Johnny replied. 'Just four weeks to go. We've got all the ads ready to run. It's all been a bit of a race against time, but Hugo wanted to get it launched well in advance of Christmas and we felt it might be a good idea to tie it in with the Paris collections. There's going to be a big bash at the Hôtel de Crillon. I hope you'll be there,' he added politely.

'So do I,' Dr Chapman agreed. 'We do tend to get rather bogged down with the technical side here. It's rather nice to have a taste of the glamour every now and then. After all, that is our business at the end of the day. Come, follow me . . .'

Fern kept her arms firmly folded in front of her as they toured through a maze of benches littered with assorted flasks and test tubes. Plastic bottles with impossible to pronounce labels were stacked on open shelves around the walls. Heads bent over pots of cream, or peered into microscopes.

'This is quality control,' the doctor explained. 'We have to test the products continually in case of contamination, or in case something goes wrong on the production line. Naturally when one is dealing with cosmetics it is extremely important that the product is in perfect condition. The skin is very sensitive and we must exercise scrupulous care over our formulations. You can't begin to imagine the sort of dire effects an allergic reaction may have. Some poor women's faces have begun to peel right off. Dear me, dear me . . .' he muttered to himself. Johnny winked at Fern as she wrinkled her nose up in horror.

They entered the lift and went down to the lower basement level. The noise of machines filled Fern's ears, only these weren't heavy clumping, machine-type noises; they were sophisticated squeaks, hums and whooshes, interspersed with only an occasional ill-mannered crash. Bottles spun around on giant carousels filled from the teats of a mega-productive cream-cow. Fern watched in fascination as the bottles shunted around in orderly fashion, and then tripped along miniature conveyor belts to have their lids clamped on.

She tried to read the labels. 'Ah, the famous Free Radical Eradicator. Hugo mentioned it. It sounds like an insect repellent. What does it actually do?'

Dr Chapman smiled at Fern benevolently. Here was a question he was pleased to have been asked. 'As you know,' he began conspiratorially, 'free radicals are rogue molecules which damage the cells, thereby preventing them from communicating with other cells. When this happens, cells suffer all sorts of damage, from moisture imbalance to even precancerous development. And, of course, we mustn't forget, *premature ageing*.'

'So how do we get these, er, free radicals?' Fern asked, hoping the question didn't sound too stupid.

'Oh, my dear girl, we all have them,' the doctor cried enthusiastically. 'Some are just there naturally. Others, and these,' he pointed his finger towards Fern, 'are the ones we are interested in fighting, are caused by external factors, such as pollution, UV light, smoking, all those dreadful environmental factors that none of us can avoid. So, we use our Free Radical Eradicator.' He produced a jar from one of the counters and thrust it proudly under Fern's nose.

She read the ingredients: 'Antioxidant, Vitamin E, wheatgerm, evening primrose oil, extract of chamomile . . . hyaluronic acid and sunfilters. Sounds impressive.' She handed the jar back to the doctor.

'Keep it, my dear. Ah yes, we've moved on a bit from the old cold cream days. Of course, that was just glorified petroleum jelly, you know. Very effective, of course. In fact many dermatologists insist you can't do better than cover yourself in the stuff every night, but aesthetically . . . Well, you can imagine. Makes the pillow awfully sticky, I gather.'

Fern giggled. Dr Chapman was certainly proving to be an informative guide. She hoped that they were getting near to Vitale. As they walked through the plant, the doctor reeled off the product names over his shoulder, gesturing to the variety of enticing bottles, jars and tubes with their silver tops and wine-red lettering. They reached a closed door and the doctor punched in a security code and then put his face close up to a security camera.

'Can't be too careful,' he confided. A few seconds

later the door clicked open. 'And here,' he said proudly, 'is Vitale!'

Fern rubbed her hands together gleefully. She recognized the distinctive silver lids and the green lettering. The silver OR logo of Oscar Rees glittered proudly in the centre of the lids.

'Please, tell me all about it, everything – if you've got time, that is.'

'Of course, of course.'

Dr Chapman ran through the production methods as Fern tried once more to scan the small jars spinning on the machines.

'Our production is nearing completion. Very soon we shall be getting everything down to distribution, when it will go out to the shops. We have special press packs to get ready – you know the sort of things, little trial packages of the range which can be put into a glamorous case ready for the launch. Of course, that's all down to the packaging chaps. They work in New Bond Street, getting all the designs ready, deciding on the bottles, the labelling, the colours. We just have to deal with the technical problems such as whether the bottle they've chosen is actually practical. It's all very well them coming up with some marvellously inventive shape, but we've got to get it onto the machines.'

They came to a halt outside another locked door. By the same process the door eventually opened. 'And here it is. Fern – I hope I may call you that – meet Vitale.' Fern peered delightedly at the small collection of cosmetics. Lipsticks in ribbed silver casing; solid cream foundations in simulated jade tortoiseshell compacts with silvered snap fasteners which slipped into neat little green velvet pouches, and blushers and eye shadow compacts all in the same matching green and silver. Then there were the bottles of foundation mousse, and the eye and lip pencils, everything co-ordinating in the Vitale colours of green, silver and white.

Dr Chapman picked up a tall slim bottle. 'Alpha Hydroxy Acids, or more simply fruit acids, were discovered by a Chicago dermatologist named Dr Eugene Van Scott in the seventies. You might call his discovery a bit of a miracle for anti-ageing. Now if you remember I was saying earlier how free radicals can damage communication between cells?' Fern nodded enthusiastically. 'Well, the exciting thing about AHAs is that they can *help* the cells to communicate with each other. You see as the skin gets older, the message to shed dead cells gets weaker, and so we find a build up of dull, dead skin. AHAs bring the skin's surface pH to its optimal level of 4.6. And, as you know, at this acidity, the enzymes, or mortar if you like, which hold the old, dead cells on the skin's surface, break down, therefore allowing the new cells to come up to the surface to replace those nasty dead things, much as happens when the skin is young.'

Fern nodded. It all seemed so logical, but there was so much to remember.

'And this here,' the doctor held the bottle up, 'is Vitalize, containing the magic, vital ingredient, glycolic acid which, as you know, is from sugar cane. We call this our Skin Life Accelerator. Of course, as we all know, other fruit acids do the same job: malic acid from apples, tartaric acid from grapes, and then there's pyrruvic acid from papaya – very exotic, that one, and we mustn't forget the old sour milk lactic acid. But in my opinion, the original – glycolic – is the best!

'Now here we have Vitality, the moisturiser. You will remember I was telling you about the enzymes which hold the cells together? Well, this *marvellous* formulation helps repair the cracks between the cells we don't wish to lose by matching the intercellular cement and merging into the skin. This has been achieved by the formulation of a new type of liposome which as you – '

Fern couldn't stand it any longer. 'What exactly is a liposome?' she interrupted politely.

'A tiny bubble, my dear, which carries the vital, ha, forgive me, no pun intended, ingredient straight to the skin cell. Ceramides. Acts just like Polyfilla, really, pastes in the cracks.' He added thoughtfully. 'And most importantly of all, we can now put both Vitamin C, which is water-soluble, and Vitamin E, which is oil-soluble, into the same cream, whereas in our original Free Radical Eradicator we only had Vitamin E because of the incompatibility problem. We can do this by putting the Vitamin C complex into the little bubbles, or liposomes, so that they remain separate until they reach the skin.'

Fern's head was beginning to spin. Johnny picked up a dark green, transparent brick of what looked like soap.

'Ah yes, my boy. That is our special neutral pH cleansing bar. Of course if you use ordinary soap and then plaster all this lot on your face, you'll be wasting your time and money. So, what do you think?' he said finally.

'It all sounds so complicated, technical and scientific. I suppose I'll have to get to know my way around it.'

'Indeed you will,' said Johnny. 'You're the ambassador for it, Fern. You'll be the one all the journalists fire their questions at, and you can bet your last million that they'll be trying to trip you up – prove what a bimbo you really are.'

'Terrific. That makes me feel really confident, Johnny.'

Dr Chapman squeezed her arm. 'Don't you worry about it. I'll give you some information to take away. It'll soon begin to make sense to you. You just give me a call if you need anything explained. Now, come along, we've still got the "colours" to do, and there's someone waiting to meet you.'

The tall dark-haired man looked remarkably familiar, yet Fern couldn't recall ever having met him before. Johnny whispered in her ear. 'Watch your back, lovey.' She didn't have a chance to ask what he meant. 'Fern, I'd like to introduce you to Alexander Easton, our Assistant Head of Product Development. Alexander, this is Fern Donleavy, our new face for Vitale.'

Fern eyed Lucienne's twin brother warily, wondering whether he would subject her to the same hostile reception as his sister.

He took her hand and shook it warmly. 'Fern, I'm so delighted to meet you at last.' His voice oozed silky, well-bred charm. His dark eyes glittered warmly at her.

She felt herself relax, returning his smile. 'Hello. I didn't realize you were based here.'

'We boffins tend to keep a low profile, don't we, Dr Chapman? Occasionally we dust ourselves down and venture into the glamorous world of New Bond Street, but mostly we tuck ourselves up with our test tubes. How are you, Johnny?' he said, finally acknowledging Johnny's presence.

'Alexander,' Johnny grunted.

Alexander let his eye rove rather obviously over Fern's tall figure. She felt her cheeks colouring. 'Yes,' he said finally. 'I can quite see why you were so keen,

Johnny. Come,' he said turning back to Fern, 'let's go and have some lunch and we can get to know each other.' He clutched her elbow and led her out of the room. Fern shot Johnny a helpless look over her shoulder while Johnny and Dr Chapman trotted behind them. 'What do you think of the product?' Alexander asked her.

'It's wonderful. I've been totally befuddled by all the technical stuff, but I'm pleased it has such a natural product base. I'd hate to involve myself with anything that was tested on animals, or used animal extract or whatever it is they stick in cosmetics these days. Sugar cane sounds fine to me. What is it you're working on?'

'Oh, I get involved in a bit of everything here and there. I help with the formulations.'

'So you had a hand in Vitale?'

'Both hands, actually. I'm afraid I can't claim all the credit, though. These AHAs are being used right across the industry. It was just a question of getting our own formulation right. It's not quite the same as having discovered the magic ingredient ourselves. As I'm sure you can imagine, a scientist always dreams of making the miracle discovery himself – or herself, I should say. So I spend a fair bit of time concocting strange potions, don't I, Dr Chapman?'

'Oh yes, Alexander. He's always got some breakthrough up his sleeve.'

'So what's your latest one?'

Alexander tapped his nose conspiratorially. 'Top secret, I'm afraid. But soon I shall have found the key to the fountain of eternal youth.'

Fern giggled. 'Then you will be extremely rich and extremely famous.'

'I know. Exciting, isn't it?' His dark eyes sparkled at her merrily. 'Of course, there is just one slight problem.'

'Oh?'

'Well, once I've done that, there really won't be any need for cosmetics any more. I might just put you out of a job.'

Fern didn't answer. She looked at Alexander unsure of whether he was teasing or not. Still, at least he was easy company.

'I've never been to Moscow. Let me come with you!' Lucienne leaned forward, balancing the glass of champagne in her right hand, resting her left on the edge of the bath. The bubbles swirled around her breasts in a ticklish fashion.

Alexander began to soap her back. 'Mmm,' she sighed blissfully. 'That's so nice, darling.' She leaned further forward as his hand slid soapily over her wet skin. She almost purred with delight. 'Well?'

'You've got work to do here. This chap that Nikolai has set up – he's expecting only me. He doesn't want a posse, does he?'

'Oh, come on, Alexander. You know perfectly well what an aide I can be to you. I'm really quite an asset.' She reached behind her head and grabbed his upper arm. Then she slid right around so that she now faced him. Alexander's hand was no more than an inch away from her left nipple. She looked him directly in the eye, and then dropped her gaze so that it rested suggestively on her breast. Slowly, she smiled up at him. She thrust her shoulders backwards, so that Alexander's hand made contact with her nipple, then she slid her knees apart, squirming in the hot soapy water luxuriously.

Alexander's laughter gurgled in the back of his throat. 'You're like a little cat, Lucienne. A cat needing a damn good fuck.'

Still clutching his arm, Lucienne carefully placed

the glass of champagne on the floor, then she took hold of his hand and pressed it over her ripe breast. As she did so, Alexander's fingers closed around the moist pink globe. Lucienne gasped.

'Oh . . . yes . . .' She opened her knees wider and then rocked them together, apart, together, apart, pushing the water in little waves that eddied deliciously between her legs. Alexander flicked the tip of her nipple with his forefinger.

'I thought you were getting plenty from your banker.'

'Quantity isn't the same as quality,' she said huskily. 'He's not like you, Xan. There's no one like you.'

As Alexander plucked her from the bath and held her wet body against his, he murmured against her shoulder, 'I can't imagine there are too many like you either, Sin.'

Alexander unbuttoned his trousers. 'Bend over!' he ordered.

Lucienne folded at the waist, resting her fingertips on the floor, a couple of inches from her toes. Alexander stepped back to admire the view, his cock already in his hand. Then he slipped it against her so that its head stroked against the warm flesh of her buttock down over her arse, and into the folds. She raised herself onto her tiptoes, pushing herself against him, rubbing at him up and down, up and down, frantic to feel his swollen penis push into her. 'Come on . . .' she cried. 'Please . . .' She made small grunts of pure sexual need.

Alexander pushed the head of his penis against her while Lucienne helped him slide in.

When at last she could take no more, she screamed out, and her whole body shuddered as if some giant electric current had passed through her, making her convulse and jerk like a string puppet. Then she flopped down, out of Alexander's grasp. Alexander stood over her limp body.

'I take it you're satisfied, Sin?'

'Mmm,' was the only reply.

'Good. I'll call you from Moscow when I get chance. Take care of your banker.'

Lucienne's eyes remained closed, but she lifted a heavy arm and waved goodbye to her twin.

Chapter Sixteen

❦✄❦

'Olivia!' Hugo's bellow echoed around the marble-floored hallway and up the staircase. 'Olivia, where the hell are you?'

Hugo had already searched most of the ground floor, vainly trying to locate her. Where was the bloody woman? He chased up the stairs, two at a time, flinging open his estranged wife's bedroom door.

Olivia's shriek of surprise confirmed her presence. All that was visible of her was a small head poking above a sheet which was firmly tucked under her chin.

'Hugo! How dare you march in here like this? Please get out!'

'Well, I must say I hardly expected to find you in bed. It's the middle of the afternoon, for God's sake! Are you ill?'

'I . . . er . . . yes, I felt a little queasy. Now please, Hugo, be good enough to leave.'

'Very well, but I would like to see you in the library in ten minutes – if of course that's convenient to you, Olivia,' he added sarcastically.

As he spun on his heel he could have sworn he could see the faint outline of another head emerging from under the covers. He fought the desire to look back. Whatever Olivia did with her time was of no interest to him. It was probably that dyke of a masseuse who was always hanging around the place. He turned his nose up distastefully. Getting rid of

Olivia was an item on his agenda long overdue. He'd been stupid to let things drift on for as long as they had. Twenty years! Lord, was it really as long as that? A lifetime! A life sentence, more like.

If only he'd known then what he knew now. Even his father might have seen reason if he'd known he was pushing his only son into a marriage with a lesbian. Of course, Hugo really had no one to blame but himself. If he'd had a stronger character he'd never have allowed himself to be coerced into it, no matter what amount of emotional blackmail had been loaded on to him. He could have followed his heart instead of his filial duty and life would have been very different and very happy, of that he had no doubt. He paced the polished oak library floor, staring sightlessly at the sun-bleached boards and the priceless Persian rugs. 'Bah! You old fool!' he chastized himself. 'She's probably old and toothless by now.'

He stopped mid-stride when Olivia entered. 'Do give your friend my apologies,' he said coldly.

Olivia flushed. 'I can't imagine what you're talking about.'

'It is hard to imagine, I grant you that,' Hugo muttered. 'Thing is, Olivia, I've had this damned silly letter from your lawyers.'

'Oh?'

'I trust you know of its contents?'

Olivia shrugged. 'I leave things up to them. They are the experts, Hugo.'

'Oh come, come, Olivia. They might advise you, but they follow your instructions, and you must have instructed them to demand from me a sum of £20 million.' Hugo almost choked on the words. 'If it wasn't so sick it would be almost amusing.'

'I can't see why. You seem to forget, Hugo, that

209

your father and mine were partners. Therefore not only do I have a claim on the company as your wife, I equally have a claim because I am an heir. However, as you will appreciate, I do not wish to work in the company or get in your way, I simply wish to realize what is rightfully mine so that I may start a new life.'

'Olivia, you make it all sound *so* simple. The fact that as you well know we're in the middle of a potential hostile takeover bid – which you and your bloody family are a party to – and the fact that I need all the cash I can raise to keep any of the company at all, should make you understand that if I accede to your request I shall have nothing.'

'As ever, Hugo, you are being overdramatic.'

'*Overdramatic!*' he bellowed. 'Are you of this planet, woman? Those are the facts, plain and simple.'

'My lawyers have advised me not to discuss matters directly with you.'

'I'm sure they have. Well, you can tell your lawyers to stuff their demands up their scheming little arses! Twenty million is out of the question. Ten million would be out of the question. You have your shares in the company. That is your legacy, Olivia. You have not worked in the company, but you have benefited enormously from being my wife. You don't stand a cat in hell's chance of succeeding with your ridiculous demands.'

'We shall see, Hugo.'

'Indeed, Olivia!' he retorted as she closed the door behind her.

Hugo sighed into the newly settled peace of the room, his eyes roaming over the book-lined shelves. The library had been a passion in his father's life, and in his grandmother's before that. He trailed his finger along the lovingly waxed leather spines of the numerous first editions. Yes, he'd be sad to see the old house go, but in his heart he knew it was an impossible dream to hang on to the Rees home as well as the company.

He stopped in front of the portrait of his father which filled the wall above the mantelpiece.

'You've got a lot to answer for, you old bugger!'

'I just don't believe this, Fern, I really don't.'

'Excuse me.' Fern pulled the bulging suitcase off her bed and onto the floor where she struggled with the zip. 'Damn,' she swore under her breath.

'Will you please listen to me.'

'I am listening, Paul. But there's nothing more to say. I'm sorry. But I feel it's best if we don't see each other any more.'

'Just like that?'

'It can't be a surprise to you. We hardly see each other these days, anyway. You know how we fight, Paul. Every time we do meet it turns into a destructive point-scoring session. Look, I've thought about this a lot. I can't see that it's making either of us very happy. And,' she lowered her voice, 'I don't love you.'

'And what about me?'

Fern looked at him blankly.

'Why do you think I came here?'

She shrugged. She wanted to say that she thought he was probably bored and had nothing better to do, but she thought better of it.

'Because I love you, Fern. Because I want to be with you. You know how good we are for each other.'

'But that's my point. We're not at all. Our relationship just makes me unhappy.'

'Then I think you're very selfish.'

Fern looked at her watch. 'Look, I'm really sorry, Paul, but I have to go. The taxi's going to be here any minute.'

211

'So that's it then. You swan off to Paris and have a great time, having dumped me.'

Fern turned round and looked at him properly, taking in his slumped shoulders and his withered expression. She knew him better than that. He was just playing a part – the part of the hurt man. Wounded pride, that was all that was wrong with him.

'I'm sorry.' She bit her lip and turned back to her suitcase.

'No you're not. You're too hard to be sorry.'

She flinched, but said nothing.

His voice sounded ugly and bitter. 'You really think you're something special, don't you, with your million-pound contract? Well let me tell you, you're nothing. A nobody! You couldn't even write a decent article, could you? I bet *Faces* were delighted to get shot of you.'

Fern felt the tears prick behind her eyes. She kept her face turned away from him and concentrated on her suitcase.

'I have to go.' she pleaded. 'You must leave, Paul.'

'Oh I'll leave. It'll be a pleasure. You were a lousy fuck, anyway.'

'Then you shouldn't be upset, should you?'

He stepped towards her and unconsciously she braced herself, scared of what he would do next. Then suddenly he spun on his heel and walked towards the doorway.

'You're a bitch, Fern Donleavy. A hard, calculating little bitch!'

She held her breath, listening as the sound of his footsteps receded down the stairs, only daring to relax when she had heard the reassuring slam of the front door. She picked up her jacket, took one last look around the flat, and then started to lug the heavy case to the door, ready for the taxi. It was only when she was finally locking up that she realized Paul still had a set of keys. Well, there was nothing she could do about it now; she had a plane to catch. She'd have to get the locks changed when she returned.

When Fern stepped into the arrivals hall at Orly Airport she was blinded by flashing white lights. She brought her hand up to shield her eyes, squinting into the crowd. A sea of photographers had lined themselves up against the ropes and were leaning forward, faces obscured by their giant lenses, popping their flashes like a strobe machine.

Fern glanced behind her to see what all the fuss was about. A lone businessman strolled a few yards back, frowning curiously at Fern. She felt a rising surge of panic as the realization hit her. She knew the publicity machine had been getting its wheels oiled, but she had no idea it had roared into this much action. She heard her name being called as the ratpack fought to get a good shot of her. She blinked in all directions, struggling to put on a reasonable smile. The flashes hurt her eyes but she remembered she had to try and ignore them, otherwise all the pictures would show her with her eyes shut. Suddenly the photographers were all around her, gabbling at her in unintelligible French. *'Ici! Fern – ici, s'il vous plaît. Un petit sourire pour nous, allons-y.'*

'Une pose . . . Ah, Fern, très belle . . .'

She couldn't believe this was happening. She tried to push her laden trolley through the throng. Another crowd of travellers seemed to have formed beyond the pack, no doubt wondering what all the fuss was about. Fern looked around helplessly, wondering how on earth she was going to find Bea,

Dominique Lefevre's assistant, amongst all this lot. Suddenly a petite blonde head appeared from under a photographer's armpit. 'Fern . . . Mademoiselle Donleavy, over here!' She was waving frantically, then struggled breathlessly towards Fern. 'Sorry, I got held up. News of your arrival obviously filtered through to the paparazzi.'

'Yes, I had no idea . . . It's nice to see you again,' Fern said, still eyeing the crowd nervously. She had met Bea on her previous trip a couple of weeks before, when she had been vetted for Chanel's catwalk show. Fern had then endured the dubious privilege of parading before Madame Lefevre's hypercritical eye to measure up whether she could *marche* properly, and whether her proportions were sympathetic to this current season's trends. Luckily for Fern, they were, and after nervously walking back and forth in impossibly high heels at least a size too small for her, the boss had nodded her approval, finally giving Fern the smallest of smiles.

Now here she was, ready for the big one, and she felt terrified.

Bea took her arm. 'I have a car outside.'

'Thank goodness,' Fern sighed. 'I was wondering how to make a getaway from this lot.'

'You walk swiftly, and push a lot,' Bea grinned. 'Come, follow me.'

'*Excusez-moi! Pardon, messieurs . . .*' the diminutive girl shouted and a passage formed for them. Fern pushed her trolley determinedly forwards. Eventually they reached the safety of Bea's white convertible BMW. Fern eyed the car admiringly. Bea grinned. 'It's not mine, alas. It is in your honour.'

'How very nice.'

'Everyone is very excited about meeting you again. I have to take you to the salon for your final fittings –

after you've checked in at the hotel, of course – and then there is a rehearsal with all the models. I'm afraid it's going to be a rather full schedule for you, yes?'

'Well, my time for the next two days is all yours. Then on Friday we have to start getting ready for the launch of Vitale on Saturday. All the Oscar Rees lot will be arriving on Friday morning.'

'And the show on Friday night. I think you will be very tired by then.'

'I guess I will.' Fern relaxed back into the seat, stretching her legs out in front of her as the car sped them into the city and God only knew what horrors waiting for her there.

Fern stood like a stuffed dummy while two women sighed and tutted around her. She tried not to think about the fact that she was almost naked in a room packed full of people. She tried not to mind the way her waistline was prodded and her thighs squeezed. She tried not to think about the curious looks she was getting from all the other models who seemed remarkably at home with the fact that they too were nearly nude. Fern recognized a few of the faces . . . the supermodels! She fought her instinct to shrivel into a little ball with her arms folded across her, and instead concentrated on holding herself up to her lofty five foot eleven, telling herself that this was something she had done every day of her life. Next time Johnny had one of his bright ideas, she'd make sure she vetoed it, especially if it meant subjecting herself to endless probing and prodding from humourless women. How one learns . . . she groaned inwardly.

Madame Lefevre stood at the opposite side of the room, eyeing Fern as if she were an unfinished garment while the two couturiers flicked their tape measures around nearly every inch of her, clucking like French hens in overworked irritation.

'Don't worry,' Bea whispered reassuringly. 'They're always like this. We had all your measurements last time. This is just the fine tuning. They like to make a show of their art.'

'I was wondering if my scales had deceived me and I've put on weight. They seem so annoyed by something.'

'Don't take it personally. This is the climax of all their work for the last six months. Everything has to be exactly right, and everyone's temper and patience is worn very thin.'

Then Madame Lefevre pulled a sapphire-blue wisp of a gown from one of the dress rails and handed it to the two women. Fern watched as they reverentially slipped the garment off the hanger and helped Fern put it over her head. At first the cold silk lining made her shiver, but as the side zip was closed, and the shoulders were gently teased into place, Fern couldn't avoid the feeling of awe that she was inside such an icon of couture. As the couturiers brandished their pin-cushion wrist straps, pushing her this way and that, moving her arms and making minuscule adjustments to shoulder straps and side seams, Fern watched herself in the enormous wall-sized mirror. Chiffon floated away from her shoulders like gossamer wings, which were so light and filmy they seemed to defy gravity, barely coming to rest against her arms when she ceased to move. The short gown was ruched into figure-hugging swags of sapphire chiffon, which appeared to change hue as the light caught the fabric's undulations.

No other garment had ever felt so deliciously sensuous as this. Madame Lefevre strung several rows of pearls around Fern's neck, and then threaded more through her hair. She gave Fern one of her rare smiles and Fern grinned back.

Suddenly she was enjoying rising to the challenge. She looked at herself and felt proud of her height, satisfied with the smooth curve of her hip brushed under the couturier's professional hand, and at last she began to look forward to dressing up and attempting to do these marvellous clothes the justice they deserved.

When at last the fitting was over and Madame Lefevre had literally taken her through her paces, explaining how she must concentrate on squeezing her buttocks together, and letting her hips sway just the right amount, allowing her arms to swing her around when she made a turn and how she must tease the photographers with her eyes. There was a fair bit to remember and by the time the lesson was over, Fern's head was spinning along with her body.

Bea handed Fern a white silk robe. 'Come on, I'll introduce you to the rest of the girls. I'm afraid there's going to be an awful lot of standing around. I hope you are feeling comfortable.'

Fern relaxed at Bea's kindness and put on her best smile as Bea made the introductions. Even without make-up, with hair pushed up into scarves or rough ponytails, these girls were still impossibly beautiful. Fern found herself almost awestruck by the perfection of their features.

'Have you had any lunch?' Suzy was the first to speak. 'Here, grab a sandwich, otherwise you'll faint. We all stuff ourselves with Mars bars to stop falling over – then we worry about getting spots!'

Fern took the proffered plate and started to push the food into her mouth. It seemed a long time since the couple of croissants and coffee on the plane.

'I heard about your Oscar Rees contract.' One of the other girls came and plonked herself down next to Fern. A long T-shirt almost covered her skimpy pants. Fern recognized the face, but couldn't recall the name.

'I'm Kate,' the girl said. 'This is my second season. It's nerve-wracking when it's your first, but just remember all you have to do is walk. One foot in front of the other, and that's it. Simple!'

'I'll probably fall flat on my face.'

'No. Once you get out there, you'll forget what you're doing. The people are packed in, the music's pounding, and all you're worried about is getting your next change done in time and making sure you've got the right necklace and shoes. It'll be over before you know it. How many shows are you doing?'

'Just this one.'

'You're kind of lucky. We've got another rehearsal after this one, a show tonight and two tomorrow, then another thirteen after that. Then there's the receptions afterwards. God, I don't know how we manage to get through it. Anyone who says we don't earn our money should try it for themselves.'

Fern helped herself to a glass of mineral water. Four cases of the stuff were stacked under the table. A couple of bottles of champagne stuck their necks out of silver buckets, but Fern noticed no one seemed interested in serious drinking.

One by one more girls came over and introduced themselves and Fern's nervousness subsided. These girls weren't conceited, unapproachable bitches, they were professionals using their best assets to make a very good living in the short time available and she realized with a jolt that she was exactly like them. Through no fault of their own they had been born perfect freaks – perfectly beautiful freaks – and underneath the beautiful exteriors was just an ordinary bunch of girls earning a living. Fern had been guilty of judging these girls because of their looks. She hadn't stopped to think about the minds behind the faces, which was exactly what she accused others of doing to her. She knew she would have to fight her damnedest to make sure that behind *this* particular clotheshorse was an independent, intelligent mind to be reckoned with. Oscar Rees had better watch out!

Twenty-four hours later, teetering precariously in her shoes, Fern was beginning to wonder just what had happened to all her bravado. Bea was like an island of tranquillity in a sea of total pandemonium, as dressers rushed about, security men built like Saracen tanks fought off invaders, and models elbowed each other for mirror space, putting the finishing coat of lipgloss onto already gleaming mouths.

She squeezed Fern's arm reassuringly. 'You look marvellous, and you will be marvellous.'

Fern tried to smile, but she feared if she did, her whole face might crack up into little pieces. 'Thank you, Bea. You've been so kind.'

Bea blew Fern an air kiss and disappeared through the curtain which separated the beau monde from the chosen few. Ever since her arrival yesterday, Bea had been at Fern's side reassuring her and acting as a diplomat between the fierce couturiers and demanding show producers, quietly smoothing frazzled nerves with her gentle manner. But as she waited for the off, Fern hardly dared to move for fear of putting the tiniest crease on to the white sequined calf-length gown which moulded to her body like a glove. As she moved her lower limbs the tiny circles threw off rainbow-coloured shafts of light. Two thin sequined strips ran over her bare shoulders down to the boned bodice which pushed her breasts upwards to form an impressive-looking décolletage. The dress clung like a second skin as far down as her mid thighs, but from there it fluted out into panels which swung cleverly around her calves. A swathe of heavily sequined silk had been bound into a turban which covered most of her hair, save for a few wisps which had escaped down over her left shoulder. Her head felt heavy but in a way it helped her to maintain her stiff posture, reminding her to strut instead of walk, helping to nudge her into the part of glamorous catwalk model. For the moment, the champagne was flowing and Karl Lagerfeld himself was flitting between a select bunch of journalists and his bevy of beauties, looking as cool and relaxed as royalty. He came over to Fern.

'I watched you earlier . . . on the runway.' His accent of French-softened German was strangely seductive. 'You do very well, and you look very lovely . . . very beautiful. Especially the dress on you. It feels good, *ja*?'

'It feels wonderful. I just hope I don't go to pieces out there.'

'I know you won't!' he said emphatically. 'You will walk on clouds out there.' The Kaiser brushed his famous black fan in front of his impenetrably dark glasses and moved on. Fern felt she had been truly honoured.

Finally, a respectable fifty minutes later than scheduled, the show began. The music roared into life, the lights flashed and the first group of six models strutted their stuff down the runway. Bea stood next to Fern, peeking through the curtain. Her voice was squeaky with excitement.

'Everyone is here,' she said proudly. '*Vanity Fair, Harper's Bazaar, Women's Wear Daily, Vogue* – they're the ones lined up in the front row on the left, the big buyers and the celebs always get the front row, too. Make sure you smile at the cameras. You want the fashion editors to choose a shot of you for their copy tomorrow.'

'I feel sick with nerves,' Fern howled, remembering the statistics Bea had quoted earlier: out there lay approximately one thousand journalists, three hundred and fifty photographers and fifty television crews.

'Here, take a slug of this.' Bea held out her champagne glass and Fern knocked it straight back. 'Now you'll float down the runway.'

'I hope to God you're right.'

Fern waited for the director's signal and then lined up with the others. Suddenly they were on in a blaze of light and applause. Somehow her stiff legs managed to move with the music. Her pelvis led her shoulders as she swayed her hips in the deceptively lazy way she had been taught.

She pasted a smile on her face and went for it for all she was worth. Halfway down she pulled the loose turban from her head and her hair swung around her shoulders in a blaze of russet red. The bulbs flashed and Fern posed. She trailed the unswathed fabric of the turban along behind, giving the photographers her best seductive smile. She was beginning to enjoy herself.

Leo Eden nudged India Duncan-Forrester in the ribs. 'Isn't that that girl?' he said in a loud stage whisper.

India's wire-rimmed spectacles were balanced haughtily on the end of her nose. Leo knew they were purely an affectation. 'Yes.' India's bored tone belied the fact that she had been watching Fern Donleavy like a hawk, noting the animal fluidity of her movement, watching the gasps of the audience as she twisted and manouevred herself down the catwalk. Even India secretly had to admit to herself that the girl looked stunning.

'What's she doing up there?' Leo hissed.

'You must have read the papers, darling,' India sighed impatiently. 'She's the new Oscar Rees girl.'

Leo leaned back in his chair and frowned to himself. Of course he'd read about the new face for Vitale, but he'd never made the connection. He watched, mesmerized, as Fern's wild copper mane bounced over her shoulders, and around her breasts. He followed the line of her endless legs, remembering the day he had seen her in the jacuzzi. Inwardly he congratulated Hugo. From the way the bulbs were flashing every time Fern appeared, she was the most popular model of the show, which meant Oscars would get a huge publicity boost over the week, coupled with the fact that the Vitale launch was scheduled for tomorrow night. And that meant that Lowenstein would start breathing down Leo's neck over the damn takeover once more. Leo privately felt a little sorry for Hugo, and for the future of Oscars. He'd have a chat with him later to try to persuade him to take a positive role within the new organization.

The show flew by in a blur of posing, strutting and stripping. By the time the last call came, Fern was feeling euphoric. She had actually managed to get through it without one tiny trip. As the bride came out, accompanied by Karl Lagerfeld, the models lined up on either side of the curtain and applauded their master. Fern surreptitiously scanned the faces in the audience, trying to spot the Oscar Rees lot. She couldn't see any of them but if she wasn't mistaken, she could see the haughty face of India Duncan-Forrester scowling directly at her.

Johnny splashed more champagne into Fern's glass. 'Drink up, darling. You were wonderful, the toast of Paris!'

'Thanks,' Fern grinned, 'but if I drink any more I shall look like the shrivelled old crust of Paris, and we've got the launch tomorrow.'

'Don't worry about that. It's all so well organized it will be a breeze. Come on, let's go and find Hugo and the others. He sent me to search you out. They've managed to find a quiet corner in the other bar.'

Fern obediently followed Johnny, trying to ignore her aching legs and feet and the fact that she would give anything just to crawl into a bed right now. She felt utterly drained. Johnny tugged her by the hand towards a large group of people who had taken over most of the far side of the glittering mosaic-gilded bar of which the Hôtel de Crillon were justly proud. Fern recognized the back of Hugo's head. She touched his shoulder lightly and as he spun around his face lit up in delight.

'Fern!' he cried. 'Darling girl, well done. You were magnificent. We're all so proud of you, aren't we?' he gestured to his companions.

Fern blushed and dropped her eyes in embarrassment. When she lifted them she was chilled to see that far from meeting smiling faces, she was confronted by more than one frosty glare. Fern shrank back towards Johnny as Hugo made the introductions.

'Fern, I don't think you've met Lady Pembroke . . .' Fern stuck her hand out politely and returned the charming smile of Hugo's girlfriend with

223

a melting one of her own. 'And India, Leo, you've met, of course . . .'

India nodded and Leo took her hand. Fern remembered the last time they had met and she caught herself looking into his eyes to see if she could detect that same sense of mockery which she knew had been there before. His deep dark eyes were impenetrable, but his lips brushed hotly over the cool tips of her fingers. Almost involuntarily, she pulled her hand sharply out of his grasp, and rubbed at the spot on her fingers, as if she had been burned. Watching her, Leo Eden smiled a lazy, teasing smile.

'I didn't realize Cooper Jefferson were involved with catwalk shows,' Fern said, noting with some surprise the degree of coldness in her own voice.

'Oh, Leo usually likes to keep me company,' India interrupted. 'Naturally I always get a front row seat, bearing in mind the importance of *A La Mode*, and Leo is known to be a fairly good customer, particularly of Karl's, aren't you, darling?'

'What she means, Fern, is that she generally manages to con me into buying a couple of little numbers.'

'I'd have thought with your degree of success, India, you'd be buying them for yourself!' Fern couldn't resist it.

'Well, I, of course . . . I do!' she spluttered.

'Do you?' Leo sounded genuinely surprised. 'I hadn't realized, India.' Fern caught his eye and realized with shock that he was winding India up. His dark eyes sparkled merrily at Fern. She turned away in confusion, not wishing to get drawn into some daft game between the pair of them.

Hugo grabbed her by the arm. 'Come on, Fern, come and talk to Ricci. I've told her so much about you and she's been dying to meet you, haven't you, Ricci?'

'Just dying, Hugo.' Ricci smiled at Fern warmly and congratulated her on the show. 'Let's sit down and chat. I want to hear all about you.' She patted the sofa and Fern obediently took her place beside Ricci. 'I should think it must get awfully hot and tiring standing beneath those lights for hours on end.'

'It does. And sometimes you've got to hold the same pose and you get so stiff you think you're going to die, or, at the very least, never move normally again. But I'm having a lot of fun, and I'm keen to get to know all about the products and the way the company works.'

Ricci smiled a little sadly. 'You'd better be quick then, Fern. There may not be a company for much longer. Cooper Jefferson are hoping to take it over.'

'But I thought that was just a rumour! Hugo would never sell out, would he?'

'No, but the other members of the family might. It's a bit of a long story, and I think Hugo's sort of hoping that if he doesn't mention it it might just go away.'

'I can partly understand that, but there must surely be something he can do to stop it happening?'

'Not if the shareholders want to sell, and if Hugo doesn't have the money to buy their shares.'

'How much would he need?' Fern asked.

'About £50 million.'

'Jesus!' Fern breathed. 'So there's not much hope?'

Ricci shook her head. 'Not unless the twins, Olivia and the Rees Foundation can be persuaded otherwise. Unfortunately they're all screaming for money. So really, my dear, that is that.'

'No wonder Hugo's been so short-tempered lately.'

Ricci laughed. 'He's fortunate we all put up with

225

him, isn't he?' She leaned back in the chair and crossed her long slim, black-stockinged legs. She wore a simple black jersey dress with two strands of pearls at her throat. A large sapphire surrounded by glittering diamonds held the double string together. Her pale blonde hair fell to her shoulders. She had a slight fringe, and the rest was swept back and held neatly in place with a quilted black hairband. She had the kind of aristocratic good looks that merely become refined as one gets older – more worldly, but still undoubtedly sexy. Johnny had told Fern about Hugo's impending divorce. No doubt Ricci and Hugo would get together officially once it was all through.

Eventually Fern excused herself. She needed a good night's sleep and she still had some briefing work to do in order to prepare herself for the ladies and gentlemen of the press on the big day tomorrow. And she wanted space to think about the consequences of Ricci's news and just what the sale of Oscar Rees would mean to her. It would be just her luck to be an out-of-work model on top of being an out-of-work journalist. She'd have to talk over her position with Hugo, but for tonight it was more important to make sure she got her beauty sleep or she'd be out of work one hell of a lot sooner.

Chapter Seventeen

❦

Leo collected his faxes from the hotel lobby and made his way into the restaurant. Usually he would have breakfasted in his room, but India's late-copy-driven chain smoking had forced him out into the fresh air. He had left her tearing her hair out trying to decide which little numbers she would single out for special despatches in her editorial. He scanned the bustling room, trying to find a table and then he saw a flash of bright sienna at the far side of the room. He smiled to himself and weaved his way through the tables. Fern's head was bent over a sheaf of papers and she appeared not to notice his approach, nor even the pulling out of the chair opposite.

Leo coughed. Fern started, hitting the cup in front of her. 'Oh! I didn't see you,' she flustered, trying to catch the papers, and stifle the rattling cup.

'I hope I'm not disturbing you.'

'No, just a little homework.'

'On what make-up you will be wearing tonight?'

'Actually on the history of Oscar Rees's perfumes.'

'How interesting. Do tell me.' He sounded unusually warm.

'Well, I'm sure you're not that interested . . .'

'But on the contrary, I'm extremely interested.'

'Ah yes, I suppose on reflection you would be, wouldn't you? Bearing in mind you're about to buy the company.'

Leo shrugged. 'Nothing's settled as yet. Hugo and I still have to discuss certain things. Anyway, I wouldn't have thought you'd be too concerned about it.'

Fern's lips tightened and her eyes flashed angrily at Leo. The patronizing bastard. Pointedly, she picked up her papers and continued to read.

'Really,' he said, 'I meant what I said. I'd be most interested to hear the histories.'

'If you're buying the company, I would have thought you'd have made it your own business to find out.'

'You're confusing romanticism with economics.'

'Correct me if I'm wrong, but I thought the business of cosmetics was about romanticism, selling dreams and fantasy. Some of the great perfumes were formulated around dreams by great romantics. I wouldn't mock that if I were you. After all, I gather Coopers think these dreams are worth at least £40 million.'

'You're remarkably well informed.' Leo was enjoying himself.

'For a gate-crasher?' She regarded him from underneath her raised brows.

'I'm sorry. You weren't a gate-crasher, you were a –'

'Journalist.'

'Ah yes, that's right. The interview with India. You mentioned it.'

Fern was surprised he'd remembered. 'We had a personality clash, I believe.'

Leo laughed aloud. 'India gets a little, how shall I put it kindly?'

Fern waited, feigning disinterest.

'A little insecure, shall we say?'

'That or downright unprofessional!'

'It's a tough old world out here, Fern. I expect you'll learn. Besides, you're doing far better now than you ever would have done working for India. I should be grateful to her if I were you.'

'Look, I don't mean to be rude, but I really do have some work to do.'

'Oh feel free, don't let me stop you.' He clicked his fingers and a waiter appeared. *'Deux cafés, s'il vous plaît, et des croissants avec du beurre, mais sans confiture, et une petite assiette de fruits très fraîches, d'accord? Merci.'* He grinned at Fern. 'You were saying?'

'Was I?'

'Absynthe. Let's start with that one.'

Fern grinned back at last. He was so persistent! And maybe the practice would be helpful.

'It was Oscar Rees's first major fragrance – a wedding gift to Nancy, Hugo's mother. You remember, of course, originally absinthe was a French liquor made from wormwood. It was bitter-tasting and so, almost as a ritual, a specially perforated spoon would be suspended over a glass, and the liquor would be carefully dripped through a spoonful of sugar. The thing was that the liquor was actually rather poisonous and caused blindness and madness. It was outlawed, I believe.'

'A strange wedding present, then, of something bitter-sweet.'

'I think Oscar's point was the union between himself as the bitter, and Nancy as the sweet. Between them they made a heady and formidable potion. It also goes back to Adam and Eve, I believe, as the legend of artemisia, from which absinthe is concocted, is that it is the plant which sprang up in the serpent's wake as it writhed along the ground when driven out of the Garden of Eden. Maybe Oscar was making a pun on the fact that like Adam, he had fallen victim to a woman's charms.'

'A nice little story,' Leo agreed. 'And what of the others?'

'Well, when Hugo devised his first fragrance, he stuck with the mythology connection. Orpheo was formulated when he was just twenty-five. I guess it's remarkable that even when he was so inexperienced he managed to come up with something which remains a major seller today.'

'I don't wish to sound cynical, Fern, but Hugo pumps a lot of money into keeping it well marketed.'

'Wouldn't you when it's the all-time tenth best-selling fragrance?'

'Could the marketing be superfluous?'

'That's a chicken and egg argument. You push it, it sells well, because it sells well, do you need to push it? Is it selling well because it's being pushed, or is it selling well because of huge established brand loyalty? It seems to me that Hugo's strategy of consistency little and often has worked well for it.'

'You seem to be learning fast, Fern.'

'Yeah. I like learning, Leo. But you know no one has ever got to the bottom of *why* Hugo chose Orpheo. Like his father before him, he'd just got married, and so I guess at the time people assumed that it was a wedding present for Olivia, but the legend is incredibly sad, heart-rendingly unhappy, in fact. Seems such a strange choice.'

'Do you think Hugo had some secret love then, Fern?'

'You know the legend?'

'Sure I do. Poor old Orpheus loses his wife after she's been bitten by a serpent. Orpheus does a deal with Pluto who agrees to let him go down into the underworld and bring back Eurydice on condition that he doesn't look at her until she's back on earth. When he eventually finds her in Hades, Eurydice is heartbroken that her love won't look at her and beseeches him to do so. Unable to bear her unhappiness, just as Orpheus steps back onto earth, he turns to her, and of course she disappears back into Hades for eternity, leaving him forever to mourn her.' Leo grinned at Fern smugly. 'I think that's about it. Which could lead us to suppose that Hugo had some secret love!'

'Exactly. And maybe he could never tell her why he couldn't be with her.'

'You have a vivid imagination, Fern.'

'Just a curious mind, Leo. Anyway, I've got to go. I'd better practise putting my lipstick on!'

'Touché!' he sighed as she left.

The Vitale launch party flew past in a blur of speeches, flashlights and endless interviews. Fern found it hard to come to terms with being on the opposite side of a journalist's notebook and had to bite her tongue on several occasions to stop herself from asking what angle they were going to use, how long the piece would be, what pix they would need, and so on. Tonight she would play the bimbo – after all, that was what she was being paid for. She smiled until her jaw ached and tried to stifle her yawns. The ballroom of the Hôtel de Crillon was packed solid with bodies. All the major retailers from France, the UK and America – all of whom had to be introduced to her; all the major fashion and cosmetics press; all the distributors and agents, the factory boffins, including Dr Chapman and the Easton twins, their father, Julian, whom Fern had not met before, all of them passed before her in a blur of smiles and introductions. She must have been asked how she'd been discovered about a million times, to the extent that she was wondering whether she should scribble out

231

an appendix to the press release pack and hand it around, rather than go through it one more time.

Johnny stayed close to her side, making sure she wasn't swamped by people, carefully filling her glass – with mineral water – and guiding her through her paces. His presence gave her a quiet confidence. It was so reassuring to know that he was there for her if she needed a little help.

After what seemed like many hours, she could tell that the crowd was thinning out a little. Johnny winked at her.

'Won't be long before we can escape. I think you've done your bit well and truly. Now all we'll have to do is wait for the press tomorrow. But my guess is Vitale's going to be a huge success, as are you, darling Fern.'

'Thanks, Johnny. For everything. I don't know what I'd have done without you.'

For a moment he gazed at her and she thought he was about to take her in his arms, but then he dropped his eyes and took a step back.

'Rubbish. I've done nothing except my job. Come on, let's find a quiet spot for a drink. I bet you could use a rest.'

He pulled her through reception and into a small salon. 'Wait here, I'll go and find a waiter.'

Fern kicked off her shoes, and tucked her feet up on the banquette. She shook her hair out from the tight French plait, at once feeling good to be loose and free. Then she knew that she was not alone in the small room. A large display of plants occupied the space behind the small banquette, and she realized that there must be a similar seat on the opposite side. She caught the unmistakable sound of Hugo's voice. She raised herself up on to her knees and peered through the foliage.

'Hugo,' she called, before realizing who his companion was.

'Fern darling, come and join us.'

'I'm waiting for Johnny.'

'Never mind that, I've hardly seen you all night. Come and let's have a look at you. I want to see the Vitale girl.'

'Okay.' She slipped her shoes back on and walked round. Leo moved away from Hugo so that she could sit between the two of them.

'I hope I wasn't interrupting anything,' she said, suddenly feeling very awkward about the fact that she'd maybe disturbed a high-powered meeting.

'Not really, we were just discussing the takeover of Oscars by Coopers, weren't we, Hugo?'

'We were, but I'm sure that now Fern's here we could switch subjects.'

Fern guessed immediately that she had rescued Hugo from Leo's negotiating tactics. She didn't know whether to be pleased or sorry.

'Here, have some champagne.' Leo passed Fern his glass.

'I've had so much mineral water already.'

'But you can relax now, darling. Come and tell us all about your evening.'

'As long as I don't have to smile I'll talk about anything. I swear my face will split in two if I crease it any more. Look, I know this is probably none of my business, but I've been thinking very hard about this takeover deal. Whatever is decided will have a direct effect on me, I imagine, bearing in mind I have a signed and sealed two-year contract with Oscar Rees, no matter who's running it.'

'Correct,' Leo grinned and placed his arm around the back of the banquette proprietorially. Fern leaned ever so slightly forward, unbearably conscious of the proximity of his warm limb.

'Why don't you just sell Coopers some of the lines?'

'It makes perfect sense, but Hugo would never agree to it,' Leo murmured.

'It never occurred to me that you'd want to do that,' Hugo sighed. 'You've always said that you wanted control of the company.'

'Well, you've always said that you didn't want to let any of it go. Naturally I assumed that went for the lines.'

'Oh, come on, Leo. I can always produce new lines. Naturally there are some which I wouldn't want to sell, such as Absynthe, Orpheo and Vitale,' he added patting Fern's knees. 'But without prejudice, of course, there is always Ozzie, Ingénue, La Petite Mort, maybe others.'

Leo sat upright, removing his arm from behind Fern. 'Are you serious?'

'I believe so. I mean, one has to be realistic, Leo. I need the bloody money at the moment. I've got Olivia breathing down my neck for millions of pounds. I've got shareholders leaving like rats from a sinking ship and I would, if at all possible, like to keep an independent, privately owned, bloody good company in perpetuity. Now I can't do that, as we all realize. My options are that I sell you a chunk of the shares – say forty per cent. Before I know it, I'll have Cooper Jefferson monkeys swinging around all over the place getting in the way of things. Doesn't bear thinking about really. But, as Fern says, if, say, I were to get shot of a few lines, then maybe we'd all be happy.'

Hugo broke off and stared at Fern. Leo, too, was regarding her with his mouth open.

Fern watched the pair of them silently. 'Is it something I said?' she asked quietly.

Leo was the first to speak. 'Is this a setup?'

'What do you mean, dear boy?'

'You two. You've set me up, haven't you? You planned this meeting.'

'I don't know what you're talking about.'

Leo turned back to Fern. 'You mean you just thought of it?'

'Well, of course I did. It seems to make perfect, rather obvious sense. Look, excuse me you two, here's Johnny. I'll see you later.' Fern got up and left them both gawping after her.

Chapter Eighteen

Johnny couldn't quite believe what he was hearing. It was only two days since Vitale had been launched, for Christ's sake.

'Let me get this straight, Hugo. You want *me* to be the one to tell Fern that *you've* sold her out?'

Hugo coughed awkwardly. 'I wouldn't have put it quite like that, Johnny.'

'Then how would you have put it?'

For once Johnny felt not the least bit afraid of Hugo Rees. Right now the only thing he could feel was raw-red, angry rage.

'I had no choice. I had to save the company! Coopers would have taken a controlling interest. Look, no one is more upset than I at the fact that we have lost Vitale, La Petite Mort and Bijou. But we've still got Ozzie, Absynthe, Orpheo, Florissima, Intuition and Ingénue.'

'But what am I going to tell Fern? She gets back from Paris tonight!'

'Look, she still works *here*, Johnny, it's just that she's now officially under contract to Cooper Jefferson for all promotional work connected to Vitale as and when required for the next two years.'

'Just like that.'

'Yes.'

Johnny regarded Hugo with contempt. 'You sold her out without even talking to her about it.'

'I had no option – I had to make a quick decision. You're making me sound like a pimp, man. I'm trying to save the business.' Once more Hugo coughed. 'Now look here, Johnny, I've been very straight with you. Er, now I'd appreciate it if you'd just get on with the job in hand.' Hugo picked up his telephone by way of dismissal. He didn't need Johnny Sharpe to point out to him what a dastardly deed he had done. He had fought Leo tooth and nail to keep Vitale from going, but for some reason Leo had been adamant that he would have it, and figurewise he had made an offer Hugo simply couldn't refuse. The product had only been launched a couple of days ago and yet Leo had paid more for it than La Petite Mort, which had been up and running for three years and had terrific brand establishment. Hugo would have £50 million in the kitty – enough to pay off the twins, Olivia, the Foundation and the bank. It even sorted out the divorce settlement. He would have liked a bit more cash in hand for future product development, but all in all, with a toss up between losing a chunk of the company itself, or the three lines, even if it did involve losing Vitale, it had been worth it.

Ironically, it had been Fern's suggestion in the first place. Hugo shook his head in disbelief. That girl was really something else. God, he hated having to do this to her, but he was sure she'd understand, especially when she professed to have such a strong head for business on her shoulders. She had to see the economic sense of the move. It wasn't as if she was being fired. She was simply being contracted out. Technically she would remain very much on the staff at Oscars where she could concentrate on her product development ideas. Hugo smiled benignly to himself. She might even be pleased with the arrangement. Johnny would sort it out for him now that Hugo had explained the situation. Then maybe Hugo himself would take her out to dinner, just to make sure there were no misunderstandings or upsets. He felt a lot better already.

Fern paid the cabbie and heaved her suitcase up the steps to the flat. There was a light showing through the sitting room window. She frowned, trying to remember whether she had left it on before she left for Paris. Was it really only five days ago? It seemed like a lifetime. Her head throbbed, her body ached and she felt very low indeed. It had been one hell of a day. Shopping in Paris had sounded like a good idea when Johnny suggested she try it, but it had all been too much on top of the exhausting schedule she'd had to get through.

She fished about in her handbag for the doorkey. Once inside, she struggled with the suitcase, bumping it up every stair, cursing under her breath. By the time she got to the top she was exhausted. She hesitated for a few moments to get some strength back into her arms, and then finally she was home. She slammed the door shut gratefully behind her. There was a slightly stale smell of unlived-in-ness. The vase of lilies which Johnny had given her wilted miserably, browned around the edges of their pale transluscent petals. She picked them out of the vase and slung them in the bin, flinging the rancid-smelling water into the sink. Her stomach churned, reminding her that she had eaten nothing since breakfast, having found herself unable to touch anything on the plane on the way back. She picked out an apple from the sad-looking fruit bowl and bit into it. Then she heard noises.

She froze in the doorway, the apple poised on her mouth.

'Fern!'

She let out her breath. Paul! What in God's name

was he doing here? This was all she bloody well needed. She climbed the stairs woodenly, bracing herself for what would undoubtedly be one of Paul's scenes.

She could smell the drink from where she stood, although he was at the other side of the room, kneeling on the floor by the window. A whisky bottle stood at his side, three-quarters empty. She couldn't see a glass anywhere.

He stood up and his face was twisted into an ugly rearrangement of his features. His eyes were narrow slits from which a fierce light burned accusingly at her. His lips were a tight, thin line pressed hard across his teeth, opening and closing with no sound coming through them. He took a step towards her and then weaved sideways. Instinctively she ran towards him and caught his arm to steady him.

'Paul . . . you're blind drunk.'

Her head exploded into shards of white angry pain as his arm came up and walloped her across the face. She fell away from him.

'Bitch!' His voice was like the snarl of a hungry Rottweiler. As she fought the pain, struggling to open her eyes, tears stinging the lids, she saw his hand through the mist and once more she was thrown into a world of blood-red pain that flashed across her head, spinning her away from him, conscious only of the agonizing hardness of his hand against her soft flesh.

'No . . .' Her voice was a strangled sob. She tasted the blood in her mouth and choked. Her head was on fire. The pain was terrible.

'Dirty little bitch!' he spat, watching her roll across the floor. He picked up a newspaper and threw it to her. It landed by her nose. She blinked hard, trying to see through the blur in front of her eyes. 'You're nothing but a cheap little whore!'

'But – '

'Look at you!' he snarled. 'Thinking you're so bloody clever, poncing around with fancy designers and millionaires. Getting your face in all the papers . . .' His voice was a threatening hiss. 'How many did you sleep with, Fern? Did you have them all? All the photographers? Johnny Sharpe? Hugo bloody Rees? I just bet you did, you little whore. Well, Fern, I've got news for you . . .'

Through the pain-filled mist she caught the glint of something in Paul's hand which froze the blood in her veins. 'No!' she cried. 'Paul, no! Think what you're doing! Please . . .'

He stepped towards her and brought his face menacingly up to hers. The sourness of his breath turned her stomach. 'Now, my pretty Fern,' he whispered against her cheek.

She felt his arm lift. Her body trembled uncontrollably. She tried to push him away but he moved too quickly. She felt red-hot pain shoot through her cheek. She screamed in agony, feeling the warm flood over her skin.

Paul grabbed her hair, snapping her neck backwards. 'Just so that you don't look odd . . .' He started to laugh, a ghastly, evil, maniacal sound. She felt consciousness fade away as the cold metal blade flashed beneath her eye.

Fern heard whisperings, muted voices. Searing pain burned into her face. Tentatively she raised her hand and her fingers met an uneven surface of tight bandages. She tried to speak and then flinched with the discomfort.

'Fern?'

business of babies behind you as quickly as possible, so that you can get on with enjoying life.'

'I don't know how you can complain about it. I had a nanny from the day I was born. I hardly think I cramped your style too much.'

'Oh I know, sweetie, but one's figure! It's so much easier to get everything back into the right places before you get too old. How do you think I've managed to keep your father happy all these years.'

'By turning a blind eye to his misdemeanours, mostly. And carrying on with a few of your own.'

'Those don't mean anything. We always come back to each other. I think providing one is discreet about that sort of thing then it can't do any harm. No, the fact is that your father and I really do like each other. We have a mutual respect. Anyway, we'd better change the subject. Here they come.'

'Leo's been telling me about Paris, darling. You didn't tell us that's where you were disappearing to. How is old Hugo?'

Guy Duncan-Forrester was as dark as Antonia was fair. India had inherited his fine features and her mother's sleek figure. Guy could never be described as sleek. He liked his food too much, and abhorred any sort of exercise other than getting his leg over a frisky filly, four legged or two, depending on his mood.

He swirled his cognac around a Waterford balloon glass.

'Ladies?' Leo asked dutifully, waving the bottle in their direction.

'He seems fine, Daddy. He had Ricci Pembroke with him. Now that he and Olivia are divorcing I guess they'll be getting hitched up soon.' India acknowledged her mother's approving wink.

'Weddings are such fun,' Antonia yawned. 'We simply don't have enough of them, do we, Leo?'

243

'No, no, Antonia, probably not.' Leo was barely listening to Antonia's usual inane chatter.

'Did you see the papers tonight?' she went on. 'That poor creature who was signed up to promote Hugo's new line – what was it called? Vital or something like that – well, it was all over the press . . .'

'Yes. I did read it,' India said, irritatedly tapping a cigarette on the back of her Cartier lighter. 'Seems she had a spot of boyfriend trouble. He cut her up rather badly. I gather she won't be able to work!'

'What did you say?' Leo's attention was suddenly keenly focused.

'You know, that girl – the one Hugo's signed up for Vitale. Her boyfriend slashed her face. It's been in all the evening papers. Didn't you read it? Really, darling, you spend so much of your time wrapped up in board meetings these days I wonder you ever learn of what's going on in the world.' India twirled the cigarette between her scarlet fingertips. 'Shame. She was *such* a pretty girl, wasn't she, darling?'

Leo's mind was racing. He'd just bought the bloody line for £20 million!

'Where is she?'

'Um, the paper didn't say. Why on earth do you want to know?'

Leo rose. 'Excuse me, I've got some calls to make!'

Rowena pressed her nose against the tiny window and looked longingly at the airport building. Its bunker-like façade had never looked so attractive as now. If only she could be one of those figures standing against the window of the viewing gallery, instead of being strapped into this flimsy piece of metal fatigue about to be zoomed up into the heavens and then, hope to God, come back down again. If God had meant her to fly, he'd have given her a beak and feathers, as well as wings. She clutched the arm rests and screwed her eyes shut tight as the roar of the jet engines increased. Her lips mouthed silent Hail Marys as the beast sped along the runway, and then whoosh . . . up went the nose and she was pushed into the seat back. Something went ping over her head, but she wasn't ready to open her eyes just yet.

Nothing, but *nothing*, would have induced Rowena to get onto this bloody thing, except, that was, for Johnny Sharpe's grave summons.

She'd spoken to this Johnny Sharpe person on Seamus's telephone and the man had just garbled something about how Fern had been in a fight with Paul and now she was in hospital. Rowena had better come over. Johnny Sharpe . . . Oscar Rees . . . what the hell had Fern been up to? Rowena knew there was trouble brewing from the moment Fern had mentioned this bloody job. Nothing but bad could come of it. God only knew what had happened to her.

So here Rowena was, a mere six hours later, having deposited the goat and the cat with Paddy, and then bribed Paddy to drive her to Cork.

She was persuaded finally to open her eyes when the words safety and emergency were mentioned. Hawk-eyed, she watched as the stewardess's sleight of hand made it impossible to follow exactly how she had managed to slip herself into the life thing. Ah well, she'd just have to leave it to fate and God's will.

The flight took just over an hour and the first Rowena saw of England was a kind of concrete space station with spider-like arms sticking out of forbidding-looking boxes. There were planes and buses all over the place. Rowena hated it! The last time she had left Ireland had been five years ago when Anthony had made her put in an appearance at an exhibition he had organized for her. He had dragged her to London, New York, Paris, Stockholm and Madrid. There had been other places, too, but she had refused to consider any more than five cities. How Fern could live in a dump like this was totally beyond her. She waited obediently until the stewardess told them they could unfasten their seatbelts and make their way into the terminal building and then, still shaky, she grabbed her holdall containing her few essentials and set off.

Fern thought she must still be dreaming. Was it minutes, hours, days even, she had been lying here drifting in and out of sleep? She had been vaguely aware of different voices, people coming in and out, sticking needles in her, urging her to take pills. The pain was easing slightly, but not much. Every time she tried to move her mouth it felt like her cheeks were full of broken glass. She ran her tongue over her dry lips and opened her eyes.

Leo Eden's face swam in front of her. She screwed her eyes tight shut and opened them again, trying to rouse herself.

'Fern,' he said softly.

'It *is* you.'

'Yes.' He lifted her hand up and perched himself carefully on the edge of the bed. 'What happened?'

'I'm not sure. It's all a bit of a blur, but I think I got into a fight.'

'So I see. What did he do to you?'

A small tear welled up in Fern's eye. She blinked it away and attempted to sit up, so that she could sip some water. Leo handed her the glass and tenderly held it to her lips.

'Thanks.' She tried to smile. 'He cut me. He cut my face.'

Leo's expression darkened. He felt bitter fury pulse through his veins. His knuckles tightened. It was difficult to see her face, but the eyes which stared up at him melted his heart. She looked so vulnerable and afraid. He wanted to reach out and touch her cheek, but he dared not for fear he would hurt her.

He looked away, for a moment unable to control himself. Each time he had seen her she had been full of sparks and fight. He hadn't realized until this second what an effect she must have had on him. He felt a cold, murderous anger towards whoever could have done this to such a lovely creature. As of today, *his* lovely creature. The contracts had been signed at lunchtime. The press had feted the discovery of this lovely woman. All the fashion pages had been full of her success in Paris. He had just paid £20 million and now here she was, bandaged, scarred, ruined . . .

Only a complete madman could have done something like this. When Leo got his hands on him he'd squeeze any life left out of him.

A nurse poked her head round the door. 'It's okay, I'm a friend, not a journalist,' he called.

'You'd better be. Two more minutes,' the nurse answered sternly.

Leo had had to fight his way through the press to get near the hospital. The whole world seemed to know what had happened. The room was bursting with flowers and cards. For a moment he thought he might be physically sick. He fought back the bitter bile.

'Don't you worry, you'll soon be out of here. I'm going to make sure of that.' He lifted her fingers to his lips and brushed a light kiss over them. She nodded and turned her head away. Leo reluctantly

247

tiptoed out of the room and almost collided with Hugo. His face looked ashen.

'Leo, dear boy. Ghastly business, just ghastly. You've seen her?'

Leo nodded, for a moment not trusting his voice.

'How is she?'

'Confused, and in a lot of pain, I'd say. Where's the bastard now?'

'Locked up. He's being held at Vine Street station. I gather he's been charged with GBH. Not that that is going to help her.'

'What do the doctors say?'

'I haven't spoken to them myself, but Johnny Sharpe tells me it's too early to tell at this stage, although she has major cuts to both sides of her face.' Hugo shook his head sadly. 'Terrible. I just can't believe this. I feel so damned responsible . . .'

'Get her into the Foundation!'

'What? Oh yes, yes, I'd thought of that. I'll have a word with the doctors shortly.' Hugo sounded dazed.

'I'll speak to them now.' Leo's anger gave him strength. 'You make sure that when she's moved she has the best, the *very* best.'

Hugo turned away, muttering his agreement.

As Leo made his way to the desk, all hell broke loose at the far end of the corridor. The press were pushing through the door, flashbulbs popping like crazy.

'Will ya just sod off and let me alone!'

Leo saw a flash of copper-coloured hair. He drew in his breath sharply and focused on the woman marching towards him, who had successfully beaten off the marauding hordes.

The resemblance was uncanny. She wasn't as tall as Fern, but the hair, and the face . . . He knew immediately who it must be.

'Excuse me,' he began hesitantly, touching the woman's arm. 'But are you by any chance Fern's mother?'

'And who might you be?' she snapped, tossing her wild red hair over her shoulders and hitching up her holdall.

'Eden, Leo Eden. I'm a . . . sort of, er, friend of Fern's.'

'A *sort* of friend? I'm not sure I know what a sort of friend is. I guess the bastard that put her in here was a sort of friend.'

'Not that sort of friend. I know Fern through our work. I'm very sorry, Mrs, er . . .'

'Rowena will do. Now where is she?'

Leo directed her to the room. 'Can I get you a coffee or something?'

'A whisky would be more like it, but I don't suppose there's much hope o' that in this mortuary.' Rowena strode off. It was easy to see where Fern got her fire from.

Hugo bent low over Fern's head and whispered quietly to her. 'Darling girl, how are you?' He kissed her forehead.

'Still wondering what I'm doing here,' she said. 'I'm not sure what happened. I gather Johnny found me.'

'That's right, he came over to see you and found you in the flat. You don't remember?'

'Not really. I remember Paul . . . I remember the fight, but that's about it.' Her eyes filled with fear. 'Where is he now?'

'In custody, I believe. Best damned place for him. Several of us would like to get our hands on him.'

'My face, Hugo. What's happened to it?'

'Sssh, now. You'll soon be back in front of the cameras. You just need plenty of rest.'

Hugo heard someone come into the room. He turned round and time stopped still. He gasped. He was seeing a ghost. His mind must be playing tricks. As he stared at the woman framed in the doorway, more than twenty years slipped away. He stood up and tried to speak. Dear God, it wasn't possible. Memories flooded back. Holding her on the dockside, her hot tears stinging his cheek, her slim body pressed into his . . . He felt his knees buckle and he grabbed the end of Fern's bed for support.

'Rowena!'

'Aye, it's me, you bastard!' she hissed.

'But how . . . what . . . why are you here?'

Fern shifted on her pillows. 'Ma!' she cried. 'Oh Ma! What on earth are you doing here?'

Hugo dumbly looked from Rowena to Fern, and back to Rowena. 'I don't understand,' he whispered.

'Leave us, Hugo!' Rowena commanded. Hugo's limbs had turned to wood. He hardly dared breathe. He couldn't take his eyes off her, off either of them. He shook his head. 'Your daughter?'

'Later, Hugo.'

Rowena almost pushed him out of the room and closed the door behind him. Nothing but bloody bad, she knew it.

'Oh, Ma, it's good to see you. How did you know?'

Rowena squared herself up to facing Fern. She needed all her strength to protect her daughter. She struggled to keep her voice even.

'Johnny Sharpe got in touch with Seamus and he came to tell me. You got me on an airplane, would you believe? Now what the hell happened?'

Fern went over as much as she knew, all the while clutching tightly onto her mother's reassuring hands.

Rowena smiled, and whispered in the way she used to when Fern got sick as a child. Eventually she could see Fern's eyes begin to droop. Rowena watched as she began to drift away. Suddenly her eyes flew open.

'Hugo knew your name?'

'Sssh, darling. You get some sleep.'

'And you knew his!'

'You're dreaming. Sssh now. I'll come and see you a bit later.' Rowena tucked the sheet under Fern's bandaged chin and tiptoed out of the room.

Chapter Nineteen

Hugo leaped on her. 'Rowena, I have to talk to you.'
She carried on walking, striding out, forcing Hugo to
trot to keep up with her. 'Listen, Rowena, we must
go somewhere.'

She stopped and looked at him contemptuously. 'I
can't think you and I have anything to discuss. Just
look at you, you overstuffed shirt.' She curled her
nose into a sneer, taking in his pinstriped suit, and
his striped shirt and striped tie. 'I might have known
that's exactly what you'd turn into. No balls, of
course.'

'Rowena!' Hugo grabbed her arm. 'Please.'

'You're not going to let me alone, are you? Very
well, then, you can find me a bar and buy me a
bloody drink. God knows, I could do with one.'

Hugo tried to grab her bag but she snatched it back.
'Steady on, you can have my company but not my
clothes.'

Leo's voice followed Hugo down the corridor:
'Hugo – I need to speak to you.'

Hugo called back over his shoulder, 'Not now, Leo.
I'll find you later.' He still had to trot to keep up with
the woman.

Eventually they managed to fight their way to a
seat in a crowded Paddington pub. Hugo passed
Rowena the double Jamesons and she knocked half of
it straight back.

'That's better,' she sighed with satisfaction and
slammed the glass onto the table. 'So, you bastard,

what the hell happened to you twenty-odd years ago?'

Hugo almost choked on his gin and tonic. Nothing like getting straight to the point.

'Rowena,' he sighed morosely, 'If only you knew. If I could have explained – '

'What stopped you? All those fine fancy words about how you'd come back and marry me. How you'd be gone for a couple o' weeks and come back for me. Oh sure, wasn't I the fool for you, you weak, lily-livered, spineless little shit!'

'Steady on, Rowena. That's a bit strong.'

'Huh. Oh pardon me for sure, Mr Hugo fancypants Rees, but I do believe I've good cause for feeling a little put out about it. Ah! It's all a bloody long time ago, and looking at you now I'm that glad you never came back.'

She flicked her hair back and caught him straight in the eye. Tears sprang into it. He brushed them away.

'It's no good crying. I've a heart as cold as ice.'

'I wasn't crying. You just flicked your hair in my eye!' he protested.

'Huh! Excuses. I'd forgotten how dishonest you could be.'

Hugo downed his gin and tonic. 'When I first saw her I thought of you. The likeness . . . I should have known. Never have I seen hair like yours. And the eyes . . . God, I've been blind.'

'I bet you'd forgotten all about me. Jesus, there's plenty of us redheads from Ireland anyway.'

Hugo gazed into her face like a lovesick puppy. 'There's none like you, Rowena. Or Fern, come to that. But did you know about me? About Fern's job? Does Fern know about us?'

'There's sod all to know, Hugo. Why on earth would I go telling Fern about some pathetic little affair that happened way before she was born? I can't think she'd be that interested now, would you?'

'You knew she was working for me?'

'No, not exactly. She told me when I last saw her that she wouldn't dream of working for you. I told her that she'd be chucking her life away if she did. And I was damned right, wasn't I? None of this would have happened if it wasn't for Oscar bloody Rees and you. I'm glad you never came back, Hugo. Boy, am I glad.'

Her voice was sharp enough to attract several glances. Hugo stared down into his drink in embarrassment.

'I don't know what to say. It's . . .' he swallowed hard, 'it's my great regret in life.'

Rowena roared with laughter. 'My great regret in life!' she mocked him. 'That and parting with your teddy bear, I'll bet. You were a spoilt little brat, and you wanted it all, and you got it all too easy. You just couldn't recognize a thing of value.'

'You're wrong. Every day I've thought about you.'

'Oh, come on – '

'It's true. For the last few years maybe not quite so much, if I'm honest. Memory fades, but God, Rowena, you've been in my heart always. I know I made the wrong decision, but it wasn't really my decision.' His voice dropped to a whisper. 'I had no choice.'

'Everyone has a choice. You made a choice. You didn't come back.'

'I couldn't tell you what happened. I thought it would be kinder somehow to let you think I was the bastard you believe me to be. I thought that way you'd get angry and get over me. I knew there wasn't any hope. I knew it wasn't fair for you to maybe think there was. I thought I was doing the right thing. But, dear God, you have to believe I've paid for it. Every bloody day, I've paid, Rowena.' This time the tears were real. He wanted to take her hand, but he dared not.

'I loved you so much, and I went on loving you. When I saw you today, standing there, it was as if the years just fell away. I just wanted to gather you into my arms. I yearned for you, Rowena.'

She stared down into her empty glass, refusing to look at him. Eventually she sighed. 'I'll have the same again,' she said and pushed the glass towards him. 'They say she'll be scarred for life.' Rowena's green eyes blazed at Hugo angrily.

He nodded sullenly. 'Yes.' This time he took her hand. He was pleased that she didn't snatch it away. 'There's the Rees Foundation – you may have heard of it – it's got the best plastic surgeons in Europe. We'd like to move Fern there. She'll get the best treatment.'

'I guess you owe her that, don't you?'

He flinched, feeling the cut of her words. 'I'll make the arrangements, then. She's a lovely girl, Rowena. You should have seen her in Paris. She was magnificent. So lovely . . .'

'And look where it's got her. That boy should be hanged. I gather he's locked up.'

'Yes. They've charged him already.'

'Not that it's done Fern much good.'

Hugo stared down into his drink for several moments, then he let out a long sigh. At last, he looked back at Rowena, swallowing his emotions. He had to change the subject otherwise he might break down.

'So, tell me about you, Rowena. Have the years been kind to you?'

'Sure. I've had a wonderfully happy life. I met

255

some great people. After you left I moved away from Leitrim down to the southwest. I hardly noticed you'd gone.'

'Then I'm glad. That was as I wished.'

'You married?'

'Yes, a lesbian bitch, who I'm pleased to say I'm finally divorcing.' He glanced sideways at Rowena. 'I should never have married her in the first place.'

'That was your choice, I expect.'

'As a matter of fact it wasn't, but it's a long story. And you? What of Fern's father?'

'Just someone I knew.'

'He must have been very special.'

'I thought so once.' Rowena drained her glass. 'I've got to find Fern's flat. Johnny Sharpe gave me the key. I need to lie down. It's been a long day, Hugo.'

'Of course. Perhaps tomorrow we might meet again?'

She shrugged. 'Perhaps.'

Fern was getting used to her new surroundings at the Oscar Rees Foundation. She had a large airy room overlooking a small garden area in the centre of which stood a stone fountain gently spraying out water. The nurse bustled about the room, tidying up the magazines and prodding here and there into the masses of flowers which filled the room.

'I don't think I've ever seen so many flowers in my life. Whoever sent these must have bought up the entire florists.'

'People have been very kind,' Fern sighed, glancing at the pile of cards and messages from well-wishers. Johnny had kept bringing her newspaper cuttings about herself. Hard as she tried, Fern found it hard to believe how so many people had picked up on the story and been so incensed by Paul's actions.

Unconsciously she raised her hand to her cheek. The main bandages had been removed and now she was left with just a small square of gauze over each wound. As yet, the doctors had not allowed her to see the extent of the scarring. Instead they kept assuring her that once the swelling had gone down it would look a lot less frightening than it did at the moment. The pain wasn't so bad either. At least she could begin to smile a bit – not that there was much to smile about.

'Your boyfriend obviously thinks an awful lot about you.'

Fern frowned. What on earth was the woman talking about? It was his fault she was in here!

'He's been phoning up all day to see how you've settled in. Says we're to make sure you have everything you want. And he's booked Dr Anthony Fielding. He's the best plastic surgeon there is, dear.'

She must mean Johnny, but Fern was surprised that Johnny would have booked Dr Fielding himself. It must be on Hugo's say-so. Dear Johnny, he'd been so kind, keeping her stocks of grapes, magazines and chocolates topped up.

'Leo something, that's his name, isn't it?'

'You mean Leo Eden?'

'That's it. Tall, dark and handsome. Lucky you!'

'You say he's been ringing up?'

'Yes, at least three times today already. See that bouquet over there – the really big one – ' the nurse pointed to a basket arrangement of yellow roses which stood about four feet high – 'that's from him. He delivered them himself before you were transferred here from St Mary's. He obviously loves you a lot!'

The nurse bustled out of the room leaving Fern to sink back into the pillows, dazed and bemused. As she thought about the nurse's words a lovely warm feeling oozed over her body and she smiled, as far as she was able, to herself.

Leo's phone wouldn't stop ringing. Every time he got up from his desk the bloody thing trilled. He was thinking of just walking out on it, but he knew he'd have to sort out Lowenstein and at some stage he'd have to deal with the Easton twins. 'Yes,' he barked into it. Nicky, his PA's, nervous voice informed him that Bob Lowenstein was on the line and was insistent Leo speak to him.

'Bob!' Leo's voice shouted cheerfully into the mouthpiece.

'Leo. What's going on over there? I just got your fax. I've been out of the office for a couple of days. Are you telling me you've actually *bought* La Petite Mort, Bijou *and* Vitale?'

'Sure. For just $80 million, Bob.' Leo heard the breath whistle through Bob's beautifully capped teeth.

'But I thought we were going for the company.'

'*Were* going for the company, Bob, but it wasn't up for grabs in the way we thought. This way we can cream off the profits straight away. Those lines are worth a mint.'

'I hear there's a problem with Vitale!'

'Problem?' Leo hedged.

'Sure. I hear the little lady fronting it got into an accident. Did you buy her as well, Leo?'

'She was part of the deal, but she's going to be okay, Bob. I've got the best plastic surgeons on to it. Have you any idea how much publicity this is creating? This girl is becoming a national celebrity.'

'She won't be much good at advertising cosmetics – '

'I wouldn't be too sure.' For some reason Leo was getting very irritated with Bob's pessimism. 'They can perform miracles these days. Whatever, all this will work in our favour.'

'I hope you're right, Leo. I hope you haven't just spent almost $100 million on a turkey.'

'I've got to go, Bob.' Leo slammed the receiver back into its cradle and shuddered.

'What do you mean you didn't get anywhere with him?' Lucienne screeched at her twin. 'He sold you out. You and he agreed that when the shares were sold both you and I would have a job at Coopers. He *can't* go back on it. He agreed!'

Alexander helped himself to another brandy from Lucienne's drinks cabinet and stared morosely into its depths. 'What the hell do you think we can do about it? We had no contract with Coopers. It was a gentleman's agreement.'

'Gentleman!' Lucienne spat. 'That's a bloody joke. Eden's clearly no gentleman. And just where does he think that leaves you and me?'

'I need time to think,' Alexander snapped wearily. 'I need to plan.'

'Didn't you insist, Alexander?'

'Look, Lucienne, we're not playing little games here where you can just bully your way into getting exactly what you want. I can't *make* Leo Eden employ us. Before we had something to bargain with, and that was the potential sale of the lion's share of Oscar Rees, including our own shares. Now Hugo's gone and sold off the lines, it means that there's more money in the company, our individual share-holding's gone up, but if Hugo wanted to, he could buy us out. Now we could sell out, or we could stay, and it might just suit us to hang on a bit longer.'

259

'What about Moscow?'

'Moscow's almost up and running. There's no reason why I couldn't use Oscar's resources instead of Coopers', now, is there? Nobody need know what we're up to in our own quiet way. Perhaps we might even set up a clinic at the Foundation for extra special treatments.

'And now, my little twin,' Alexander said as he stroked Lucienne's cheek soothingly, 'are you going to be my guinea pig?'

'Oh, Xan,' she sighed as her mind started to relax. 'Whatever would I do without you?'

'Don't you worry about anything. With our combined talents neither Hugo nor Leo Eden can stop us doing anything we want. You wait and see!'

Chapter Twenty

Rowena slammed the front door behind her and peered down the street, trying to remember how one went about hailing a taxi. She turned left towards where, in the distance, she could hear the main buzz of traffic, and strode purposefully forward. She had only gone a few yards when she became conscious of a huge grey shiny car crawling along the kerb beside her. She pushed her chin further towards her chest and kept on walking. She'd heard about this sort of thing going on. Either she was going to be offered business, or she was going to be held at knifepoint and raped. She decided if she ignored them they might just go away. The car came to a stop and she heard footsteps walk quickly behind her.

'Rowena!'

She turned. 'Hugo! You frightened me half to death. What were you doing creeping up on me like that?'

'I have to talk to you.'

'That's what you said yesterday.'

'This is really important. Come on, get in the car.'

Rowena peered into the comfort of the Bentley's interior, and then at the long walk ahead of her through the filthy streets into the middle of God only knew where, and she needed no second persuasion. She settled back into the corner, clutching a carrier bag full of apples and oranges and a bottle of Jamesons.

Hugo waved a piece of paper in front of her.

'What's that?' she cried, pushing his hand away from under her nose.

'Fern's contract.'

'So why are you pushing it under my nose, Hugo?'

'Look at her date of birth, Rowena.'

'I know what her date of birth is, Hugo.'

'Precisely eight and a half months after I left Ireland.' Hugo watched Rowena's face blanch.

'So.' She held her breath. 'What are you saying, Hugo?'

'Isn't it obvious?'

'I don't know what you mean.'

'She's mine, isn't she?'

Rowena shrieked. 'Yours! Don't be a fool, Hugo. Fern is *nothing* to do with you. You flatter yourself.'

Hugo clutched her arm and brought his face to within nine inches of Rowena's. She shrank away, into the depths of the seat. 'You seriously expect me to believe you had someone else?'

'Why should that be so incredible?'

'Because you loved me!'

'Huh. You arrogant . . . you . . . Of course I had someone else.'

'What was his name, then.'

'Er, Michael. And anyway, it's none of your damned business.' Rowena bit her lip and stared into her lap.

Hugo spoke gently. 'I wanted a child so much, Rowena. Why didn't you tell me?'

'Because you never came back.'

'I would have done. You know I would, if only I'd known.'

'I wanted you to come back because you loved me, not because I was pregnant. I wanted you to want me. And you didn't. Why should I have told you? Because *I* wasn't enough?'

Hugo shook his head sadly. 'What a mess. What a bloody mess.' He reached out and put his arm around Rowena's slim shoulders and drew her small frame against him. He felt the resistance soften. 'When I left,' his voice was low and hesitant, 'I left to break the news to my parents that we were to marry. Rowena, I was so full of joy and happiness, I just couldn't wait to tell them. I thought I'd come back for you and take you home to meet them, and it would all just fall into place – the romantic dream I had of you and I living happily ever after. I was naïve and stupid. I hadn't bargained for their grand plans. It seemed they had my whole life planned for me. Cambridge and then the family business. Oh, and marriage to Olivia, the daughter of my father's partner. They were furious. My father told me that he would disinherit me if I had anything more to do with you.'

'So you chose money!' Rowena choked on her contempt.

'No. It wasn't as simple as that. I was quite prepared to be disinherited. Believe it or not, you were far more important to me.'

'So what happened?'

'My mother told me that she had breast cancer. I hadn't known about it before, but apparently it was quite advanced. My father said that if I caused her stress then she would give up the will to live. He started to blame me for her illness. The next couple of weeks were a living hell. My mother took to her bed and complained of the pain she was in. My father hardly spoke to me and it just seemed that I was responsible. I began to believe them. Oh, now I can look back and see that what happened would have happened anyway, but then it was the hardest form of emotional blackmail. But in the end I made her a promise that I would marry Olivia. Two months later she was dead. What could I do?'

Rowena kept her head turned away.

'I couldn't tell you,' Hugo continued. 'I don't know why. Maybe, as I said yesterday, I thought it would be less cruel if you thought I'd just gone off and dumped you. I knew there was no hope for us.'

'Poor Hugo,' she said softly and squeezed his hand.

'Huh!' he grunted. 'Poor weak and pathetic Hugo. I could have stood up to them. Instead I let them ruin my life.' He sighed heavily and swallowed, trying to ease the hard lump in his throat. 'It must have been worse for you.'

'Sure it was hard, but I survived.'

'What happened?'

'I waited, of course, for a letter or something. Then when I realized I wasn't going to hear from you again I ran away from home. I didn't think I had any choice. Barely seventeen, a good Catholic girl, uncle a priest . . . Can you imagine the shame I'd have brought on the family?' She spoke unemotionally, as if it were someone else's story. 'So I joined the hippies, lived on a commune for a while, started to paint, sold a bit here and there. It was hard, but it was all right.'

'If only I'd known.'

'Maybe it's as well things turned out as they did. I could never have stuck your sort of life. Nor you mine.'

'I don't know. I think I could have easily taken up yours. Oscars has been my duty for so long now. It was all I had, my hair shirt, if you like. But to have a child, Rowena. You can't know how miraculous this seems . . . All these years and I didn't know. Fern. My daughter.'

264

'So now I suppose you'll be wanting to rush in like a bull at a gate and tell her all about it,' Rowena snapped, forcing him back to reality.

'Well . . . I, er, hadn't really thought much about it, Rowena. It's all such a shock.'

'I forbid you to, Hugo. She's had enough trauma these past few days. It won't help her.'

'You can't know that.'

'I know me own daughter and I know the shock won't do her any good. Wait, Hugo, until she's stronger.'

'Do you have any idea what you're asking?'

'As much idea as you have of what you're thinking. You'll listen to me and wait. I want your word.'

Hugo stared out of the window. The only thing he wanted to do right now was rush into Fern's room and sweep her up in his arms. He ached to hold his child.

'Very well. I'll wait a little. But not forever, Rowena!'

Dr Fielding's face was so close to hers that Fern could feel his warm breath against her cheek. He carefully examined the knife wounds, running his magnifying torch close to her flesh. He worked silently, deep in concentration.

After what seemed like many minutes, he sat down on the edge of the bed and smiled gently. 'I'm afraid these cuts aren't going to disappear overnight.'

Fern swallowed hard and bit on her lower lip. Her huge green eyes betrayed the fear she was suffering as she stared at the doctor. For several days she had been able to avoid looking at her face, but now she didn't know which was worse – living with her imagination or facing up to the reality. There was only one way to settle things and she knew she had to face up to it soon. It might as well be now. She took a deep breath. 'May I see them?'

Dr Fielding squeezed her hand and nodded once, silently, as if he could understand the enormity of the decision she had come to. He smiled at her reassuringly. 'Sure,' he said eventually. 'Nurse, bring Fern a mirror, would you, please?'

Fern's stomach tightened with anxiety. She knew she had to steel herself to face up to the damage, but as the nurse disappeared, suddenly she didn't know if she'd be able to handle it.

'I never used to be at all vain,' she tried to joke weakly to the doctor. 'Funny, but now I feel absolutely petrified at what I'll see.'

'Look, Fern, it's not going to be easy for you, but just remember that what you see now is bruising and traumatized tissue. I can achieve an awful lot with today's surgical techniques. As I said, it won't happen overnight. I think we'll have to whip you into the operating theatre more than once, but eventually you'll barely see any scarring at all.'

'Good job I wasn't really cut out to be a cover girl, then.'

'You'll be on the front of *Vogue* by the time I've finished with you.'

The nurse reappeared clutching a small hand mirror. She looked at the doctor uncertainly.

'Here, let me,' he said, handing it to Fern. He took hold of her other hand. Fern gasped. Her features were swollen out of all proportion. The bruising had crept under both her eyes, where it had turned an ugly shade of purple, edged with yellow. The worst cut was on her left cheek where the swelling seemed to pull her nose to one side. On the other cheek, a smaller welt of black crept vertically up to her eye. She touched the wounds gingerly, and a huge sob broke from her lungs. She tossed the mirror on to the bed.

'I look horrible. Ugly and frightening.'

'The bruising will be gone in a week. You'll be amazed at how much better you will look.'

'Oh God,' the tears flooded down her cheeks. 'I'm sorry, but it just seems so awful.' She blew her nose on the tissue the nurse had thrust into her hand. 'I hadn't realized how bad it was.'

'Now you're going to have to be a brave girl and listen to me. Because the cuts were made by a knife, they are in a very thin line. St Mary's did a very good job of sealing the wounds with butterfly stitching. You will be left with two small red lines and I can get rid of those for you. You are seeing it at its very worst.'

'I don't know how anyone can bear to look at me.' She blew her nose again.

'Sssh,' the doctor said gently. 'I want you to trust me. You're in the very best place.'

'And Dr Fielding's the very best,' the nurse added softly.

'I know. You're all being so kind to me. But why did he do it to me? He must really hate me.'

'The police want to have a word with you as soon as you feel up to it, Fern. Can I ask them to come in later? I imagine you'll want to tell them all about what happened.'

'I guess. I feel very confused about everything. I don't know what I expected . . . I knew what he'd done, I mean I could feel it, but I suppose I wasn't really prepared to . . . you know . . . to see it. I didn't think it would be that terrible. Now that the pain doesn't seem so bad, maybe I thought it wouldn't be that awful.'

'It's only natural that you should feel confused.

267

You've had a huge shock. I think you've been incredibly brave so far. Now you and I are going to become very good friends, Fern, and you're going to trust in me, and my skills, and together we're going to show the world that you're just as beautiful as you ever were.'

'It's funny, but I kind of took my face for granted. Well, you do, don't you? Every day, you wake up, go to the bathroom and there it is, staring back at you, same old face. You expect to see it looking just the same, day in, day out. I was used to the way it looked and now I just don't feel like me any more. I know you must get a lot worse cases in here and I'm not being terribly brave at the moment. I guess I'll get used to it. It could have been a lot worse, like I could have lost my eye or something. Or he could have murdered me. In fact, when you think about it, I was quite lucky . . .'
She broke off as the tears welled again.

'That's it, lovey,' the nurse said, shooing Dr Fielding out of the way. 'It's about time you let it all out. You've been brave for too long. Come on, now, that's it. You have a good cry . . .'

Dr Fielding nodded to the nurse and stepped towards the door. 'I'll pop back and see you later, Fern. Remember what I told you.'

'I suppose I look even worse now.' Fern tried to smile as she got through her sixth tissue. 'God, what a sight I must be. If I have any visitors you'd better tell them I'm indisposed. I don't want anyone to see me like this!'

'There's a whole world out there wishing you well. You were on every news bulletin for two days running, and you've made all the national papers, did you know that, Fern? You're a national celebrity. And as for that man . . . there's a mob wanting to lynch him.'

'What a way to achieve notoriety! I wonder what'll happen to him.'

'I hope he'll be put away for a very long time.'

'I don't know what I hope. Sometimes I almost wish I could do the same to him, so that he'd *know* what he's put me through! Then I think that by feeling that I'm just as bad as he is. I suppose he should go to prison but the thought doesn't give me much satisfaction and it won't change anything. I just wish I could wake up and find that all this has been some terrible nightmare.' She laid her head back on the pillow and turned away from the nurse. 'I think I'd like to rest now,' she murmured, trying to stem the tears of self-pity which threatened to engulf her once more.

'Dr Fielding!' Leo chased down the corridor after the doctor. 'Dr Fielding, can I just have a quick word?'

'Mr Eden. Yes, of course. I expect you want to know how our young patient is.'

'Yes, yes, that's right.'

'She's a little upset at the moment. She's just seen the damage for herself. As is normal practice in these sort of cases, we kept her away from mirrors for the first few days. It's always very difficult, and especially for a young lady whose face quite literally was her fortune.'

'And?'

'And what?'

'Her face? What about her face?'

'Well, it will take time. A long time. I can't possibly operate until the scar tissue settles down, and that could take quite a few months, depending on how quickly she heals, of course. After that, well, I shall have to perform skin grafts and so on, and it all depends again on how readily we can match the skin on her face. I intend to try to "grow" some skin from existing cells, but as you will appreciate, Mr Eden, the technique is relatively new and it all takes time and patience.'

'But what about the success?'

'She'll always have some scarring there, although I would hope that it would barely be visible to the naked eye, and particularly as she is so young. You see, the skin is extraordinarily elastic at this age which makes life much easier for us. If she were say ten years older, then the success of such invisible mending would be that much less.'

'Will she model again?' Leo persisted.

'I really couldn't say, Mr Eden. We'll just have to wait and see. In the meantime I'm afraid I would have to advise Miss Donleavy to earn her money in some other way. I hope she took out some form of insurance. I understand that is the norm.'

'Thanks, doctor.'

Leo stomped back down the corridor. That was not what he wanted to hear. Yes, he knew damn well Fern's face was insured. She'd be able to claim her contract money, and he'd be able to claim for any damage suffered by Cooper Jefferson for buying what Bob Lowenstein had so succinctly called a bloody turkey.

He walked past Fern's room and peered in through the open doorway. She appeared to be sleeping. He walked on and then, on impulse, doubled back on himself. He stood in the doorway for a few moments, watching the rhythmic rise and fall of the sheet across her chest. He tiptoed over to the bedside and stood looking down at her. Her loose hair covered the pillow in thick strands of deep amber silk. Her smooth brow looked untroubled; relaxed and at peace. Then his eyes travelled down to the ugly swelling. He forced his eyes away from it and instead concentrated on the soft, velvety pink pillows of her lips. Sighing heavily he turned away and walked slowly out of the room.

Fern's slippered feet padded down the airy corridor. It felt so good to be out of her room and able to stretch her legs properly. Hardly any sounds drifted from under the row of closed doors and she seemed to be the only person about. Eventually the corridor opened out into the magnificent entrance hall. She stopped to have a good look around, taking in the mahogany panelling, the huge chandelier glittering over her head, the fine ormolu-framed mirror. It all smacked of money, loads of it!

'Impressive, isn't it?'

Fern jumped and turned round. 'You startled me.'

The fair-haired man smiled, and she found herself smiling back into his friendly, open face.

'I'm Edward Hunter, the Foundation's administrator. I know exactly who you are. In fact, I was just on my way to meet you. I wondered if you'd like a tour of the place. I'm sure it must get very boring cooped up in your room, though we do try to make it as comfortable as possible.'

'More than comfortable. I've been so well looked after, but I must admit I felt like some exercise. I'd very much like to see the Foundation. If you're sure . . .'

'Of course. It would be a pleasure.' She followed him into a small lift, self-consciously tightening her robe around her. They stopped at the third floor. 'We don't have wards as such, but a small number of individual rooms in various parts of the Foundation. Our three consultants specialize in slightly different fields, so we tend to have our burns together, and our cuts together and so on.'

'How many patients can you fit in at once?'

'Up to twenty. That's quite a lot for a clinic like ours. They're not all full at the moment, which is a shame because we have scores of people on our waiting lists hoping to be given the opportunity of treatment here. It's such a long process, you see. Facial reconstruction can't happen overnight, as I'm sure you know. Mostly patients will return for a series of operations. There's only a certain amount that can be done at any one time.' He paused outside one of the rooms. 'Perhaps you might like to meet one of our other patients?'

Fern nodded. 'Please.'

'You might find it a little distressing.'

She steeled herself and followed Edward through the doorway. A little figure lay on the bed. Fern tiptoed towards it, at Edward's invitation. The small bundle was almost entirely swathed in bandages. Fern's eyes softened with concern. The head turned at the sound and a pair of eyes flew opened, startled. They stared at Fern, and the small gap where a mouth lay partly concealed below the gauze moved soundlessly.

Edward peered over Fern's shoulder. 'Hello, Lucy.' His voice was full of warmth. 'How are you today, sweetheart?'

Fern's heart pounded as she watched the pair of frightened eyes crinkle into an answering smile.

'Lucy's feeling a bit sore. She only had her op a couple of days ago. Lucy, this is Fern. She's come to say hello.'

'Hello, Lucy.' Fern smiled into the wary grey eyes. 'I hope you get out of here really soon. I'm staying on the ground floor and if you like I'll pop in and

272

see you again.' Lucy nodded. 'How old are you, Lucy?'

'She's seven – and a half,' Edward added, grinning at Lucy. 'We mustn't forget the important half, must we, Lucy?' Lucy blinked her agreement. 'I'll see you later, darling.' Edward smiled at her affectionately. Fern waved goodbye.

'What on earth happened to her?'

'House fire. Her mother left Lucy and her baby brother at home alone most nights, it seems. They had a gas fire and the baby crawled into it. Lucy tried to put the flames out. It was too late for her brother.'

'Oh my God!' Fern cried, her eyes filling with tears. 'How horrendous. That poor child. How on earth did Lucy escape, then?'

'Luckily a neighbour heard the screams through the thin walls of the flat and was quick-thinking enough to throw himself on top of Lucy. He was a real hero. Saved her life. The local hospital referred her here for remedial surgery.'

'Will she be all right?'

'Well, put it this way, she'll never be a cover girl.'

Fern felt as though she was going to throw up. She shook her head sadly and sniffed. 'It rather puts things into perspective,' she said after a lengthy pause.

'Doesn't it? I guess that's why the two old grandees decided to do something worthwhile and set this place up. It'll be a shame if it has to close down.'

'What do you mean?' she asked sharply.

'According to the accountants we're desperately short of cash. We haven't been able to open the new wing properly. We need a huge cash injection immediately, and we need some proper management on the board of governors. I suppose what would probably happen is that in the future, treatment will only be available to those who can pay – people like you, Fern, not the little Lucys of this world.'

'But that's terrible!' she cried.

'Don't I know it. Come on, I'll take you back to your room. They'll be wondering where you've got to.'

Chapter Twenty-one

❦❦❦❦❦

'So home tomorrow, Fern? I bet you can't wait.'

'No, I guess not.'

Ricci sensed the uncertainty in Fern's voice. 'Aren't you excited about it? It's been nearly a week since they moved you in here. I would have thought you'd be desperate to get back, sweetie.'

'Oh, I am!' Fern exclaimed. 'It's just that I feel so cocooned in here. It's not like the real world. People coming in to see me all the time, lots of lovely flowers and messages, it's all been a bit surreal. I guess once I get out of here I'll have to face up to reality. I still feel a bit shaky over the whole business with Paul. Something like that makes you realize just how vulnerable you really are. I don't think I ever felt afraid before. I always knew I could look after myself – *thought* I could look after myself . . .' Her voice tailed off and she stared miserably down at her hands.

'Well, he's safely locked away now. He won't come near you again.'

'I know. They want me to go down and give them a full statement as soon as I'm ready. I hear they decided against giving him bail.'

'Perhaps they think he's too dangerous, Fern.'

'He was just in a jealous, drunken rage. I don't believe he'd do it again.'

'Fern! You'd be being irresponsible if you let him get off. He will do it again. Perhaps not to you, but maybe to some other poor creature in the future. He's ruined your career, for goodness' sake.' Ricci bit her lip, wondering if perhaps she'd gone too far. 'I mean – '

'It's all right, Ricci. Remember, I never really wanted to be a model in the first place. I'd much rather learn the business if I am going to work in cosmetics. I guess now the Vitale thing is over I could go back to journalism. I've got a few things to think about once I get out of here.'

Ricci patted her hand reassuringly. 'The important thing is not to rush, sweetie. You look after yourself, first of all. Don't you go worrying about Hugo, or Leo, or any of that business.' Ricci caught the light which suddenly illuminated Fern's eyes.

'Leo came in to see me quite a bit, I gather.'

'Yes. That was nice of him, wasn't it?' Ricci tried to keep the note of cynicism out of her voice.

'I can't think why. After all, I've only met him a few times. But the nurses told me he was insistent that I had absolutely the best treatment. I must see him, to thank him.'

'No rush, Fern. Leo will understand.'

'How well do you know him, Ricci?'

'Quite well. Of course, I've known India and her family for longer. She and Leo seem to have been together for an absolute age.'

'Oh.' Fern couldn't hide the note of dejection in her voice. 'It's serious then?'

'No one knows with those two. It's been quite an extraordinary relationship over the years. Each has periodically gone their own way but they always seem to get back together. I really don't know why India puts up with Leo. Naturally he's used to having his pick of women and he has a tendency to *take* his pick. India seems to just turn a blind eye. Personally I think it's because she's desperate to marry him. He is quite a catch, but I couldn't put up with the womanizing.'

Fern felt unutterably low. It was all so confusing. When she'd first learned that Leo was visiting her she'd felt surprisingly pleased by the fact – even excited. Despite his worldliness, which at times bordered on the arrogant, there was something unavoidably attractive about him. Perhaps it was to do with his self-confidence, and that aura of power that he exuded. It was something she had never encountered in the past. Leo was so much older than any of her previous boyfriends. Like Johnny – who was far more like her type of man. He'd called in to see her every day without fail and he was such easy company, making her laugh despite all her problems. But since that night in his flat he had been more like a brother to her. Whilst he'd peck her on the cheek and give her hand a reassuring squeeze every now and then, he hadn't even attempted to kiss her again. Anyway, she was stupid to think that either of them would be interested in her now, after what Paul had done to her.

'In other words any sane woman would avoid Leo like the plague.' She tried not to let Ricci see how disappointed she felt.

'Oh, sweetie, I do hope you aren't falling for him. I'd hate anyone I was fond of to get involved with Leo. It only ever ends in hurt and you really don't deserve any more upset in your life, darling. And Hugo must have told you about the deal he did with Leo.'

'No, what deal?'

'Well, I understood it was partly your idea, you clever girl. Hugo arranged to sell Leo some of the lines, in order to save the company.'

'So what happened?'

'You mean nobody's told you about Vitale? I can't believe they wouldn't . . .' Ricci bit her lip. Now she'd really gone and put her foot well and truly in it. 'Leo bought Vitale,' she said quietly, watching Fern's face like a hawk.

'No! Hugo wouldn't do that!'

'I think Leo put him in a position where he couldn't avoid it. He made him a very big offer.'

'Hugo sold me out!'

'I'm not sure of the details, but I think it was along the lines of you still being employed by Oscar Rees, but being contracted out to Cooper Jefferson for Vitale's promotion as and when necessary. To be frank, Fern, I've hardly seen Hugo at all for the past few days. He seems to have been rather tied up elsewhere . . . doing what I have absolutely no idea. But, Fern, there's no need to be upset about it, because you won't have to work for them at all now.'

'Won't I? Isn't it amazing how much better informed everyone else seems to be than I am? I mean, it's only my future we're talking about here. Why the hell didn't Hugo tell me? And Johnny! He must have known about it, too!'

'I imagine it's because neither of them wanted to upset you while you were in hospital.'

'But Hugo made the decision – about Vitale – without talking to me about it.'

'Fern,' Ricci gazed at her steadily, 'Hugo is a shrewd businessman. He had to save the company. He may be fond of you, but you were part of a commodity which helped save the company. I don't suppose he thought it would make much difference to you . . .'

'Leo!' Fern cried. 'That's why he's been so damned interested. Because I was a bloody commodity. No wonder he's been demanding the best care in the world. No wonder he's been creeping in and out every day to see how I am. He wants to know

278

whether his investment is all right. And to think I thought – '

'I'm sure it's not that at all.' Ricci tried to pacify her.

'Oh, Ricci, I'm not completely stupid. I was beginning to think he was actually concerned about me, and I was feeling *grateful* to him. All he was interested in was his bloody deal. What a filthy business this is, Ricci. People, as you say, are commodities, to be bought and sold at whim. Just wait till I see Hugo.'

'Rowena, I'd like you to meet David Llewellyn. David, this is Rowena Donleavy, Fern's mother. David is my lawyer, Rowena, and we have to talk to you about Fern. There have been some important developments which both David and I feel you should know about.'

Rowena was still wondering how she had allowed herself to be dragged along to the Connaught, at Hugo's insistence, for what he termed a 'business lunch'. The sooner she could get Fern sorted out, and herself back to the cottage, the better. She set aside the enormous menu.

'So you've told David about Fern?' she cried accusingly.

'When you hear what David's got to say, you'll realize it was imperative. And the sooner we tell Fern, the better. There are wider implications here, Rowena.'

'More trouble, you mean, knowing you lot.'

David coughed, trying to hide his embarrassment. 'Fern's grandfather, Oscar Rees, made it clear in his will that if there were any surviving children of Hugo's upon his death, then such children would be entitled to inherit ten per cent of shares in the company. Those shares are currently worth £10 million, Mrs Donleavy.'

Rowena picked up her glass and knocked back its contents in one gulp. 'So what are you saying?'

'It's all rather complicated, Rowena,' Hugo interrupted. 'But because I didn't know I had a child, Fern's inheritance passed to the Rees Foundation, according to the terms of my father's will. It seems that the Foundation are now wishing to sell their shareholding, which is actually mostly Fern's, and if the Foundation do sell that shareholding in the immediate future, it will be difficult for Fern to claim back the shares.'

'She would be entitled to some compensation, of course,' David added, 'but once the shares passed to a third party, she would lose her entitlement to them.'

'I'm afraid I haven't a clue what you're talking about,' Rowena muttered. 'Shares, inheritances, claims and whatnot. It's all nonsense to me.'

'In simple terms, Rowena, if Fern doesn't acknowledge her legal right to shares currently being held by the Foundation, and the Foundation sells those shares, she will lose them.'

'So you're telling me Fern's an heiress.'

'That's right. She should be worth around about £10 million.'

'Holy Mary . . .' Rowena held her glass out for a refill.

'I had a meeting with all the shareholders this morning. Loosely, Oscar Rees is owned by myself, my wife, her brother, her brother's two children, the bank, and the Foundation. Because of recent, shall we say, problems, certain members of the family have announced their desire to cash in their holding. Now it may be that due to the recent sale of some of Oscar Rees's assets I will be able to buy in those shares myself, or persuade the investors that they would be better served by receiving a payout from the profits of the sale of assets. But in the meantime, in order to clarify the situation so far as everyone is concerned, we must advise Fern of her position.'

'So what you're saying is that you want my permission to tell Fern about you?'

'Precisely. Otherwise Fern might suffer a considerable loss.'

'As if the money would do her any good!'

'Bearing in mind her current situation and the unfortunate, er, accident, I would have thought the money couldn't fail to benefit her.'

Rowena looked at the pair of them thoughtfully – Hugo, lean-featured and drawn-looking, impeccable in his dark business suit; David, ultra-confident, oozing smoothness and money. It all seemed so alien to her, seated amidst a sea of gleaming white tablecloths, and sparkling silver, listening to the well-mannered hum of polished conversation. Was she really here? Hearing all this? The man sitting opposite her – Fern's father? And Fern an heiress?

Suddenly Rowena felt exhausted by the whole thing. It was so beyond her. She'd been swept up on some tidal wave of millionaire corporations and million-pound deals of which she had no comprehension. She couldn't swim against it. She simply wasn't equipped with either strength or skills. She'd known from the minute Fern told her about the Oscar Rees job that she would eventually be beaten by it, despite all the struggles of her life to raise her daughter properly, with real values and a healthy disrespect for materialism. But Fern was Hugo's daughter, too. Rowena had had Fern all to herself for twenty-odd years. Now perhaps it was time to set her free, let her find her true self. This was Fern's world and Rowena had no right to deny her daughter her destiny any longer.

'Very well,' she said finally. 'But we'll break it to her together.'

Chapter Twenty-two

Ricci switched on the nine o'clock news. Every day there'd been some comment on Fern's situation and Ricci wanted to catch up on whether there was any news on her discharge. Poor dear girl. Ricci had grown terribly fond of her in spite of the fact that Hugo appeared to be so totally besotted with her. What with his visits to the hospital, and all his commitments with the company, she'd only managed to catch him on the telephone, and even then only for what amounted to a brief couple of words. In true Hugo fashion he had promised to call her back. To date he clearly hadn't made the time. Paris had seemed so promising, too. Once he had made the decision to divorce Olivia, Ricci had been nursing secret hopes that maybe he might feel finally able to commit himself. Of course, she'd never pushed him. As ever she must just be patient and wait and see.

'And finally,' the newscaster was saying, 'good news today on Fern Donleavy, the model who has been recovering from the vicious attack by her former boyfriend.' The cameras zoomed in on the front of the Foundation. Ricci saw Fern, accompanied by her mother, whom Ricci had previously seen on the news bulletins, and Hugo! The camera closed up on Fern's face. The dressings had been removed and the scars were clear to see. In spite of everything, Fern was smiling broadly. Ricci smiled too.

'Dramatic news today,' the voice continued, 're-vealed that Fern Donleavy is the daughter of cosmetics magnate Hugo Rees. The story is yet to be confirmed, but sources close to the family tell us that it was only a few days ago that Mr Rees became aware of the existence of his daughter upon the meeting of Mrs Donleavy, from whom he had been estranged since 1971. We understand that Fern has only just been told of this dramatic turn of events.'

'What do you think of your new father?' The microphone was thrust into Fern's face.

'I . . . er . . . haven't had chance to think it through,' Fern smiled weakly.

'So, Mr Rees, you really had no idea of the true identity of Fern?'

'None whatsoever.' Hugo clutched the arm of Rowena and squeezed her close to him. 'Thanks to this wonderful lady I have the gift of a daughter. Now if you'll excuse us, I wish to spend time with my family.'

The three of them pushed their way through the crowds of reporters and climbed into the Bentley.

Ricci sat staring sightlessly at the screen. She felt a sharp stab like a knife wound in her gut. How could this be? It must be some sort of mistake, some publicity stunt that Hugo was trying to pull off. And the way he was looking at that woman – Fern's mother . . . Ricci picked up the phone and punched out Hugo's number.

'Hugo,' she breathed, 'is it true?'

'Ricci darling,' he cooed back at her, 'isn't it the most marvellous news? I'm so thrilled. Can't stop now, darling, I'm just having supper with Rowena and Fern. I'll call you tomorrow.'

Ricci threw the receiver back into its cradle and curled up into the sofa, hugging her knees tightly to her chest. Was she forever destined to take a back seat in Hugo's life? It all seemed so desperately unfair.

'I was actually going to bite your head off when you came in to see me today,' said Fern.

'Because of Vitale? Well, it was your idea.'

'Not to sell Vitale. I didn't mean you to sell *me* to Leo Eden.'

'Well,' Hugo beamed at her over the rim of his brandy glass, 'it's all turned out rather well. You don't have to work for him.'

'It's a bit of a rash way of getting out of a job.'

'The doctor says the scarring will disappear, Fern. He assured me of that.'

'I know. God, I feel exhausted by it all. I still can't believe what you and Rowena told me. It just seems so bizarre that you and she . . . that you . . . you know. You're both so different.'

'We weren't in those days. If it hadn't been for my parents I could very easily have gone off and lived Rowena's life in the wilds of Ireland. I was tempted. And I was deeply in love with your mother.'

'But you left her.'

'Rowena told you the story, didn't she?'

'She said you were blackmailed into staying here. I guess only you knew whether you were making the right decision or not. No one can really imagine what it must have been like.'

'How right you are. And it was a living hell. Come on, Fern, no one can accuse me of wanting to live with Olivia, for God's sake. We barely consummated our marriage. I've lived like a monk for years until Ricci and I . . . oh, there were a few others in between but I never forgot your mother. That day when I first saw you at the ball – it was like seeing her standing in front of me. But it never occurred to me that there was a connection. I thought it was just a coincidence, a strange quirk of memory, the light playing tricks. But it brought the pain back to me as if it were yesterday. She's still just as I remember her, wild and beautiful.'

'You're still in love with her?' Fern whispered, watching the expression on Hugo's face.

'What? I . . . er . . . don't know,' he flustered. 'I hadn't really thought about it.'

'She chews men up and spits them out for breakfast,' Fern warned. 'As a race I think she'd probably prefer to have them put down.'

'I gathered that,' Hugo laughed. 'Listen, isn't it fortunate that Olivia's moved out? I'm so glad you agreed to come and stay for a while.'

'It feels really weird, all this grandeur, Thomas and Nancy waiting on us. It's all so odd. But I didn't want to return to the flat by myself, and Rowena insists on going home tomorrow. Besides, I suppose we really ought to try and get to know each other.' Fern kicked off her shoes and tucked her feet underneath her bottom, settling into the corner of the rather cold leather chesterfield sofa. She yawned conspicuously. 'I shall have to go to bed. I'm not used to being awake all day. Isn't this library magnificent?' She stared around the room at the thousands of books lining the walls from floor to ceiling.

'Indeed. I was afraid I would have lost it with Olivia's divorce demands.'

'But you haven't.'

'Thanks to the sale of Vitale and the other lines, I can afford to pay Olivia off, at least I think I can. That's if she's prepared to show an ounce of reasonableness. I've got a big meeting with them all tomorrow. In fact, Fern, I'd like you to come if you feel up to it.'

'Won't they think it a bit odd if I'm there?'

'I really couldn't care less if they do. They're going to have to get used to it, aren't they?'

Fern clutched Rowena's hand as Thomas sped them down the M4 towards the airport. 'Are you sure you'll be all right, Ma? I know how much you hate flying.'

'I'll be fine. Don't you worry about me. It's you that needs the looking after right now.' Her eyes travelled with a maternal hunger over her daughter's face. 'Promise me something, darling.'

'Of course.'

'Don't let them corrupt you. I'd hate you to turn into one of those empty-headed bimbles, or whatever you call them.'

'Bimbos, and I won't. How could I with a mother like you? I've got all my values from you. No one's going to take that away from me, or from you, Rowena.'

'I guess you're right. You're not a bad girl, you know, Fern.'

Fern laughed quietly. 'Nor you a bad mother. You know if all this hadn't happened, would you have told me in the end?'

Rowena shrugged and stared out at the traffic before answering. 'I don't know if I would have had the courage,' she confessed. 'I knew in my heart it wasn't right that you shouldn't know. I was terrified . . .'

'Of what?'

'That you'd turn against me,' she said quietly.

'Because of Hugo?'

'Because of the secret, because of Hugo, because I hadn't been honest, because of who he was . . . Oh, I don't know, hundreds of reasons.'

'Well, I haven't turned against you. And Hugo's not such a bad person.'

'I don't know. I'm still working it out in my head. He never knew I was pregnant when he left Ireland. I never told him. God, I still can't help feeling angry, Fern. All those hard years when life was such a struggle and there was he, living the life of Riley with all his money and status and all. I guess I've been a bit like a woman scorned. I didn't want him to know about you, because I wanted him to pay.'

Fern nodded slowly. 'Now I understand why you were so weird when I came over to visit you. It must have been one hell of a shock, me breezing in and talking about him and all.'

'I thought I was going to have a heart attack. I'm sorry I didn't tell you, darling. I just couldn't face it. I was scared, and I wanted to keep you to myself, not share you with him. I just felt he didn't deserve it, but I had no rights. I realize that now. He's not such a bad person. A little weak, maybe.'

'He still cares about you.'

'Nonsense. He's in love with a dream. Always was, probably.'

'He asked me to give you something,' Fern suddenly remembered, and delved into her rucksack, pulling out a small, beautifully wrapped parcel.

'What is it?'

'He didn't tell me. He just said I had to make sure you got it before you left.'

Rowena's fingers picked open the small parcel. 'Perfume,' she said, holding the bottle up for Fern.

'Orpheo. I was right. I knew it,' Fern cried.

'Mmm, smells all right.' Rowena sniffed the neck of the bottle and then dabbled a couple of spots onto her wrists. 'Reminds me of the old lavender water your gran used to make. Lavender and roses soaked in distilled water, with a bit of poteen to help 'em along. 'Course, this stuff smells much better.'

'Hugo made it for you.'

'This bottle? He's gone to a lot of trouble.'

'No, Ma. He made the perfume itself for you – after you and he split up. He developed it. You remember the story, Orpheus and Eurydice.'

'Sure I do. You mean he made *this* . . . for *me*?'

'Yes, it's one of their best-selling perfumes now. There must be hundreds of women out there wearing *your* perfume.'

'Essence of goat would be more like it these days. Well, what an idea,' Rowena sighed, turning the small, leaf-shaped bottle in her hand. 'Fancy that.'

Fern could tell that her mother was chuffed to bits. 'I'll tell him you liked it.'

'You'll do no such thing. I'll tell him myself when I see him.'

'But when will that be? You're hardly likely to be coming back to London in a hurry.'

'Never you mind.' Rowena's eyes sparkled mischievously at Fern as she turned the small bottle over in her hands.

Fern took her seat to Hugo's right. Self-consciously she fingered the pleat at the back of her head, checking on the pins which Nancy had so professionally flourished this morning.

Thomas had been sent to Fern's flat to collect some clothes, including the white linen Versace shift she knew would do her – and Hugo – justice at the board meeting.

One by one the others filed in. Fern noticed that Hugo barely looked up from his pile of papers. Olivia, whom Fern had never been introduced to, dropped her jaw in astonishment when she saw Fern. Then the twins arrived together. They took their seats across the table from Fern and Lucienne glowered at her. Julian ambled in a few minutes later, followed by two men who appeared much older than Hugo. She had no idea who they were, and from the looks on their faces they were very much wondering what on earth she was doing there.

Once all the seats had been filled, and the orders for coffee taken, Hugo opened the meeting.

'I'm sure you all know why I've called this extraordinary meeting,' he began, 'but in case there are any of you in any doubt, you will recall that at our last meeting we had a majority in favour of the sale of La Petite Mort, Vitale and Bijou to Cooper Jefferson for an agreed price of £50 million. Now I know that some of you were rather keen to sell out your holdings, and before we move on to that, I wanted you to hear my proposals.'

He paused and flicked through his papers while Laura poured out coffee for everyone. Fern could see that they were all on the edge of their chairs waiting to hear what he was going to come up with.

'I propose,' he began, raising his voice so that it carried easily around the large conference room, 'that we divide the Coopers revenue between the various shareholders on a percentage basis. In essence I shall retain forty per cent, i.e., £20 million, and the rest of you will divide the remaining £30 million according to your shareholding.'

'So I would be entitled to £3 million,' Olivia was the first to speak.

'Exactly.'

'And Alexander and I would have just under £2 million each.'

'£1.95 million to be exact,' Hugo confirmed. 'And

no doubt Humphrey, seeing as you're a banker, you can work the figures out for yourself . . .'

'£3.6 million,' Humphrey Morrison murmured, avoiding Hugo's eye.

'What about the Foundation?' Lewis Bloomfield barked. 'That's a fifteen per cent division so that makes – '

Hugo put his hand up and stopped Lewis midflow. 'Ah, I was just coming to that, Lewis. You've rather pre-empted me. I expect you've already noticed that we have a new face with us today.' Hugo beamed at Fern proudly. 'I'd like you all to meet my daughter, Fern.'

Fern grinned at Hugo, but then glancing around the table, met the hostile faces levelly.

'Just a moment,' Olivia once more was the first to speak. 'What the hell are you talking about, Hugo? You have no daughter. I heard there was some daft rubbish on the news last night, but I can't believe it's true. I imagined this was some sort of publicity hoax – '

'Anyone can tell she's just a scheming little fortune-hunter,' Lucienne interrupted her aunt. 'You aren't so naïve as to believe her story are you, Hugo? We all thought you were approaching a mid-life crisis, dear uncle, but we none of us can imagine you'd be so taken in by a . . .' Lucienne curled her nose in distaste as she regarded Fern across the table. '. . . by an adventuress.'

Fern felt her cheeks flush with sudden anger. She squeezed her fists together and stared into her lap, waiting for Hugo's response.

'I shall continue on the basis that I didn't hear those comments of yours. I do not have to explain myself to you. As I was saying, I'd like you all to meet my daughter, Fern. Now aside from my considerable pride in being able to formally introduce her to you all, my reason for inviting Fern along to this meeting of shareholders will become clear. Some of you may be aware of the terms of my late father's will in which he left ten per cent of Oscar Rees to the Rees Foundation on the basis that I had no surviving children on the date of his death. Of course if I *had* known of Fern's existence at that time, then the ten per cent would have been bequeathed straight to her. Now we shall be taking immediate steps to transfer the ownership of such shares back to Fern, their rightful owner.'

'But this is preposterous,' Lewis Bloomfield spat. 'Absolutely out of the question. I demand to take legal advice before this discussion continues any further.'

'Of course you must do that, Lewis, but I have already researched the full legal implications and I have to tell you that Fern has a prima-facie claim.'

'But what about the money? You know we were counting on selling those shares for the Foundation's survival. The Foundation will have to close down.'

'Oh, come, come, Lewis. Don't be so dramatic. The Foundation can raise money very easily, particularly,' he glanced at Olivia, 'if the fundraisers get themselves organized. Besides, I understand that my wife will be donating some of her money to the Foundation's pot. Am I correct, Olivia?'

'Um, yes. I haven't yet decided quite how much. Naturally I shall have to calculate my own overheads and various, er, financial commitments . . .'

'Quite so. In any event, the bare facts are that Fern will have her shares. Let's not forget, Lewis, that you still hold another five per cent of Oscars as willed to you by Alfred Easton. If you choose to take a share in the profits that will give you a hefty payout. You're not completely broke yet.'

Fern caught Hugo's attention. 'May I speak?' she asked him quietly.

'There's no need, darling. I can handle this. You just sit tight and listen.'

'No, really, Hugo. I think it's important.'

Hugo studied his daughter, noting the firm line of her jaw, and her cool gaze. 'Very well. The floor is yours, my dear, if you're sure . . .'

Fern stood up and swallowed hard, noting the mixture of expressions now eyeing her from around the table, ranging from the curious to the downright hostile. Her smooth voice carried clearly around the large room.

'I have just spent a week being cared for by the Foundation and I am eternally grateful to all the staff there for their kindness, care and concern. I had a chance to see first hand the expertize offered by the Foundation in terms of reconstructive surgery, and to get to know the skills and capabilities of the many leading surgeons involved.

'But not only did I see how the Foundation functions from the medical side, I also got to know some of its patients, including one brave little seven-year-old who in her short life has suffered more trauma than many of us have ever experienced in our entire lives. Lucy has third-degree burns to her legs and back. She cannot straighten her fingers out properly, because of the scar tissue causing her skin to quite literally shrink. Unlike me, Lucy's mother isn't in the fortunate position of being able to afford the likes of Dr Fielding and his colleagues. She relies upon the Foundation's charity.'

Fern swallowed hard as her voice cracked with nervous tension. 'Lucy was just one of the many patients I met. I can't sit back and watch the Foundation struggle. And certainly not because of me. I therefore propose to donate half of my share of the profits from the Cooper Jefferson sale to the Rees Foundation.'

'Fern!' Hugo gasped. 'You haven't thought this through. I cannot allow you to – '

'I have thought about it very hard, Hugo. I will only pursue the ownership of the shares on the basis that this is agreed.'

'Well, I think that's very noble of you,' Olivia cried. 'On behalf of the Foundation, I accept. Lewis!'

'Er, yes. Thank you. The Foundation is most grateful to you. Under all the circumstances that seems more than fair of you.'

'More than fair indeed!' Hugo said grimly. 'Are you absolutely certain, Fern?'

'Deadly certain, Hugo. But there is just one small thing.'

'Yes?'

'I'd like a seat on the governing board of the Foundation. I got rather attached to the place and I gather I may be spending a little more time there. So I hope the other members of the Board would appreciate my intention to contribute positively and effectively to the Foundation's future.'

'Of course we shall have to put it to the vote,' Lewis blustered, 'but in all the circumstances . . . Olivia?'

Olivia could barely bring herself to speak. Just who the hell was this upstart of a girl, marching into her life, taking over the bloody Foundation and no doubt taking over Oscar bloody Rees next? And now she'd have to work alongside her. It was all too much! 'I, er, can't see there'll be any objection,' she spluttered through tight lips.

'Good,' Fern said delightedly. 'Then we can ask David to draw up the papers. Thank you, all of you,' she said, taking her seat.

Across the table she caught the broad smile on Alexander Easton's face. 'Well done,' he mouthed silently to her and he put his hands together in mock applause.

'Yes, well, er, I think that brings the meeting to an end. I trust everything meets with your satisfaction. I suggest any further discussion you may require should be carried out with me privately.' Hugo closed his file and stood up. As everyone started to move out of the room Humphrey Morrison collared him.

'Hugo, we must speak.'

'Yes, yes, Humphrey, but not now. Fern!' Hugo called out as he saw his daughter disappearing through the doorway. He desperately needed to speak to her. Alexander was buzzing after her like a bee after honey. 'Fern!' he called vainly as she disappeared from his view.

'Oh, very well, Humphrey. Let's get this over with, then.'

'It seems, Hugo, that the bank may have been a little hasty.'

''Twas ever thus, I believe,' Hugo grunted.

Humphrey cleared his throat nervously. 'Hugo, we have always had a good relationship.'

'Not quite as good as I thought, Humphrey.'

'The fact is,' Humphrey continued, 'that we've been carrying out some internal investigations and it seems that the, er, report on you and the company may well have been, um, ill-conceived.'

'Ill-conceived?' Hugo bellowed. 'Ill-conceived! What the hell does that mean? Surely you considered the information you had before you properly before taking such a risk with my business. And what do you expect me to say now? "Thank you"? I really would doubt my sanity if that were to be my response. And, of course, there is nothing wrong with my sanity, is there?'

Humphrey shook his head miserably. 'No.'

'Quite. So what are you doing about it? To make amends, as it were?' Hugo rubbed his hands together, enjoying the other man's discomfort.

'One of our executives, Charles Allen, it seems was having an affair with your niece. Miss Easton was feeding him information about you and the company and the fool used it to try and influence the Board at the bank.'

'"Try" is perhaps the wrong word, Humphrey. It *did* influence the Board, damn fools that you all are! So now what, eh, Humphrey? You going to give me a free piggy bank to make me feel better?'

'Naturally Charles Allen has been dismissed.'

'Naturally!'

'And naturally we shall not be selling our shares in the company. Of course, we reserve our right to dispose of the shares if we wish at some stage in the future, but you will be given first option, and then we would ask you to recommend a buyer. I'm afraid we can't go any further than that. After all, we must protect our investment.'

Hugo nodded sagely. 'How very wise of you, Humphrey. Well, thank you so much. Now if you'll excuse me I have several matters needing my urgent attention.'

'But – ' Humphrey Morrison stopped as Hugo raised his hands to silence him.

'Thank you, Humphrey. We will no doubt be in touch.' Hugo strode off, leaving the banker miserably in his wake.

Fern was nowhere to be seen. Hugo scanned the corridor and cursed under his breath. He had to speak to her.

'Hugo, there you are. I want to speak to you.'

'Oh, not another one,' he sighed. 'Not now, please, Olivia. I really have to – '

'Now!' she insisted. 'If you want a public scene that's fine by me, but I suggest we adjourn to your office.'

'Very well.'

Once the door had closed behind them he turned to his soon-to-be-ex-wife. 'Is there something wrong?'

Olivia's face reddened and twisted into the most unattractive contortions. 'Yes, Hugo. There is something extremely wrong, if you really want to know.' She leaned forward over his desk and brought her face unpleasantly close to his. 'I would like to know,' she hissed, 'what the hell all this nonsense about *that* girl is all about. How can you possibly start parading her around as your daughter? Apart from the embarrassment it's causing all of us, you're making an absolute fool of yourself.'

'I'm not sure I understand you. I'm sorry if Fern's existence is causing you embarrassment, though I can't for the life of me understand why, and as for making a fool of myself, well, I fail to understand whatever gives you that idea.'

'You've been conned. She's not your daughter. For God's sake, man, any number of women could march in here and say the same presumably. I know you've had several affairs over the years.'

'I suppose it's possible, but the fact is they haven't. And you have to realize that it was I who discovered her existence and not she who discovered mine. As I said in the meeting, I do not need to explain myself to anyone. The fact is I am satisfied that she is my daughter. It may interest you to know that if I had been less of a fool in those days, I would have married her mother then instead of allowing myself to be put into a life of purgatory with you. No doubt you wish the same. Just be grateful that the two of us now have the opportunity to rebuild our lives. Please concern yourself with your own affairs, and not with mine. Good day, Olivia.'

'You're a fool, Hugo Rees, and I intend to prove it.'

'Like your niece tried, Olivia? If I were you, I'd concentrate on trying to retain some semblance of dignity. God knows, there's a sad lack of it in your family at the moment. Now I really must get on.'

'You disgust me, Hugo, you really do. I hope you rot in hell!'

'It couldn't be any worse than being married to you, now could it?'

'Well, you can cheer yourself up with the thought that I shall push this divorce through as quickly as I possibly can.' She stood up.

'Then I suggest you get on with it,' Hugo shouted.

Olivia stormed out of the office, slamming the door as hard as she could.

Lucienne could barely contain herself. She ran her red-tipped fingers through her sleek black hair and then fiddled absently with the brass buttons on her navy Yves Saint Laurent blazer, watching Alexander and Fern through the smoked glass office partition. Just what the hell was Xan playing at? Eventually she tore her eyes away, unable to stand the sight of them laughing together a moment longer. Who the hell was she anyway? Hugo's daughter indeed! It was the biggest load of utter nonsense she had ever heard and somehow Lucienne would find a way to prove it. She glanced at her desk and saw the list of telephone messages. It seemed that Charles had called her four times in the last two hours. She picked up the list and, scrunching it into a tight little ball, threw it pointedly into the wastepaper bin. Shame really – he'd been such a good fuck. But his mind could be a bloody bore! He'd soon get tired of calling her when he realized that she wasn't going to speak to him. All the effort that she'd put into her side of the operation and it damned nearly worked. If that stupid old fool Morrison hadn't got suspicious and if Leo Eden hadn't blown the deal by agreeing terms with Hugo . . .

There'd be some other way to sort things out. Like Xan said, between them they could do anything. Lucienne stood up and took another look at her brother and the tart. Against Xan and herself the girl stood no chance. Finally Lucienne smiled to herself. Now that the Charles Allen project was over, she needed something else to get her teeth into, and the exposure of Fern Donleavy would be very satisfying indeed.

Chapter Twenty-three

'Please, David, try and talk some sense into her,' Hugo pleaded.

'So far as I can see it, Hugo, Fern is fully aware of what she is doing, and she's clearly made up her mind.'

'Thank you, David,' Fern grinned. 'I have explained to Hugo exactly that. I want to do something positive to help the Foundation – not just pumping money into it. I'd like to get really involved with it. I couldn't bear to see it close down.'

'The Foundation wouldn't close down, Fern. You've been emotionally blackmailed by them. They weren't that short of cash. It's just mismanagement on their part.'

'You know, Hugo, I don't understand how you could just stand by and let it suffer. It was your father who set it up, after all. Yet you seem to have distanced yourself from it totally.'

'Don't be fooled, Fern,' David butted in. 'Hugo gives the Foundation a substantial amount of money each year. He just chooses not to tell anyone about it.'

'David!' Hugo admonished him. 'That's enough.'

'No, Hugo. It's important that Fern knows the situation. While Olivia was involved to such a large extent, Hugo decided that his role must be, how shall I put it, that of a sleeping member.'

'I knew we'd only fight,' Hugo explained with a wry grin, 'so I just let them get on with it.'

'Why didn't you tell me? I thought that you – '

'Didn't care? Oh, but I do, very much. That is why the Foundation would never have gone bust. And quite frankly, I'd prefer to have used my money, rather than yours, to prop it up. Ideally I would have liked the Board to see what a pig's ear Olivia was making of everything and then get shot of her.'

'And I've blown it!'

'No, of course you haven't. There was no guarantee that they would have asked for her resignation. I was playing a waiting game, just to see.'

'I have blown it, haven't I?' Fern said quietly.

'No, darling. You mustn't think that. There was never a definite plan. And now you've got your seat on the Board you'll have a wonderful opportunity to sort her out, won't you?'

'I hope so. Although I think my best plan will be to keep out of her way as much as I can. I'm not interested in the politics, I'm purely interested in the work.'

'Good! And I wish you the best of luck, Fern,' David said cheerfully. 'Now I've just got some papers for you to sign and thereafter I'm proud to tell you that you are the owner of ten per cent of Oscar Rees. Excited?'

'Yeah,' she grinned. 'Now Hugo will have to find me something to do.'

'I have a feeling that I shall be more concerned with trying to find things for you not to do,' Hugo laughed.

Ricci checked her hair once more, squinting into the shadowy mirror. She had killed all the lights, so the room was flatteringly illuminated by the candelabra on the dining table. She realized with surprise that this was the first time she had invited Hugo to dine with her in the flat. They both enjoyed eating out enormously, so it had never seemed appropriate to suggest a night of home cooking – until now. She popped into the bathroom and gave herself an extra spray of perfume – Florissima – and then poured herself a rather large gin and tonic.

Her critical eye roamed over the table, double-checking that everything was in its place. The small arrangement of tea roses and oak leaves still looked fresh and delicate. The crystal sparkled invitingly. The oyster mousse was chilling in the fridge, the boeuf en croute was just about to go into the oven, and the vegetables were in the steamer, ready to be cooked at the last minute. She felt well-satisfied with her efforts.

She checked her watch. Hugo should be here any moment. Having selected some Debussy to fill the silence, Ricci settled down beside the fire, letting the mellifluous strains wash over her. It wasn't often that she let herself admit quite how lonely she had felt since Rufus died. Along with convincing others of how well she was coping, she had almost managed to convince herself.

Rufus had been a very dear husband and, indeed, a kind friend to her. Of course, physically the relationship had been rather restrained, bearing in mind the twenty-eight years that separated them in age, but Ricci had basked in the intellectual stimulation Rufus's companionship afforded her. Ever since they had married ten years before, Ricci had known the chances of her being a relatively young widow were fairly high, but the knowledge and vague expectation had in no way diminished the tremendous sense of shock, and loss, and agonizing pain of grief she had endured following Rufus's death.

The only balm had been her business. She couldn't bear to keep on the large house they shared in the country. It held too many memories, and besides, there was little point in her rattling around an eight-bedroomed mansion by herself. Instead she had purchased this rather sensible pied-à-terre in Drayton Gardens where she could be centrally placed to carry out her blossoming interior design consultancy, and where she could be near her friends. Life had assumed a fairly routine-like normality when Hugo had called to invite her to lunch. Despite her initial misgivings about becoming involved with him, Ricci soon found herself drawn in by his charm. He wooed her thoroughly and, eventually, successfully. Hard as she tried not to, she found herself becoming more and more emotionally involved with him. She fought it, and at times she refused to see Hugo so that she might recover her independence once more. Ricci knew that she couldn't cope with weathering another hurt so soon after Rufus. She wanted her protective coating intact. She wanted her independence to shield her if ever Hugo lost interest. But life didn't always work like that and now, here she was, terrified out of her wits she was about to lose him. Since the shock revelation they had only exchanged the briefest of phone calls. Tonight's dinner would be the first opportunity to discuss everything properly.

A log spat a spark onto the carpet and Ricci jolted out of her reverie to stamp it out. She realized her glass was empty and she looked at her watch. Hugo was half an hour late. She decided she'd better put the beef in the oven, otherwise he'd be weak with hunger by the time they sat down to eat.

'A table for three?' Fern asked curiously. 'You're expecting someone to join us?'

'Yes. Leo. Hope you don't mind. I've got some things to talk over with him, and as some of them concern you I thought it would be a good opportunity for us to get together. You don't mind, do you?'

'Well . . .'

'Oh look, here he is!'

Hugo stood up and Fern sensed Leo's body behind her chair.

'Hugo.' She turned around. 'And Fern, what a pleasant surprise.' Clearly he hadn't been expecting to see her either.

'Leo,' she said, politely, trying to hide the weird mixture of emotions churning up her mind and gut. Since Ricci's revelations in hospital as to the real reason he'd been so solicitous towards her, she had tried to push him to the back of her mind. Fortunately all details regarding the Vitale contract had been dealt with via correspondence passed through David. As she clearly had no role as The Face any more, it was all down to the insurance companies assessing both her loss and that of Cooper Jefferson. She'd heard through Johnny that even now Coopers were trying to find a replacement 'Face' to front the line. Leo took his seat beside her and Hugo filled his glass.

'I understand congratulations are in order.'

'Indeed.' Hugo beamed at Fern proudly. 'Aren't I the lucky man?'

Leo's dark eyes glittered at Fern. 'Exceedingly lucky, Hugo.'

Fern looked quickly down at the table, cursing the warm glow flooding across her cheeks. 'I haven't had chance to thank you, Leo, for all the flowers, and for all the support you gave me while I was at the Foundation.'

'It was Leo who first suggested we move you to the Foundation, Fern,' said Hugo. 'He really was most concerned . . .'

For his investment, Fern thought cynically.

'It was most kind of you, of Coopers,' she added.

'Your face, it's looking good, Fern,' he said kindly.

'Thanks. The doctors tell me the scars are coming on well. Soon I'll be able to have the first op. Apparently I'm a fast healer.'

'So I see.'

'I'm sorry about Vitale.' She wanted to draw him out.

'Forget it. There are other faces. That sounded awful. I didn't mean . . .'

'Don't worry. I think I know what you mean. You must have felt you backed a loser, though.'

'No, no.' Leo lied smoothly. He was still trying to soothe Lowenstein's nerves over the whole damned deal. 'You did a fantastic job of launching Vitale. It's selling fantastically well.'

'The sympathy vote.'

'Maybe,' Leo shrugged. 'That boyfriend of yours, what's happening over the charges?'

'He's being held on remand. I'm told it could take several months to get to trial. Then I'll have to give evidence against him. Frankly, I try not to think about it. If it were up to me I'd bury my head and forget the whole thing. Because of all the publicity I think he'd be lynched if it didn't go to trial. I'm told he'll probably get a suspended sentence – clean record and all that. The way I look at it is that whatever time he spends on remand will give him time to think about what he did. I thought maybe I should go and see him, and then I thought it would be too painful. I still feel so angry.'

'So do I,' Leo sighed, studying her face carefully. Despite the scarring, she still looked lovely. 'If I were him, I wouldn't be able to live with myself. He should be put away for a very long time.'

'Funny, isn't it, how you think you know someone and then you find you don't know them at all.'

'You should never take anyone at face value.'

Like me, Fern thought to herself, remembering his arrogance towards her in Paris, and his awful teasing when they had met before that.

'So what are your plans now, Fern? We could do with some advice over Vitale if you fancied a change from Oscars!'

Fern studied him curiously. It was impossible to judge whether he was serious or not. She had the feeling he was probably mocking her again.

'I think I'm going to be rather tied up at Oscars, but thanks for the offer. I plan to find out exactly how Oscar Rees works.'

'Bit of a chip off the old block, wouldn't you say, Leo? I think she's very like me.'

'She's certainly much prettier than you, Hugo.'

Fern's hand flew to her cheek and self-consciously she pulled her hair around her face. Leo watched her, his eyes narrowing.

'It's a good company, Fern. In fact, it's one I'd quite like to dabble in myself.'

'I think we know that. Isn't that what all the dealing's been about?'

'I don't mean Coopers. Hugo knows how I really felt about Coopers having a say in the running of Oscars. I didn't think it was any good for the company, either of the companies, in fact. No, I'm talking about me personally.'

'But wouldn't there be a conflict of interests, bearing in mind that strictly Coopers and Oscar Rees are in competition?'

'Not really.' Leo grinned at Hugo. 'The marketing strategies are somewhat different, the management structure is somewhat different, and the company philosophy is *very* different.'

He studied his fingernails thoughtfully and then he glanced up, directly meeting Fern's gaze. 'I thought I might join as a sleeping partner – keep my options open. What do you think, Fern?'

She flushed to her hair roots. 'I, er, think you might be spreading your interests in too many directions, Leo, which at the end of the day would be of no benefit to either party.'

Leo raised his glass to her. 'You learn fast, Fern.'

'Thanks, Leo.' She raised her glass in acknowledgement. She had a very strong feeling that neither of them had been discussing business!

The leaves on the trees were just beginning to show the slightest touches of gold around the edges. In a few weeks' time the whole forest would be ablaze with rich autumn colours. Johnny and Fern had called in at Burley for lunch in a pretty old pub which was far enough off the beaten track to escape the main drifts of tourists. Nearby Lyndhurst tended to bear the brunt of it, so Johnny told her. They sat in the garden, enjoying the soft September sunshine. Fern was content to soak up the rays while Johnny secretly admired the flames of colour in her lustrous Barnet.

'You and Alexander seem to be getting on very well. Where did you disappear off to?'

'He took me into the lab to tell me about what he was doing.'

'Something unsavoury, knowing him.'

'He seems harmless enough, Johnny. His sister's the one that's pure poison. He's come up with an idea which I think could be of benefit to the Foundation. It could be a good source of revenue.'

'Such as?'

'Stop sounding so suspicious! Such as some fairly innocuous-sounding beauty treatments which could be run as an offshoot clinic based at the Foundation itself. He wants to set up a rather exclusive kind of salon giving what he calls autologous fat transfer injections. They're a kind of glorified collagen injection, only instead of using animal products the fat is taken from over-endowed body zones, such as the bottom, and pumped into where it's needed on the face.'

'It sounds disgusting.'

'I think it sounds a lot less disgusting than using essence of dead cow. The fact is, Johnny, it seems to me that this is far more natural, it doesn't hurt anybody else, and it actually works. There's no risk of the body rejecting the fat cells and if it's done under the guidance of the Foundation we could get ourselves a reputation for excellence in all aspects of cosmetics. I was rather impressed.'

'I think he's bamboozled you with science.'

'Look, Johnny, the fact is the Foundation needs to get some more money in. It can't rely on Olivia's charity balls forever. This way, if a clinic was set up, then more funds would be available for treating those that really need it: the poor Lucys of this world.'

'All I'm saying is be careful, Fern. Don't trust him. I know what those two are like. Remember it was their idea to sell Hugo out in the first place.'

'I know,' Fern sighed. 'But if I can oversee it, together with the team of doctors at the Foundation, then I can't see that Alexander could get away with anything. Everyone can reform, you know.'

'Not Alexander.'

'Well, nothing's been decided. But there's an

empty ward doing damn all at the moment. It would cost hardly anything to set up.'

'You sound as though you're already converted.'

'I'm thinking about it, that's all. And stop worrying about me.'

'I can't help it. How are things at home?'

'Okay. Hugo still seems to be on cloud nine. He treats me a bit like a doll at the moment, but I'm sure the novelty will wear off soon.' She downed the rest of her half of bitter. 'He's not at all as I ever imagined my father to be. I thought Rowena would have had it off with some hippie artist or musician, a kind of wandering minstrel-type. But Hugo!' She laughed. 'I still can't imagine them ever getting together. Between you and me I think he's headed for some kind of mid-life crisis. He keeps talking about Rowena and how he regrets everything.'

'What about Ricci?'

'Precisely. Poor old Ricci. I had lunch with her yesterday. She hadn't heard the details – can you imagine? I had to tell her all about it. I felt dreadful. I think it's very cruel of Hugo to leave her out in the cold. I know he's been busy, but you'd think he could make the effort to see her.'

'Sounds to me as if you were doing Hugo's dirty work,' Johnny said gruffly.

'Yeah, I felt like that too. He really needs to sort himself out. I just hope he's not nursing any secret fantasies about Ma.'

'You think he might want to go back to her?'

Fern shrugged and stuffed the last pickled onion into her mouth. Through satisfied munches she answered thoughtfully. 'It's like unfinished business between them. I think maybe they're both still a bit in love with the idea. Crazy, isn't it? You'd think at their age they'd know better.'

'Love's a funny thing. It doesn't seem to know how to stick to the rules of convenience and form.'

There was something about Johnny's voice – a kind of cracked quality – that sent a tremor across Fern's skin. She looked at him sharply and noticed that he hurriedly pulled his eyes away from her. She swallowed, trying to formulate the right words. Now was the time to ask. She had to know about whatever it was that made him remain so distant from her. Had he been damaged by something in his past?

'And what about the women in your life, Johnny?'

He dragged his eyes back to her face and studied her for a few moments. Fern could see sadness in those dark blue depths. She wanted to reach out and touch him, but she dared not. Johnny coughed, before finding his voice, then he tried to make it sound light.

'Too busy. Wouldn't have the time to fit in a woman.'

'Oh,' she said quietly, lowering her glance to the floor. 'I thought . . . well, never mind what I thought.'

'Hasn't been anyone for a long time,' he continued as if he hadn't heard her. 'Last one was married and it was very messy indeed. I ended up getting cited in divorce proceedings, private detectives on us, the whole bit. It put me right off romance. I decided to wait,' he grinned a lopsided grin. 'And you?'

Clearly he had chosen to forget about their one and only clinch. She could hardly blame him. She couldn't imagine that any man would be that interested in her now that Paul had rearranged her face. 'Well, after Paul I've rather lost the inclination.'

'Funny, I thought Leo Eden was getting rather keen.'

'If he was, I didn't know about it. Besides, he's well and truly tied up with India Duncan-Forrester. I hear he likes to stray, but always goes back to her.'

'Yeah. You're wise to stay clear of him. He has a reputation for leaving a trail of broken hearts in his wake. Oh, he's a nice enough bloke, Fern. But not exactly what I'd call stable.'

'Perhaps we should form a celibates club then.' Fern punched his arm playfully.

'In which case I'd better get you back to London, or your father will become suspicious!'

'What an idea!' she giggled. 'I guess I'll have to get used to the possessive father bit.'

Hugo smiled when he saw the vast arrangement of roses gracing Ricci's table.

'Ah, you got them, I see.'

'Yes, thank you, Hugo.'

'Ricci, I'm most terribly sorry. I hope you hadn't gone to too much trouble. I got involved in a meeting and I simply couldn't get away. I know I should have telephoned. Well, to be honest, Ricci, I was so involved that it quite slipped my mind.'

'It's all right, Hugo, really. I understand. Would you like a drink?'

'Let's go out,' he said cheerfully. 'I need to make up for the other night. I'm going to treat you to an absolutely slap-up evening tonight. You choose where you'd like to go.'

'That's very kind of you, Hugo, but if you don't mind I'd like to stay here for the moment. There's something I must talk to you about.'

'Oh, well, if you're sure. I know how you like to eat out, Ricci. And so do I.' His stomach rumbled loudly, right on cue. Ricci chose to ignore it.

'I had lunch with Fern yesterday.'

311

'Did you? She didn't mention it. Isn't she wonderful?' He oozed new-found paternal pride.

'Yes, she's a lovely girl, Hugo. She filled me in on the story. Of course, up until then I had only heard via the press what had happened. It was very nice to hear it from her.'

'Oh, Ricci, I'm sorry. I really should have talked to you earlier. I just can't think where the time has gone, what with the sale to Coopers, and Fern, and sorting Olivia out. God, it's been hectic.' He started to loosen his tie.

'I think perhaps we both of us need a little space, Hugo. So much has happened in such a short time. The divorce . . .' she glanced at him, 'everything's so up in the air. I think it would be best if we had some time to ourselves, give us chance to think things through, sort out what we want.' Ricci felt the lump rise in her throat. She swallowed hard. Her pride would not allow her to give in to tears or hysterics.

'But, Ricci, what are you talking about? I love seeing you.'

'And I love seeing you, Hugo. But I think you need some time to adjust. Perhaps I do, too. You seem to have so many commitments in your life.' And I don't want to be second best, she wanted to add. 'I think it would be better if you spent some time with Fern, get to know your daughter, and Rowena.'

'Yes.' He nodded firmly, confirming her worst fears. 'You're right as usual, Ricci. I do seem to be spreading myself a little thinly at the moment. But could I be free to perhaps call you? I shall miss you, my sweet.'

'Of course,' she smiled, cursing the moisture in her eyes. She turned away quickly. 'Thing is, Hugo, I've got tickets to the theatre tonight. I'm afraid I have to leave in about ten minutes, if you don't mind. I really think it's best.'

'Oh, but . . . I thought we might, you know . . .'

Ricci squared her shoulders bravely. 'Take care, Hugo. I wish you luck with everything.'

Sullenly, head bowed like a small boy, he stood up and shifted awkwardly from one foot to the other. 'Goodbye, Ricci,' he muttered. He leaned forward and she offered him her cheek. His lips burned her soft skin. She raised her hand to the spot and turned away. 'Goodbye, Hugo,' she said and closed the door firmly shut behind him.

Charles Allen held the phone in mid-air, unable to believe what Lucienne had just said. He brought the receiver back to his ear, just to make sure that she had really gone. The cold empty hum of the dialling tone confirmed it. 'Bitch!' he swore under his breath. 'Cold, heartless, fucking bitch!'

It had taken him damned nearly three days to get hold of her. He either got her secretary or the bloody answering machine. Eventually, in desperation, he had pretended to be a journalist and the secretary had put him through. What was it the bitch had said? 'Too busy to see you, Charles. Think we'd better cool things down.' And, besides, she was seeing someone else! Subconsciously he rubbed at the back of his neck where it still ached from keeping yesterday's all-night vigil outside her flat in the vain hope of seeing her. She hadn't bloody showed. He'd already guessed she was fucking elsewhere. God, he thought he might go mad with jealousy. He picked up the whisky bottle and sightlessly splashed some into the tumbler, filling the glass almost to the top. He gulped the stuff back, enjoying the burning hit at the back of his throat.

As he felt the warmth flow into his veins he took another slug, and then another, knowing that eventually he would feel oblivion. He had no job any more. His reputation was ruined – no one would be interested in employing him now, thanks to Morrison's meddling. No notice! Just get out now. Bloody Morrison had had his phone tapped. The bank had decided he had acted improperly by not divulging his relationship with Lucienne. And Lucienne had been feeding him adverse information about Hugo in order to influence the buy-out. Damn, damn, damn! Just what the hell was he expected to do? He'd already lost his car and without a salary the flat would be next. It was mortgaged up to the hilt thanks to the fact that his ex-bloody-wife had managed to hang on to the marital home. What he wouldn't do just to have somebody to talk to. There were no friends he could turn to now. His name was dog shit! Who'd want to see a failure like him? He refilled the glass with more whisky and drank from it. Lucienne had set him up and now he was ruined. His dick had been his downfall! He walked out on to the balcony, letting the tears of self-pity flow freely down his cheeks, barely noticing them, save for the salt taste on his mouth.

He leaned on the balcony and looked down at the sight of all the cars, and all the people leading their normal, comfortable little lives. What did he have to live for now? The scene swam in and out of his vision as the lights dazzled him, exploding from single points into starbursts. He tried to fight the mist of blackness that followed, and the nausea. What was the point? The glass dropped from his hand and smashed at his feet, but Charles was beyond noticing. He was already halfway over the balcony. It was all going to be so easy . . .

*　　　*　　　*

'Shame about your friend Allen.'

'What? Oh yes. Wasn't it? Just goes to show what a weak character he was.'

'So you're not too upset about it, Sin?'

'He had certain attractions, but quite frankly he was becoming a bit of a pain, bombarding me all day with his telephone calls. Still, I'd have preferred it if he hadn't topped himself. You know what these bloody journalists are like. Next thing you know my name's going to be plastered all over the damned papers. God, it's all a bit of a mess, Xan. What are we going to do?'

'All in hand, dear Sin. Our new cousin is delighted with my clinic idea. She's probably making her recommendations to the Board at this very minute. Which leaves me in the happy position of being able to visit our friend Nitchkov in Moscow and get everything set up in readiness.'

'Let me come with you this time. I promise I wouldn't get in the way.'

Alexander laughed quietly. 'I know you, I'd never get outside the damned hotel room. And if you were out of my sight I'd be worried about you. It's like the Wild West goes East over there.'

'That's why I want to come. There's something about those great big hairy Russians I find irresistible.'

'Tell you what, maybe I'll bring you one back. Now, darling, I have to go. Be good while I'm away.'

Chapter Twenty-four

'Fern!' Hugo's shout echoed around the hallway. 'Fern!' he cried again. He threw his briefcase down, and flung open the library doors. 'Ah, there you are, darling!'

He paused in the doorway, relishing the wonderfully warm feeling he always got when he found her at home. The early evening sun poured through the tall windows, turning her luxurious hair into flaming liquid amber. She uncurled herself from her corner of the chesterfield, stretching her bare feet out from underneath her. 'Hugo,' she cried, returning his grin with affection. She still couldn't bring herself to call him Dad. She carefully set the book aside.

'I knew I'd find you in here. You must have got through almost the entire collection by now.'

'Nothing like, but I have come across something fascinating. I must talk to you about it.'

'Yes, yes. But I want to tell you my news.'

She could see the flush of excitement on his face. His eyes shone with happiness. 'What's happened?'

'I've just bought an airline ticket.' He waved an envelope under her nose. 'I leave tomorrow.'

'For where?'

'Cork!' he said with relish.

'Cork! Rowena?'

'Exactly. Isn't it exciting? I finally made up my mind, Fern. I'm not going to let life pass me by any longer. You only live once. Now that my marriage has ended I intend to do all the things I should have done with my life – starting with Rowena.'

'Does she know about this?' Fern said warily.

'No,' he beamed. 'I thought I'd surprise her.'

Fern had a terrible sinking feeling. 'Are you really sure this is wise, Hugo? She's not much of a one for surprises. Perhaps you ought to just let her know, so that she can make arrangements.'

'Nonsense. It's far more romantic this way. I can't wait to see the look on her face when I turn up. Now be a dear girl and tell me exactly how to find the place, would you?'

Fern shook her head thoughtfully. 'Well, good luck, Hugo.' She had a feeling he might need it.

Fern decided to wait until supper before telling Hugo of her discovery. She hugged it to her all through Nancy's pâté, listening to his plans for the next few days, and then as the lamb arrived, she couldn't contain herself any longer. She had to speak to him before he went away, otherwise she'd go crazy with impatience. 'Hugo, I have to talk to you about one of the books I found today in the library.' She waited to get his full attention.

'Oh yes?' he said, reluctantly dragging himself away from the wilds of southern Ireland.

'A book which must have been written by my great-grandmother, Oscar's mother. Her name was Eugenie.'

'That's right. I barely remember her. She died when I was about ten. I gather she was quite a force behind the empire.'

'Well, that's the point, Hugo. You see, the book I found gives details of all her formulas. It's quite beautifully laid out. In fact after supper I'd like you to have a look at it. She's written down the formulas in the

317

most beautiful handwriting, and then illustrated the ingredients. There's recipes for soaps, toilet waters, bath essences, shampoos . . . there must be over a hundred. And the drawings are really exquisite.'

Hugo mopped his lips with the napkin. 'I knew there was a book lying around somewhere. My father mentioned it to me, though I confess I haven't actually looked at it myself.'

'I'm surprised you never used it. Surely the company would have manufactured some of the formulas at one stage?'

'Oh, in the very old days, before Oscar Rees was officially started. Cosmetics have been in the blood for many generations. But you see, in the thirties everyone wanted modern ideas, bright lipsticks and face powders. Nail varnishes, that sort of thing, and of course women mainly wanted French perfumes. There really wasn't much call for homespun recipes.'

'But it seems such a shame, such a waste!'

'Life moves on, darling. It's our history, if you like, museum stuff. We've progressed a long way from those recipes,' he laughed affectionately. 'Shall we take a look at it over coffee?'

As Hugo obediently flicked over the pages of the faded leather-bound tome, Fern rehearsed her speech in her head. The more she thought about her idea, the more the small seed of excitement grew in her belly. She knew exactly what she wanted to do.

'Marvellous, isn't it?' he laughed. 'What a woman she must have been. Such artistry, as you say, Fern. And such attention to detail. Even tells you where she picked the chamomile for her shampoos, and where the oat grains were harvested. Quite lovely. We should have the book on show at the offices perhaps.'

'Hugo, I've had a wonderful idea.'

'What, glass case, that sort of thing?'

'No. I don't want to put it on display at the office. I want to recreate those formulas and market them properly, and package them using those wonderful drawings. Can't you just see it? It's just like *The Country Diary of an Edwardian Lady* all over again. We could produce beautiful glass bottles. I can just see it . . . that marvellous essence of the past. Hugo, it's an absolute goldmine.'

'Calm down, darling. It's just not compatible with the sort of thing we do these days. We're not a homespun sort of company, as I explained. We're into hi-tech developments based on scientific formulas, not formulas found in Granny's attic.'

His voice softened when he saw Fern's crestfallen face. 'Believe me, darling, I do know what I'm talking about. I love the way you've thrown yourself into the business. I think it's quite marvellous how you've shown so much enthusiasm towards the Foundation and for the marketing side. I'm quite thrilled by your potential. But you have to learn to walk before you can run, and you need to learn all about the business before you can go headlong into developing and launching whole new product lines. When I was your age I had to work in each department and get to know the entire business. And that's precisely what I'd like you to do.'

'By the time you were twenty-five, which is precisely a year older than I am now, you had formulated Orpheo, all by yourself, if I'm to believe the publicity blurb.'

'Well, er, yes, that was slightly different. Your grandfather was set against it. I had a lot of proving to do. Fortunately it was hugely successful.'

'Perhaps because you had a burning ambition to do

it. You were fuelled by a purpose, weren't you, Hugo? Your love for Rowena!'

'You *are* very well informed. But even so, Fern, I still had to learn the business first. And apart from anything else, it just isn't complementary to what we are doing now.'

'You hardly make any toiletries at all, apart from the odd facial bar or luxury body moisturiser. That's hardly exploiting much of the gift market, is it?'

'There's too many others more established than us in that particular field. I'll find you reams of market feasibility studies, if you like, to prove my point. We are not interested in boxed soaps and scented drawer liners – or bubble baths and body lotions. We leave that sort of thing to the Body Shop!'

'They seem to have done all right out of it.'

'Well, it's just not us.'

'I want you to think about it, Hugo.'

'I have thought about it, Fern. It's out of the question. While I'm away I suggest you busy yourself starting from the bottom. You're such a fast learner you may well have reached the top by the time I return.'

'Huh. You probably think you'll be there for months! In any event, I intend to do a feasibility study on it.'

'Darling,' he spoke gently, 'listen to me. I *know* our business. I don't want you to spend any time on this. Now I know how keen you are not to be singled out for special favour just because you're who you are, so I should treat you like any of my other employees and tell you that I wish you to follow my instructions. And those are to put this book on one side and concentrate on what Oscar Rees is best at: and that is the future, not the past.'

'And that's your final word on it.'

Hugo's jaw set stubbornly. 'Indeed.'

'Hugo?'

'Yes, Fern.'

'The book. May I have it? As a gift, I mean. If you don't intend to do anything with it then I'd like to have it.'

Hugo was relieved that the battle at last seemed to be over. 'Of course, my darling. After all, it belonged to *your* great-grandmother. I'm sure she'd be thrilled at your having it.' He stood up and put his arm around her shoulder. 'I'm sorry, Fern. But you do understand, don't you?'

'Yes, I do. So, I'd better tell you how to find the cottage, hadn't I?'

'Ah yes. Honestly, Fern, I feel like a nervous teenager again.'

After three cramped hours of driving, Hugo at last sighted the cottage. He pushed the map into the door-pocket, and drew up beside the steep bank which marked the boundary of the front garden. He switched off the engine and clambered out, feeling annoying little tweaks across the small of his back. He stretched, and shook his legs, trying to revive the flagging circulation. The car was ridiculously small, ludicrous for a man his size. He scowled at the offending red Fiat Panda which the effusively charming girl at Hertz had introduced him to. At his protests she had assured him this was the only car available unless he wanted to hang around for two or three hours until something else turned up.

He was almost wishing he'd damn well waited. He lowered himself back into the car to retrieve a much-wilted bunch of roses from the back seat. As he raised himself back out of the car, he hit his head on the roof with a resounding thud.

'Oof!' he cried, rubbing the large lump which had immediately appeared. A cat strolled up to him, its tail held haughtily aloft, and rubbed itself on the leg of his trousers. 'Get off!' he snapped, and gave it a helping lift with the side of his foot. The cat and Hugo regarded each other with mutual distaste, and then the cat pointed its small pink anus in Hugo's direction and sauntered off.

Hugo decided he'd leave his suitcase in the car for the time being. It wouldn't do to appear too forward. He straightened his hair, and started to whistle silently as he headed for the ever-open front door.

The air inside was cool and still; gloomy after the bright sunlight. He knocked on the door as he entered, but there were no distant answering footsteps. All was silent. He wrinkled his nose. He detected the faintly acid smell of sour milk which seemed to be wafting through from the kitchen. As his eyes became accustomed to the gloom, he could see there was something hanging suspended from a beam over the kitchen table. His nose told him this was what was responsible for the smell. A bowl placed below the muslin bag contained a foul-smelling watery, milky-looking liquid. Several flies buzzed interestedly around it. Hugo's empty stomach lurched threateningly.

There was no sign of life other than the cat, which had reappeared. It leaped up on to the table and blinked at him. Still clutching the roses, Hugo went out through the kitchen door into the garden. He could hear vague humming coming from the direction of a shed at the bottom of the garden. Swallowing hard to rid himself of the taste which had developed from the smell, he walked briskly towards the building. The humming stopped abruptly.

'Shit!' The expletive shattered the tranquillity. This was followed by a torrent of further obscenities which halted Hugo in his tracks. Just as the silence descended once more, Hugo was almost knocked sideways by an ear-splitting scream. An airborne grenade of small paint brushes launched itself with some gusto from the doorway of the wooden hut, and spread out in the space above his head, from where they rained down on him like arrows. He dropped the roses and shielded his face and head with his arms.

'Good God! What are you doing here?'

Hugo lowered his arms and found Rowena framed in the doorway. His heart raced and, the roses temporarily forgotten, he bounded towards her.

'Rowena!' he cried. He closed the gap between them, intent on sweeping her into his arms. Rowena thwarted him by turning on her heel and disappearing back into the studio. She was seated in front of a large canvas, her back towards him, by the time he reached her.

'Rowena . . .' his voice was nervous and uneven.

'Sssh.'

'Rowena.' This time he whispered.

'Quiet!' she snapped, without turning her head. 'I'm thinking.'

'Oh,' he whispered again. He studied the canvas. Nothing recognizable could be discerned from the red brush sweeps which covered the foreground, or the paler, pinker brushstrokes occupying the top half of the canvas. Rowena sat as still as a stoat, eyes fixed on some intangible point in the fledgling painting. Hugo hardly dared to breathe. Clearly some deeply spiritual level of communication was taking place here. He stood, silent as he had been bidden, for several moments, until he began to see the ridiculousness of the situation.

323

'H'm-m.' He cleared his throat. Rowena started, but continued to ignore him. 'Rowena!'

'Sssh,' she hissed vehemently.

'Rowena! I've come to see you, Rowena!' He held his arms out towards her, almost touching her shoulders. Then he dropped them uncertainly. 'I wanted to surprise you. I thought you might . . .' His words shrivelled along with his confidence.

'Holy Mary! What kind of a surprise is this?' At last she turned to face him, her jade eyes round as saucers. She slapped her forehead melodramatically, leaving a splurge of red paint. 'How the hell did you find me?'

'Er, Fern. She sort of gave me a general idea of the direction, though I have to say the detail was sadly lacking. It's taken me quite a time to locate you,' he added proudly, hoping she might sense the degree of his achievement.

'How long are you stopping?' she demanded, eyeing his starchy new corduroys and his Gucci loafers with ill-concealed derision.

Hugo struggled to retain his composure. This was not going at all according to plan. 'I hadn't exactly thought. I was hoping . . . I, er, thought . . . per-haps . . .' He took a step towards the door and turned to face the wilderness, shoving his hands into his pockets. Suddenly he felt rather ridiculous. It had never occurred to him to think that she might be less than pleased to see him. He'd gone through the scene many times in his head, replaying the moment when she would run into his arms and he would sweep her up in a passionate embrace and then . . .

He looked back over his shoulder, feeling the mood of enchantment slide off him like a warm overcoat in a bitter wind. 'I thought you might be pleased.'

'You came all this way?' Her voice had softened.

'Yes. I was desperate to see you,' he said gently, but afraid to move. 'Perhaps it's inconvenient,' he added, at a loss to know what to do next.

Rowena sighed heavily. 'No. It's not inconvenient. Come on, I'll make you a cup of tea.'

Hugo followed her meekly. She strode through the long grass, her youthful figure clad in what appeared to be an enormous man's shirt, and a pair of tattered jeans which had been roughly cropped just below her knees. She sighted the roses.

'Oh, Hugo, look! How lovely!' she gathered them up and then picked her way through the tangle of paint brushes. 'I hope I didn't hit you,' she grinned sheepishly.

'Er, no, not much.'

In the kitchen Rowena placed the kettle on the stove.

Hugo's nose caught the unpleasant smell once more. 'Rowena, what is this stuff?'

'That, Hugo, is the most delicious cheese you're ever likely to taste. I'll give you some for supper tonight. That's if you're staying to supper?'

'I, er, well, I . . . I guess I am. If that's all right.'

'Sure, whatever.'

She busied herself with the tea, giving him an opportunity to study the chaos of the room. The walls were covered with drawings and paintings of all sizes and shapes, some framed, some merely scraps of paper pinned up on the crumbling plaster with drawing pins. A large sofa was pushed against the wall behind Hugo, and although it was covered with bright rugs he could see patches of horsehair escaping from the arms where the fabric had worn away. The floor felt gritty beneath his smooth leather soles and he crossed his legs feeling self-conscious and ill at ease. He wiped away the group of stale breadcrumbs gathered in front of him and smiled nervously as Rowena splashed watery-looking tea into mugs. Then she picked up an impossibly large tin pitcher and expertly aimed milk into the mugs. Hugo tried not to notice the small white flecks which floated up to the surface of the pale brown liquid, or the slightly rancid smell which crept under his nose as he manfully sipped at it. Rowena sat down opposite him and spooned two large teaspoons of honey into her tea. Then she sipped at it loudly and appreciatively.

'Ah, that's better,' she sighed, leaning back on the creaking wooden chair.

Hugo would have liked to have been able to see her better. The late afternoon sunlight barely filtered through the small window above the old stone sink, and her face was in shadow. He could not read the expression in her eyes.

'So,' she said, 'why did you come?'

He was taken aback by her directness and for a moment he studied the menacing globules in his mug. He sighed and continued to stare downwards. 'I wanted to see you.'

'Why?'

'I couldn't stop thinking about you, Rowena. After all this time, seeing you again like that, I realized . . .' His voice trailed off as his courage failed him. She seemed so strong, so composed, so matter-of-fact. She was making him feel foolish and uncomfortably out of place. He cleared his throat. 'I told you in London, I've thought about you all these years, I thought about how we were together – how much in love we were, the girl you were, and the woman you are. God knows how many times I dreamed of you, Rowena. I just wish my life had been different. I wish I'd done the right thing. I wish I could turn back the clock and start all over again – with you. I've loved you for over twenty years, Rowena. I realized that the moment I set eyes on you again. I still love you. I just had to come.'

Without speaking she stood up and collected a small bottle from the dresser and splashed the clear liquid into her tea. 'Want some?'

'What is it?'

'Fire water,' she said. 'It's good for the heart – and the mind.'

'Thank you,' he said, cursing his voice for its stiff politeness. He took a sip and choked. 'For Christ's sake, Rowena, it nearly took the roof of my mouth off!'

She chuckled. 'It gets better with the second slug. Go on, try it again.'

Uncertainly he took a tentative sip and simultaneously felt the warmth of the alcohol seep through his chest. He took a larger gulp. Perhaps if he were drunk he might not notice his folly.

Still Rowena didn't speak. Instead she stayed calmly watching him, as if she were studying an object of curious interest, or even one of her precious paintings.

'I had hoped,' he murmured eventually, 'that you might be feeling a bit the same way.'

'In love with you, you mean?'

'Well,' he tried a light laugh which came out as a strangled grunt, 'maybe not necessarily in *love*, but perhaps a little, um, fondness?' His voice rose hopefully.

'After what you did?'

He raised his hands in surrendering motion. 'I know, I treated you abysmally. I can't excuse what I did. You must have had the most dreadful time, and all because of me. I suppose you must hate me. I can imagine you must!' His voice, although it trailed off, lacked conviction. Hugo could usually talk his way round an awkward situation, and he knew he did have a certain charm. Ricci had always told him so.

'But you still felt that I might *want* to see you?'

'I thought you might remember how it used to be, how we used to be. And then, of course, there's Fern.'

'Fern is a biological fact, Hugo, not the foundation for a resumed love affair. Just because we have a daughter between us doesn't mean that you and I have a relationship.'

'But, Rowena!' he cried. 'Of course we have a relationship. We are her parents. We share her, Rowena.'

'She's not an item of property, Hugo, like a car or a house.'

'I didn't mean that,' he said exasperatedly. 'I just meant to say . . . oh God,' he groaned. 'I don't know what I mean. It all sounds wrong. I should never have come. It was stupid of me, stupid and presumptuous. Of course I should have realized you must hate me so much that you'd never want to see me again. I'm not a creature of impulse, really. My life is laid out so neatly, all planned and scheduled. I can't remember the last time I did something impetuous, or vaguely adventurous.' He ran tired fingers through his hair and rested his head on his hand. He felt utterly exhausted and defeated. He downed the remains of the lukewarm tea, appreciating the burn of the alcohol. Its warmth felt reassuring, giving him much-needed strength. 'I think the last time was with you. You probably don't remember, but we walked for miles in the hills, and then we rested by a lake. You let me hold you and I wound your hair so tightly around my hands, I never wanted to let you go. I wanted us to stay like that, bound together for always. Then you suggested that we go for a swim and we both stripped off and you ran into the water. I followed you and the water was icy cold. So cold that every bit of me shrivelled so that it hurt. I remember our limbs turning blue. But you stood there laughing and splashing, your skin so pale and beautiful, almost translucent, and with your hair . . . well, you looked like the Lady of the Lake. Afterwards we shivered together, clinging to one another until the heat of our bodies warmed us through, and then, my darling Rowena, we made slow, delicious love. You gave yourself to me completely. I remember the curve of your throat as you arched your head back, surrendering yourself to our love. The little cries you made as I moved inside and the way you clung to me with such strength. I remember being surprised by your strength. That's why I came to you, Rowena. Because I cannot forget.'

Unsteadily he rose to his feet, making the chair squeak on the stone floor. 'I'll go now. I'm sorry. Please forgive me, but I understand if you can't.'

'No!' The strength of her command stopped him. He turned to her, defeated and humiliated. She saw the hurt through the shadows and the dejected slump of his shoulders. 'No,' she repeated, this time softly. 'Don't go. I don't want you to go.'

He shook his head. 'It's all right, Rowena, you don't have to say anything.'

'But I don't want you to go, Hugo.' Her voice was almost a whisper that swept through the stillness like a caress. She stood up slowly and walked around the table. He felt his whole body tense, afraid to move, afraid of what was about to happen. He watched her, transfixed, as she swayed towards him. She took hold of his hand, which hung stiffly at his side, and clasped it in her firm warm grasp. 'Please stay,' she murmured.

As if in a dream, he grabbed her and pulled her towards him, squeezing her so tightly that she cried out. Then his mouth was on hers, burning into her sweet cool lips, tasting her, devouring her. He felt her shudder against him as her soft body moulded itself to his. His fingers tore into her hair, pushing her face towards him, afraid that if he were to release her the dream would fade. But her body felt real enough. Frail and small, beautifully vulnerable, but wonderfully real. The next few moments of Hugo's life were forever to remain a blur to him, but somehow between them they managed to divest themselves of all their clothes. His only awareness was the immaculate curve of her breasts and the firm mound of her belly, yielding under his eager hands, and the tantalizing scent of Orpheo filling his soul.

Fern rechecked her tattered note and confirmed the name on the wall plate with that in her hand: R. H. Harrison & Partners, Commercial Property Agents. This was the place. Shoving her note back into her jeans pocket, she adjusted the weight of her canvas rucksack and climbed the stairs, two at a time. She pushed open the opaque glazed door at the end of the corridor and came face to face with a receptionist.

'Can I help you?' the girl said in a decidedly snooty voice.

'I hope so,' Fern grinned at her warmly. 'I'm looking for a property.'

'A commercial property?' The receptionist pushed the spectacles back onto the bridge of her nose and regarded Fern with a mild irritation, having interrupted a rather complicated bit of figurework

Mr Harrison was at this very moment awaiting from her.

'Yes. A shop, actually.'

'We only deal with properties in Covent Garden,' the girl said, turning back to her word processor as if that would end the matter.

'Well, I assumed that.' Fern cleared her throat and tried again. 'I'm actually looking for a shop in Covent Garden.'

'We haven't got anything below £50,000 a year.'

Fern exhaled slowly. 'Phew, that much, huh?'

'Yes. Property's frightfully expensive here. Sorry I can't be more helpful.' Again she returned to her word processor.

'Perhaps I might have details.'

'Of what?' The girl reluctantly turned back to Fern.

'Of the shops – at £50,000 a year.'

'Very well.' She pushed the intercom. 'Mr Miles, there's someone here who requires assistance with a shop. Perhaps you could spare her a few moments?' She listened and returned to Fern. 'Mr Miles will be with you shortly. He's the partner in charge of retail premises.'

'Thank you.'

A few moments later a door behind the reception desk opened and a man Fern assumed to be Mr Miles stepped through. His smile of welcome slipped as he took in Fern's ripped jeans and battered leather jacket and, much as she tried not to think about it, she knew the still-red scars on her cheeks gave her the appearance of someone inclined to a good brawl. Uncertainly he held out his hand. 'Miles, Jeremy Miles. Er . . . I gather you're looking at retail premises, Miss, er . . .'

'Donleavy. Fern Donleavy.'

The man frowned, wondering why there was something vaguely familiar about the name.

'Perhaps you would like to come into my office and we'll have a chat.' He adjusted the knot on his red-and-white spotted tie, unsettled at the girl's appearance. Most of Harrison's clients did not sport ripped denim jeans to the offices. She was, without question, a time-waster, one of these silly young things (though she was in fact a year older than he) who got an idea in their heads that they could rent a shop in the Piazza for twenty pounds a week and make a fortune selling some form of ethnic crap. Still, for the sake of the company he had to go through the motions.

'Do sit down.' He gestured to the small chintz sofa sitting beyond the reproduction yew coffee table. He pulled a wicker chair close up to the table and joined her. 'Now,' he said, clicking his pen into action and poising it over a clipboard, 'what exactly is it you're after?'

Fern pored over the estate agents' details. The one huge pile was fast diminishing into two smaller piles: one of absolutely useless, and one of almost useless. The shops were either too small, too large, in a grotty position away from the main centre, or in such a state of disrepair that it would take months of work to get them together. What had started off as being a really exciting day's work, full of eager anticipation of what she might be able to find, had turned into a soul-destroying realization of how finding the right sort of premises was not going to be an easy job. Eventually, too tired to focus on any more of the ridiculously small snapshots, she pushed the piles aside. Nancy had brought her a tray of salad which had remained untouched and forgotten for the past couple of hours.

Half-heartedly she chased the food around the plate, glancing down her newly made list of 'things to do'.

She circled point 3, where it said chemist, and chewed thoughtfully. Alexander Easton's face flashed in front of her, probably because he was the only chemist she had come across, apart from good old Dr Chapman. While she could maybe ask Alexander's advice, she could hardly ask him to work with her. Perhaps she could call him tomorrow to see if he could think of anyone who might be keen to try something different. On the other hand, it could be better to keep the whole operation separate from anyone at Oscar Rees in case there was ever any accusation of foul play.

She flipped through her copy of *Soap and Cosmetics Magazine* and read the small ads once more, circled a couple of the ads and rubbed her tired eyes. She had a lot of ground to cover in a short space of time, but she had no doubt she could do it. After all, she was Oscar Rees's granddaughter.

Chapter Twenty-five

Lucienne followed Alexander through the door of the fledgeling Clinic. She placed her hands on her hips, and regarded the reception area with satisfaction. 'Well,' she said, 'this should do nicely. Very nicely.'

Alexander followed her gaze and his lips lifted into an identical replica of his sister's smile. 'I think you're right, Sin. It's going to be abso-bloody-lutely perfect. Come on, I'll show you around.'

He led her along a corridor where a series of six or so doors opened off. 'We can accommodate the over-nighters in here. These rooms will be kitted out to the highest specification: television, video, luxury bath-room, the works. Coming to stay here will be like booking into a five-star hotel. They just won't want to leave.'

'Marvellous. What about the consulting room?' she asked eagerly.

'Down here. Come on. Here's the first,' he said, pushing her gently in front of him.

'My God, Xan, I had no idea they were going to give you an entire operating theatre.'

'Pretty impressive, eh?' he said, grabbing her slim waist and whirling her around the bank of stainless-steel cupboards which flanked the central surgical bed. 'Could have this whole thing up and running in, what, four weeks or so?'

'Are you serious?' she squealed. 'What about Nitchkov? Will he be able to supply all the stuff by then?'

'Darling girl,' he sighed indulgently, 'Nitchkov's got freezers packed full of the stuff. It's like an over-stocked cash and carry. I should think he'd be delighted to ship out the first batch on the strength of a phone call. We have done all the business already, don't forget.'

'Ironic, isn't it? All those Russian women getting off-loaded Oscar Rees stuff on the black market, and we're getting – '

'Yes, yes, Sin,' he interrupted her swiftly. 'Walls have ears, dear girl, walls have ears.'

'But there's no one around here. I haven't seen a single solitary soul since I arrived half an hour ago.'

'Don't be deceived. The place is crawling with nurses and administrators. It's just that you can't hear them. They've got those bloody crêpe-soled shoes on – like vicars in a brothel. Besides, I've got our new cousin coming in for a chat in half an hour or so, about some testing of a little sideline she's thinking of launching.' He looked at his watch. 'Perhaps you might feel it politic to make yourself scarce. It's hardly as if you and she have got off to a good start, is it?'

'I don't know how you can call her cousin. She is not our cousin, Xan. She's Hugo's bastard and I'm still convinced she's an imposter. Stupid old fool that Hugo is, he'd have believed anyone who'd walked off the street. I knew we were right to question his sanity.'

'Look, darling,' Alexander's voice was filled with fraternal impatience, 'impostor or not, the fact is that Hugo seems to believe her for the moment. But if we bide our time for a while, keep our noses clean, then one never knows just what sort of opportunities could arise, do we?'

'I still think the entire situation is outrageous. Just

look at what's happened, Xan. She's got herself a seat on the Board, she's bloody Assistant Product Manager at Oscar Rees, she's been on every newspaper's front page in the past few weeks and now, to cap it all, you seem to be creaming up to her in a revolting fashion and are even contemplating testing some cosmetics for her! Not for Oscar Rees, but for her!'

'Darling sister.' Alexander reached out and rested his hand on his twin's shoulder. 'You have already made an enemy of this creature. I, on the other hand, have her eating out of my hand. You should remember that it was at her recommendation that we were granted the space here within the Foundation for our clinic. She's very stupid, easy to manipulate. I can control her,' he said flicking out his long fingers and curling them, clawlike, while he studied his perfectly manicured nails. 'She will do what I want.'

'I think you want to get between her legs, you shit!'

'I must confess that so far as legs go, they are rather attractive, but you must always remember,' his voice dropped to a rasping whisper, 'the only legs I *really* enjoy getting between are yours!'

'Well, here she is.' Lucienne's snarl rearranged itself into an almost charming smile. 'Why, Fern,' she cooed, 'how delightful.'

'Lucienne,' Fern could barely keep the shudder out of her voice. If Lucienne was attempting to be nice, then there was without question some bitchy reason behind it. So far Fern had dealt only with Alexander, and despite what everyone else had told her about him, she had found him helpful and friendly. And she had always been a great believer in making her own mind up about people – which is why she now felt exceedingly irritated to be confronted by Lucienne. This was one person *all* her instincts told her was bad news.

336

'I was just saying to Alexander how thrilled I am with the Clinic. Alexander says that we might have it up and running within a month or so!'

'Yes, so I understand. Um, Alexander,' Fern tried to bypass Lucienne's duplicitous simpering, 'I was hoping to be able to have a little chat with you about a few things.'

Lucienne, unable to hide her true character, narrowed her eyes into venomous slits and snapped, 'Fine. I was going in any case.'

Xan smiled at her sympathetically. 'I'll catch you later, Sin. Ciao, ciao.'

Once more Fern fought the urge to shudder. Ciao, ciao. Ugh, she thought to herself, and watched Lucienne disappear in a cloud of what she now knew to be, unmistakably, La Petite Mort. Alexander placed his hand against her elbow and led her back down the corridor into what would become the luxurious waiting area.

'Have a seat, Fern. I hope you're pleased with the way everything's coming along.'

'It's all looking very good. I had a word with Edward Hunter, the Administrator, and he told me he was sure one of the consultants here already would be pleased to discuss overseeing the treatments at their normal rates.'

'Fern, you're so thoughtful,' Alexander beamed at her. 'But in actual fact I do have somebody in mind who's *rather* a specialist in this sort of thing. I gather he's a bit of a whizz at sticking needles in people.'

'Yuk!' Fern screwed her face up at the thought of the technique. 'I can only comfort myself with the thought that at least they'll get it done properly here, rather than by some charlatan making false claims about what can be achieved. Anyway, the Board are thrilled about the revenue coming to the Foundation.

All in all everything seems to have worked out very well.'

'So that's me sorted out,' Alexander relaxed back in his seat. 'Now what about you? What's all this about Great-granny's formulas?'

Fern tugged a folder out of her rucksack and opened it up on her knee. Several scraps of paper fluttered onto the floor.

'Thanks.' She grinned as Alexander collected them up and handed them to her. He had to stop himself from rolling his eyes with disdain.

'Ah, here it is,' she said, having shuffled through sheets covered in messy scrawl. 'I've written out three of the formulas for you. What I'd like you to do, Alexander, is to get them made up and then tell me what you think from a chemist's point of view. If they are okay then I shall go ahead and get them produced in quantity. I've got a place lined up already. I can't think for one moment there'll be any problems but I obviously want to be sure of things before I go spending lots of money in getting loads of the stuff made up.'

'You are serious, then?' Alexander asked.

'Yes. I really think I can do it. I've got my eye on a couple of premises, I've got the packaging design being mocked-up and I've got all the ideas for what I want to do. If Oscar and your grandfather did it all those years ago, I don't see why I can't have a go now.'

'But surely you could do it under Oscars' umbrella.'

'Oh, Alexander, you must understand. I don't want to achieve something just because my father owns the business. If I were to be a success you can imagine what everyone would think. I'd just be like some puppet figure that no one would ever take seriously.'

338

Alexander nodded slowly, sympathy and understanding oozing out of his face. 'I *do* understand, Fern. Why do you think Lucienne and I were keen to move on? Like you, we both felt – well, me particularly, really – that we would never really *achieve* anything worthwhile just being with the old man's company. Everyone thinks you're there just because of who you are, not because of what you are.' He placed his hand on his chest, wondering at the same time whether he might be overdoing it slightly. 'I mean, Fern, I've got nothing against Hugo at all. I like him *very* much. Wouldn't have done anything to harm him or mess up the company for him. It came as quite a shock to me when Olivia and the Foundation decided to be wooed by Coopers, too. I'd never have got the ball rolling in that direction had I realized that Hugo might end up in such a poor position. As it has turned out, with you appearing and everything, well, I'm so delighted. It's all worked out for the best, hasn't it?'

He beamed at her with pure affection. Fern grinned back. Alexander took her hand and squeezed it tightly. 'And I have a cousin all of my own.' Fern started to speak, to explain that that wasn't quite the case. Alexander put his hand up to stop her. 'Don't say it. I *know* you're not a true cousin, but we could pretend, couldn't we? I would so like that.'

Fern shrugged, feeling the infectiousness of his warmth. 'Okay. Why not?' She sighed with contentment. 'I guess we're all at quite a turning point, aren't we? Even though there's Oscars in the background, we're still doing our own thing, you with the Clinic, and me with my shop. I guess it would be nice to have some family support.'

'You've got it, Fern. If you need any help at all, you only have to ask. You know I'd be delighted to do all I can. I'll get these looked at . . . and I'll pop the product into the office – in plain brown paper, of course.' He laughed and patted her on the knee, leaving his hand resting lightly over the hole in her jeans so that it touched her warm flesh underneath. Fern looked at the hand and then looked at Alexander. He laughed again, lifting it up and shrugging nonchalantly. 'Forgive me, I was just feeling full of familial emotion.' He jumped up and she followed. Then, placing an arm around her shoulders, he led her along the corridors and out of the grand entrance of the Rees Foundation.

Hugo was having a hard time getting to grips with consciousness. He lay supine, eyes tightly closed against what he assumed to be raging sunlight aimed directly on his face. Behind his eyelids a layer of grit had formed which chafed against his strangely dry eyeballs. His tongue rasped against a mouth lined with foul-tasting felt. He tried to swallow but his mouth was as arid as a desert. As he lay, feeling the strangeness of his surroundings – the scratchy cottton sheets, the soft mattress which groaned and sagged under his weight and caused his back to ache in protest – he smiled to himself. He listened and caught the sound of another's soft breathing beside him; the rustle of the sheets as a hand moved in annoyance at the fly buzzing over bare skin.

Slowly Hugo opened his eyes and turned his head. The sight hit him with a lurch in his stomach, sending warm oil through his loins. A storm of conker-coloured silk spread over the pillow, snaking towards him as if some wind had billowed through it in the night. It framed her small pale face like the flames around a sun. He was filled with such warmth, such heat of desire. Tenderly he reached out and stroked

340

the delicate skin, marvelling at the downy softness beneath his fingers. She stirred slightly. Her lips moved in silent speech and she arched her back, causing her buttocks to brush against his thigh. Her eyes flew open with a start and she turned to face him. As he watched, he caught the briefest flicker of disbelief, and then echoed the small smile which curled her lips and which wordlessly told him that she was remembering with a good deal of pleasure that which they had shared before they had finally collapsed into a deep sleep, totally spent and exhausted.

Rowena sat up and Hugo watched with admiration as the sheet fell away from her breasts. He resisted the temptation to reach out and cup the inviting curve in his hand. Much as he would like to, his head warned him of dire consequences.

'A cup of tea?' she said chirpily. Hugo nodded and then suddenly remembered the grim liquid she had fed him the day before. 'Let me do it. I bet you never have tea brought to you in bed, do you? I insist that I will do it.'

'As you want,' she yawned and fell back onto the pillows. 'I've usually been up three hours by now, so I might as well revel in the decadence of the day for a change. You'll find everything – it's more than obvious. Oh, and the cat'll want his breakfast. He won't leave you alone till you give him his food. You'll find it in the larder at the end of the kitchen.'

Hugo leaned over the bed and planted a tender kiss on her forehead. 'Don't you worry, I'm sure I'll manage. You have a nice doze until I come back.'

Rowena drew the sheet over her head and sighed a contented sigh.

Hugo pulled on his striped boxer shorts and feeling the cold of the bare wooden floor, searched through his trousers in order to locate his socks. He tiptoed out of the bedroom and stood at the top of the narrow staircase, leaning against the wall to balance himself as he pulled on his knee-length dark grey worsted socks. Feeling more than a little stiff he made his way down the steps which led into the kitchen.

His stomach heaved as the sour smell of the day before hit his nose. Today it seemed to have amplified itself and he concentrated on breathing through his mouth as his eyes adjusted to the gloomy kitchen. The cat appeared from the shadows and screeched at him, threading itself between his legs, making it difficult for him to cross the room.

'Bugger off,' he hissed as he aimed his sock at its backside. Trying not to notice the dripping bag of curds or the gathering oily-looking whey which was arousing such interest in the bluebottles, he filled the kettle and placed it on the comforting warmth of the range. After several false starts he found a tin containing strong-smelling tea and the small teapot which Rowena had left full of the previous day's brew. He watched it trickle down the drain in the old stone sink and wondered what he should do about the swarm of tea leaves which clogged the plughole. Grimacing with disgust, he scraped the slimy brown leaves up with his fingers and flicked them into a bucket hidden behind the curtain under the sink. He scowled at the chunks of solidified grease which had somehow got themselves mixed up with the tea dregs and were now adhering to his fingernails. He ran the hot-water tap, waiting an age for the warmth to run through and then after several moments tried unsuccessfully to rinse his hands under the cold water. In frustration he picked up a tea towel and scraped his fingers over it. By now the water was ready for making the tea. In the larder, the giant pitcher of milk stood on a shelf, covered with a round of tattered muslin. Hugo lifted the muslin and peered into the jug. A crust of pale yellow had formed around the very edge of the white milk which remained stuck to the sides as Hugo swilled the liquid around. The smell was not dissimilar to that of the cheesemaking process underway in the kitchen. Steeling himself, telling himself not to be so wimpish, he splashed far too much milk into both mugs, dribbled honey over the table and down the sides of Rowena's mug, and then remembered to feed the bloody cat. By the time he made it back up the stairs, Rowena was flat out on her back, mouth open and snoring contentedly. Helplessly Hugo looked around for somewhere to place the tea. There was hardly any furniture in the room at all, save for the small double bed, a couple of bentwood hat stands littered with Rowena's clothes, and a bookshelf stacked full of books. He bent down and placed the mugs on the floor and then climbed into bed beside her. He listened as the snoring got louder and then he poked her arm, waking her with a start.

'Darling,' he said joyfully. 'Tea has arrived.'

Chapter Twenty-six

'Well, what do you think?' Fern stepped over a pile of sagging cardboard boxes, sending a cloud of dust upwards. Johnny choked. Through a watery-eyed mist he took in the sorry shelves which were hanging away from the walls, the depressing red-and-black vinyl tiles covering the floor, and the ghastly fluorescent strip lights overhead. He felt he had to say something positive.

'Well,' he said, playing for time, 'it's, er, certainly got, um, potential. Hasn't it?' he added brightly.

'So you can see it?' she said with satisfaction.

'I . . . er . . . Yes, I can.'

'You don't think I'm bonkers, then?'

'Bonkers! Not in the least. Why on earth should I think that?' he lied uneasily.

'Liar!' she cried, and burst out laughing. 'It's written all over your face, Johnny Sharpe. You think I'm *completely* bonkers, you think the shop's awful and you're far too nice to admit it to me.'

'Well, maybe not *completely* bonkers; just a small bit bonkers.'

'Yep,' she said, looking around at the sad state of disrepair. 'Anyone who could think they'd make a silk purse out of this dump would have to be. Bert's Bakery. I wonder what happened to Bert?'

Johnny blew the dust off the wooden countertop and hitched himself up onto it. 'So, what's the plan?'

'The lads arrive on Monday and by Friday all this crap will be out, and the transformation begins.'

'Lads? What lads?'

'Me old mates Mick and Sean, that's who. The brickie and the chippie. We were at school together. I called them up and asked them if they'd be interested and they said they'd be over on the next boat. I had to persuade them to wait a couple of days. But believe you me, Johnny, they're brilliant. I'm designing some old apothecary-type shelves and drawers and things. I thought mahogany would look good against dark green walls, old pine floorboards, and "DON-LEAVY'S" in large gold letters on a dark green background across the front. Or maybe painted in an arc across the window. What do you think?'

'God knows, Fern. If you can pull this lot together it'll be a bloody miracle. And that's just the start of it. What about the product?'

'All in hand. I'm going up to Malvern tomorrow to see a company about producing the stuff. I've already decided on the bottles. Four different sizes, plain glass, with heavy round stoppers in the top – all recycleable and refillable. I'm talking to the bottle people about having "Donleavy's" embossed into the glass, but I'm not sure of the cost yet. There's going to be a line of twenty lotions, all available in various sizes, six different floral soaps, four toilet waters, six bath salts, four shampoos, and a special limited edition of silver-lidded jars which a silver-smith in Wales is designing for me, for the "top end of the market".'

'And dried flowers, I suppose,' Johnny sighed. 'You'd better have some of those, hadn't you?'

'Not *dried*, Johnny. Where *have* you been? Everyone knows they're dreadfully passé these days. Parchment flowers – that's what I shall have – huge bowls and jugs filled with parchment flowers. I've already seen a couple in Gloucestershire about

345

supplying me with those. Oh, and I've found a Victorian till,' she added as a triumphant after-thought.

'So when do you think you'll be opening?'

'Dunno yet. A month, six weeks, something like that.'

'You really are crazy. You couldn't possibly get all this sorted out by then. You need at least three months. You're planning on getting at least forty different products formulated, packaged and on to the shelves in a saleable state in a matter of weeks?'

'Sure, why not? Everyone I've spoken to who's going to be involved in helping me thinks they can come up with the stuff very quickly.'

'But believe me, Fern. I know about these things. When Oscars launch a product it can take a year – even two years.'

'But it's not like one of Oscar Rees's products, is it? That's all scientific baloney about finding miracle ingredients and marvellous new formulas. This is all about simplicity – returning to Victorian times when only natural stuff was available. So long as the pro-duct doesn't go off or cause some ghastly reaction then that's all there is to it. I've got Alexander look-ing into it for me at this very moment.'

'You should stay well clear of him. I've told you before. He's exceedingly bad news. You shouldn't trust him with anything.'

Fern pushed her bottom up onto the counter top and shuffled her way to Johnny's side. She smiled at him benevolently. 'I know what you've heard about him, Johnny, but I can only go on what he's been like to me. He's been helpful and nice. I've got to make my own judgements. You should know that by now'.

'Like with Paul, you mean?'

346

'Ouch! That was below the belt, Johnny.' She jumped down and headed off towards the door.

'Fern!' he called after her. 'Stop! I'm sorry. I know I shouldn't have said that. It just slipped out. It was a rotten thing to say.'

'Yes, it was. Rotten and cruel, Johnny.'

He took her by the arm and pulled her back from the doorway. 'Look, don't you realize I'm only saying these things because I worry about you? I think you've had enough trouble lately without getting into any more. I just want to warn you. I guess I felt maybe your judgement hadn't been so hot in the past. I know it sounded cruel, but I had to say it!'

'Thanks,' she said frostily. 'I appreciate the advice. Thanks for coming,' she tried to pull her arm away from him but Johnny's grip tightened. Suddenly she was staring straight into his eyes. He could see the darting flames of anger light the smoky emerald eyes.

Then, as suddenly, he released her. 'Sorry. Didn't mean to do that,' he muttered and pushed past her. 'Got to go,' he mumbled and shot through the open doorway, leaving her watching his back disappear, in puzzlement.

Olivia stabbed her cigarette into the ashtray and promptly lit another one. Then she sloshed some more whisky into her glass and drained it. She paced the room agitatedly, flicking ash distractedly in her wake.

'Olivia, for God's sake, sit down and relax. I've never seen you in such a dreadful state.' Linda propped herself up on the pillows and watched Olivia's rather emaciated-looking naked body move jerkily towards her. She was one lump of stressed-out flesh. 'How about another massage?'

'Linda, I've had three already today. And at the moment I'm afraid I'm finding the whisky does the trick more successfully.'

'You're only punishing yourself,' Linda sighed.

'Punishing *myself*? For God's sake, girl, I hardly need to do that, now do I? Everyone seems to be doing a thorough job of that on my behalf.'

'Look, you've got to do something constructive, Olivia, instead of hitting the drugs like this. Surely there must be something you could do?'

'Short of murdering the little bitch, I really don't think there's anything else.'

'She's only a snippet of a girl, for heaven's sake.'

'I know. That's what makes it so bloody maddening. In the space of just a few short weeks, that little bastard has elbowed her way into the Clinic, brainwashed all the trustees with her bountifulness, got Alexander apparently eating out of her disgusting little palm, wrapped Hugo round her little finger, moved into *my* house, become a shareholder of Oscars, turned into a celebrity through the fact that her boyfriend didn't do a proper job of finishing her off and no one can see that she's really a complete and utter *nobody*! And you tell me she's a snippet of a girl. I KNOW THAT!' she screeched, reaching once more for the whisky bottle.

'Do you realize, Linda, that because of her generosity, I am expected to match, if not beat, her donation to the Foundation? H'm? And if I do, then I shall either have to sell my shares or ask Hugo for more money. I'm going to be poor, Linda. Do you hear that? Poor!'

'Down to your last ten million, you mean,' Linda muttered under her breath.

'Oh, it may sound a lot to you, you little tartlet, but I have a position to uphold. I have to buy a decent

348

house. I *have* to live in Chelsea. There's my wardrobe to consider, holidays, visits to friends – you have no comprehension of what it's like to be poor.'

'Olivia, if you weren't such a good lay I'd give you a jolly good smacked bottom. You're sounding ridiculous. And if you really think you're going to be so hard done by, why the hell don't you tell your lawyers to get more money out of Hugo?'

Olivia drew hungrily on her cigarette and blew the smoke out in a furious jet.

'Can't you blackmail him or something?'

'Blackmail Hugo? You have to be joking. He's such a boring old sod that he's never done anything remotely naughty in his life, bar bonking that wimpish Ricci Pembroke and adopting stray bastards. No, I can't think of anything at all. He's too squeaky clean. I'll just have to make his life difficult through the lawyers – stick in a demand for an extra ten million, something like that. Maybe he'll be so desperate to get rid of me he'll crumble. We'll see. God, that bloody girl!'

Hugo was feeling far from squeaky clean at this very moment. He was standing watching a miserable sheet of rain sweep relentlessly down on the window, much as it had done for most of the day. The hills beyond the cottage were shrouded in dank grey mist, which swirled oppressively over the fields towards the cottage. Rowena had locked herself up in the studio leaving him to pace around boredly. He longed for a hot shower and a delicious, Connaught-style meal. His isolation was increased by the fact there was no tangible contact with the outside world. Even the sound of a telephone ringing would have been a welcome diversion, or a snippet of Radio Four. Looking out on this lonely vista, one could

349

imagine the world had completely passed one by. No traffic, no bustle, no people, no communication, just lots of rain and solitude.

He tried to settle himself down with a book, but found Rowena's choice of literature somewhat different to his own. He flicked through *The Creation of Patriarchy* and decided to give it a miss. Then he picked up *Outrageous Acts and Everyday Rebellions* by someone called Gloria Steinem, who sounded vaguely familiar. Here were rows of books designed to make him feel guilty for wielding a penis. Is this what he had done to her? He swallowed hard, feeling close to tears, afraid of the unfamiliar emotion. He never cried. Never much to cry about it, really. Rowena would call him arrogant for believing himself responsible for her 'feminism'. A humble man couldn't wield that kind of power over a woman. Not an emancipated, liberated woman like Rowena. She had turned into a hermit crab which had crawled into a shell a touch too tight for it and now was unable to get back out. It had welded itself to her body and now she was stuck there, inviolate and unreachable.

Last night she had almost escaped, letting him near her vulnerability, but since they had dressed the mood had broken. She had bustled around, coldly efficient and brusque, treating him like an awkward intrusion into her life. She had mocked his manners, his clothes and his character, making him feel as out of place as a duck in a hen house.

He moved over to the doorway and stared for several moments at the studio where he knew she was busy painting, or thinking, or whatever it was she did. He considered going to see her, but something, some instinct, stopped him. He took one last, slow look around and then sadly, with wooden steps, he made his way through the cottage, closing the front door finally behind him.

Rowena caught the sound of the car engine firing into life. She threw down her brush and raced back into the cottage. 'Hugo!' she called out, running through the kitchen, bumping into the chair and sending it flying in front of her. She reached the front door just as the small red car rounded the bend beyond the cottage, so that although she could still hear it, she could no longer see it.

With heart pounding loudly, filling her ears, she walked back into the kitchen, searching for a note, for some indication as to what had happened, why he had decided to go. But there was nothing. She sat down heavily and rested her head in her hands, waiting for something, whatever emotion, to take hold of her. For some time she remained, motionless, emotionless, just waiting, and then slowly at first, tears started to spill silently down her cheeks.

There she remained until the daylight faded and the silent darkness filled the cottage. With infinite care she found one of the paraffin lamps and made her way out to the studio. She struggled through her artist's debris and opened up the large chest. Then she pulled out the painting. She knew what she had to do.

Carefully she carried it out of the studio. The moon showed its light from between the clouds and cast a ghostly glow over Hugo's young face. Tenderly she smiled at the features of the man who no longer existed. She picked up some dry kindling from the woodpile and built a small heap in the middle of the stone courtyard to the side of the cottage. She removed the glass globe from the lamp and exposed the blue-rimmed flame, picked up a small twig and teased it into fiery life. Then she put the burning twig into the pile, and blew gently on to the flame, to fan its efficiency. She unscrewed the cap from a bottle of white spirit and sprinkled it over the edges of the canvas. When she was finally satisfied with her makeshift incinerator, she ceremoniously laid the painting down.

She stepped back and watched as the flames searched and licked their way around the canvas. As they found the dry varnished wood, they hissed and crackled hungrily. Shadows fell across his face, and then flame brought it once more to life. As the pyre grew hotter, the holes started to appear. The centre seemed to form a cavity and the paint melted and bubbled into huge blister-like wounds. Rowena forced herself to watch the systematic destruction of her dream.

Maybe now she could be free.

Chapter Twenty-seven

As soon as Hugo had settled himself down in his chair, Laura appeared. 'Thank God you're back!' she cried. 'The whole world's been trying to find you. Where on earth have you been?'

'Nowhere important,' he grunted, avoiding Laura's curious eyes. 'I just took a couple of days off. I needed to sort something out, and now it's sorted, so that's that.'

'Good. I'm glad. David wants to speak to you urgently. Leo Eden wants a meeting with you. Johnny wants to speak to you about Fern . . . '

'Anything else?'

'Isn't that enough to be going on with? I'm sure I can come up with a few more bits and pieces if you want.'

'All right, Laura, thank you,' he snapped a little too coldly. He wasn't in the mood for her wisecracks. 'Get me David, will you?'

'Certainly, sir.' She reversed out of the room.

'Bloody women,' Hugo mouthed silently.

'Where the hell have you been?' David's urgent tone immediately put Hugo's back up even further.

'Look, what is this, some kind of interrogation? I went away for a couple of days. It's *allowed*, isn't it?'

'No, not when you're head of an international company and nobody knows where the hell you are. The whole world could collapse around you. As a matter of fact it probably has.'

Hugo had a mental picture of vultures, in the form of Rowena, David, Ricci, Olivia, circling round his head, all closing in on him, waiting for a stab at his flesh.

'What do you want, anyway?'

Charming as ever, David thought, ignoring Hugo's brutal tone. 'Olivia is being exceedingly difficult over the divorce. Her lawyers have slung in a demand for another £10 million. They say they'll advise her to go for the house if you don't cough up.'

'So tell them to eff off. She's not getting it.'

'She's going to take you to court, then.'

'Let her. Everyone should have their day.'

'Yes, Hugo, but perhaps not at your expense.'

'So, what are you saying, give in?'

'What I'm thinking is that because of the complexity and diversity of the business, because she's Easton's daughter and because of the length of the marriage, because she doesn't actually work and because you get to keep the company et al., I want you to think about the likely implications of a costly court battle and all the attendant publicity.'

Hugo whistled through his teeth in annoyance. 'Telling me to give in, are you, David?'

'No. But maybe you should up the ante a little. Listen, I've been through some figures, and I'd like to pop over and see you later today, if it's convenient. Then we can chat about it in more detail. We've got fourteen days to get back to them, though I have to tell you two have already gone.'

'H'mph!' Hugo grunted. 'Come in at three.' David was still saying goodbye as the phone clicked down on him.

'Get me Leo Eden!' Hugo snapped into his intercom.

'Thank you,' Laura snapped back as she picked up

her telephone. God, Hugo really could be an absolute pig to work for at times.

'Leo, I gather you wanted to talk to me.'

'Hugo.' Leo sounded delighted to hear him. 'How are you, old chap?'

'Not so much of the "old", thank you, and I'm fine. You?'

'Never been better. Listen, remember we chatted about Oscars and a certain arrangement? Well, without going into it over the phone I'd like to meet you, talk a little further. I've an idea which might interest you. Dinner perhaps?'

'Four o'clock this afternoon.'

Hugo slammed the phone down and buzzed Laura. 'David at three, Eden at four, okay?'

'Sir!' she snapped. 'Anything else?'

'Yes. Send Johnny Sharpe in.'

'Why is it everyone around me seems to be constantly wingeing,' Hugo moaned almost to himself as he listened to Johnny. 'What the hell is going on here? I leave the office for two days and during that time you let my daughter get some totally harebrained idea into her head and seemingly condone her plans by visiting shops with her, and then come complaining to me that you're worried about her. Why the hell didn't you stop her, man?'

'Because she's too damned stubborn!' Johnny cried. 'She's your daughter, Hugo. I've been in agonies about whether I should talk to you, and if it wasn't for the fact that she was getting herself involved with Alexander I probably would have minded my own business. I've tried to tell her several times that Alexander is an evil little shit but she just won't listen. And now she's got this idea into her head of renting a shop and producing cosmetics, as if it were as easy as setting up a WI stall.'

'Then why don't you stop her?'

'I told you. She won't listen. Maybe you could.'

Hugo laughed humourlessly. 'Oh, she won't listen to me. I've got no bloody hope. Wouldn't even try and waste my breath. That is one hell of a determined girl. All we can do, Johnny, is sit back and watch. Keep our eyes on her, inconspicuously, as it were.'

'Spy on her, you mean?'

'I wouldn't put it quite like that, Johnny. Just watch out so far as Alexander is concerned. Try and make sure he's not conning her.'

'Thanks. That's all I need, a brief to watch that snake.'

'All in a day's work, dear boy.'

'I'm a Product Manager, not a spy.'

'But she is your assistant, and you are responsible for her.'

'She's your daughter!'

'Then I shall help you. Don't worry, Johnny. She'll soon get bored with this little idea of hers when she realizes it takes a lot more than a few bottles full of Granny's potions and a shop in Covent Garden to be successful in cosmetics. But I get the feeling she has to find out the hard way.'

'Too bloody true. Shall I tell her you're back?'

'I'll pop down and see her later.'

In truth Hugo wasn't particularly looking forward to facing Fern. He was dreading her asking him about how his trip went, about what had actually taken place between her mother and father. Equally he wasn't too keen on being reminded of red-haired Irish women. More than twenty years was one hell of a long time to nurture a dream. Two days was a hell of a shocking way to come down off that dream.

*　　　*　　　*

356

By the time Leo came in, Hugo was feeling battered, bruised and exhausted both emotionally and physically. He was sick and tired of Olivia's divorce demands, sick of the bloody money. He just wanted to get shot of her so that he could get on with his life. He knew now that the time for living in the past had finally been exorcized. He had to get on with his life, make what was left of it a hell of a lot more fulfilling than that which had gone before. He had sat and listened to David's earnest advice.

'Give her another five million, Hugo, and get rid of her. Full and final settlement,' he had said.

God, that sounded good. It seemed to be the week for full and final settlements. Perhaps he should take it as an omen.

'Thing is, Hugo,' Leo's voice cut into his thoughts, 'I've been thinking that since the sale of the lines to Coopers, and bearing in mind the divorce – which I hope you don't mind my raising – I feel you might welcome a small cash injection into the company. And I'd quite like to get involved with Oscars on a personal basis.'

'You want a job?' Hugo tried hard not to sound incredulous, but failed.

'No,' Leo laughed quietly. 'Not a job. I've enough with the one I've got for the moment. I'd like to become a shareholder, sort of non-executive director, if you like. That's if there are any shares up for grabs at the moment.'

Hugo's grin spread across his face. Hadn't he just told himself that he was about to start a new phase in his life? Get shot of all the old rubbish; start afresh?

'How's ten per cent sound?'

'Ten per cent sounds pretty okay to me.' Leo's grin echoed Hugo's.

'Good. I'll have the papers drawn up by my lawyer. I'll sell you some of my personal shares. £12 million to you, Mr Eden.'

'Phew . . . that's two million over the odds.'

'I know. Take it or leave it.'

'I'll take it.'

'Good.' Hugo stood up and stretched his arm across the desk. 'Welcome aboard Oscar Rees, Leo.'

'Of course this will be a private arrangement, you understand.' Leo gazed unfalteringly at Hugo. 'I wouldn't wish Coopers to get the wrong idea.'

'A private investor? Of course. I'm sure you'll be well satisfied with your investment.'

'I have no doubt of it,' Leo said enigmatically.

Leo strolled down Long Acre, hands in his trouser pockets, whistling quietly to himself. He knew exactly where he was headed, having driven past it the previous night. As he neared the shop front he slowed his pace and came to a halt outside the shiny new plate-glass window. 'Not bad,' he muttered to himself as he examined the gold calligraphy across the window.

'Donleavy's' was spread in a huge arc across the front, in letters a foot high. Two standard bay trees stood sentry outside the shop doorway. He tutted to himself. 'They'll soon develop legs . . . ' He peered in through the glass, scowling into the dark interior, a hand on his brow to shield the daylight from his eyes, and then caught sight of a movement towards the shelves. Fern was balanced somewhat precariously on the top of a wooden step ladder, clutching an armful of glass bottles. He watched for a few moments longer as she carefully deposited the load on to the shelves, and then climbed back down. Leo walked jauntily through the open door.

Fern was bent double over a huge cardboard box. Her hair was swept up in a triangle of cotton and there was an interesting glimpse of bare flesh where her T-shirt had parted from the waist of her jeans. She stood up carefully cradling a further armful of bottles.

'Want a hand?' he asked nonchalantly.

'Good God!' she cried, struggling to hang on to her burden. 'You gave me a fright!'

'Sorry,' he grinned at her. 'I didn't mean to. You're obviously very involved.'

She placed the bottles down on the countertop and adjusted the scarf, pushing it back from her damp forehead. Then she wiped her hands down the front of her striped butcher's apron. 'I am. There seems to be such a lot to do. We open in a week and most of the boxes are still to unpack. I keep arranging and rearranging bottles. I'm even doing it in my sleep.'

'Don't you have any help? Where are your staff?'

'I've sent them both out to buy a sandwich and some polish.'

'Polish?'

'For the shelves.'

She folded her arms in front of her, feeling awkward and shy. Why was it he always made her feel like that? As ever, he looked annoyingly at ease, standing there with his hands stuffed into his pockets, grinning at her, laughing at her.

Leo glanced around the shop, letting his eyes roam over the old-fashioned shelves. Flower names had been carefully lettered in gold to match the contents of the bottles arranged above them. He picked up one of the large bottles. It felt nicely heavy in his hand and he touched the smooth round stopper, noticing how well it fitted into his palm. 'Nice,' he commented, 'very nice.' The label had been beautifully decorated with a soft watercolour wash depicting a bunch of lavender tied with a pink ribbon. 'Donleavy's' followed the curve of the top of the label, again carefully scripted in gold. The paper was slightly uneven, giving the appearance of parchment. He replaced the bottle on the shelf and picked up another, while Fern watched him silently. He followed the line of all the shelves and then spotted the small silver-topped jars which Fern felt particularly pleased with.

'What on earth . . .?' He picked up the small pot and peered at the miniature label. 'Rose and honey enriched face cream. It sounds almost edible.' He picked up another. 'Hawthorn and cucumber facial tonic?'

Fern watched his face, for some reason hardly daring to breathe.

'And what's this, orange and magnolia cream bath? It sounds as if you're opening a food shop, rather than a cosmetics shop. And all these sizes, let's see, you've covered a wide price range.'

'The smallest start at £3.99, and the biggest is £8.99. The silver ones are £25. That's because they're a bit special.'

'Well, I have to congratulate you, Fern. It all looks marvellous.'

Despite her reticence she beamed at him. 'Do you really think so?'

'I do. I should think you'll have them queueing down the whole of Long Acre. What are you doing about publicity?'

'I've got a small crowd coming round next Friday night for drinks, a few press and some friends, then it's all go on Saturday.'

'Has Hugo seen it yet?'

'No. He's waiting until Friday night. He's one of

the many who think I've gone totally barmy.' She looked at her watch. 'I shouldn't really be here now. It's my lunch hour so I thought I'd just pop over and have a look. It's hard to resist. I'm just itching to get my sleeves rolled up and wait for the till to start ringing.'

'Do you think I might invite myself then, on Friday night? I'd like to help give you a good sendoff.'

'Sure,' she said, taken aback. 'If you've got nothing better to do.'

'I wouldn't miss it for the world, if you'll have me,' he grinned.

'It's, er, seven o'clock.'

'Fine, I'll see you then,' he said and strolled back out of the door. Fern started to hum softly to herself, feeling more light-hearted than she had in days.

When Fern returned to Oscars she found Johnny pacing up and down outside her office in a foul mood.

'Oh you're back at last!' he grunted.

'I've only been gone an hour and a half.'

'Fern, you're gone an hour and a half every bloody lunchtime. You disappear off at 5.30 on the dot. You're turning into a real little clock-watcher.'

'I didn't realize it was a problem. I've been doing my work, haven't I?'

'Yes, yes, of course you have, brilliantly. It's just I'm finding it difficult to work with someone whose mind seems to be permanently elsewhere!'

As soon as he saw the look of hurt in her eyes he immediately regretted his outburst. He couldn't fault her work, that was partly the trouble. He'd like a reason to be angry with her, he was almost spoiling for a fight, and for the life of him he couldn't work out why.

'Look, it's okay, forget I spoke.'

361

'It's all right. I'm very conscious of trying not to let Donleavy's interfere. You obviously feel it is.'

Johnny ushered her to her chair. 'Sit,' he said gently. He perched on the edge of her desk and studied the floor, unable to meet her eyes. 'You did an excellent job on the marketing plan for Ozzie. You know how much Hugo loved the idea of sponsoring St Martin's Fashion School's annual show. It's exactly the right market for Ozzie and it was an inspired idea to give the students a T-shirt to design. That'll give us a lot of press coverage, and then there'll be the merchandizing on the top. And it was your idea to get the shop-in-shop managers along to an annual training session where we can update them on what's going on with the products and give them a chance to feel good about Oscars. Just think how hard they all are going to be working when they know there's the quarterly draw for a weekend in Paris at the George V, courtesy of Oscars, for the highest sales target?'

Fern shrugged. 'It seemed kind of obvious.'

'The best ideas always are – once someone's thought of them. And you did. How can anyone fault you?'

'Then why are you so cross with me?'

'I dunno. Maybe you intimidate me, you're so bloody wonderful.'

'Johnny!' She looked at him hard, trying to find out whether he was serious. 'You can't mean that.'

'I guess not.'

'I'm not after your job, you know.'

'I should think not. You wouldn't be able to fit it in. Besides you're already doing half of it.'

'But I thought that's what I was supposed to do, be your assistant,' she said indignantly.

Johnny stood up and paced the small room. 'Look, forget it. I shouldn't have said anything, okay?'

362

'Okay. And by the way,' she said in a small voice as he headed for the doorway, 'I've got Paul's trial starting tomorrow. So I won't be here then, either. I don't know how long I'll be needed for.'

Johnny thumped the side of his head. 'Jesus Christ, I'm sorry, Fern. What a bloody clot I am. Look, I'll come with you.'

'Forget it.' She tried to smile, but it went all crooked. 'You'd better man the fort here. We can't have two of us out.'

Johnny marched out of the room, wishing he'd got the guts to garotte himself.

Fern shook her head. Maybe she, too, had been below the belt this time, but it was true she had the trial, and she didn't quite know how she was going to handle it. The only good thing about it was that the lawyers had told her Paul intended to plead guilty and that meant it would all be over quickly. Her presence was just a formality in case the judge had any questions, or in case anything went wrong with the plea. She had been trying not to think about it at all.

The phone on her desk trilled to life.

'Fern?' She recognized Alexander's smooth voice immediately. 'Dear Fern,' he continued, 'how's it all going?'

'Oh fine, thanks, Alexander. Exhausting but fine. What's happening at the Clinic?'

'We should be ready to run next week. Marvellous, isn't it? Anyway I just wanted to give you a quick buzz to ask a favour.'

'Sure,' she said, 'ask away.'

'Well, we've had a slight hiccup with one of the consultants over here. Thing is, he's a bit "old school", if you know what I mean. Seems he's a little dubious over the idea of us giving cosmetic treatments under the guise of the Foundation. He's rabbiting on about it demeaning the Foundation's work. Anyway, I thought it might be a good idea if you could perhaps have a word with him, being as you're on the Board and all that, perhaps let him know that a substantial amount of revenue from our little venture will be going to line the Foundation's coffers – which,' he laughed, 'at the end of the day pay these silly old duffers' salaries. Would you mind awfully?'

Fern sighed heavily into the phone. This was the last thing she bloody well needed. 'No, Alexander, of course I wouldn't mind. Which consultant is it?'

'Cameron Hope-Dickins. I hope you manage to sort him out. You're a brick.'

Fern put her face in her hands. She had two reports to put together for Johnny, and after his outburst just now she had to make sure they were shit hot. Then she had to convince Hugo that she wasn't wasting company time. She had to get to Malvern tonight to have a meeting with the Product Head there about future deliveries of Donleavy's goods, and then do a final ring round of all the press who were supposed to be coming on Friday night. And she had to get to court for 11.30 tomorrow.

Through the haze of her anxiety, she caught sight of a number which she had valiantly ignored for the past few days, and then without a second thought she punched out the digits.

'Josephine Adams Public Relations.' The girl sounded efficient and businesslike.

'This is Fern Donleavy. I'd like to speak to Josephine Adams. I've got a project I need help with . . . a party . . . in four days' time. Think you can handle it?'

What the hell was the point in having all this

money if she killed herself before she had a chance to enjoy it?

Leo was reading the paper with particular intensity. The small photograph of Fern caught his attention. There was an item on that bastard Paul's trial. He felt the knot in his gut tighten as he read the few lines. A guilty plea had been accepted by the judge, and sentencing had been delayed, pending reports. Leo's eyes narrowed dangerously. For his own good, that boy had better pray he'd be locked up for a long time to come. If Leo got his hands on him he'd be lucky to walk again! He swore at the intrusive ringing of the telephone and snapped into the mouthpiece.

'Leo, thank goodness,' India's smooth voice purred down the telephone. 'I've been trying to reach you all day. You're becoming frightfully elusive, darling.'

'Really? I'm sorry.' Leo struggled to keep the impatience out of his voice. His eyes fell on the pile of messages left by his secretary. 'I've been rather tied up.'

'Well, I rather gathered that. I was just ringing to remind you about Friday.'

'Friday?'

'You haven't forgotten, darling?' she sighed with exasperation. 'The ballet, remember? I've got tickets for Covent Garden. Then we're meeting Mummy and Daddy for dinner. So what shall we do? Meet there at 7.15?'

Leo's dark brows knitted together in a deep frown. It had completely slipped his mind. 'Um, look, India, something's come up. I don't think I'm going to be able to make it.'

'Leo! You've *got* to make it. I've had these tickets booked for weeks.'

'I know, I know. I really am sorry. But I've got to look at a new business proposition. It's very important. I really don't think I can get out of it.'

'Can't you switch your meeting? Please do try, darling. We hardly seem to see each other these days. And you really did promise me.' Her wheedling voice irritated him.

'No,' he said firmly. 'I can't switch it. I'm truly sorry, but there's absolutely nothing I can do. Perhaps your mother – '

'I want to go with you, not with my mother, Leo. For God's sake, we are supposed to be having a relationship, you know. Lately I'm beginning to wonder whether you're that interested.'

Leo couldn't be bothered to get into a heavy discussion. He had several calls to make before he left the office, and he didn't have time to spend on sorting out his love life right now.

'Of course I am, ' he said placatingly. 'Tell you what, why don't we have dinner on Saturday? You book wherever you like, and I promise we'll have a lovely evening together. I really am sorry about Friday, but there's nothing I can do.'

'I'm very upset,' she said, sounding like a spoiled child. 'You're very naughty, Leo.'

'These things happen, India. You know how busy I am.'

'Well, I'm busy, too, but it all depends on one's priorities, doesn't it?'

'Look, India, I've got to go. Call me on Saturday morning.'

There was no way in the world he intended to miss Fern's opening night. He had an idea it was going to be a most interesting evening.

India was seething with silent indignation as Fenella,

her assistant, marched into the office. 'What now?' India snapped fiercely.

'Sorry, but I was just bringing you your faxes. I thought – '

'What is it? Is it important?'

'I don't think so. Just the stockists' details you asked for for the piece on Tibetan jewellery. There's only a couple of places in the whole country and they're both in the southeast.'

'Well, anyone who wants it will just have to get it by mail order, won't they?' She sighed in exasperation. 'Pass it on to subs, will you? I imagine you've checked it out factually.'

'Yes, I have.' Fenella started to retreat. She hated India when she was in one of her moods. She could be a real cow. Lately she was becoming a bore to work for.

'And what else?' India's tone stopped her.

'Just an invitation to a shop opening. I'll pass it to one of the girls in Features, if you like. I don't think you'll want to go.'

'I can't imagine why people seriously expect the Deputy Editor of *A La Mode* would be interested in every little tinpot shop that opens up.' Her eyes scanned the press release. 'Wait a moment,' she said, suddenly. 'Fern Donleavy. That's the Oscar Rees girl! So she's opening a shop selling her grandmother's cosmetics, is she? What a silly idea. You know, I'm almost tempted to go along. Let's see, when is it? Friday . . . h'm.' She considered the fax. 'Listen, Fenella, do you like ballet?'

'I quite enjoy it, but it's a while since I've been. It's so damned expensive these days.'

'How do you fancy going to Covent Garden on Friday night? I've got two tickets and, er, I can't go. You can have them, if you like.'

'Well, if you're sure . . . that would be lovely. Er, thanks, India.' Fenella was trying to cover up her shock. India was not generally known for her largesse.

'Good. I'll bring them in with me tomorrow.'

Fenella closed India's office door behind her. One day she'd be able to work that woman out. Maybe.

Chapter Twenty-eight

As Fern listened to Cameron Hope-Dickins' affected
voice drone on and on, she was busy doing mental
time-and-motion studies, working out whether she
could get two hundred press releases written, printed
and collated by five o'clock this afternoon when she
only had two and a half hours to go. She tried not to
wriggle in her seat, containing her impatience in
clenched fists hidden beneath the desk. Smiling sympathetically through gritted teeth, she nodded atten-
tively as the doctor made his point for about the tenth
time.

'Miss Donleavy, you have to understand my position. I am one of the world's leading plastic surgeons
and I have to be most careful about my reputation.
I'm sure you understand that.'

'Of course, Mr Hope-Dickins.'

'And I have always been proud to be associated
with the Rees Foundation.'

'Yes.'

'But if there is going to be the slightest suggestion
that dubious cosmetic treatments will be carried out
there under the guise of the Clinic's expertise, then I
shall be duty-bound to resign my services. Do I make
myself clear?'

'Crystal clear, Mr Hope-Dickins. I can only repeat
my assurances that Alexander Easton will be working
under the close supervision of eminent specialists,
and that the process in use has been tested in the US.
We will be doing an important service to the future of

cosmetic treatments such as this by getting them carried out by professionals, rather than some backstreet, unqualified, exploitation merchant. I do hope you will be able to give the Clinic your full support.'

'H'mph! I think the whole thing's a load of baloney. Now take someone like you, dear girl . . . '

Fern's hand flew self-consciously to her cheek. Over the weeks she had become a dab hand with concealing make-up techniques. In some lights the scarring was almost invisible, and she found she could forget about it for longer and longer periods.

'Now there's a worthy case for treatment if ever I saw one. But I fail to see the ethics in women having their skin messed about with in order to chase after some daft idea of youth.'

'Mr Hope-Dickins,' Fern said firmly, 'thank you for passing me your opinion, which of course I must take on board. I would just like to reassure you that the Foundation will benefit enormously from the Clinic's revenue.'

'Yes. But I shall be watching them very closely, Miss Donleavy, very closely.'

'So shall I.' She struggled to keep the smile off her face. 'Now I really mustn't keep you any longer.' She rose to her feet.

'Until next time, Miss Donleavy,' the doctor smiled graciously.

'Phew!' Fern breathed, as she escaped the Dickensian claustrophobia of the Harley Street rooms. But if Alexander cocked up with the Clinic, it would be *her* head on the block.

She shook her hair free from the restraining ribbon and broke into a run. Two hundred press releases, back to Queen Anne's Walk for a shower and quick change and then the shop by 5.30. She'd never make it!

At seven o'clock Fern put the finishing touches to the hanging clusters of green and gold balloons, festooning them with giant silk ribbons. The PR people were clucking around, checking on the drinks and food and Fern was quietly wondering just how two hundred bodies were going to cram themselves into what had suddenly become an impossibly small area.

Soon, as she cupped a reassuring glass of champagne in her hand, a handful of guests filtered through the doorway. Fern introduced herself and chattered away, making gentle small talk about her products. Politely she excused herself as she noticed Hugo's Bentley pull up outside. He struggled out of the car bearing an enormous bunch of red roses which obliterated the top half of his body.

He had to turn sideways to get through the door. He handed them to her with relief. 'There you are, darling, to wish you all the luck in the world.'

'Thank you,' she beamed at him. 'They're lovely. I'll find somewhere prominent to put them. Come and have a drink.'

While Fern disappeared into the back room for a vase, Hugo had an opportunity to look around at the beautifully stocked shelves. His eyes travelled over the assorted bottles and jars and Fern watched from the rear of the shop as a small smile spread over his face. Returning to his side, she waited.

'Marvellous!' he cried. 'Well done. I knew you could do it!' Fern thought it might seem churlish to remind him that he had thought her idea ridiculous. 'Looks absolutely super. How on earth did you manage it all in such a short time, and in your spare time, darling?'

'It was bloody hard work – and I'd never have managed if Johnny hadn't put me in touch with some of his contacts who helped me find the bottle company and the manufacturers in Malvern. I'm exhausted, but I think it's been worth it. I guess the next few days will tell. All I need after tonight is customers.'

Fern had to break off from chatting to Hugo as crowds of people began to arrive. Unfamiliar faces were grinning at her, congratulating her and telling her how simply marvellous it all was. The buzz of conversation filled the room, so that she was finding it difficult to hear. A few flashbulbs went off, and someone from a radio station asked her if she might step outside for a couple of minutes' worth of interview. So far so good . . .

Too excited to feel nervous, Fern breezed her way through the questions, noticing that the pavement was fast filling up with bodies. She caught sight of Johnny in the distance, accompanied by Zak the photographer. He waved to her and she blew him a kiss. Then she felt a firm hand at her elbow and turned to find herself looking up into Leo's dark-eyed grin.

'Congratulations!' he murmured, putting his lips so close to her ear that she could feel his warm breath on her skin. 'Looks like the party's a raging success.'

'Thank God,' she laughed. 'But I hardly know *anyone*. I chickened out and gave the whole thing to a PR company to deal with. I just ran out of time.'

'I should think that was an extremely sensible decision. Are you enjoying yourself, Fern?'

'Yes,' she nodded. 'I'm having a wonderful time. I can't quite believe it's all done. The last few weeks have been an organizational nightmare. Let me find you a drink.'

'No, no, I'll get you one. You are much in demand, I can tell. I'll find you in a little while.' She watched his tall frame move almost effortlessly through the sea of people. As she turned back she saw Johnny watching her. She tried to move over to him, but found her way blocked by a shaven-haired female. Fern's mouth dropped open in horror as she stared into Alix's scheming eyes.

'Fern!' Alix cried delightedly. 'How are you? I've been meaning to get in touch with you for *weeks*. What a busy time you've been having.'

'What are you doing here, Alix?' Her voice was full of undisguised loathing.

'I was invited. Nice champagne,' she said, raising her glass and knocking back its contents with satisfaction. 'Nice grub, too,' she said, cramming her face full of smoked-salmon canapé.

'You've got a bloody nerve!'

'I really don't understand what you mean. I was thinking I might run a little story on you, a nice rags to riches exposé. What do you think? Perhaps you might be prepared to give me an interview. I'm sure you'd be glad of the publicity.'

'I can just imagine what sort of exposé you'd give me, Alix. Thanks, but no thanks.'

'Suit yourself,' she shrugged. 'It's your loss. So, how's it feel being a shop girl?'

'I suggest you finish your champagne and leave.'

'Is that a quote I can use?'

'Go to hell, Alix!'

'Fern?' The familiar, slightly tentative voice rescued her.

'Ricci!' Fern exclaimed happily. 'How nice to see you. Come on, I'll show you around. 'Bye, Alix,' she called over her shoulder.

'Till soon, Fern.'

Fern shuddered. 'Awful female,' she hissed. 'Should have been drowned at birth.'

'Unusual for you to be so direct, Fern.'

Fern laughed. 'Cruel, you mean. Believe me, she's an absolute vixen. So, come and tell me what you think.'

Ricci put a restraining hand on Fern's arm. 'Is Hugo here?' she said a little nervously.

'H'm-m, though God knows where.'

'I assumed he would be. Perhaps if I just stay on this side of the room, then . . . '

'Don't be silly. You shouldn't cower in some corner, Ricci. Come on, I'll help you break the ice.'

Ricci's 'NO' was said with such vehemence that Fern stopped dead in her tracks. 'I just wanted to congratulate you, darling. I really can't stop. I'm accompanying friends to dinner. They're waiting for me outside.' She kissed Fern's cheek lightly and disappeared, leaving Fern disappointedly shaking her head. God, the older generation could be really stupid. Then Fern was swept into a corner by a couple of journalists. Automatically, she reeled off the answers to their questions.

'Excuse me, thank you. Excuse me . . . would you mind . . . ' the high-pitched female voice cut through the babble like a strangulated foghorn. 'Hey, um, Fern! Yes, that's right, you!'

Fern turned her head. 'India! What – ' She bit her tongue to stop a repeat of the conversation she had just had with Alix.

'Got your invitation and thought I'd pop in for five minutes. Course, it's all been done before. Nothing original is there?'

Fern raised her eyebrows and waited.

'Sort of up-market Body Shop, really. Who's backing you?'

'No one. I'm backing myself.'

'Oh, of course. I was forgetting. You got all the money from Oscars, didn't you? Quite a little windfall, I remember reading. Well, I'll give it six months.'

'Give what six months?' Fern regarded her incredulously.

India's eyes circled the room. 'Your venture. Very difficult to break into this sort of market, especially at this time.'

'Well, thanks for the advice, India. I'll remember it. I'm sure you'd like a drink?'

'Champagne? Thanks,' she said dismissively.

'Arsenic, more like,' Fern muttered under her breath.

'Ah, Fern, there you are. Here's that drink I promised you at least an hour ago.'

'Leo! What the hell . . . '

'India!'

Fern stood between the pair of them, taking in the look of horror on Leo's face, and the sheer disbelief on India's. Her presence seemed to have been temporarily forgotten.

'Business proposition!' India screeched. 'You said you'd got some bloody important business proposition. You lied to me!'

'I did not lie. This is it.' He grinned at Fern. 'I'm sorry, Fern, but you'll have to excuse India's outburst. I told her I had an important business proposition to look at, and so I have. Anyway, India, I wasn't expecting to see you here. I thought you'd be half way through Act One by now.'

'I bet you did,' she snarled at him. Then, as if seeing it in slow motion, Fern watched with amazement as India took one of the full glasses clutched in Leo's hand and poured the contents over his head.

Leo's mouth dropped open. Fern was caught between the urge to burst out laughing or gasp in horror. She grabbed a tea towel off a passing bottle and offered it to Leo. Streams of champagne were running down his face, dripping from his collar and onto his lapels. The babble of voices silenced as the crowd became aware of the drama unfolding before them. Cameras flashed and journalists fought their way through the crush to get a better view of the action.

India was standing, frozen, with the empty glass clutched in her hand. She seemed to be almost as surprised by her action as the rest of them. Without another word, she spun on her heel and swept out of the room.

'Women!' Leo sighed as he mopped himself up.

'Maybe you deserved it,' Fern said unsympathetically. 'And what did you mean about a business proposition? Is that what you think I am?'

'Too early to tell. But I like to keep my ear to the ground. I told you I was impressed by what I've seen, but as you said yourself, you haven't actually opened yet. We shall have to see.'

'I am not a business proposition,' she said defiantly. 'That's the only way you've ever looked at me, isn't it? When I was in the Foundation, when you were so helpful to me, that was because I was a business proposition, wasn't it?'

Fern was losing her temper. And the fact that they were surrounded by an intrigued crowd did nothing to cool her down.

'I was concerned for you, that's all.'

'Crap! You were concerned because you'd just bought Vitale and you thought you'd bought a turkey. That's the sum of your kindness.'

Leo took a firm hold of her arm and led her through

376

the circle of people, out onto the street, his face a mixture of anger and disbelief.

'Listen to me, you silly girl.'

She tried to break out of his grasp. 'I am not a silly girl, you arrogant – '

'Okay. Not *so* silly. But I visited you in the Foundation because I cared. I had you moved there because I cared. You've no idea what the sight of you lying there, all bandaged up like that, did to me. Now I'm sorry that I broke up your party. I had no idea India would be here. It's been embarrassing for you and I apologize. I'd better go.'

Fern couldn't believe her ears. He *cared* about her? He released her arm and took a step away from her.

'No.' The word was out before she could stop it. 'I mean – '

'You don't want me to go?'

'I'm not sure,' she shrugged, fighting her emotions. She was mixed up, confused. He did weird things to her. She felt unsettled, almost ill. Nothing made much sense. Suddenly she felt herself pulled towards him. He threw his arms around her and brought his mouth down heavily on hers. She felt herself sinking into some deep abyss, drowning, spinning around as if all will were leaving her, melting into him, unable to tear herself away. Her breath came in short gasps. His mouth was so hot, so demanding. Then suddenly he released her.

'There,' he murmured, 'what does that tell you?'

Fern brought her hands up to her face and placed her fingertips on her temples. 'I don't know,' she cried. 'I just don't know.'

'Have dinner with me!'

'But – '

'Your smart PR company will take care of everything. There's nothing more you can do. Besides, the longer you stay, the longer all the hangers-on will stick around drinking free champagne. It's stylish to leave your own party!'

'I don't care about that.'

'No,' he laughed quietly, 'I don't suppose you do. But please have dinner with me. It's long overdue, Fern.'

'Okay.' She felt as if she had just set the seal on something which could well turn out to be more than she could handle.

Zak watched Johnny's intent face. 'So, me old mate, you're hung up on her. Stop being so obvious. You look like a sick dog.'

'Don't know what you're talking about,' Johnny snapped gruffly, tearing his eyes reluctantly from the scene outside the window. 'I gave up women long ago, and well you know it!'

'Hey, man, no hard feelings. I'm not your keeper. But I don't like to see someone I care about makin' a fool of themselves. And I think that rather tasty-lookin' piece of rump steak just beat you to the lady.'

'Yeah. So it seems,' Johnny said morosely. 'Come on, let's get out of here.'

Alix downed the last drop of champagne and readjusted her rucksack. Tonight's little chain of events had been most enlightening. She was well pleased with herself for deciding to come along, just to see what snippets she could pick up and hopefully use against Fern sometime in the future. That girl had a bad habit of making enemies in the wrong places. Judging from India Duncan-Forrester's well-aimed drenching of Leo Eden, she wouldn't be at all happy about the fact that her boyfriend looked set to get his leg over Fern. She and India might have a little mutual interest, so to speak. Alix already had an idea of what she needed to do.

It seemed somehow inevitable that Leo would take Fern back to his house for coffee. It seemed more than inevitable that the coffee should be completely forgotten and, instead, she should be led gently through into his bedroom. She stood, hardly daring to breath as Leo gently slipped the soft wool jacket from her shoulders. She watched his face as he expertly undid the small pearl buttons on the front of her filmy crêpe de Chine blouse, and pushed it from her shoulders, revealing her naked breasts. Trembling now, he unzipped her trousers and helped her step out of them. She stood, arms by her side, shivering with desire as he reached out and drew her towards him. Her breasts pushed against the crisp cotton of his shirt. It felt cool against her nipples. His hard body, reassuringly strong, pressing into her loins. Slowly and tenderly he pushed her down onto the bed, letting his eyes roam luxuriously over her body as he pulled his shirt off.

She placed her arms above her head and crooked her knee and waited . . . She marvelled at the sight of his powerful body, his glowing olive-toned skin – the fine dark hairs that spread between his nipples and tapered down his belly. Her eyes rested on his proud penis, on the taut, silken skin which she ached to touch.

Leo lowered himself on top of her, almost squeezing the breath from her body. His mouth burned down on hers, hungrily devouring her, teasing her tongue, bruising her cheeks and neck with a delicious wet warmth. Fern threw her head back and moaned with sheer pleasure. Then Leo's lips tightened over her nipple while his tongue darted in an agony of ecstasy. She clutched his head to her breast, squirming against him. His searching fingers found the moist cleft between her legs. She heard the low gurgle of laughter in his throat.

Almost beyond consciousness, unaware of time and place, lost on some aching plane of urgent need, she urged his body towards hers. Her legs parted and at last she felt him lower himself against her loins. She felt the warm hardness of his shaft search probingly against her soft folds. He rocked into her, tentatively at first, oh so gently. Then she felt him push deep inside her. The fire started in her groin and spread up through her belly, into her breasts. She grasped his head, putting his mouth against hers, clutching at him frantically. Her legs slid up over his thighs, locking his pounding buttocks against her pelvis. 'Leo!' she cried out. 'Oh my God . . . Leo!'

Her body shuddered as the tiny convulsions overtook her, flooding her mind and her body. Then Leo was with her, slamming harder into her, gasping now, until he too cried out with the ecstasy of the moment. He flopped against her, finally spent. She opened her eyes and felt the warmth flow over her as she watched the smile of sheer delight spread across his face. She squeezed her arms around his broad back and wriggled underneath him.

'H'm!' she sighed. 'That was so nice!'

Leo pushed his arms under her and squeezed her tightly to him. 'It was wonderful, darling,' he sighed. 'And long overdue. But definitely worth waiting for!'

Fern snuggled into the warm safe circle of his arms.

Chapter Twenty-nine

Still drowsy from sleep, Fern felt Leo's body leave her side. She opened her eyes just in time to find him bending over her, kissing her firmly on the mouth.

'Morning, sweetheart,' he sighed warmly. 'I'm just popping out to buy the papers. Won't be long. Maybe there'll be something about the party.'

She couldn't believe his energy. They must have made love at least three more times during the night, and each time more slowly than the last.

She could close her eyes again and sleep forever . . .

She dreamed she was at the office. She was struggling to order more bottles for the shop, Johnny was shouting at her that Hugo was about to fire her and her phone was ringing. She tried to ignore the phone. She wanted Johnny to explain why . . . then Johnny started to fade. She swam back to consciousness. The phone trilled relentlessly on the bedside table. She continued to ignore it. Leo would get it. Then she remembered that Leo had gone out.

She reached out and knocked it off its cradle. With clumsy fingers she struggled to connect it with her ear.

'Hello,' she said at last.

'Oh, is that 584 0987?'

Fern tried to focus her eyes. 'Sorry,' she muttered, 'I'm afraid I don't know.'

'Oh!' the voice said abruptly and slammed the phone down.

Fern stared aggressively at the deserted receiver and leaned over to replace it. No sooner had she snuggled back down under the safe depths of the duvet, than the telephone rang again.

'Damn you,' she hissed at it. She wished Leo would hurry up. 'Hello!' she snapped unsolicitously.

'Look, I'm trying to get hold of Leo Eden. I'm sure I've got the right number.'

'You have.' Through the fog of exhaustion Fern had the nasty suspicion that she recognized the brittle female voice at the other end.

'Who is this?' the voice demanded arrogantly.

Fern's better nature told her that she should put the phone down but India Duncan-Forrester in no way deserved Fern's better nature.

'Hello, India, this is Fern. Would you like me to give Leo a message? He's just popped out.'

'Fern! What on earth are you doing there?'

'Trying to sleep,' Fern sighed, and put the phone gently down.

India Duncan-Forrester screamed in rage. 'Oh, how dare he!' she railed to the empty room. 'The bastard! How could he? With her! Oh!' She stamped her foot angrily. Then she picked up the small Herend rabbit Leo had given her for her last birthday and smashed it against the far wall. It rained down onto the table below in satisfying shards. 'Damn you, damn you, damn you!' India screeched.

Then she punched out her mother's number. She'd know what to do.

Leo's nose caught the tempting smell of fresh coffee as he entered the flat. He found Fern in the kitchen looking completely edible in his cast-off white shirt.

He threw the papers down on the side and grabbed her. 'What a sight to come back to,' he whispered, placing his hand searchingly against her bare buttock. He squeezed the warm flesh. She slapped him off playfully.

'I'm hungry,' she said. 'I need sustenance after all that exercise. I've found the orange juice, now all I need is glasses. And bacon and eggs, that's what I feel like. How's it sound?'

'Delicious.' He patted the carrier bag by the papers. 'Luckily I had the same idea. Everything's in here. We'll cook together, shall we?'

'Okay,' she grinned.

'But first, I thought you might like to see this.' He picked up one of the newspapers and thrust it under her nose. 'Turn to page 3.'

Fern opened up the front page and then saw her own face stare back at her from outside the front of the shop. There was a good three hundred words about her, the shop, and her Oscar Rees connection, and about the 'accident' with Paul.

'Blimey!' she said. 'That's unbelievable. Listen to this: "Entering Donleavy's one finds a delicious Aladdin's cave of mouthwatering ingredients blended together into a marvellous collection of Victoriana cosmetics. These delightful bottles would grace the grandest of bathrooms but are available at a price to suit everyone's pocket. I for one will be rushing round to the shop today to stock up on the Donleavy's range. I know what I shall be giving for Christmas this year!" I can't believe it!'

'Well done. There's more, but perhaps you should wait until after breakfast.'

'Why, is it bad?'

'Not exactly bad. Let's say it's slanted in a different way.'

'Where? Show me now!' She riffled through the pages.

'Here. Front page of this one.'

Leo's drenched head stared back at her. India stood looking guiltily up at him, while the look of shock on Fern's face was clear for all to see.

'"Leo Eden tests out champagne shampoo at cosmetics launch . . . "' Fern read on. 'Well it could have been worse, I suppose. At least they mention the products.'

'H'mph. I must say I'd rather two and a half million people didn't have to see the results of India's misbehaviour. But – '

'Talking of India, she telephoned while you were out. She didn't sound terribly happy about hearing my voice.'

'She wouldn't be. That's something I have to sort out, darling. India and I are finished, have been for a long time, really. It's just that she doesn't give up easily. I have tried on many occasions to spell it out to her, but she can be very thick-skinned.'

Fern shrugged. 'Sometimes you have to be cruel to be kind, don't you? Perhaps you should try being honest with her.'

'My darling, after last night, I have no choice, do I?'

By 10.30 Fern was back in the shop. She couldn't believe her eyes. The place was absolutely packed. Jackie was at the till while Anna was busy helping customers select what they wanted. She was so grateful to have found them both. They were cousins of Sean the carpenter, desperate to get jobs in England. Fern had interviewed them over the telephone and had heard the real enthusiasm in their voices. Jackie was nineteen; while Anna was

384

twenty-one. Fern had moved them into her old flat – an arrangement which had suited everybody very well indeed.

'Thank God you've come,' Jackie cried between ringing up numbers. 'We've had queues of people here since 9.30. And they aren't just buying one item. They're buying up the entire range. They all say that the bottles are so pretty they want to have the complete set. I've never know anything like it.'

'How are we doing on stocks?' Fern said, feeling a butterfly nervousness.

'I don't know. I haven't had a chance to find out. That's the one trouble with having an old till, Fern. If we had a modern computerized one we could have all our stock control running with the sales.'

'But none of us dreamed it would be necessary, did we? I'll check it out myself and then I'll come and give you a break.'

'Would you? Thanks. I'm beginning to go cross-eyed.'

Fern eyed the shelves in disbelief. Rows of bottles which had been stocked four deep were now down to two rows. There were small gaps appearing in places. She read the labels and fetched the stocks through from the store room. Anna helped her pile them back onto the shelves.

'It's like the first day of the January sales in here, Fern. I've never seen anything like it. I thought people weren't supposed to have much money at the moment? Jackie says the average sale is £30. That's two hundred per cent up on your projections.'

Fern grinned. 'Yeah, but remember it's our first day. It's bound to slow down after today. Who knows, we may sell nothing else all week.'

But by Thursday, Fern was rushing up to Malvern

to have an urgent meeting with the suppliers. The bottle manufacturer was running out of bottles and couldn't get the quantity needed over to the factory in time. The goods could be made quite quickly, providing they could still get all the ingredients delivered on time, but even there Fern was warned that she might have to spread her net a bit wider. The Product Head, Roger Markham, warned her that if she was going to have such a fast production rate, then the present suppliers of raw ingredients wouldn't be able to meet the demand. 'I suggest,' Roger told her, 'that you find some more suppliers in the next few weeks.'

Fern confided in Leo. Over dinner she told him of the imminent crisis. 'I know it's wonderful, but sometimes I think I'm going to have a nervous breakdown with the strain of it all.'

'That's because you're having to run before you've really learned to walk. You never expected it to take off like this, did you?'

'No way. I thought the stuff might dribble out at first, no pun intended, and then as people got to like it we'd build up sales that way. But this has been a consistent, huge demand. We've even had people ringing up from around the country who've read the publicity, telling the girls they want the items posted to them. They're asking if we do hampers for Christmas. I tell the girls to say that of course we do hampers, and of course we do mail order, but somebody's got to bloody well organize it. I'm stuck at Oscars for most of the day and nearly all the responsibility for running everything is falling on those two. I've already given them rises. Thank God they're so efficient and loyal.'

'I'll only proffer my advice if you want it.'

'Leo, I want it. The last thing I need is to turn into

some kind of overworked martyr disappearing up my own orifice. For God's sake, advise me!'

'First, you're spreading yourself too thinly. You're trying to be a jack of all trades . . . '

' . . . and master of none,' she added ruefully.

'I wouldn't say that. So far you've done pretty well.'

'Thank you, Mr Eden.'

'But now you're finding you can't be in all the places you're needed all at the same time, right?'

'Right. Take this week, for instance. I've got meetings set up with half a dozen separate raw materials suppliers, an alternative bottling company, a basket importer and the Post Office!'

'As well as doing a full-time job at Oscars. So maybe what you should do is take on some more employees. Start delineating the separate areas of expertise, and get in some experienced people to take care of it for you.'

'But, Leo, I'm talking about a little shop in Covent Garden, and while we'll soon be making profits, those profits aren't going to pay loads of salaries. While I've got plenty of capital, I don't want to spend it because the business isn't viable enough to finance itself.'

'So open more shops instead of concentrating solely on mail order to meet countrywide demand. You could start with, say, Bath, Cheltenham, Edinburgh. Maybe even Dublin, too. You've got to think big. And delegate.'

'That's scarey,' Fern sighed. 'But exciting! You really think it's viable?'

'I haven't seen the figures, but if you like I'll have a look at them.'

Fern was filled with such a wonderfully warm

387

feeling as she studied Leo's face, his fine features and his dark, almost black eyes which shone back at her with affection. Never before had she felt so much support in her life. Leo just seemed so genuinely interested in everything she did. There were no cruel barbs, no jealousies, or hidden meanings behind his words. A shiver of passion ran across her shoulders and she reached out to touch his hand. Talking about the business was certainly exciting, but bedtime was drawing rather close . . .

Alexander stood at the back entrance of the Rees Foundation and watched as the van reversed up to the supplies entrance. The two men plonked the generator on top of the metal casket and manhandled it towards Alexander.

'Careful with that thing. I've got frozen medical supplies in there. Do be careful,' he warned as the box nearly slipped through their hands. 'For God's sake – ' He shot forward, but thankfully they tightened their hold.

'Where do you want it, guv?'

'Follow me!' Alexander said haughtily. 'And be careful!'

'We do this all the time, you know, guv.'

'Could have fooled me,' Alexander grunted under his breath.

Eventually he closed the closet-sized freezer on the shipment. Now all was on schedule. The first patient was booked for her initial treatment tomorrow. Alexander could hardly wait. Her fifty-year-old wrinkles would be gone in a few days' time. He was convinced she would look like a twenty-five-year-old, and there'd be no risk of rejection of these special cells. He took one last look around the place, nodded to the security guard, and left, satisfied that the

388

means to making his fortune was safely tucked up for the night.

Johnny was beginning to feel like some soft-shoe private dick. Dickhead, more like, he chided himself. Lurking around corners, spying on Alexander. He was a product manager for Christ's sake, not some cloak-and-dagger detective. His trainer-clad feet moved noiselessly over the Foundation's tiled floor. He followed the corridor towards the Clinic. All the lights were off so it looked as if the coast was clear. Even so, his heart thumped loudly in his ears. He could almost hear the rush of blood surging through his veins, overdosed on adrenalin. He could see double doors ahead of him. He felt for the small torch in his jacket pocket. He slipped through the doors. To his right he could see the eerily moonlit quadrangle of garden; to his left a row of numbered doors. He peeped through the small window in the first door. He could just make out the shape of a bed against the far wall.

Then he heard a movement, so faint he wondered if his ears had played tricks on him. He crouched back into the doorway, afraid to open the door lest it might alert whoever was out there to his hiding place. He felt dizzy with fright. He was no bloody hero. This was not his game at all. Damn Hugo! Damn Fern! And damn the whole bloody family! He made up his mind to start looking for a new job – if he ever got out of this place.

Hardly daring to breathe Johnny watched as a slight figure detached itself from the shadows of the corridor. But something wasn't quite right. Through the mist of his panic it suddenly dawned on him how strange it should be that somebody else should be tiptoeing around the place at the dead of night –

somebody who clearly didn't want to bump into anyone either! He did a quick mental calculation. This person was a good foot smaller than Johnny. As the figure unwittingly narrowed the gap between them, Johnny knew he would be discovered. But he had the advantage of surprise. Like a missile he launched himself bodily at the other intruder from his hiding place.

'What the . . .!' a female voice squealed as they both fell onto the ground in a struggling heap of arms and legs.

Johnny squinted into the darkness and made out a bald female head. 'Who the hell are you?' Johnny demanded gruffly in an urgent whisper, hoping he'd disguised his voice sufficiently. The body squirmed under him, and he felt sharp fingernails stab into his arm. He tightened his grasp on the body. 'Oh no you don't,' he said shaking her. 'I'm not letting you go until you tell me exactly who you are, and what you're doing here.'

'Well, just who are you?' the girl demanded.

'Mind your own business. I'll ask the questions.' Johnny was really getting into his role now. Eat your heart out, Philip Marlowe.

'Let go of me then.'

'Not bloody likely. I know your game.'

'I can't . . . breathe . . . ' she choked.

Johnny softened his grip and as he did so he felt her leg move. Too late, a blinding pain exploded in his groin. 'Why you fucking little cow,' he moaned as, releasing her, he doubled up in agony.

She wriggled away and broke into a run. Johnny tried to stand, but the pain crippled him, tearing through his testicles like red-hot fire. She disappeared through the double doors and he knew he would never catch her.

'Fucking idiot!' he told himself. 'Stupid fucking idiot!'

It took Johnny a good few minutes to recover enough to move, but once able to walk he decided that for tonight at least, he'd better get out of this bloody place. There'd be other nights to find out just what the hell Alexander Easton was up to.

Chapter Thirty

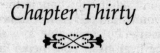

India eyed the bald-headed female with a mixture of distaste and annoyance. Really, had she known what a spectacle the girl made, she wouldn't have invited her for lunch at the Groucho Club. As it was, India had scurried for the darkest corner in the vain hope that she wouldn't be spotted by anyone.

'Thing is,' Alix continued, 'I think what I've got could be worth an awful lot of money to you, India. It could bring down Fern completely. Believe me, there's some disgusting stuff going on at her precious Clinic. She'll be dead meat once this story breaks.'

'But you won't tell me what it is?'

'All I can tell you is that the Easton twins are up to no good at that smart new Clinic. I can let you have some hard facts in a few more days. And then it will be the end of Donleavy's . . . and Fern!' Alix didn't add that she was getting desperate to offload the story before someone else did. For all she knew, that bloke at the Clinic who nearly clobbered her last night could have been another journalist. Luckily for her, it had been very easy to get India Duncan-Forrester hooked on the idea.

India managed to stop herself from breaking into a smile. 'So I suppose you'll want a hefty fee for this . . . er . . . piece?'

'Yes. I could easily sell it elsewhere, but I thought that given your personal interest in Fern you might want to have first bite at the cherry.'

'You're right,' India muttered. 'Come and see me

when you're ready. Then we'll talk money. Obviously you won't sell it elsewhere in the meantime?'

'I think you could give the story the kind of exposure I'm after.'

'I'll wait to hear from you then.' India stood up from the table and nodded her goodbye to Alix. She did not wish to give the girl the satisfaction of knowing just how pleased India was with this new development. Leo would be much easier to deal with now.

Leo smashed the squash ball against the rear wall of the court and sent it whistling round his opponent's ears, against the side wall, and back on the service wall, where it made contact just above the base line and then landed several satisfying feet away from Tom Cochrane's racquet.

'Leo, you're playing like a demon,' Tom groaned, wiping the dripping sweat from his brow.

'I wouldn't say that.'

'Don't be modest. You've thrashed me 9-1,9-1,9-1. I'm beginning to wonder if we should cancel next week's game,' he laughed. 'I have to consider my health, you know.'

Tom held the door open for Leo and patted him on the back. 'Thanks for the runaround, anyway.'

'You're looking a little hot, darling.'

Leo's smile froze on his lips. India was leaning against the wall outside the court.

'India, I didn't know you were going to be here.' Leo's eyes shot to his watch. He was meeting Fern right here in fifteen minutes' time. 'I've been trying to get hold of you all week.'

'I know, darling,' she pouted. 'I've been *frightfully* busy. Haven't had a moment to pick up the phone. Anyway, never mind. Here I am now.'

Tom Cochrane stood looking embarrassed. 'I, er, will go and change. See you shortly, Leo.'

'I wanted to talk to you, India,' Leo said gruffly, zipping his racquet into its cover. He put his hand into the small of her back and pushed her along the corridor beside him. 'About us . . . '

'Really, darling? What a coincidence. Me, too.'

'It's time to – '

India put her forefinger on his lip. 'I know. I know just what you're going to say, and it's all right, darling. Really all right. I know the time has come to sort ourselves out. We really couldn't carry on as we were. I agree with you absolutely.'

'You do?' Leo sounded incredulous. This was going a lot better than he had planned.

'Yes. I know you, darling. And I know what you want . . . and what you need. I suppose that's why we've got on so well together.'

'Yes,' Leo said uncertainly. There was no point in provoking her if she was going to take it as well as all this.

'So, don't you worry about a thing, just leave it all to me.'

Leo nodded, not entirely sure what it was that he was leaving all to her, but he thought he'd better humour her. He had to get rid of her, get into the shower, and be ready to meet Fern. The last thing he wanted was for her to get the wrong damned idea if India was around.

'Okay, India. Look, I have to run. You do understand?'

'Of course I do,' she said cheerily. 'Besides, my class starts in two minutes. We'll speak soon, sweetie.'

Leo smiled insincerely, and watched her skip off in her skin-tight black cycle pants and matching skimpy bra-top. She looked like a physically challenged spider.

Whenever Hugo opened his front door these days he hoped to find his daughter in residence. However, since Donleavy's had opened a month ago she had absented herself nightly, and he intended to ask Leo just exactly what his intentions were towards her. The house seemed somehow cold and lifeless without Fern's presence, but at least he didn't have to worry about keeping out of Olivia's way any more.

The kitchen door opened and Nancy appeared, wiping her hands on the front of her pinafore.

'Ah, Mr Hugo,' she said warmly. 'Good evening. Will you be wanting supper tonight, sir?'

'Er no, Nancy. I'll probably eat out. Or I'll help myself to something later on. Please don't worry about me.'

'Very good, sir.'

'Perhaps if I could just have some ice in the library?'

'Certainly, I'll get it for you right away.'

Hugo stepped into the book-lined room and closed the door gently behind him. There was such a comforting smell of old books and worn leather, of dry parchment and lavender polish. He could understand why Fern chose to spend so much of her time in here.

He walked over to the windows. The light was fading so that the room was cast in a restful gloom. He looked across the narrow street at the blank characterless buildings opposite, formal and regimented; neat, bland and unimaginative. Sterile. Like his previous life with Olivia. Everything was so damned organized. Even the back copies of *Country Life* stacked to the side of him were organized chronologically.

Everything in his life revolved around order. And he now knew that was precisely why he had left Rowena in that manner. He couldn't change. He bore as little resemblance to the wild bohemian he had imagined he could be as the lifeless stone log in the fireplace bore to a fragrant piece of applewood. He stared at his delicate, office-trained fingers and shook his head. How long had he deluded himself? He could have saved himself twenty years of anguish. Rowena had been right. They were worlds apart. She could no more cross over into his than a wild bird could enter a gilded cage and survive.

He poured a glass of whisky and downed it straight, relishing the sharp heat shooting through his gullet. Here was the real world, his world, and it was time he started taking responsibility for it. He'd moped for the last eight weeks since his return from Ireland and now he wanted to get on with his life.

Would Ricci take him back? Dare he hope that she might forgive his stupidity? He certainly had some difficult bridges to build. And wasn't it a strange irony that with Fern's arrival, so many changes had happened in his life? She seemed to be a catalyst, who altered his very perception of himself. For the first time in his life he was forced to examine himself and his motives, and he was rather afraid that he wasn't too impressed with what he had found.

Not normally disposed towards serious introspection, Hugo was somewhat relieved when Nancy announced Leo's arrival. 'Here, join me,' he said gratefully, handing Leo a whisky.

'Thanks.'

'Sit down.' Hugo gestured to the club armchair.

Leo nodded but remained standing, leaning his elbow casually on the mantelpiece. 'I've been sitting all day.'

Hugo shrugged and seated himself. He studied Leo from over the rim of his glass. He cut an impressive figure. His height – six two at least – gave him a commanding presence, coupled with his thick black hair and wide, reliable shoulders. He was the kind of man never to suffer fools. Hugo was glad Leo had bought the shares. But he wasn't sure quite how glad he was that he was bedding his daughter.

'I wanted to talk to you about Fern,' said Leo.

Hugo drained his glass in one hit. Suddenly he had a premonition that he might be drinking with his future son-in-law. He'd only just found Fern himself. It seemed grossly unfair that some other chap was about to steal her away from him already. 'Yes?' Hugo said slowly, bracing himself for the worst.

'About Donleavy's, the business.'

'Oh.' Hugo's relief was visible. 'About Donleavy's. Right.' He poured himself another Scotch.

'I've been giving it a lot of thought. My feeling is that Fern's getting out of her depth. She's going to be a victim of her own success.'

'Really?'

'Yes. I'm not sure she can manage the thing any more. It seems to be snowballing at an enormous rate. She's ripe for expansion already. I've told her so. I've even suggested that she open up six more shops. But as I said, I'm not sure she can handle it, should be handling it, by herself. Especially when you consider that she's got a full-time job on Oscars' staff.'

'So what are you suggesting I do? Fire her?'

'No, no, Hugo, something far more constructive than that. Here's what I think we should do.'

Hugo listened carefully, and with interest, as Leo outlined his proposal.

'So what do you suggest we do next?' he said, when Leo had finally finished.

'Put it to her. Call a meeting with her tomorrow morning, at 10.30 a.m., say? I'll be there.'

'Well done, Leo. I'm sure she'll be thrilled. It's a much sounder idea all together.'

'Good,' Leo sighed with satisfaction.

Johnny placed a cup of black coffee on Fern's desk. 'Thanks,' she said gratefully. 'That's really sweet of you.'

'Drink it.'

'Jesus, what have you laced it with?' Fern choked and spluttered.

'Trust me!'

'Oh, I've heard that one before. Every time someone says trust me I should do the complete opposite. For heaven's sake you're as bad as Rowena! What's in here?'

'Brandy.'

'At nine in the morning!' Fern shrieked. 'Are you feeling all right, Johnny?'

'I'm feeling fine; it's you I'm worried about.'

'But I'm feeling fine, too. At least I was before you started plying me with laced coffee. What's it all about anyway?'

Johnny threw *The Times* down on her desk.

'Thanks, but I don't read it. It's far too grown-up for me.'

'I suggest today you read it, especially page 19.' For some reason Fern had a rather unpleasant feeling in the pit of her stomach. 'Why?' Her voice cracked uneasily. Then she picked up the coffee and drank it straight down. She felt the brandy hit her with its satisfying warmth. She stared at Johnny. 'What is it?'

'The engagements. You know, fiancées and all that crap. I'm sorry to do this to you, but I didn't want you to find out from somebody else.'

'It's Leo, isn't it?' she groaned.

Johnny nodded. 'I'm sorry, Fern. I did try and warn you.'

Fern opened the newspaper and forced her eyes to focus on the page. She scanned the columns. Twice she missed it in her blind panic, but then she saw it. India Duncan-Forrester and Leo Eden. She scrunched the paper up and threw it onto the floor. Her cheeks burned red hot. She felt dizzy. She opened her mouth to speak but no words came. She looked at Johnny silently.

'I'm truly sorry, Fern.'

'The bastard!' she spat. 'The out-and-out pig! I'll kill him!'

'Steady on, Fern.' She sounded so dangerous that Johnny was half afraid she meant it. 'He's not worth it.'

'No, you're right. Killing's too good for him. More like a slow, deliciously tortuous death, starting with castration.'

Johnny shuddered. 'There's a great saying that I always rely on at times like this: don't get mad, get even.'

Fern's eyes were aflame with a wild anger. 'Believe me, Johnny, by the time I've finished with Leo Eden he'll be begging for castration as the easy option!'

Somehow, through a supreme effort of will, Fern had managed to push Leo to the back of her mind as she knocked tentatively on Hugo's office door. She did not wish Hugo to get the idea that she was an emotional wreck. Not when she'd spent the best part of two months convincing everyone that she was Superwoman.

'Come!'

She opened the door and froze. Leo and Hugo stood up to greet her.

'What are you doing here!' she demanded.

'Fern!' Leo cried. 'Darling, Hugo and I have a plan which we're dying for you to hear.'

'I know all about your plans,' she hissed, and then aware of Hugo's bemused scrutiny, she squared her shoulders and took her seat. She intended to deal with Leo privately, in her own way. She answered his warm grin with a glower of anger.

She turned her face away and fixed her eyes on Hugo, determined to ignore him completely.

'H'm-m,' Hugo cleared his throat and spread his fingers out in two fans on the edge of the desk. 'Leo has told me about the marvellous success you've achieved with Donleavy's.' She regarded him silently. 'He's also told me of the struggle you've been having, trying to keep everything running smoothly.'

She narrowed her eyes. Bloody, traitor, she thought. Just you wait . . .

'Thing is, Fern, we feel – that is, Leo and I thought – that it might be in your best interests if we were to take Donleavy's under the Oscar Rees umbrella.'

'What?'

'I think it's time to bring Donleavy's back into the fold, as it were. I suggest we give you a cash sum for whatever shares you care to nominate in the business, naturally you can keep a sizeable proportion yourself, and then we can let Oscars take over the day-to-day running of everything. Which, of course, will free you up for other things.'

'What on earth are you talking about?'

'I'm sorry if I'm not being clear enough, Fern. I'm suggesting that Oscars buy Donleavy's. After all, darling, don't forget it is my grandmother's formula you're using. It seems only right that now, now that you've shown me what a success it can all be, it comes back into the control of the company.'

Leo cringed at Hugo's total lack of tact and diplomacy. He was hardly going to put Fern in a receptive frame of mind speaking to her like *that*.

'Why you . . . I don't believe this, Hugo. You *gave* me those formulas. You told me categorically that you weren't interested. And now that I've done all the hard work, all the setting up, all the bloody graft, you have the bloody nerve to sit there and complacently – no, *arrogantly* – tell me that you'll have it back.' She turned to Leo. 'And it was *your* idea? You are an out-and-out traitor. A cheat and a liar.' She stood up, pushing the chair violently backwards. 'All your grand speeches about nepotism and all the struggles you had to make your own mark. About how brave I was to do the same thing, how you understood! You really are full of total crap, Leo! And you, Hugo. *I've* built Donleavy's and I will carry on building it, by myself. I don't need either of you to help me.'

Both men stood up automatically. 'Fern!' Hugo cried. 'Just a moment, let's talk about this. We were only trying to help you.'

'Well, you can both stuff your help up your backsides. I don't need you. And as of today, you can have my resignation, Hugo. I no longer wish to be associated with this particular branch of the organization. It stinks – and you're going to need more than your smart line of perfumes to fumigate it.'

She swept out of the room.

Leo shook his head. 'I don't understand it. Whatever's the matter with her? Yesterday she was as gentle as a kitten. Perhaps it was a bit tactless of you to mention the fact that the formulas were yours, Hugo. You did give them to her, didn't you?'

'I . . . er, yes, I suppose I did.' The words nearly stuck in his craw. 'But I don't feel you handled her particularly well either, Leo. Otherwise she wouldn't have mentioned all that stuff about nepotism which you've obviously been filling her head with.' Hugo was damned if he was going to take all the blame. 'And so much for your idea, Leo. I don't think she thought anything of it.'

'Leave this to me. I'll talk to her. It's probably PMT, something like that. You know what women are like.'

'Good idea. Let me know how you get on. We must talk her out of resigning. She's become quite an asset.'

'I'll do all I can,' Leo said sincerely. But he had a feeling he was in for a tough time ahead of him.

He raced down the corridor after her. Johnny Sharpe looked up from his desk. 'She's gone out,' he said.

'Where to?'

'She didn't tell me. But I get the impression she wanted to be alone. After all, she had some pretty bad news, didn't she?'

'What bad news?' Leo's voice was filled with concern.

'Can't imagine,' Johnny said sarcastically, turning back to his papers.

'So you've finally done it!' Nicky shrieked. She bounced into his office and planted a loud kiss on Leo's cheek. 'Congratulations!' she cried.

402

'What? Why is everyone behaving so bloody strangely today? Just what the hell is wrong with the world?'

'Don't be so stuffy, Leo. It's not every day you get engaged, is it?'

'What?'

'Your engagement. It's in *The Times* today.'

'You're joking!' Leo's face was turning a rather dangerous shade of purple. 'To whom?'

'As if you didn't know,' she giggled. 'To India, of course. I'll get the paper.'

Time froze as Nicky disappeared. Leo's heart raced with a cold fury. Just what the hell had India done now? If this was one of her silly pranks . . . She really had gone too far this time. He scanned the five lines, feeling sick. Then he picked up the telephone. Within seconds India's answer machine droned at him.

'It's Leo. I'd like a word with you,' he barked.

He had to get hold of Fern, let her know of the dreadful mistake.

Alix returned from the coffee machine, clutching the flimsy plastic cup, concentrating on not spilling the black coffee over the edge. She didn't notice the figure follow her down the corridor, until she was just about to resume her seat.

'It took me a while to place you,' Johnny sat down opposite her, 'but then I remembered. Now would you like to tell me just what the hell you were doing at the Foundation the night before last, when you nearly castrated me?'

'I don't know what you're talking about,' Alix hissed. 'Get out of here before I call security.'

'Oh no, I'm not letting you get away with it this time. I know it was you, and I'll have you charged with trespass if you don't answer my questions. I took a photograph of you,' he lied smoothly, 'with my infrared camera before I jumped on you. It shows your face quite clearly. So don't bother to lie.'

'And what were you doing there, sneaking around, anyway?'

'I work for Oscar Rees. I was there on legitimate business.'

'Oh yeah?' she said cynically. 'If that's the case why were you hiding in the shadows?'

'Because I knew I'd caught an intruder. You could have been armed.'

'I was,' she laughed, rubbing her knee conspicuously.

'So, now that we've established who we are, and where we were, perhaps you'd tell me why.'

'I was researching a story.'

'Spying, more like.'

'Sometimes it amounts to the same thing. I've been hearing a lot of interesting things about this Clinic of yours.'

'Mine?'

'It's Oscar Rees's, isn't it? You just told me yourself that you're a company man.'

'Okay, then, this Clinic of *ours*.'

'Yeah. Sounds a bit dodgy.'

'Dodgy? In what way dodgy?'

'Thing is,' Alix said, enjoying herself now, 'I've been watching your colleague Alexander Easton, and he seems to be getting hold of some rather interesting stuff from Moscow.'

'Such as?' Johnny was trying hard to maintain his cool. Nonch was the order of the day.

'Human tissue,' she said with relish. 'He's shipping over human tissue to use in his nasty little injections. And I've got proof.'

'Absolute bloody crap!' Johnny snapped. 'You've been watching too many movies.'

'I've got pictures and papers to prove it. And what's more, you can tell your chums back at the factory that I intend to run the story when I've pieced it all together. I shall enjoy seeing the downfall of Miss hoity-toity Fern Donleavy. She needs to be brought down a peg or two, if you ask me.'

'You're crazy.' Johnny forced himself to laugh. 'How do you know? What facts have you got?'

'It's all here,' she said, tapping a pink folder on her desk, 'the name of the supplier in Moscow, the dates of the shipments. This story is going to be the scoop of the century. I predict the downfall of the entire Oscar Rees organization and there's nothing you can do about it.'

Johnny snatched the pink file and sprinted. Through the doors, down the corridor, he rushed towards the stairway.

Alix's shouts echoed behind him. 'Stop!' she screamed. 'There's a thief in the office! Call security! Stop him!'

He raced down the stairs, willing his legs to keep going. At last he came to the bottom. The stairs led on down to the basement. If he went through the main entrance he'd be bound to be stopped by security. He almost threw himself down to the basement. There was a small window, just wide enough to get his head and shoulders through. Bracing himself he smashed his elbow against it, and then took his jacket off and used it as a shield to push out the remaining glass. He vaulted up and squeezed through the tiny opening. He was out on the street. Without looking backwards he raced along the road, and then, thankfully, found a taxi just dropping off its fare.

He leaped into the vacant seat.

'Bond Street,' he cried, through his gasps. 'Oscar Rees.'

Chapter Thirty-one

Leo was in a filthy mood. He'd had Bob Lowenstein
breathing down his neck for an hour over some new
acquisition he was into, Fern had not returned any of
his calls despite the fact that he'd chased her all
morning at the office, and left several messages on
her answering machine at home; and now he had
lunch with India to look forward to.

He hardly bothered to speak to the maître d' at
Marco's, but sullenly allowed himself to be led to the
table. India's head was bowed over a notepad on
which she was busy scribbling, her hair, in its immaculately precise geometric bob, swung forward
over her cheekbones, matching exactly the black piping on her red Chanel suit. Her slim black-stockinged
legs were elegantly crossed to the side of her chair.
Once he would have found the sight appealing.

'India,' he said, as he reached the table. She looked
up and beamed at him.

'Leo, darling.' She kissed the air in front of her with
her scarlet lips. 'I feel as though I haven't seen you for
days. I've been so terribly busy. Mummy and I
popped round to the General Trading Company this
morning – '

'India!' Leo snapped, cutting her off mid-sentence.

'We thought we'd do a sort of preliminary list, and
save you the boredom of having to traipse around – '

'India . . . ' he hissed again.

'What, darling?' She regarded him innocently.

'What the hell do you think you're playing at?'

'Darling?'

'I said, what the hell do you think you're playing at? And what ever induced you to put that ridiculous announcement in *The Times*?'

'Ridiculous, what do you mean ridiculous?' She affected a hurt expression.

'Our engagement!'

'But we agreed, darling, remember, that you'd leave everything to me. So I assumed you wouldn't mind a bit my putting it in the rag.'

'I said nothing of the kind!' The waiter arrived with the menus. Leo snatched his and set it to one side. India opened hers out and started to scan the list.

'India, are you listening to me?' Leo's voice was rising.

'Of course I'm listening to you, and so is half the restaurant. It's just that your words aren't making any sense.'

'Dammit, India,' he said, bringing his hand down heavily on the table, 'I said nothing about our getting engaged. What I thought I'd said was that you and I were *over*. Are my words plain enough now?'

'But . . .!'

'I do not want to marry you.'

Heads turned. The waiters eyed them nervously. India's bottom lip quivered threateningly. Her face flushed and she stared down at the tablecloth.

'You tried to manipulate me into this . . . ' A tear splattered onto the plate, followed by another, then another. India sniffed loudly.

Leo glanced around the restaurant. He noted the disapproving looks cast in his direction. He suddenly felt like the big bad wolf. He reached into his pocket and pulled out a large white handkerchief.

'Here, have this,' he said as solicitously as he could manage.

'Thank you,' she spluttered. She took it and blew her nose. She mopped up the tears, being careful not to smudge the mascara under her eyes. 'We might have had this discussion in a less public place, Leo.'

'India, if you remember it was your suggestion that we meet here. You left the message with Nicky. This is the only opportunity I've had. What did you want me to do, send a fax?'

She sniffed again. 'Well, I can't believe you mean what you're saying, Leo. Perhaps you're over-wrought. We've both known that we would marry eventually. Do you know how long we've been together, Leo?'

'I'm sure you do.'

'Four years . . . '

' . . . on and off.'

'Mostly on. And I've been more than understanding over your little dalliances. I never complained.'

'Perhaps because you were having a few of your own. Look,' Leo's voice softened, 'I know it's been a long time, India, and maybe there has been a sort of complacent sense that this would continue. Maybe marriage was something you thought we were headed towards. Maybe we were. But the fact is,' he cleared his throat, 'the fact is that I don't want to marry you. I'm sorry.'

'Oh but I think you will, Leo,' India said, her voice hardening.

'Look, India, I didn't put the announcement in the paper, you did. And you know damn well you were tricking me the other day. Did you seriously think that I'd just meekly sit back and say, "Fine India, you bamboozle me into it, and I'll just trot along with you"? Is that what you seriously thought?'

'Yes, Leo. I knew that would be what you wanted. I've always had a very good knowledge of what you wanted – what makes you happy. That's why we've stayed together for so long. I'm prepared to overlook your dalliance with Fern. She's very young, Leo, and she'll get over it very quickly. Believe me, it's for the best.'

Leo was almost beyond speech. The woman was out of her tiny mind!

'I love Fern,' he spluttered, 'and I am not going to give her up. Now stop this nonsense, India, it's most unbecoming. You're only going to make a complete fool of yourself. Have more dignity.'

India's mouth twitched. Leo's declaration of love had cut through her like a knife, but she gathered her strength, knowing her armoury was well equipped for the ensuing battle.

'Then if you love her you'll want to protect her, won't you, Leo?'

'Of course I will. What the hell are you going on about?'

'I have received some very privileged information, Leo, about Fern and about the Clinic which she is so involved with. Of course I'd hate to do anything to upset somebody so important to you, and I can only guess at the implications it would have on Donleavy's, but I fear she would be put out of business, and I imagine that you'd do anything to stop her from being damaged – if you love her.'

'Are you trying to blackmail me, India?'

India's eyebrows shot up in horror. 'Good Lord, no. What do you take me for? I'm trying to *help* you Leo, to protect Fern. I'm acting in *both* your interests. I'm sure I could find a way of making sure that this disturbing information about Fern doesn't see the light of day – with your help, Leo.'

Leo stood up. 'You really are beyond belief, India. You seriously thought that you could manipulate me into marrying you with your empty threats. You disgust me! I hope I never have to set eyes on you again!'

'If I were you, Leo, I wouldn't be quite so hasty in my judgement. Think about what I said. Fern's career depends on it.'

He glowered at her fiercely and, spinning on his heel, marched out of the restaurant.

India coolly took lipstick and a mirror from her handbag and carefully repaired the fading scarlet. Then she snapped her bag shut decisively. Once she had the information from Alix she would make sure that Leo knew she wasn't bluffing.

'This is unreal,' Johnny cried as Zak refilled his wine glass. 'It's like something out of a horror movie.' He felt sick to the pit of his stomach. 'I just can't believe it. Even of Alexander. I'd never have thought the guy could be as sick as this.'

'*If* it's true,' Zak cautioned. 'That bird Alix could have made it up.'

'Yeah, she could have, but I've a terrible feeling she hasn't. Christ! Can you imagine what would happen if any of this stuff got into the press? Oscars would be dead, and Fern along with it. It's fucking dynamite, Zak!'

'You'd better assume what you have isn't the only copy around. My guess is that Miss Baldy can still do a helluva lot of damage.'

'You think I haven't thought of that?' Johnny snapped.

'Sorr-y, man. Only trying to help.'

'I know.' Johnny pushed his bony fingers through his long hair. 'What the fuck am I going to do?'

'Well, so far as I see it, you've got several options. Number one, you go and have a chat with Easton and find out what he's up to.'

411

'I think we can knock option one on the head, can't we? As if he's going to say, "Oh, yes, of course, Johnny. Come and have a look, I'll explain it all to you," if you bloody please.'

'Okay. Then there's number two. You tell Fern what's goin' down, and let her decide how to handle it.'

'She's got enough on her plate right now. I don't think she could take it.'

'Or you do nothing. Pretend you haven't seen any of this stuff. Let them all get on with it. At the end of the day, mate, it's not your problem.'

'Take the cowardly way out?'

'Sounds sensible to me. *That's* what I'd do.'

'Know something, Zak? I don't believe you. You're full of shit,' Johnny laughed at his old friend affectionately. 'I know exactly what you'd do.'

'Yeah?'

'You'd get on a plane to Moscow and find out for yourself.'

'Then you're round the fuckin' twist, Sharpe, round the fuckin' twist.'

Johnny stared into his wine as if it were a crystal ball. 'You know people over there, don't you?'

'A couple of guys. Not your type, man. They're a little *rough* around the edges, keep bad company. Sergei was a merchant seaman. I picked him up in a bar in Berlin years ago . . . he keeps in touch occasionally. What a wild night that was!'

'You know where he is now?'

'I could find him.'

'Would you, Zak? I might need some help over there. My Russian's a little rusty.'

'Don't do this, Johnny.'

'Ah, life was getting dull. It'll do me good. Time I had a holiday.'

* * *

Fern had just left Donleavy's, her head full of plans and worries, when a familiar and unwelcome voice startled her: 'Mind if I walk with you for a bit?'

Fern jumped. 'What the hell did you do that for? Oh, Alix, not you again. Look, I can't think we've got anything to say to each other so I really think it's best if we stay out of each other's way. Sorry I can't stop!' Fern strode away from her. Alix was all she bloody needed. How many more people was she expected to have to dodge? Hugo, Leo and now flaming Alix!

'I've got something you might want to know, something very important, Fern. I think you should listen.'

'Not now, Alix. I'm in a hurry. Save it for your cronies at *Faces*.' She tried to dodge away from her.

'I think you ought to listen, Fern,' Alix persisted. 'It's about your precious Clinic – and certain Moscow connections!'

'More scandalmongering, eh, Alix? Don't you ever give up?'

'Johnny Sharpe seemed to find it interesting enough. He came into my office and stole an entire file on the story I've been researching. Bit of a pain, but of course I had it all backed up. He seemed pretty shit scared, Fern. I think he realized how important my story is.'

'Oh, go away, Alix. You really expect me to believe that? Go and wind somebody else up. I'm busy.'

'Suit yourself, Fern, but don't say I didn't warn you. I'd ask your friend Johnny about it if I were you.' Alix stomped off.

God, would that girl never give up? Fern had far too many important things on her mind to worry about Alix's empty threats. She'd known her too long to take any of what she said seriously. Still, perhaps when she got into the office tomorrow after-noon she'd have a chat with Johnny, just to see.

She had booked into a hotel so that she'd be well out of the way of Leo's pestering calls and Hugo's attempts at persuading her to retract her notice. She had a breakfast meeting planned with a couple of interviewees for the job of Products Co-ordinator, and she had to run through her list of questions and check over the CVs. After that she had to take the train down to Bath to look over a potential site. At least all the activity helped keep her mind off things.

By the time Fern got into the office the following day it was almost five o'clock. She threw off her jacket and flipped through the pile of messages. No less than ten from Leo. Well, he'd soon get bored with trying. There was a note from Hugo asking her to look in and see him 'if she had a minute'. She felt very tired and worn. Already it had been a long, hard day. The Bath visit had been a total waste of time and she intended to ring the agent and give him a piece of her mind. The property was just about signed away to somebody else! They could damn well pick up her expenses for the wasted trip. She saw Janie hover outside her doorway.

'Hi,' she called out. 'Is Johnny in?'

'No, Fern, he isn't. He's gone away. Zak, his photo-grapher friend, called in this morning and told me he's gone off for two or three days. I could have sworn he said Russia. I guess I must have misheard him.'

'I should think you did,' Fern laughed. 'I can't think what would make Johnny rush off to Russia. Funny that he didn't mention anything about it yesterday morning.'

'He didn't say anything to me either. Oh, well, perhaps he got an exciting offer.'

414

'Hope so. He's been looking pretty tired lately.'

'Yeah, you, too, Fern. Look, if there's anything more I can do to help, any phone calls, stuff like that, I'd be only too pleased, especially while Johnny's away. It's going to be pretty quiet.'

'Thanks, Janie. I'll bear it in mind.'

Fern tried to concentrate on the pile of reports on her desk, but her mind kept wandering. Something Alix had said was niggling away at her, and she couldn't for the life of her think what it was. She pushed the reports away and tried to recall the exact conversation. It was hard, bearing in mind Fern had barely been listening to the vicious little cow.

'Shit!' Suddenly she sat bolt upright. Moscow. Alix had said Moscow.

She pulled out her Filofax. Zak was in here somewhere, she knew it. Her fingers scrabbled over the pages. At last! She punched out his number and got an answering machine. 'Zak, it's Fern. I have to speak to you urgently about Johnny. I'm in the office, call me . . . '

Johnny pulled the leather collar hard around his ears, and tried to sip nonchalantly at the gnat's piss lager, but it was hard to remain nonchalant when nearly every head in the place was turned towards him. He glanced expressionlessly at the rows of hostile faces. He lowered his eyes, concentrating on the urine-coloured liquid in front of him.

Johnny checked his watch for the second time. Sergei was late. 'Come on, Sergei,' Johnny sighed to himself. Soon he'd have to take a leak, and he wasn't sure he'd make it back in one piece. He looked up hopefully as the door to the bar swung open. Tarzan's understudy walked in and stood in the centre of the room, hunched and glowering from

415

pale, crazed-looking eyes. This guy probably ate guys like Johnny for lunch. Johnny hunched further down inside his jacket, trying to render himself invisible. He saw the figure loom towards him. He looked up, taking in the long, straggly, filthy-looking hair, the yellowing teeth and the stinking clothes, and then he realized that this was the man he had arranged to meet.

'Sharpe!' The man barked by way of introduction. Johnny nodded and attempted a grin which only succeeded in baring his teeth. The man shouted to the barman and roughly pulled out the chair opposite Johnny. He looked once around the bar, and all faces turned back towards drinks. No eyes met Sergei's glance.

'Good,' he said. For what reason Johnny couldn't have said. The weather? The bar? Certainly not the beer. 'Zak, he's a friend of yours?'

Johnny nodded. Zak had some strange friends.

'Mine, too. We met in a bar in Berlin.' Sergei broke into what could only be described as a highly suggestive laugh. Johnny himself had been known to indulge in a bit of rough on occasion, but Zak had really taken a whim to its extreme.

'So you want information.'

'Yes. As I said on the telephone, it's all a little delicate. There is a hospital – twenty-five, I think it is.'

'There are many hospitals.'

'Yes, I'm sure. Only this one might be slightly different' Johnny coughed. He had no idea how much he could trust this man. Maybe he and Zak had just shared a one-night stand. Johnny wished he'd hung around to find out more from Zak. Still, he had no other options at the moment. If he didn't seek Sergei's help, he'd have to be out on the street asking directions. 'This one I believe is an abortion hospital.'

Sergei's gaze didn't falter.

'I believe it's run by a Dr Yuri Nitchkov.'

Immediately Sergei's very blue eyes narrowed. He glanced nervously over his shoulder. He moved his head closer to Johnny and lowered his voice to almost a whisper. 'Did you say Nitchkov?'

'Johnny felt his skin suddenly chill. 'Yes.'

'I know that bastard all right. He's a Chechen.'

'Chechen?'

'From Chechenia. It's a self-proclaimed republic. They have their own Organizatsiya, like mafia. Very dangerous.'

'Terrific!'

'He runs many things, black market, drugs . . . He has many friends in high places. You don't mess with Nitchkov. You don't ask questions about Nitchkov in bars. You want my advice? Put yourself on a plane back to London. That's the information I give you.'

'What does he do?' Johnny persisted

'I told you. He does everything. Come on, let's take a walk.'

Johnny was happy to leave his drink and the depressing bar. They stepped out into the cold damp air. 'You know what happens to people who mess with men like Nitchkov?'

Johnny wasn't sure he wanted to know, but Sergei's gesture left him with no illusions. 'Forget this trip. Go home. We guys, we just play at the market. A few cigarettes here, some jewellery there, underwear, cosmetics – tame stuff. Nitchkov, well, he's involved in heavy things. Nothing I would mess with. There's a line of respect. I can't help you, Sharpe.'

'Then tell me where I can find him.'

'No. I will not.'

Johnny was fast losing patience with this over-sized apeman. 'Look, I've come a long way. I'm tired. If you don't tell me I shall just take a cab to Hospital Twenty-Five and sit and wait for Dr Nitchkov to surface.'

'Then you are a fool.'

'Yes, I expect I am, but just tell me where I can find him.'

'You have paper? A pen?' Johnny withdrew both from his jacket. 'I tell you where Nitchkov has his club. It's a brothel. I tell you, then you can go home.'

'Okay, then I can go home,' Johnny sighed.

He glanced at Sergei's scribbled note, then he slipped it into his pocket. Sergei grinned at him as Johnny watched his pen disappear into Sergei's pocket. 'Thanks,' he said.

'I'll give your regards to Zak.'

'I hope you're able to.'

Sergei watched as Johnny walked briskly away from him. He turned to walk in the opposite direction. He took a couple of steps, and then cursing loudly, he turned round and walked after Johnny. He owed his friend something.

Chapter Thirty-two

Lucienne's reassuring smile concealed her rapidly increasing suspicions.

'Date of birth?' She continued filling in the form in front of her while studying the strange female sitting opposite.

'Seventeenth of April 1971.'

'You're very young for this kind of treatment. Are you sure you really need it?'

'Just look at this slack skin down here,' she cried, pulling at non-existent jowls. 'I need an injection desperately. I've felt like it for years, but I've never had the money to go ahead with it before, and besides, I've been a little wary of other clinics. Now that the Rees Foundation are doing something, I feel quite safe. These injections are totally without side effects, you say?'

'We can guarantee it. There's no risk of rejection whatsoever. And you'll probably find that unlike most treatments, you won't have to keep coming back every six months for another course.'

'What is this miracle stuff you're using?'

'I'm afraid that's a closely guarded secret,' Lucienne grinined. 'A lot of our competitors would very much like to know. So when can I book you in?' she said brightly.

'Tomorrow?' the bald girl grinned back.

'Okay, tomorrow at eleven o'clock. Goodbye.' Lucienne ushered her out. As soon as she had disappeared down the corridor, she telephoned Xan.

When Zak received Fern's telephone message he rushed straight round to Blake's Hotel, where she was staying. By the time he had finished telling her what he knew so far, Fern was pacing up and down, shaking her head.

'This is just too crazy for words, Zak. I just don't believe it.'

'Neither did Johnny, until he saw Alix's file. That's why he's gone off to check it out for himself, to make sure before he started goin' and treadin' on people's toes. These aren't the sort of accusations that should be thrown at anyone. And that bloody woman's threatenin' to blow it all sky-high. He was a total fuckwit to go. I told him, but he wouldn't bloody listen,' he said darkly. 'And now I haven't heard from him in over thirty-six hours.'

'Doesn't sound like too long a time, Zak.' Fern tried to sound comforting.

'He said he'd call me yesterday. It's possible he can't get a line out, but I'm worried.'

Fern chewed on her fingers, trying not to let Zak know how shaken she was. He looked worried half to death. 'I'm sure he'll be okay. I need time to think, Zak. I need to work out what to do.' It was her bloody Foundation that was about to be well and truly fucked up. She had to find out just what the hell was going on.

'Are you in the studio tomorrow? I'll call you when I've decided what to do,' she told him.

'Don't go and do anything crazy, Fern, will you?'

'Like what?'

'Like followin' him. Sergei'll look after him. He's a good mate. I trust him.'

'Then get hold of him. Find out if he's seen Johnny.'

'Fern, I've been tryin' all fuckin' day.'

'Okay, okay, sorry,' she sighed. 'I guess I'm not thinking straight. I'll call you tomorrow, once I've . . . well, whatever. I'll call you.'

'Cheers, Fern.' Zak rubbed her cheek with his finger. 'You're a good kid, you know.'

'Thanks. I'll remember that.'

Once Fern had let Zak out of her suite she collapsed onto the sofa with her head in her hands. It just couldn't be true. It was all so crazy. She wished she had the comfort of a certain pair of strong male arms around her. She could do with a cuddle right now – a cuddle and someone to talk to, to get into perspective all this crazy nonsense Zak had come up with. She sighed into her arms. She had to handle it by herself. She couldn't expect to go involving anyone else. Hugo and she were hardly speaking, Ricci had enough on her plate. Besides, it was with Fern herself that the buck stopped. She was the one who had pushed the idea of the Clinic through in the first place, in spite of the opposition on the Board. Fucking Alexander! His slimy guts wouldn't be fit for dog food by the time she'd finished with him!

Alix didn't stir as the shadowy figure padded silently past her bedroom door. Nor did she drift back to consciousness at the vague plumbing sounds going on in her bathroom. She slept deeply and peacefully as the intruder, finally satisfied with his handiwork, quietly let himself out again.

The next morning, as Alix filled her morning bath tub, she tried to open the window, but the wood seemed to have swelled. It just wouldn't budge. She closed the bathroom door, and hummed to herself as the room filled up with steam. The old gas water heater roared and gurgled, sending piping hot water into the tub. She slipped out of her robe and dipped her toe into the water. Today was the day when she'd have first-hand experience of the Rees treatment. She felt very smug and self-satisfied. Pouring some Donleavy's apricot and almond oil bath essence in first, she stepped into the inviting water and settled back. She closed her eyes and started to dreamily drift away, thinking about her story, and how famous she would become. Alix Green, News Editor, *The Times*.

She slipped gently into sleep, blissfully unaware that in a very short time she would be completely comatose.

'Where is Alexander?' Fern hissed at Lucienne. 'I want to see him *right now!*'

'He's busy . . . in a meeting. Hang on a minute.' Lucienne got up and followed Fern. 'You can't go marching in on him like that! Just who the hell do you think you are?'

Fern gave her a withering look and ignored her. Lucienne grabbed her arm.

'Let go of me.' Fern's dangerous rasp shocked Lucienne into releasing her grip immediately. She took a step backwards. Fern's eyes were blazing with rage. She threw open the door and barged in. Alexander was hanging on to the end of a telephone.

'I want to talk to you.' She was surprised by the cold authority in her own voice.

'Fern! What a wonderful surprise,' Alexander sighed with his sickening charm, slowly replacing the receiver in its cradle.

'Forget all that, you worm!' she shouted. 'Now you can tell me just what the hell you and your evil sister have been playing at.'

'Fern, remember where you are. We have patients here. What on earth are they going to think?'

'Shut up!' Her voice cracked the air like a whip. 'Shut up and listen!'

'Very well.' Alexander eyed her with something almost akin to amusement. 'I must say you look very attractive when angry, dear Fern.'

'Tell me about Moscow!'

'Well, let me see, it's the capital of Russia. It's rather cold, I believe – '

'Tell me about aborted babies, Alexander. And the "special injections" you're pumping into poor unsuspecting women under the protection of my Foundation?'

'*Your* Foundation? You're a little premature, aren't you, dear? I know you're ambitious, but I really don't think you can refer to it as your Foundation just yet. You ought to be a bit more careful. You might injure some large toes, you know.'

'It's true then!'

'What, about offending people? Oh, I'm sure that's the case.'

'About these special consignments of yours. These special consignments of dead babies!'

'That sounds awfully dramatic. And totally ridiculous, my dear. I think you might be getting a little confused between placental extract and foetal extract. The former is used quite widely in the cosmetics industry. If you'd thought to spend a little more time on your education rather than running around setting up shops you might know that.'

'I'm not talking about placental extract, Alexander. You know damn well what I'm talking about. These special cells of yours, guaranteed rejection free. They're not taken from fat reserves at all, they're taken from . . . God, it's obscene!' she cried. 'You're a monster!'

'You're talking rubbish.' Alexander's voice was

dangerously low. 'You can't prove a thing. It's all crazy nonsense.'

'And your Dr Nitchkov, I suppose he's crazy nonsense, too, is he?'

'I've been doing some cosmetics deals with him. There's a very lucrative market in Oscar Rees products.'

'Crap. That's not what you're up to. Now I want to know exactly where this doctor friend of yours is. I'm intending to pay him a visit.'

'You could just pick up the phone!' His eyes gleamed at her merrily.

'Well, I could. That's if I wasn't concerned over the disappearance of Johnny Sharpe. It seems he went over to see your *friend* and now he's gone missing. So, if you'll just let me have his address . . .'

Suddenly Alexander's face changed. His mouth hardened and his eyes narrowed schemingly. 'Very well,' he said, starting to scribble on a piece of paper and then thrust it towards her.

'Thanks.' She turned on her heel and walked quickly away.

As soon as she was out of earshot Alexander snapped at his twin: 'Get me Nitchkov on the phone, fast. And get me booked on a Moscow flight. I don't care which bloody airline it is, but I've got to get to Moscow before she does.'

Zak played Fern's message on his answer machine and groaned aloud. 'Fuckin' stupid woman,' he cursed. 'Air-headed fuckwit.' What the hell was he supposed to do now? Send in the seventh fucking cavalry? He might just as well invite them along to what was turning into some crazy party over in Moscow.

He stormed around the studio, pushing tripods

bad-temperedly out of his way, punching out at the paper backdrops. Damn the pair of them. Fern was not his responsibility. Johnny maybe, but not Fern, too. He wasn't some bloody baby-minder. He had work to do, commitments. Besides, he didn't have the cash to go leaping across continents at the click of a pair of nail-varnished fingers. It was not his fucking problem! Leo Eden could damn well sort her out. Sergei would look after Johnny. He picked up his twentieth cigarette of the day and stuck it in his mouth. He pulled in the smoke as if it was his dying breath, and punched out the telephone numbers. Soon Leo Eden's voice was on the other end.

'Listen, Eden, I've got something important to say to you.'

'Who the hell are you?' Leo's smooth voice snapped irritably.

'I'm a friend of Fern's. She's in trouble. I think she could do with your help. Got a pen ready?'

Nicky herself greeted Leo at the airport. She held up a small attaché case. 'Everything's in here. Money, loads of it, passport, et cetera. I'm afraid I couldn't put clean pants in for you.'

'Okay, okay, which flight am I on?'

''Fraid you just missed one, Leo.'

'Shit!' The elderly couple in front of them turned around in surprise. Leo ignored them. 'Which airline?'

'Air France.'

Leo looked around the terminal building, and eventually managed to locate the relevant Air France representative.

'I'm sorry, sir, but I cannot tell you if your friend is on the flight,' the smart woman said.

Leo tried once again, speaking slowly, as if through

425

doing so he might make himself more clearly understood.

'I'm sorry, sir,' she repeated automatically. 'I cannot give you that information.'

'Why not?'

'Because it's against our security policy. Unless it is an extreme emergency, I am unable to help you.'

'This is an extreme emergency.' Leo banged his hand down. Somehow he guessed this whole damned thing had to be tied up with what India had been hinting at. Why the hell hadn't he listened to the damned woman? Then he might have been able to prevent Fern from rushing off. Anything could happen to her . . .

Nicky put her arm warningly on his. 'Leo, this won't help,' she said quietly.

'I'm sorry,' Leo struggled to control himself. 'But I fear that once she gets to Moscow she could be in a great deal of danger. I really need to know if she was on that flight.'

The girl looked from Leo to Nicky. Nicky tried to look as pleading as Leo. 'Look, I'm not supposed to do this.' She tapped into the computer and then concentrated on the screen. 'What was the name again?'

'Fern Donleavy.'

'Ah, yes. According to this list she was on the 11.30 flight.'

Leo didn't know whether to be relieved or disappointed. 'What time's the next flight?'

The woman tapped away at the keyboard. 'There's a BA flight at 14.00. Check in is at 13.00, desk 63.'

'Thanks.' Leo strode off leaving Nicky to make the necessary noises of gratitude.

She trotted after Leo. 'What's going on, Leo? Why all this sudden drama?'

'I haven't got time to explain now, Nicky, but I have to get that flight. Call Hugo Rees. Tell him Fern's gone to Moscow after Johnny Sharpe, and I'm going to look after her. Tell him . . . tell him not to worry.'

Nicky grabbed his arm. 'Look,' she whispered, 'over there – isn't that . . .?'

'Alexander Easton.' Leo stopped dead in his tracks and pulled Nicky backwards, turning quickly away from Alexander's line of view. 'Sit down!' he ordered. He bent his head low over his knees, as if he were tying a non-existent shoelace. 'Keep your head down, I want to see what he's up to.'

'That's going to be a bit difficult from this angle, isn't it?' Nicky peered over Leo's bent head. 'He's heading for gate 63. Moscow's suddenly become awfully popular.'

Leo looked up. He could just see the back of Alexander's dark head. He watched as he talked to the girl behind the desk, and then after several moments, walked towards the departure gate.

'He's bound to see you if you're on the same flight,' Nicky said, matter-of-factly.

'I'll just have to make sure that he doesn't, won't I?'

'What do you intend to do? Go in drag?'

'Nicky, if you haven't got anything sensible to say, then don't say anything.'

'Sorry. It just strikes me as being a little out of the question, you know, being on the same flight as someone – '

'It's not like a bus, you know. Come on, I'd better get my ticket. Let's hope he's not the only one on the flight.'

Leo craned his neck over the seating plan and tried to ascertain which end the stewardess had started from. 'I'd like a seat at the rear of the plane in

427

economy,' he said firmly. Nicky smiled to herself. Leo travelling in economy was about as much in character as his turning up to the office wearing a mauve shell suit.

'Aren't you going through?'

'Not until the very last minute. I intend to lose myself in the crowds. Listen, Nicky, you'd better get back and make that call. I'll ring you when I know where I'm going to be. Thanks for coming out.'

'Are you sure there's nothing else I can do? Shirts, et cetera? You won't get anything out there, Leo, and anyone with any sense takes stuff to barter with.'

Leo looked at Nicky as if she had just revealed the meaning of life. He took her arm. 'Let's go shopping.'

Dr Nitchkov eyed the young woman curiously. She stood nearly a head taller than himself. She was certainly very attractive, despite the curious scarring on both her cheeks. Alexander's description had hardly done her justice. He smiled at her. 'So Miss Donleavy, you think I can help you find your friend?'

Fern nodded. 'I hope so, Dr Nitchkov. I understand he was coming to Moscow to see you, and now he's disappeared. I'm afraid something may have happened to him.'

'I don't recall the name.' Nitchkov looked puzzled. 'Sharpe, you say?'

'Yes, that's right, Johnny Sharpe. Tall, slim and long dark hair. He was supposed to be arriving at least three days ago.'

'I'm sure I would remember him. It's not often we have visitors from the West here.'

Fern shuddered. Nitchkov had kept her waiting in this horrible little room for nearly two hours. She was cold, tired and hungry. And there was something about this anaemic-looking man that made her feel

428

deeply uncomfortable. He was being charming enough, but there was something in his eyes . . . a kind of cold hardness, almost cruel.

'Do you know what he wanted to see me about?'

'Not really. Alexander Easton told me where to find you.' She watched his face closely. 'I gather you might have something to do with the Eastons' Clinic,' she hedged carefully.

The doctor's eyebrows lifted slightly. 'Ah yes, Alexander, of course. Perhaps Alexander knows something of the whereabouts of your friend?'

'I think not.' She shrugged. 'Otherwise I wouldn't be here.' Suddenly Fern sensed he was toying with her. 'You do know where he is, don't you?'

Nitchkov looked affronted. 'I told you, I have never heard of this man. Are you suggesting I am lying to you, Miss Donleavy?'

'I don't know. Perhaps. Look, I'm sorry, but I'm very worried about him. I thought maybe you could help . . . ' The last thing she should do was to antagonize the creep.

'I'm sure I can,' he said softly. 'Why don't you come back with me to my office? Perhaps someone there might know what's happened.' He checked his watch. 'In fact, it is time for me to leave now. I'd like to help you, if I can.'

'That's very kind,' she said. 'If it's no trouble.'

'No trouble at all,' he smiled again. 'Come. It will be a pleasure.'

Leo watched from the safety of his taxi as Alexander climbed out of the one in front and entered through the anonymous, bleak-looking doorway.

'You want woman?' the cab driver said disinterestedly.

'What?'

'You want woman? That place. You go for fuck?'

Leo peered again at the building into which Alexander had disappeared. It looked plain and dreary: almost institutional. There were no flashing red lights, neon signs or scantily clad girls strolling about. Thinking quickly, he made himself smile suggestively at the driver. 'Yes, I want fuck. But first I want hotel. I am hungry.'

'You cannot fill a woman when your belly is empty,' the driver laughed. 'I take you to the best hotel in Moscow.'

'Is it close?'

'Sure, five minutes.'

'What's the name of this street?'

'Lubyanka Street.'

Fitting name, Leo thought bleakly. He needed to get hold of Sergei.

The queue for phones reminded Leo of the queue for cabs at Waterloo Station on a wet Monday morning. At this rate he'd be here all night. He walked up to the cashier's desk and placed the brand-new holdall bought at Heathrow on the desk. Crisp dark denim showed through a chink in the zip.

The cashier looked at Leo, and then at the zip. She swallowed hard and smiled. 'Can I help you, sir?' she asked in perfect English.

'I need a telephone urgently.'

'The girl pointed towards the queue. 'It's over there, sir.'

Leo undid the zip a few inches. 'Jeans,' he said, with all the subtlety of a Skoda on a recovery truck.

'Yes, sir.'

'I need to make an urgent telephone call.'

The girl reached under the desk and then placed a shiny plastic telephone an inch away from Leo's hand. He started to unzip the bag. 'No!' she protested. She handed him a carrier bag, also from under the desk. 'After, you put them in here and then you give me the carrier bag,' she insisted.

Leo delved into his pocket for Sergei's number. He dialled quickly – too quickly. He replaced the receiver and then he tried once more. 'Slowly,' the girl advised him. He waited for the clicks to subside, and then after what seemed an age, he heard what he assumed to be a ringing tone. A minute passed, maybe two. Then there was a voice on the other end. Leo cleared his throat. The tension was beginning to get to him.

'Sergei?'

'Who is this?'

'My name is Eden, Leo Eden. Zak gave me your number.' There was silence. Leo thought for a moment that the phone had gone down.

'Where are you?'

'At the Intourist. Can we meet?'

'Walk down Gorky Street. You'll see St Basil's Cathedral. Walk across the square and I shall meet you. Ten minutes . . . '

'How will we know each other?'

'I'll know you.' The phone went dead.

'Here we are,' Nitchkov said, solicitously holding the car door open for Fern. She glanced up at the grim-looking building. This was not at all what she had expected. She felt the doctor's hand against her back, guiding her firmly towards the door.

Once inside, her fears mounted. What kind of an office was this? She heard faint music coming from some way ahead. She could smell stale beer and nicotine.

'Come,' the doctor said, guiding her elbow up the

431

narrow flight of stairs. The knot of fear tightened. 'Where are we going?' she asked quietly.

'My office. Come.' Woodenly she walked up the stairs and through the large door off the landing at the top. She looked around, taking in the expensive furnishings. It was all so contradictory to the rest of the place. 'Please, sit down,' the doctor gestured her to the large leather sofa beside the fire. 'I shall order some refreshments for you, and then I expect you'd like to freshen up. I shall make a few phone calls for you, see if we can find out about your Mr Sharpe.'

'Thank you,' Fern said meekly. A girl appeared a few seconds later carrying a tray of coffee. She smiled warmly at Fern. Fern was startled at how young she looked: fourteen, fifteen, certainly no more than that.

'This is Tania. Have your coffee and she will take you to your room.'

'No. It's quite all right. I can wait here,' Fern insisted.

'I think you will find it more comfortable to go with Tania.' Nitchkov spoke in Russian to the young girl. She nodded, and stood waiting as Fern sipped the bitter black coffee.

'Take your coffee with you, if you like.' Again Nitchkov smiled, and his gold-capped teeth glinted in the light. She replaced her cup on the tray and stood up. 'I take you,' the girl said in hesitant English.

'Okay. thanks.' Real fear filled her belly as Fern realized she was now totally in Nitchkov's control. She bit her lip and resolved to try to appear calm.

'I shall see you later,' Nitchkov said, as she left the room. Fern followed the girl down the dimly lit corridor.

Tania opened one of the doors to the left of them. Fern paused in the doorway. What the hell was this place? The girl took her hand and led her inside, closing the door behind them. Fern looked along the wall at the floor-to-ceiling mirrors. A vast bed, large enough for half a dozen, occupied the centre of the room. There was a pervading smell of sickeningly cheap perfume which caught in her throat. A table stood against the far wall. Along with a hair brush and comb, and a bottle of the offending perfume, sat a basket full of condoms. Fern looked at them in horror, realization fast dawning on her. She opened the first drawer. It was full of sex toys! Extraordinarily shaped dildoes, vibrators and creams. An evil-looking bunch of leather straps had been pushed into the bottom drawer. She turned back to the girl. Why hadn't she realized before? The fact that the girl was dressed only in what appeared to be a flimsy kimono; her thick red lipstick; her youth! This was a brothel! Jesus Christ! She had just allowed herself to be led into this . . .

Fern ran to the door. She turned the handle, but nothing happened. The girl looked at Fern nervously.

'How do I get out of here?' Fern shrieked at her.

'I no understand,' the girl whispered, stepping back from her.

Fern scanned the room again. There was just one small window in the far wall. She rushed over and tried to force the sash. It wouldn't budge. The catch was firmly locked. She was a prisoner. She turned around helplessly. The only person who knew where she was was Zak, and he wouldn't be much help, stuck in London. And what of Johnny? Now she knew without any doubt Nitchkov had done something to him. She bit her lip hard, trying to fight back the tears. The young girl looked at her kindly. She reached out to touch Fern's arm. Fern

433

snatched her arm away. 'Don't touch me!' she hissed. She threw herself down onto the bed, and glowered at the girl.

'I am Tania,' the girl said.

'I know!'

'Your name?'

Fern looked up at the child beside her. It wasn't the girl's fault that Fern was here. She was presumably just one of Nitchkov's young victims. Perhaps Tania was a prisoner here, too. 'Fern,' she said, softening.

'Zurrn.' The girl struggled with the name. She came and sat beside Fern on the huge bed. 'You very pretty.'

Fern smiled. 'Thanks.'

Tania ran her hand along Fern's jeans. 'Nice,' she sighed. Then, brightening, she said, 'You have make-up? Lipstick?'

Fern opened her bag and took out a small purse full of Oscar Rees goodies. Tania grabbed the bag hungrily, her eager fingers handling both the lipsticks as if they were precious jewels. 'I try?' she asked, her young eyes glittering with excitement. Fern nodded. Tania rushed to the mirrored wall and preened to her reflection.

Then she returned to Fern's bag and eyed it longingly. Fern delved into it once more. She pulled out the small bottle of Absynthe. She handed it to Tania. Tania splashed it on her arms, her neck, her legs, until Fern thought she would be asphyxiated with the smell of it. She screwed her nose up. 'It's very strong,' she explained.

'Ah yes . . . ' Tania laughed. 'I like.'

'Keep it,' Fern said. She needed all the friends she could get.

Leo couldn't believe his luck. Throughout his entire

life things had a habit of always falling nicely into place. He had been born lucky. Whenever his luck had seemed to be out, fortune would raise her lovely face and smile on him. All he had to do was trust to it. Up until now, that was. And this was Sergei, the great surly, unwashed Sergei. He glowered at the seaman. Sergei wasn't too impressed with Leo either.

'You know Russian?' he demanded.

'Of course I don't.'

'You expect to infiltrate these people and you don't know Russian?'

'Infiltrate? I'm not a bloody terrorist, Sergei.'

'Chechen!' Sergei hawked spectacularly on the ground. Leo's stomach heaved.

'What's Chechen?'

'Nitchkov. He's part of the Organizatsiya, the Mafioski. Have you any idea how dangerous these men are?'

Leo shrugged hopelessly. 'What am I supposed to do? Turn around and catch the next plane home?'

'Yes, if you had sense.' Sergei spoke angrily. 'Why should I help you? I have no need to risk my life. It's already too late for Johnny.'

'What do you mean?'

'Johnny. He's finished. Gone!'

'Gone as in dead?' Leo felt as if a knife had been plunged into his stomach.

'Yeah. I think so.' Sergei spoke quietly. 'I heard a rumour. A body was dumped earlier outside the British Embassy. I don't know the details yet, but it's the kind of nice little touch Nitchkov likes to add, you know. Like his signature.'

'But if everyone knows it's him, if he's responsible, how come he's not arrested? Locked up?'

'You British, you know nothing!' Sergei sneered. 'Because half the police are in Nitchkov's pay.

Because half the officials are in his pay. Money buys you everything here, and nothing. The only thing you can buy is people! Nitchkov owns too many to ever get into trouble.'

'Then how can we get to him?'

'You tell me, Mr clever Englishman.'

'You must know. You're a dealer, aren't you?'

'Huh! Compared to Nitchkov I'm still swapping badges with the little boys.'

Leo felt nauseous. 'There must be some way . . .'

'Money. That's the only way.'

'But I have money.'

'You need lots of money.'

'How much?'

'Ten thousand dollars!'

'Done. You'll have ten thousand dollars if you help me get Fern out alive.'

Sergei looked at Leo. 'Hey, you're a crazy man, you know. You're lucky. Today's the day I like crazy men.'

Leo shook his head. 'And to think I thought my luck had run out.'

Chapter Thirty-three

Fern lay on the bed, curled up in a tight little ball. She'd been over and over the room. Apart from the door, there was just no way out. Her only chance was to try and get Tania to help her. But Tania had been called out, and she had been left alone for what felt like hours. She heard a key turn in the lock and she sat up quickly.

'You!' she cried. 'What the hell are you doing here?'

Alexander Easton smiled his sickening smile. 'Come now, Fern. I'm here to help you – if you'll let me, that is. It seems my friend Dr Nitchkov is a little upset about all these visitors he seems to be getting.'

'Johnny. I knew it. He's done something to him, hasn't he?'

'Let's not talk about that little wimp.'

Fern leaped off the bed and stood facing Alexander. 'If you and your stinking friend have done anything to hurt Johnny, I swear I'll kill you both.'

'Ooh, brave words, Fern, especially when you're not exactly in a position to do anything to anyone.'

'He'd never get away with it. If anything happened . . . ' Fern's voice faltered.

'My dear girl,' Alexander said arrogantly, 'do you have any idea how much power Dr Nitchkov holds? He can do anything he likes. So, don't be foolish. Let me help you, and you can help Johnny.'

Her green eyes blazed at him. 'How could I possibly help Johnny?' she snapped.

Alexander walked across the room and opened the

door of the tall cupboard. She could hear the clicking of metal coathangers. He pulled out a black lace corset-type garment. He held it towards Fern, and looked at it, and then her, thoughtfully. 'I think you might be more comfortable in this,' he said.

'You must be bloody joking!' she cried.

'No, actually I'm deadly serious. You see, if you don't co-operate, Fern, your friend Johnny will have his little balls chopped off.'

Fern's hand flew to her mouth in horror. 'You wouldn't . . . '

'I wouldn't. But I know someone who would just love to oblige. So I suggest you be a good girl and try this on for me. I think it looks rather fetching. Of course, you may be a bit skinny for it.'

'You bastard! You evil, wicked bastard.'

'You flatter me,' he said drily. 'And isn't that rather hypocritical, under the circumstances? Put this on!'

'No!' she screamed.

'Put it on now, or else I shall give the order to deal with Johnny.'

'Leave the room, then.'

'Oh no, Fern. I intend to watch every little movement of yours. And you'd better make it worth watching.'

Fern's eyes filled with angry tears. 'You'll pay for this, you evil little shit!'

'On the contrary. This is completely on the house.'

'You know, for someone who talks about badge-swapping, you've got a surprising amount of influence.'

Leo looked in fascinated admiration at the small army which met them a couple of blocks from Nitchkov's place.

Sergei smiled. 'I told you, money buys you friends.'

The motley crew of ruffians regarded Leo with studied indifference. Leo noticed the flashy pump trainers and the uniformity of their jeans. 'I won't bother with introductions. Here, ever handled one of these before?'

Leo took the small handgun from Sergei. It felt surprisingly heavy. His gut churned and his mouth felt dry. He couldn't remember the last time he had felt like this – so out of control of his life, and dependent on others. He swallowed hard as he weighed the weapon in his hand.

'It's for a woman. You should manage,' Sergei said disparagingly.

'Thanks. Very thoughtful of you.'

'That's the safety catch. You've got six bullets in the chamber. Here's some more.'

Leo pocketed the handful of ammunition.

'Okay,' said Sergei. 'This is what we do . . .'

Fern stood in front of Alexander. She held her head loftily, almost proudly. The black lace bustier forced her breasts high. The bones cut into her ribs.

'This what you wanted?' she said scornfully.

Alexander sat on the bed. He looked at her long graceful legs, at the deliciously creamy colour of her naked skin. His eyes travelled on up to the lace cut high over her hips, her slim waist and her tits busting out of the top. 'Shoes,' he said. 'You'll find some in the cupboard. Put them on.'

'You get them!' she ordered.

Alexander smiled. Perhaps she was entering into the spirit of things after all. 'Okay,' he said. He leaned into the cupboard. Fern kicked his butt as hard as she could, sending him shooting into the

439

door. He shouted as his head made contact with the wood.

'Why you little bitch!' He picked himself up.

Fern made a fist with her right hand, and then swung at him, catching him on the chin and sending him sprawling onto the floor. She rushed to the door and tried it. Damn! It was locked. She looked around the room for something heavy. But there was nothing. Alexander was getting up. She stepped back, away from him. He threw himself across the room at her, pushing her down on the floor. She was pinned under him. He sank his teeth into her naked shoulder. She screamed.

'That's better,' he hissed. 'I think a bit more respect would be in order, bitch!'

Fern struggled, trying to push him away, but he grabbed her arms, pinning them to the floor. He released one arm and ripped at the tight bodice, exposing her breast. She cried out again, and tried to wriggle free. He forced his hand down between her legs, pushing his finger painfully inside the crotch.

'You bastard!' she spat. 'Get off me.' She grabbed a handful of his hair and pulled as hard as she could. His hand came down hard across her face. She tasted blood in her mouth.

Alexander undid his zip. He was pulling at the thin lace of her corset. She felt his penis against her thigh. She tried to lift herself, but his hand came down once more across her cheek. She was exhausted. The fight was draining out of her. Alexander propped himself up.

'Now, bitch, see how you like this!'

Fern screamed.

Then they heard the shot. Alexander stopped. 'What the hell was that?'

Another shot. Alexander released her and she

440

crawled away as he went to the door. She heard the thunder of feet coming along the corridor. There were shouts. Alexander struggled to put the key in the lock, then he opened the door.

Leo followed Sergei's army up the stairs. The door-man was left lying in a pool of blood and Leo knew these guys meant business. They stopped at the top of the stairs, and then a blond heavy appeared through the first door on the right. Sergei signalled his men in. More shots.

Leo could smell Fern. That was her perfume. 'Fern!' he screamed. Then he saw Alexander. 'You!' He ran towards him, but Alexander stepped back into the room, and locked the door quickly. Without thinking Leo aimed his gun at the lock, it gave and he flew into the room. His brain struggled to make sense of the scene.

'Fern?' He could hardly believe his eyes. Alexander stood behind her, a small penknife held to her throat. 'You take one step towards me, Eden, and I'll slit her throat.'

Leo stopped. Alexander's left arm was tight against Fern's waist. Leo growled at Alexander. 'What have you done to her, you slimy little cunt?'

'Nothing yet. Drop your gun and get out of here, Eden, slowly.'

Leo stepped back, but the gun remained in his hand.

'I said drop your gun!' Alexander screeched. Leo looked at Fern, at her lovely white neck stretched back so painfully, at the sharp glint of steel in Alexander's hand. He threw the gun on the ground.

Alexander pushed Fern forward, keeping his grip tightly around her. He bent to pick up the gun. Fern pushed with all the strength she possessed. The knife nicked the side of her throat. 'Leo!' she screamed. She threw herself on top of Alexander, toppling him to the floor. The knife spun out of Alexander's grasp. 'Leo!' she shrieked again. Leo raced to pick up the gun. Fern snatched up the knife.

'That's better,' Leo said, trying to keep his breathing even. He aimed the gun at Alexander. 'Over on the bed,' he ordered.

Fern rushed to the drawer. She pulled out the leather straps and held them up, trying to make some sense of them. 'Here,' she said, 'we'll tie him up with these.' She looked up as a man burst in through the room. 'Leo!' she cried. 'Look out!'

Leo turned to find one of Sergei's men behind him. 'We go. Now!' The Russian looked at Alexander, pointed the automatic rifle and fired. Alexander's body bucked and twitched several times. Leo and Fern looked on in horror. 'What the fuck did you do that for?'

'Nobody see us!' the man shrugged. 'Now go!'

Fern looked at the pool of blood spilling out of Alexander's head and flowing onto the bed. She held her hand over her mouth. She thought she was going to throw up.

Leo took his jacket off. 'You'd better put this on,' he said, thrusting it at her. She looked around for her jeans and picked them up. She started to pull them on.

Sergei's man pushed her. 'Go. Get.'

'My bag,' she cried.

'Leave it!' snapped Leo.

'My passport.' Fern, still clutching her jeans, ran across the room and grabbed it, then she and Leo raced out into the corridor. Sergei's man had run ahead of them, leaving Sergei to collect the stragglers, the butt of his gun still smoking. 'Come on. We'd better get out of here. This place will be crawling with police in a minute. Get the fuck out of here.'

They threw themselves down the steep stairs, two at a time, their heels drumming out like thunder. 'The taxi's round there. Run like hell!' Sergei commanded. Leo needed no second telling.

'Hurry!' Sergei shouted.

'Leo!' Fern cried. 'What about Johnny?'

'Come on. I'll explain in the cab.'

'Is he all right?'

'Come on, Fern. We must do as Sergei says. You don't want to end up back in there, do you?'

'But – '

'Look, I'll carry you if I have to.'

Leo pulled her arm and they raced along the street. They could hear sirens getting closer. 'Come on . . . faster.' Her bare feet raced along the cold pavement. The cab door stood open. They leaped into it, falling over each other.

'Sheremetyevo!' Leo commanded.

They sped off into the Moscow night.

'Leo!' Fern screamed. 'We can't just leave him. What about Johnny!'

Leo looked at the blood dribbling down her neck. He reached out to touch the wound. She grabbed his hand. 'What are we going to do about Johnny?' she repeated.

'He's dead, Fern.'

She choked. 'No!'

'Sergei said so. There's nothing we can do.'

'No!' she cried again. 'He can't be. Not Johnny. Oh, Leo,' she wailed. The tears spilled down her cheeks. Her lips trembled, and her body was racked with great choking sobs.

He pulled her tightly to his chest and buried his face in her hair. 'I'm sorry, Fern.'

'But we can't just leave him,' she said through her broken sobs.

'The Embassy will sort everything out. There's nothing we can do. We've got to get out as fast as we can. You do understand, don't you, Fern?'

She nodded dumbly. 'Poor Johnny, he must have been so brave to come here. And he was such a softy, Leo.' She plucked at his sleeve, over and over, all the while the tears streaming down her cheeks. She shivered uncontrollably.

Leo touched his handkerchief to the gash on her neck.

Fern flinched. 'Is it deep?' she spluttered between sobs.

'Not very,' he said reassuringly. 'I think you'd better get some clothes on, Fern, before you catch pneumonia.'

She let Leo push her legs into her jeans. He tried to pull them over her legs, but it was too awkward in the confined space. 'You'll have to help me, I'm afraid.' He noticed the rip in the crotch of the ridiculous lace garment. He was desperate to ask what had happened, but could not just yet. Instead, he cradled her tightly against him, letting her grief flood out. He wouldn't feel safe until they were safely on a plane out of this law-forsaken country.

Chapter Thirty-four

Fern walked along the corridor feeling weak with apprehension. She brushed at the creases which had formed across the front of her cream linen trousers, and fastened the two buttons on the front of her chocolate-coloured blazer. She'd made an extra special effort with her wardrobe today. A soft cream chiffon scarf caught her hair into a loose ponytail and she'd even put on full make-up in his honour. She clutched a giant box of chocolates under her arm and a huge bunch of flowers in her hand. Leo had warned her not to expect too much. She spoke to the nurse at the desk, who took her to the room. She knocked lightly on the door and stepped inside.

Johnny was sitting propped on a sea of pillows. His face was covered in bandages, but his eyes beamed at her. He threw his arms out and very gently she bent towards him, being careful not to brush his face.

She swallowed hard, trying to get rid of the huge lump in her throat which threatened to send the tears flooding down her cheeks. But she fought in vain. She blinked the water away.

'If you ever do that to me again, I'll kill you,' she said, trying to laugh.

His mouth was restricted by the bandages. 'Sorry!' he said.

She sat back on the bed and clutched his hand. 'How're you feeling?'

'Sore. But at least I'm alive.'

'Thank God,' she grinned.

'Well, I suppose there is one good thing to come out of all this.'

'Yes?'

'I won't be called "nosy" again.'

'Johnny!'

'No, no, it's okay, Fern. Dr Fielding is going to build me a nice new one. I'm going to choose one to my taste – or should I say smell!'

'Johnny!' she shrieked in horror. 'You're incorrigible. Trust you to make a joke about it.' She giggled and turned sideways. 'I guess this one might be a bit big for you, then?'

'Oh, huge! Grotesquely huge! No, no, I'm going to pick an attractive one!'

She squeezed his hand. 'How soon can you get out of here?'

'A week, ten days, maybe. They've got to sort of rebuild it in stages. But I tell you something, they can't keep me here long, the food's terrible.'

'You're joking. We stole the chef from the Dorchester. I'll have words.'

'Oh, would you, Fern? It's really bad. Boeuf en croute last night, soufflé omelettes for breakfast, warm salmon salad for lunch . . . I shall be *so* fat. You've got to do something about it, Fern!'

'Fool,' she said, laughing.

'Anyway, what's the latest? Leo told me Lucienne didn't take the news too well.'

'No. She's gone off to Switzerland, to some clinic, would you believe? The word is she's had some sort of breakdown. So far as I'm concerned the longer she stays there, the better. Even Olivia's out of my hair now that she's gone on her screw-the-world cruise with that dyke of hers. Unfortunately I'm not exactly the Board's favourite person at the moment as it was me who persuaded them to let the Eastons run their

Clinic.' She sighed. 'If I dare, I'm going to suggest that Olivia should be honourably retired. Whatever they think of me at the moment, I know they'll be pleased to be rid of all Easton connections. I shall just have to try and persuade them.'

'Knowing you, I'm sure you'll manage. And the Clinic?'

'What do you think? Closed, of course. The official P R line is that it's out of respect for Alexander. Sick, isn't it? But the press have been having an absolute field day trying to find out how such an eminent person as Alexander Easton could have ended up being murdered. The Russians have persuaded the Foreign Office to accept the story about him being just a victim of street crime over there. Under the circumstances, the authorities seemed to think that was fair enough. Just goes to show how bent the whole system is. However, there's still the question of Alix Green's mysterious death.'

'You and I know damned well who was responsible, but there's not much point in proving it now he's dead, too, is there? And what did the authorities say about your involvement in the Moscow massacre?'

'What involvement? It's a case of the three wise monkeys. That's the deal. We keep shtum, and there are no charges. Wicked, isn't it? Nobody wants to damage trade, you see. I had no idea this sort of thing went on. I guess some other enterprising journalist will root around for the real story. It won't be me, though. I've had enough excitement to last a lifetime.'

'Yeah,' Johnny sighed. 'And I think any sensible journalist would lay off stories connected with the Rees family after Alix's untimely death.'

'The police still think it could be accidental. That

old gas heater was definitely faulty. The coroner said she died of carbon monoxide poisoning. She wouldn't have known what was happening.'

'Shame, she deserved some pain after what she put us all through.'

'Johnny, where's your spirit of charity? You shouldn't speak evil of the dead.'

'Once a Catholic, always a Catholic, eh, Fern?'

She blushed with embarrassment. 'Not so's you'd notice.'

'And Leo?' Johnny watched her face. 'What about India and the engagement?'

'All a hoax. Would you believe India actually wrote to me to apologize for her foolishness? It was actually quite a nice letter.'

Johnny leaned back on his pillow. 'Don't trust her,' he whispered. 'She's probably got some ulterior motive.'

Fern laughed. 'After all that we've been through I guess it's going to be hard taking anyone on face value any more.'

'So you'll stay on at Oscars?'

'I've renegotiated my contract,' Fern smiled triumphantly. 'I'm going to be a consultant director.'

'Meaning?'

'I only have to put in a certain amount of hours each month. That means I can devote the rest of the time to Donleavy's – which is what I really want to do. One day I might let Hugo buy me out, but not until I've had some more fun on my own first.'

She grabbed his hand, sensing he was tiring. 'Now you get plenty of rest. I want you fit and well in time for a very special opening next month. Can you keep a secret . . .?'

Chapter Thirty-five

The bulbs flashed repeatedly, blinding her with their sharp, blue-white lights. She tried not to blink, concentrating instead on keeping the smile plastered across her face. She adjusted the thin chiffon wrap around her shoulders. Soon, pray God, they'd let her go back inside. The wind tugged at her hair, whipping it around her face. She caught sight of Zak in the crowd and grinned directly at him. 'Fab,' she heard him cry out. She leaned back against the hard stone wall, setting her jaw firmly against the chattering of her teeth. Her arms were beginning to turn blue. Please, please, she begged silently, make this over, soon.

The photographers parted, and her heart lifted to see Leo striding purposefully through them. 'Okay, guys,' he called. 'That's enough of the outside shots. We don't want Miss Donleavy to catch pneumonia, do we?' Leo pushed his way through them and removed his jacket.

'Darling,' he smiled, 'you'd better put this on.'

She laughed up at him. The cameras continued to point and flash at them. 'I wondered where you were. I thought it's usually about now that my hero comes striding along to lend me his jacket.'

He bent his head forward and swept her up into his strong arms, smothering her in a heavenly kiss. The chill left her. Her only awareness was the feel of Leo's hot lips burning deliciously against her own.

Finally, she allowed herself to shiver at last. 'Thank

God you came. I thought I was going to die of cold. Anyone would think it's the middle of summer the way they expect me to cavort around in next to nothing.'

'You do look stunning!' Leo's eyes roved admiringly over the wispy chiffon gown that clung seductively to Fern's body, the fabric artfully shaded from the palest cream through to a deep marine blue.

'No, I don't. I look as if I've died. Look at the colour of my arm. It's the same blue as the dress!'

'Blue and ghostlike. I expect the rat pack will have got some great shots of you. Anyway, there's a few speeches inside, and loads of journalists waiting to ask you all sorts of questions.'

She snuggled deeper into his arms. 'Do you know what I wish? I wish we could just run away, just the two of us . . . just jump into your car and go.'

'Well, you can't. Speaking as your business adviser, I'm afraid I cannot allow you to do that. You have responsibilities.' His voice was teasing.

'I can't get used to this idea of being labelled a business entrepreneur. All this jet-setting around, opening up shops, it's like being caught in a whirlwind.'

'I know you wouldn't have it any other way. Just so long as you take the odd break every now and then.'

'For long holidays with you, you mean?'

'Yes, holidays, and maternity leave.'

'Maternity leave!' she screeched as they walked through the shop doorway, into the throng of people. Heads turned to look at them. Hot colour flew into her cheeks. 'What do you mean?' she hissed, through barely parted lips.

'Babies. You'll have to take time off to have our babies, won't you?'

'Aren't you being a little premature?' Her eyes

sparkled at him with barely concealed excitement.

'I don't think so. Come on, you've got work to do.'

'But . . . ' Leo pushed her forward and she was lost in a sea of beauty editors and retail buyers. She looked back helplessly over her shoulder towards Leo. He shook his head, waving her on and smiling.

Hugo was at his shoulder. 'Do you know, Leo, I don't know what I'd have done if anything had happened to that girl. I was going out of my mind with worry. I'm still having blasted nightmares.'

Leo studied Hugo sympathetically. 'I know. Sometimes I wake in the middle of the night and – ' he broke off and stared at the floor. 'Oh never mind. She looks fantastic, doesn't she?'

'I'm so proud of her, Leo. Are you and she . . .you know . . . are you intending to – '

'Marry her? She may not have me, Hugo. You know as well as I do how stubborn she can be.'

Hugo put his arm around Leo's shoulders. 'Take my advice, my boy. Don't let her get away. If you really love each other, then you must do all in your power to make it work. I'd hate you and Fern to go through what I did. I'm beginning to realize what a rare gift true love is. Don't let her get away.'

Leo watched the copper-coloured head amongst the crowd. If only Hugo knew. He loved that girl so much it hurt. There was no way she was going to be parted from him. Not now, not ever.

He looked back at Hugo's pale, drawn face. He had aged ten years in the last few weeks.

'What about Ricci?' Leo asked quietly.

'Oh, um, I don't think she wants to see me.'

'You know that for certain, do you?'

'No, but . . . I wouldn't want to see me if I'd behaved as, er, badly as I have.'

'Perhaps you should let her be the judge.'

'Oh, I don't know, Leo. Perhaps I'm too old for all this.'

'Hugo, don't be so bloody stupid. We're not a generation apart, you and I, and you're talking as if you're seventy. Pull yourself together, man. Here you are telling me not to pass up the chance of happiness while you seem to be doing exactly that, again!'

'Leo! I really must ask – '

'No, you'll hear me out, Hugo. Believe me, it's entirely my own self-interest forcing me to do this. The last thing I want for Fern is to have some morose old cobweb of a father in the background. Get your arse into gear, man, and get after her. I happen to know that if you take a direct line across this room, you will find Ricci at the other side. I believe she's waiting for you!'

'Are you serious?'

'Yes, I am. Quite serious. And that was Fern's idea, not mine. She thought it might be a nice present for you. So be a good chap, and accept it graciously, would you? For Fern!'

Hugo cleared his throat nervously, and fiddled with the knot of his tie. 'Well . . . I . . . er . . . um . . . '

'Off you go, Hugo. You know what to do.'

'Of course, of course,' he said disgruntledly.

Leo raised his dark eyebrows in amusement. 'Go on then.'

'Right. I, er, I'll go and say hello, then.'

'Good idea. See you later.'

Hugo had forgotten quite how blue Ricci's eyes were. Two deep sapphire pools of loveliness smiled up at him. 'Ricci,' he said hesitantly. 'You look beautiful!'

'Thank you, Hugo.' She glanced down at her dress. 'I bought it for tonight. Do you like it?'

He took a long hungry look at the way the soft pink jersey moulded itself to the lovely curves of her body. 'Yes,' he said gently, 'I like it very much.'

Unable to stop herself, Ricci reached out her hand and stroked his gaunt cheek. 'Hugo, you look exhausted. You haven't been looking after yourself very well, have you?'

He shrugged like a small boy. 'Oh, I don't know. I guess I haven't been getting that much sleep. Everything's been a bit upside down.'

'To say the least. It must have been simply dreadful for you, all that worry.'

'Yes,' he nodded. 'It has been pretty bloody. Look, Ricci, I have to say, that is, I . . . well . . . I've been very stupid.'

A small smile lifted the curve of Ricci's mouth. 'Everyone's entitled to be stupid sometimes, Hugo, even you.'

Hugo stared at his feet. 'I suppose so, but I feel so dreadful.' He lifted his eyes and realized with shock that Ricci was actually laughing at him!

'Don't be too hard on yourself. Sometimes we all need to lay our ghosts to rest. I do understand, Hugo. Now, be an angel and get me a drink, would you? I got caught up talking to some buyer and I'm absolutely desperate for a top-up.'

Hugo sighed with relief. He took the empty glass from her fingers. Then he caught her hand in his own. 'Ricci, do you think we might try again? I really would like that very much. I have missed you! And maybe now, with the divorce almost final, well, who knows what might happen in the future? But perhaps we could give it a try?'

She looked at him serenely. 'Perhaps we should start with a drink, Hugo. Who knows what these things might lead to?'

He took a couple of steps away, then he turned back. He gazed at her for a few moments, then he nodded, half smiling. Everything was going to be all right. He moved away with a new-found lightness to his step.

The music stopped. Fern spoke into the microphone. 'Good evening, everyone,' she said. The entire crowd turned towards her. The applause was deafening. Again the bulbs flashed, causing red spots that swam blindingly before her eyes. She was conscious of her voice echoing back to her. It sounded oddly disjointed as if it didn't belong to her. She stumbled over a couple of sentences, and then, with confidence growing, she got into the body of her speech.

'This is a very exciting night for me as it marks the grand opening of the sixth Donleavy's shop. But this one is particularly special to me as it's here in the heart of Dublin, in my home country, dear Ireland. I feel so proud of the team who have tirelessly worked to make this possible and I'd like to thank them all individually . . . ' She reeled off the names, giving warm, personal comments to all of them. ' . . . And finally, there's someone else I'd like to say a special thank you to. Where are you, Johnny? Mr Johnny Sharpe, a very brave and special and dear friend, someone without whom I wouldn't be here tonight. Someone who pestered me and cajoled me into accepting the job with Oscar Rees in the first place. Johnny, where are you?' she called. She looked across the floor and saw the white-nosed face approaching.

Johnny climbed onto the rostrum and swept Fern into his arms. 'You monkey,' he whispered. He fingered the bandage self-consciously.

'I don't really know what to say,' he began haltingly, 'other than how thrilled I am to know such a lovely lady. I guess you could really call it a bit of a fairy story. I for one am delighted that Oscar Rees has a real live daughter in its clutches and I know from my own personal experience of Fern that it won't be too long before there's a Donleavy's store in every high street. In America, too. I can't wait for the exciting times ahead of us. I love you, Fern!' He pulled her into his arms once more, and they were deafened by the cheers.

Fern's eyes were moist. 'Thanks!' she said in a muffled voice. 'If I'd known you were going to say that I'd never have pulled you up here, you monster.'

Johnny laughed. 'I meant every word of it. Now, if I'm not mistaken, there's a man down there looking extremely hungry. You'd better go and find him before he gets jealous. My nose couldn't cope with any more punches right now.'

Fern searched the crowds for Leo's face, but she didn't have to look for long. He walked towards her, his hand out. She took it, feeling the warm strength of it wrapped around her fingers.

'Come on, vixen,' he said. 'I've got plans for you, and they've been held up long enough. I think it's time to make our escape.'

'I thought you'd never ask,' she giggled.

He bundled her into his car. 'Where are we going?' she asked.

'It's a surprise. I suppose I should tell you to keep your eyes shut, but it's so bloody dark, it won't make much difference. It's not very far away.'

'Leo,' her voice was hesitant, wary, even a little shy, 'what did you mean earlier?'

'About what, darling?' he asked guilelessly.

'When you said about maternity leave.'

455

'Oh, that. Well, you do want a family, don't you?'

'I hadn't really thought about it, to tell you the truth. I guess I thought I'd one day get married to a nice man and maybe think about babies after that. Perhaps I'm secretly rather an old-fashioned thing. Probably something to do with my Catholic ancestry.'

'I can't believe you mean that,' Leo laughed quietly. 'There's nothing remotely conventional about you. But, if you insist, then I guess we could get married.' His hand reached out into the darkness and found her own.

'It's not necessary,' she whispered into the night.

'I know that, darling, but strangely enough I can't think of anything I'd like better. Here we are,' he sighed, pulling the car to a halt outside a brightly lit, vast Georgian mansion.

Two dogs bundled out of the front door and leaped around the car. Fern opened her door and spoke to them, fighting off the cold wet noses.

A warm Irish voice carried across the breeze to her. A woman stood framed in the doorway. 'You must be frozen,' she called. 'Come in and get warm.'

Leo put his arm around Fern's shoulder and led her into the grand hallway.

'What is this place?' she said, looking around at the beautifully polished wooden floor, and intimidating faces peering down at them from the many oil paintings hung over the walls.

'It's a rather select hotel. We can have dinner first, or we can go to our rooms, or we can have dinner in our rooms, whatever you like, my darling. The night is yours.'

Fern stood rocking backwards and forwards from her heels to the balls of her feet. She glanced at Leo impishly. 'I think I'm rather hungry,' she said after a few moments' consideration.

'Very well. Then we shall ask for dinner – '

'For you,' she giggled and then threw herself into his arms. His hand flew up into her hair, pulling her head close to his in a vice-like grip. His kiss was an almost violent surge of want.

They heard a cough from somewhere outside their own world.

Reluctantly, slowly, Leo lifted his head. 'Ah, Mrs O'Connor, thank you,' he said sheepishly, as the woman handed him the key. 'I think we're rather tired.' He grinned down at Fern. 'It's a little late for dinner. Perhaps we might have a little bread and cheese later on. Oh, and a bottle of your best wine.'

'Certainly, Mr Eden. Now if you and Mrs Eden would like to follow me . . . '

Fern glanced at Leo. He winked at her. 'See how easy it can be?'

'Perhaps I'd better just give it one more try, just to make sure.'

'After tonight, my love, you'll never be more sure of anything.'